William J. Clough
THE LOOM

William J. Clough
THE LOOM

IRKHAM PRESS

THE LOOM by WILLIAM J. CLOUGH

PUBLISHED BY Irkham Press, Manchester UK
ISBN 978-0-9557332-0-8
COPYRIGHT © William J. Clough 2008

The right of William J. Clough to be identified as the author of this work has been asserted by him in accordance with the Copyright, Designs and Patents Act of 1988.

All rights reserved. No part of this publication may be reproduced, stored in or introduced into a retrieval system, or transmitted, in any form, or by any means (electronic, mechanical, photocopying, recording or otherwise) without the prior written permission of the publisher.

This is a work of fiction and is the product of the author's imagination. Any relationship with real events, places, people or incidents is entirely coincidental.

EMAIL williamjclough@hotmail.co.uk
TELEPHONE 07970 881606
www.irkhampress.co.uk

CONTENTS

CHAPTER 1	Mr Johnson Goes to Work	1
CHAPTER 2	The World of Sales	10
CHAPTER 3	Judy Orion	24
CHAPTER 4	Sales Training	35
CHAPTER 5	Organisational Theory	50
CHAPTER 6	Leonard Bragby	62
CHAPTER 7	The Conceptual Initialisation Department	74
CHAPTER 8	The Distribution Tangents	90
CHAPTER 9	Brainstorming	115
CHAPTER 10	Bilfred	120
CHAPTER 11	The Presentation	136
CHAPTER 12	Mr Johnson's Project	143
CHAPTER 13	All Change at the Top	152
CHAPTER 14	The Personnel Manager	161
CHAPTER 15	Nikolai	178
CHAPTER 16	The Cleaning Function	195
CHAPTER 17	Juniper	214
CHAPTER 18	The Golden Clock	236
CHAPTER 19	The Loom	253

CHAPTER ONE

MR JOHNSON GOES TO WORK

On his first day in his new job, after being issued with directions by a helpful security guard in the main entrance hall, Mr Johnson climbed a short flight of stairs to a first-floor landing, where a set of double doors with glass circles at head height opened into a small reception area.

Behind a low, wooden desk sat a smartly-dressed woman in her late fifties or thereabouts murmuring into a telephone. Mr Johnson waited politely at some distance from the desk until she had replaced the handset, whereupon he stepped towards her and introduced himself.

'My name is Mr Johnson. I'm starting work here today. I've been told to report to a Mr Bannister. I'm afraid I am a little late. Can you tell me where I have to go?'

The receptionist replied to him in a warm and creamy voice.

'Good morning, Mr Johnson,' she said. 'Have you come a long way? Oh my goodness. You must be exhausted. At this time of day the trains and buses are quite dreadful. May I get you a cup of coffee or a cup of tea? Tea? Would you like sugar? Just the one? Please, make yourself comfortable.' She put out a call for Mr Bannister.

'I'm sure he won't be long. Do sit down and help yourself to newspapers and magazines.'

Mr Johnson sat on a low armchair next to a table on which were spread a selection of newspapers and magazines.

Some minutes went by. A young man with a hot and fiery face entered the little reception area, stared at Mr Johnson, and left. The receptionist put out another call for Mr Bannister and then spoke to someone on the telephone. From this call, Mr Johnson gathered that the receptionist's name was Margaret. Mr Johnson finished his tea.

'I'm awfully sorry,' Margaret said when she had replaced the handset. 'Mr Bannister has been unavoidably detained in a meeting. He'll be with you as soon as he gets out of it. May I get you some more tea?'

Mr Johnson said yes, and when Margaret returned she not only brought him a drink but a plate of biscuits – bourbon creams, ginger snaps – and a pink paper serviette folded into a triangle. He munched slowly through the biscuits and read the financial pages of one of the broadsheets.

The fiery-faced man came back in and exchanged words in an undertone with Margaret. When he had disappeared through a fire door in the corner of the reception area she put out another call.

'Roger Dobley contact reception. Roger Dobley, do contact reception.'

Moments later her telephone rang and she passed on an instruction to Roger Dobley that presumably had been issued by the fiery-faced man. Mr Johnson drank the last of his tea. A soggy biscuit residue clung to the rim of the cup, which he wiped away with the serviette. He noticed that he had spilled biscuit crumbs on his new suit and brushed them from his lap and put the empty plate with the serviette carefully scrunched up on it to one side. As an afterthought he picked up the serviette and dabbed at the corners of his mouth, which felt a little gritty and sticky, and put it away in his right-hand trouser pocket.

A stout man in a light-grey suit swung across the foreground and left a sheaf of papers on Margaret's desk. Shortly after this a young woman in a black skirt and jacket crossed the carpet, stopped, looked inside her briefcase, and turned back on herself. Mr Johnson picked up another paper, put it down, picked another up, put this one down. He pulled up his socks and tightened his shoelaces.

'I'm terribly sorry,' Margaret said. 'He will be with you as soon as he can.'

Her telephone rang again and shortly after replacing the handset she put out another call for Roger Dobley. This time a well-built man in shirtsleeves breezed into reception and received a yellow message note from Margaret. Although she didn't address him by name, Mr Johnson assumed that this was Roger Dobley himself. Roger Dobley thanked Margaret and they both laughed at a private joke. Then Roger Dobley left by the door he had entered.

The reception area was empty again except for Mr Johnson and Margaret. Mr Johnson walked over to the desk and asked Margaret where the toilet was. Following her instructions, he passed through the door from which Roger Dobley, the fiery-faced man and the woman in black had emerged and found himself in a long, clean corridor.

On either side at regular intervals were wooden doors with finely-chequered fire glass at head height. In time the corridor opened out onto a broad stairhead. The toilet was where Margaret had said it would be, to the left before the first step of the downward flight.

Inside, he opted for one of the cubicles rather than the row of porcelain urinals. Two men stood at the urinals but they didn't turn their heads when Mr Johnson entered. When he pulled the cubicle door to it made a terrible rasping noise. He heard the two men laugh and one of them say, 'Excuse me.'

Instinctively, Mr Johnson wanted to call out that it wasn't him, it was the hinges, but his voice was dry from the tea and biscuits, and before he could say anything he heard the main toilet door swing to with a quiet schlunck.

When he had finished, he left the cubicle and washed his hands and dried them on a coarse piece of blue paper towel that was cast out from a spool in a plastic case by means of a lever on its right-hand side. When his hands were almost dry he scrunched up the blue paper and dropped it into a tall stainless steel waste bin that opened by means of a pedal at its base.

Back in the corridor two men went by. He thought they might be the men who had been in the toilet with him. One of them made a snorting noise as he passed and the other laughed. By the look of them, as they disappeared down the corridor, they were older than the men in the toilet but Mr Johnson couldn't be entirely sure and he felt relieved to be heading in the opposite direction, back to Margaret and the reception area. Mr Bannister hadn't been in yet and he hadn't called Margaret on the telephone.

She apologised to Mr Johnson once more for the wait, which was really quite exceptional, she had to admit. Mr Bannister hated to keep people waiting. He was quite particular about this and was renowned in the organisation for his punctuality and consideration. However, there was a meeting going on for most of the day that many of the managers were involved in and she knew that Mr Bannister had been expected to attend it for a short while. It must have overrun, as meetings often do.

Margaret offered Mr Johnson another cup of tea, which he accepted, although when she returned with a cup on a tray there were no biscuits accompanying it. He pulled out a letter from his pocket.

Dear Mr Johnson, I am delighted to offer you the position of Market Intelligence Consultant subject to satisfactory references. Please report to Mr L Bannister in the Strategic Development Department at 9.15am on Monday 1st August, when you will be given a comprehensive induction into all aspects of the company's business. Yours sincerely, Margaret Cletheridge, Personnel Executive.

'Excuse me,' Mr Johnson said, 'may I confirm that I'm waiting for the right person? It's occurred to me that in an organisation this size, there could be one or more people with the same surname. It is the right Mr Bannister that I've asked for, isn't it? I've been recruited as a Market Intelligence Consultant in the Strategic Development Department, it's Mr L Bannister, Bannister with two ns.' He handed Margaret the letter.

'As a matter of fact,' said Margaret, 'there are two Mr Bannisters who work here but there's little chance of a mix-up since one is indeed based in the strategic development department, while the other works in the post room. As it happens, the Mr Bannister who works in the post room as a despatch executive isn't well today and is at home recuperating. He hopes to be back in again tomorrow but to be honest with you I don't expect him to be.' She gave Mr Johnson his letter back. 'I think that the worst thing one can do when one is unwell is rush back into work when one should be safe at home taking one's time to get better. Aside from any other consideration, one must think of one's colleagues. A poorly colleague can place a tremendous strain upon an office. I must confess to an interest in this matter,' she added, and reached under her desk and brought up a green first-aid box. 'I'm a member of the company's first-aid team and have overall responsibility for the first-floor reception area and two adjoining offices.'

'Really? That's quite a responsibility.'

'Yes, it is. I volunteered for first-aid duty here when the personnel manager set up a first-aiders network three years ago. It's a standard business procedure. Happily, beyond dispensing the odd sticking plaster, I've never put my training into practice but one never knows when one might be called upon to do so.'

'Are you involved in first aid outside of work too?'

'No, no, not at all, although my husband is in the St John's Ambulance, so you could say I have something of a private as well as a professional interest.'

'I suppose that people must think he's very lucky, attending sports events and concerts and so on.'

'I've never thought about it before but I suppose people might. My husband isn't much of a sports fan, however, so it's not an issue for him.'

'Well, at least I know where to fall ill while I'm here.'

'I hope you don't,' laughed Margaret, 'but one can never predict what may happen. A few months ago one of the canvassing agents fell awkwardly in the sales office and banged her head on the floor. She was knocked out, but the worst of it was that a pin that was holding her hair in a bunch stuck into the back of her head and caused quite a lot of bleeding. The situation looked worse than it actually was but it was upsetting for many of the people involved, including the young lady who was responsible for first aid in that section. She screamed louder than anyone at the sight of all the blood and almost fainted herself. Fortunately, the lady who was knocked out came round soon afterwards and had nothing worse than a cut and a bump on her head to show for it all. But it illustrated that all the training in the world can't prepare you for the moment when you are called upon to assist in a live situation. I hope that I wouldn't react hysterically to the sight of blood or an unconscious person. I suspect that I wouldn't, but one never knows.' Margaret smiled beatifically at Mr Johnson.

'Would you mind paging Mr Bannister again?' he asked.

'Not at all.' Margaret put a call out for him. 'Still no joy,' she smiled.

Mr Johnson sat down and Margaret turned her attention to her computer screen. No one entered the reception area for a long time. Mr Johnson went to the toilet again. When he returned he asked Margaret if Mr Bannister had rung through or left a message. He hadn't. Mr Johnson sat down and leafed through a magazine, which included a piece on email etiquette and a lengthy feature dealing with the writer's fear of flying, which he had endeavoured to overcome by attending an intensive aversion therapy programme with a number of fellow phobics. It hadn't worked.

Mr Johnson declined another cup of tea, partly because he was awash with drink and partly because he sensed that Margaret hadn't offered it with any enthusiasm, although she remained uniformly polite. Shortly after he had declined this drink, Margaret came out from behind her desk and disappeared through the doors through which Mr Johnson had passed on his way to the toilet.

A minute later the telephone rang. Mr Johnson remained in his seat. It stopped on the twelfth ring. Then it rang again, stopped; rang again, stopped. Mr Johnson left his seat and pushed open the doors through which Margaret had passed. The corridor was empty in either direction. The telephone rang again. It was ringing with greater frequency than when Margaret had been behind the desk and Mr Johnson had the feeling that it was the same person trying to get through.

Mr Johnson stepped behind the desk and picked up the receiver. 'Hello?' he said. He could hear a faint voice at the other end in a cloud of hiss. Then the line went dead. Mr Johnson replaced the receiver and immediately it rang again. 'Hello?' he said. A faint voice crackled at the other end. Again the line went dead.

A tall young man in a purple shirt entered the reception area.

'Excuse me,' said Mr Johnson, 'I'm trying to answer the telephone. Margaret's disappeared and the phone hasn't stopped ringing but I can't seem to get connected. I'm new here.'

The man came round to Mr Johnson's side of the desk and pointed to a flashing red button on the console.

'When it's an internal call, press whichever red button is flashing. Apart from the button, you know it's internal because of the ringing sound. It's shorter than an outside line.'

As soon as Mr Johnson replaced the receiver the telephone rang again. The man in the purple shirt left the reception area through the fire door. Mr Johnson pressed the red button, which was marked 'Group 6', and before he had a chance to say 'Hello?' a man said: 'Where's Margaret?'

'She's just popped out, can I help?'

'Who's that?'

'My name is Mr Johnson. I'm new, I'm waiting to see Mr Bannister.'

'Les Bannister?'

'Yes, I think so.'

'He's not in today.'

'No, I think it's the other Mr Bannister in the post room who's not in today.'

'Who are you again?'

'Mr Johnson. I'm starting work in the strategic development department. Mr Bannister is off sick, apparently.'

'He's what? I thought that he'd gone to a conference. Do you mean Les Bannister?'

'No, the other Mr Bannister in the post room.'

'I didn't know there was a Mr Bannister in the post room.'

'I'm new here. Can I give Margaret a message?'

'Are you supposed to be working for Les?'

'I was told to report to him. It's my first day. I'm a market intelligence consultant.'

'In strategic development?'

'Yes.'

'Are you sure?'

'That's what my letter says.'

'Who wrote the letter?'

'It's from, let me see, Margaret Cletheridge.'

'What, Margaret Cletheridge in personnel?'

'Yes, that's what it says.'

'I don't know what they're playing at. There are no market intelligence consultants in strategic development. Who interviewed you?'

'It was a woman, Debbie Jackson I think her name was, and a man called Howard. It was at a hotel, not here.'

'Is Margaret back yet?'

'No.'

'When she does get back, could you ask her to call Mike Bignall please? Soon as she can. Thanks.'

Mr Johnson sat down again and the phone rang once more before Margaret returned but he didn't answer it. He explained about his conversation with Mike Bignall and she called him straightaway. They had quite a lengthy conversation. When she had finished, she said: 'I must apologise. It seems that

Mr Bannister isn't in the building today after all. He's away at a conference. Somebody has given me misleading information.'

'Is there someone else I can see?'

'Yes, I'll have a word with Jackie Stevens, who works with Mr Bannister. I'm really sorry. I can't understand why Mr Bannister asked you to report to him when he was going away. It's not like him at all.'

'In fairness, the letter came from Margaret Cletheridge in the personnel department. Perhaps there's been a communication breakdown between her and Mr Bannister.'

'Whatever the root cause of the problem, I'll make sure that you get sorted out. Take a seat again and I'll be with you in a minute.'

'Before I sit down, I should tell you that when I spoke to Mike Bignall he told me that there are no market intelligence consultants in strategic development. Could you tell me what he means by that? My letter is quite explicit – market intelligence consultant in the strategic development department.'

'I'm not sure. As far as I am aware, there are consultants of some sort in that department, although I'm not exactly sure how it all works. Who interviewed you?'

'Debbie Jackson and a man called Howard. It was at a hotel.'

'Let me see your letter again.' Margaret looked at it closely. 'What was the job you actually applied for?'

'It was a general graduate management trainee position.'

'Where did you hear about the position?'

'I saw an advert in the local newspaper.'

'And you wrote off for an application form?'

'No, it just asked for a covering letter and a CV. Then I was invited to come for an interview at a hotel in town. With Howard and Debbie Jackson. I didn't catch Howard's surname. I think he was a recruitment consultant of some sort. Debbie mentioned that they had some openings in the strategic development department.'

'Was that what you were looking for?'

'Not initially but when Debbie outlined what the role entailed, yes, I was very interested.'

'What does the role entail, exactly?'

'The role is primarily concerned with building relationships with key clients and finding market-specific business solutions for them. That was the sort of thing I'd started to do in my last job and wanted to develop.'

'Did Debbie mention Mr Bannister during your interview?'

'No. The letter was the first I'd heard of him.'

'I'll try Jackie Stevens straightaway.' Margaret dialled a number and spoke to someone at the other end. 'Hello Julie, it's Margaret. Is Jackie Stevens there? Is she? All right. Ask Debbie to call me as soon as she can. Thank you, Julie.' Margaret replaced the handset. 'I'm terribly sorry, Mr Johnson. It seems that Jackie Stevens is away on a training course and can't be contacted. You're not having much luck, are you?'

'Is there anyone else in that department who can help me?'

'Yes, Debbie Stewart is going to call me back as soon as this morning's motivational meeting has finished. Debbie Stewart manages the admin side of things up there.'

'Motivational meeting? What's that about?'

'Every morning between 9.30am and 10.00am the strategic development department get together to talk through their plans for the day and buoy each other up. It's a collective pep talk, essentially, and they have a rotating chair so that every member of the team gets to run the show, as it were. It was the first thing Judy Orion instituted when she started here.'

'Judy Orion?'

'Yes, she has overall responsibility for sales incentives and development. Judy Orion has single-handedly revolutionised the commercial profile of the organisation in the two, no, three years that she has been here. She has ensured that we have all become customer focused. The sales department used to be known informally as Sleepy Hollow. Now it's central to the fortunes of the organisation.'

'Is the strategic development department the same as the sales department?'

'Yes and no. Strategic development covers what was at one time just the sales department and the company's marketing and product development activities. It's a catch-all title, if you like. There's also a creative department called conceptual initialisation, which is quite new. But strategic development is mainly sales, if it's anything in particular – certainly as far as the daily motivational meetings are concerned.'

'That's a lot of departments. At the last place I worked there were only twelve of us in the company.'

'I know. I can hardly keep up with it myself,' said Margaret. 'Knowing who to put calls through is a job in itself. But I expect everything will be explained to you in good time.'

'Yes, I'm sure it will. At least, I hope it will. The letter does mention a comprehensive induction period, after all.'

'One thing this company is very hot on is inductions. You will be sure to meet all the key people. If you don't mind taking a seat, Debbie Stewart will attend to you before long.'

Mr Johnson had hardly sat down when the telephone rang. 'Yes, Debbie, Mr Johnson. His letter asks him to report to Mr L Bannister in the strategic development department. Yes, today. If you would, thank you. That was Debbie Stewart,' Margaret told Mr Johnson. 'She's on her way down.'

A few minutes later a tall young woman came into the reception area.

'Mr Johnson?' she said as she approached him, and extended her hand. He got up and shook it. 'I'm Debbie Stewart. I'm sorry about all the confusion.'

'That's quite all right,' said Mr Johnson.

'I'm afraid Mr Johnson is something of a lost soul,' said Margaret from behind her desk. 'I hope you look after him properly.'

'Don't you worry about that. We'll sort Mr Johnson out,' said Debbie. 'If you'd like to come with me.'

'When I find out how everything works, I'll come back and let you know,' said Mr Johnson to Margaret. She smiled and waved at him.

'Good luck,' she said, and he left the reception area.

CHAPTER TWO

THE WORLD OF SALES

Mr Johnson followed Debbie through the doors which led to the toilet. They turned right instead of left and walked down a broad corridor, up a flight of stairs that opened off to the left, and went up for two storeys before going through another set of double doors into a wide and open office in which sat thirty or more people at grey desks on swivel chairs of varying pastel tones. Every desk had a computer terminal and telephone. The wall at the rear of the office was dominated by a long white board divided into numerous grids containing words and figures with obvious financial significance. Motivational posters of dolphins, mountains at sunset, and the earth from space decorated the walls. The air was full of chatter and murmur.

'This is the sales section of the strategic development department,' said Debbie with an airy wave of her arm, 'which is where you will be based.'

'Where will I be sitting?'

'It's too early too say. They will have to determine the appropriate team for you first and think about desk arrangements later. You will need to see Judy Orion as soon as possible. But for the moment, I'll leave you in Margaret's capable hands. Margaret will sort you out one way or another.'

'I've spent quite a lot of time with her. You do mean Margaret on the reception desk?'

'No, Margaret is the sales and marketing liaison section supervisor. You must be thinking of Margot.'

'Perhaps, but I'm sure that she referred to herself as Margaret.'

'On the reception desk?'

'Yes. Where you came in to meet me. I suppose it could have been Margot. I hope I didn't get it wrong – I'm sure I addressed her by her name once or twice.'

'No, no, I see what you mean now. You were in the first-floor reception area. I'm sorry, we don't call that the reception desk. Yes, that was Margaret, although usually it's Sheila. Margaret's covering for Sheila while she's on holiday. Margot, on the other hand, works on the ground floor but there aren't any seats opposite her. The seats on the ground floor are to the right of the reception desk. No, not that Margaret. It's the other Margaret I mean.'

'Where does the other Margaret sit?'

Debbie pointed across the busy office to an island of grey desks on the far side of the room.

'The small woman with the grey curly hair and glasses to the left of the pillar, yes, that's Margaret. You can talk to her about your seating arrangements and while you're at it find out about your induction programme.'

'Yes, I was wondering about that. The letter that was sent to me mentioned a comprehensive induction into all aspects of the company's business. Naturally, there are a lot of questions that I would like to ask. I'm already confused about the company's structure.'

'Join the club,' laughed Debbie. 'You'll certainly get every opportunity to ask lots of questions during your induction period. It will be nothing if not thorough.'

'Will I get a schedule or a timetable of activities?'

'Yes, I think Margaret will be able to give you one.'

'There seem to be hundreds of Margarets working here. That's three already, including Margaret Cletheridge who wrote to me in the first place.'

'I know. I sometimes wonder whether there isn't a law which stipulates that every organisation must have a certain number of Margarets. I've worked for several other companies and there has always been more than your average number of Margarets. They are usually the heart and soul of the place, too.'

'Well, I might as well get on with it. Thanks for your help,' said Mr Johnson, and he walked across the room to Margaret's desk. One or two people looked up as he went past.

'Hello,' he said, holding his right hand out, 'my name is…'

'Just a minute love,' said Margaret, as she picked up her telephone. 'Hello, Margaret, hello Diane love, yes I have, yes I will, yes love, thanks, see you later. Yes love,' she said to Mr Johnson, 'can I help you?'

'Yes, my name is Mr Johnson. I've started today and…'

The phone rang again. 'Just a minute, love,' said Margaret, and picked up the handset. 'Hello, Margaret, hello Vicky love, yes they are love, no I haven't, no I didn't, yes, next week love, thanks Vicky, see you later, bye love, thanks. Now then,' she said, turning to face Mr Johnson again, 'what can I do you for?'

'Yes, I've started work here today and I've been told to see you about my seating arrangements.'

'Seating arrangements?'

'Yes, I'm starting work in the strategic development department' – he held out his letter of appointment – 'but Mr Bannister hasn't been able to see me yet, and I think I need to see Judy Orion but I'm not sure whether she's available either. Debbie Stewart told me to see you about sorting out a desk.'

Margaret looked around the office. 'I'm sorry, love, but nobody has told me about this. I don't know about any new starters. No-one's told me that someone would need a desk. We're chock-a-block in here. There's no spare room.'

This appeared to be true. A fan of desks spread out from where Margaret sat, each one occupied by a young man or woman, the men dressed predominantly in blue shirts, the women a little more variously. It looked as though every inch of the big office was taken up with people, desks, storage cupboards and computer equipment.

'Just a minute, love,' said Margaret. 'Can you get on the phones, please?' she shouted across the room, with a weighty emphasis on the word 'phones'. This had a galvanising effect on her charges, and Mr Johnson realised that until she had reminded them, they had been talking among themselves, exchanging banter, bringing drinks back from the coffee machine. Now each one retreated into a private communication with the telephone and an atmosphere of earnest dedication prevailed.

'Sorry about that, love. They need a little motivation from time to time. What were you saying?'

'I need to sort out somewhere to sit until I can see Mr Bannister or Judy Orion.'

'Which department are you supposed to be in again, love?'

'Strategic development. I am in the right department?'

Margaret laughed and looked away. 'I'll say,' she said. 'We're chock-a-block, I'm afraid. Nobody's told me about any new starters. But that's nothing new. You're going to have to work-shadow until they sort you out with something proper.'

At that moment, a young woman appeared and pressed hard on a brass bell on Margaret's desk.

'Well done, Joanne, how much was that for?'

'£1,450. I'm at 93% of target now.'

'I want a few more of you to ring that bell before the end of the day,' said Margaret to the room in general. 'Well done, Joanne love. You should hit target before four-thirty. What I suggest you do, love,' she said to Mr Johnson, 'is get a chair and go and sit with Tony over there. Tony, love, I want you to – what's your name again, love? – I want you to do some mentoring with Mr Johnson. He's just started here.'

Tony smiled and waved across to Mr Johnson, who waved back.

'Get a chair from over there and go and sit with Tony, love. I'll have a word with Debbie Stevens about what you need you to do when Judy Orion gets back in.'

'Do you mean Jackie Stevens?'

'No, Debbie Stevens. She's Judy Orion's PA.'

'Do you know when Judy Orion or Mr Bannister are going to be back?'

Margaret chewed her lip violently. 'Haven't a clue, love. Nobody tells me anything. It's poor bloody infantry in here. Debbie Stevens should know, though. I'll give her a ring in a bit. Anything else you need, come and see me.'

Mr Johnson was about to ask Margaret about his induction itinerary but thought better of it. He supposed that Judy Orion would know more about it. He pulled a faded blue swivel chair over to Tony's desk and sat down. Tony was a tall, brown-haired man in his mid thirties. He wore a dark blue shirt and a yellow tie. His desk was tidy. On it sat a computer and telephone, a pile of yellow papers and a big blue coffee mug. On a low partition at the back of desk were pinned a postcard of a football player and a green and red leaflet from a sandwich company. The mug was streaked with coffee.

Tony swivelled round to face Mr Johnson. He had very striking brown eyes. 'What are you supposed to be working on, then?'

'I'm a market intelligence consultant. I've been told to report to Mr Bannister but he's not around. Neither is Judy Orion. Are you in market intelligence too?'

Tony laughed. 'Sort of. Strictly speaking, I'm in straight sales but there's a strong market intelligence element to it. What did they tell you at the interview?'

'They said I'd be building client relationships and devising market-specific solutions. It's the strategic development department I'm supposed to be based in. This is the strategic development department, isn't it? Nobody seems very sure.'

Tony laughed again. 'You could say that. Everything is strategic development these days. And sales.'

'Is Mr Bannister your boss?'

'Not immediately. I report direct to Judy Orion, although Margaret is responsible for most of the canvassers. Les Bannister is sort of over this general area.'

'I don't understand how things work here. There seem to be a lot of different departments and sections all in the same broad sales and marketing area. I'm sure my induction will make things clearer.'

'Yes, I expect it will. How do you want to do this? You can sit and listen to me go through some sales calls if you like or I can show you round first. I was going to nip out for a cigarette. Do you smoke?'

'I've given up but I'll come out with you if you don't mind. I could do with a break.'

They left the office together, picking up three other smokers on the way. Mr

Johnson asked if they were given proper breaks or just popped out when they felt like it. Tony said that there was supposed to be a policy about smoking breaks but it was always slipping, and in any case Margaret herself was the worst offender, often going out for four or even five cigarette breaks a day.

'She's all right, though. But just watch how she chews her lip, especially when she's thinking hard.'

They walked along a long grey corridor and down a narrow concrete stairwell that opened suddenly to the left. At the bottom of the stairs they went through a fire door and entered a small courtyard hemmed in by pebbledashed walls punctuated by the exhaust outlets of air conditioning and heating units. A small square of blue sky capped the little yard but at quite a height and as far as Mr Johnson could see there was no other exit from the area save for the door they had just passed through. Wrinkled and crushed dog-ends, the dead filters spilling fluff, littered the flagstones.

Tony introduced Mr Johnson to Gavin, Mark and another Tony, each of whom was wearing a blue shirt and primary-coloured tie. Mr Johnson was keen to immerse himself in his colleagues' working culture and he asked a succession of interested questions, most of which were dealt with by Tony. Most of all, he wanted to know how everything fitted together and how the reporting structure worked.

'The thing is,' said Tony, 'there has been so much change here recently that nobody really knows who is working for whom.'

'Is that a problem?' asked Mr Johnson.

'Not really. At the end of the day, if you keep making the sales, you're all right.'

'It used to be a lot quieter,' said the other Tony. 'When Judy Orion started, everything became more driven. Summers used to be dead. Now it's busy all the time.'

'Are you all in sales?' Mr Johnson asked. They all nodded. 'I didn't realise that the job was as much about sales it seems to be.'

'Neither did we,' laughed Mark. 'I bet the advert said something about a graduate management trainee programme.'

'Yes, it did. Then they told me at the interview that there was nothing available on the programme at this time but that they had a vacancy for a market intelligence consultant.'

They all laughed at this.

'Have you done sales before?' asked the other Tony.

'A little in my last job. But I was primarily interested in developing my marketing and customer-relations skills. I worked for a research company and got more interested in the commercial side of things as I went on.'

'You'll get plenty of opportunity to develop your customer-relations skills,' said Gavin.

'I'll certainly relish the opportunity to get out and meet people face to face,' said Mr Johnson. 'That's something I didn't get the chance to do in my last job. It was totally office bound.'

They all laughed again and Tony clapped him on the shoulder. 'Good luck to you, Mr Johnson. If you ever get outside the office, let us know what it's like.'

'To be honest with you,' said Mark, 'you'll be lucky if you leave this place without a telephone glued to your ear. Most of us haven't left the office in years.'

'There used to be a few field sales reps here,' explained Tony, 'but it was all streamlined when Judy Orion started. She didn't think sending people out on the road was necessary. Now everything is done over the telephone. It's supposed to be more efficient.'

'Even when I'm at home,' said Mark, 'I automatically dial nine when I'm making a call. It's time to get a new job in a different field.'

'That's what we always say,' said Tony. 'Everyone talks about leaving but no-one does anything constructive about it. There is an escape committee of course, Mr Johnson. I'll let you know about membership when you're ready. Everyone joins eventually.'

The door into the courtyard opened and Margaret appeared, chewing her lip. She lit a cigarette and puffed furiously on it.

'What's up, Margaret?' asked Tony.

'Bloody phone system's on the blink again. It's the third time this week. How can we be expected to do any bloody work when the bloody phones are always on the bloody blink?'

The sales executives stood around her and tutted sympathetically. Tony lit another cigarette. 'Can we go home, then?' he asked.

Margaret scowled and looked away. 'We all might as well bloody well go home, love. That's what happens when you get a bloody consultant ordering the bloody telephone system. They don't ask the people who actually have to use it, oh no. Bloody consultants.' She ground the cigarette out beneath her heel.

'When is it going to be up again?'

'How do I bloody well know? The systems manager is coming up to look at it when he's out of his meeting. He's always in a bloody meeting. You might as well stay out in the sunshine and make the most of it.'

Gavin, Mark and the other Tony reached for their cigarette packets.

'Not a good start for you, is it Mr Johnson?' said Margaret.

Mr Johnson shrugged and gave a rueful grimace.

'Are you a smoker, love?' she asked.

'No. I've given up.'

'Good lad. Hang around this lot long enough and you'll soon be starting again. I'll see you all later.' She went back inside.

'What a shame,' said Gavin.

They all sat down with their backs to the pebbledash wall.

'What did I tell you about her lip?' said Tony.

'She seems a bit brusque but quite nice really,' said Mr Johnson.

'Margaret's all right. She's got a rotten job,' said Mark. 'She used to be a sales executive, pretty good too. But when Judy Orion came in she made her a team supervisor. She hates it. I'm not doing her an injustice when I say that her people-management skills are not all they could be.'

'She takes her frustration out on her staff,' said Gavin.

'Sometimes she does,' said Mark. 'I ignore her. It's the best way.'

'She's one of those traditional sales characters,' said Tony, 'the type who learned everything the hard way – you know, cold calling out of a portakabin on the edge of an industrial estate, doing deals with garage owners. She's got a very basic view of things. I've worked with a lot of people like that but you don't get too many of them here. Fundamentally, she distrusts graduates. She's a University of Life sort.'

'What does Margaret always say – it's a numbers game?'

'Yes, get your head down, work the numbers, get on the phones.'

'Get on the phones,' Mark mimicked, chewing his lip violently.

'God bless her.'

Mr Johnson thought about his last job. There hadn't been any characters like that there. He had worked with a small team of information researchers, two of whom possessed a postgraduate qualification. The work was intellectually satisfying but financially unrewarding. The atmosphere had been friendly and informal. If he was honest, the sales aspect of his role had been very low key, nothing more than dabbling. In fact, he had had the opportunity to test his commercial acumen on only one occasion. He had made an impromptu sales presentation when an interested enquirer had rung in. But his colleagues had admired his tenacity in this instance and, only half-jokingly, had referred to him as the 'commercial expert'. This had been one of the reasons he had decided to apply for his present job. He wondered how well his experiences would translate.

More cigarettes were extinguished, lit. Mr Johnson put his head back against the wall and closed his eyes. He was tempted to ask for a cigarette. But he knew that if he had one he would regret it immediately, although he would probably have another one soon afterwards. It was time to stop for good. The wall behind him was cool but enough sun came into the courtyard to warm his face. He stretched his legs in front of him like the others. They seemed to have settled in for the duration.

'What's Judy Orion like?' asked Mr Johnson, opening his eyes.

Nobody spoke for a moment. Then Mark said: 'You'll find out for yourself soon enough. She's a sales fanatic.'

'She lives and breathes sales,' said Tony. 'For most people it's just a job. For Judy, it's a way of life. Everything changed when she started.'

Tony's words fell away and he lit up again. None of them was in a hurry to get back upstairs. The courtyard was filled with sunshine. Mr Johnson closed his eyes.

Gavin drew sharply on his cigarette. 'If you're talking about sales characters, nothing beats a bloke called Graham who was at the last place I worked. He used to be a senior field rep and then became sales manager – the traditional route. Came up through the ranks. He left before I did but he'd been there over twenty years, a hard bastard, old school. I remember when I started there – what, seven years ago, eight more like, when I come to think of it – he was departmental manager by then, the day I started he took a bunch of us out, the new boys and some old hands, big bonding session, went round a few pubs, he bought all the rounds, then on to an Indian restaurant, a smart place, not your bog standard curry house, didn't do chips or English dishes for one thing, and we're all pretty pissed by then, it's about ten o'clock. He did all the ordering, everyone left it up to him. Natural authority, the manager seemed to know him quite well, he ordered a tandoori mix for everybody for starters, all served up on a big platter. Proper restaurant – candles, warmers, tasteful stuff on the walls. Not your average high street curry house by any means. Pricey, too. Real Indian artefacts. But all the way through he doesn't eat much himself, just picks at some salad and a bit of rice, has a couple of whiskies while the rest of us are on pints of lager, like he's keeping his distance intentionally. All the lads get stuck in, they think it's fantastic. When we leave the manager shakes us by the hand individually, Graham's got his arm round his shoulder. Afterwards, he takes us to a late-night drinking club, basement place, fiver to get in after eleven o'clock, that sort of thing. Everyone's far gone by then, jackets off, bottles of lager. Graham's very mellow, telling stories about legendary expense account days and the pioneering boys who set up the first professional sales arm in the organisation when it was a very different sort of company than what it is now, I mean what the company I used to work for is now when Graham was telling the story but in a way it's also about the now now, things change so quickly in this business, and the great times they used to have at conventions and conferences, hotels, and exhibition centres, and I remember feeling that I was being inducted into a world of infinite sensual promise in which foaming pints of chilled lager were poured and ready in every pub you entered, restaurant managers made a special welcoming motion with their eyebrows when you walked in, tough, humorous guys with a wealth of experience and a night-time's supply of anecdotes would seek you out at hotel bars the length and breadth of the motorway network, and genial accounts clerks would overlook the odd little manipulation of your expenses with a rueful, amused shake of the head and a wink. I know it sounds ridiculous in retrospect but that's what I felt back then. Then something very strange happened. Somehow it ended up just him and me talking at the table – the other boys were shuffling on the dance floor, at the bar, throwing up, out of earshot, whatever – and he's next to me in his shirtsleeves, the table thick with bottles, crumpled cigarette packets and sodden and torn beer mats, and he's just rounding off a story about a scam pulled on a supplier at the end of the 1960s, when he suddenly veers off the main road as it were and begins to tell me some really weird private stuff, right out of character, or what I assumed was his character, although I'd only known him a day at that point, but even so, this really weird stuff about how when he's driving home from work late at night on the motorway and the traffic starts to thin out to towards the estuary, these are pretty much his words, and he sees the shining lights across the river (I didn't know what he was on about at the time but I realised afterwards he meant the big refinery and chemical plant) at the point where the estuary tapers to a river proper, the banks and frames of glimmering future-past lights reflecting on the dark waters, innumerable pipes and spheres so silent and still at the great estuary's throat, he starts to get these feelings. The illuminated plant, he says, looks like metallic, shining whale teeth and he gets the feeling of awe and wonder that the first sight of a mountain in the distance after heavy rain has cleared or the blue band of sea meeting the sky on the way to a holiday cottage engender (I know it sounds strange but these were his words, more or less, odd as they are); then it is that he leaves the running ribbon motorway and follows an A-road back into the hills, then a country lane, and finally a farm track to a private place he knows at the top of an eminence (I'd never heard the word used in that way before) not all that far off the beaten track but high and solitary enough to feel the March wind cutting and buffeting the car, a private place where he stops the car, checks the central locking is on, and turns off the ignition and the in-car stereo system. He's safe inside and he doesn't want to go home yet. The traffic pulses leftwards, rightwards on the motorway far below, and directly opposite, so wide and bright that they seem almost within touching distance, that incredible bank of chemical lights like a vision of heaven in a science fiction film or a shimmering mechanised paradise you've visited in a dream. He wants to go nearer to the lights, which means driving straight at them from the hill, but an external force stays his hand and he doesn't switch the engine on. But he thinks about the possibility all the time, at his desk, in sales meetings, on the road, the possibility of revving up the engine and driving straight off the hill towards the lights across the river. He doesn't want me to think he's an unhappy man. In all sorts of way, he has an enviable life. Field sales and middle management have been very good to him. Car replaced every eighteen months, lovely wife Carol, two healthy kids, the converted barn. But work, Gavin, it takes over your whole life. Sometimes I wake up in the night – not properly, because my body is still sleeping – and this small part of my brain that never shuts down properly is flooded with light, clear as day, and it's off, thinking, thinking. Can't stop thinking. Write up that proposal, get on the supervisor's back, collate the third quarter's figures, go up and see the finance manager, have a look at those dockets, motivate, organise, lead. You've got to develop that training manual, take people out for lunch, get your departmental budget into some sort of shape for the board, try and find new ways of selling things. Then there is the insecurity that comes with the territory. It takes a very special kind of person to be a successful salesman, Gavin. All the time, you know that there are at least a dozen other blokes working the same hours as you, covering the same ground, watching you, waiting for you to put a foot in the wrong place, say the wrong thing, lose a client, misread a spreadsheet, get sick, lose your nerve. They are your mates, colleagues, brothers. Every day you crawl through muck and bullets with them and on some wild nights you drink and feast and see things together at two in the morning that you couldn't share with anybody else, not even your own wife, and yet not one of those guys, Gavin, they wouldn't piss on you if you were on fire in the street if they thought they could step into your shoes. So then you think, all right, everything stops, I lose my job, what do I do? What on earth do I do? Get another job? I'm forty-eight, I'm over experienced and under qualified. Everything I know in life is tied up in this organisation. I work off instinct, the smell of men, and the possibility of making a sale. I don't know much about computers and the internet – sure, I know which end of a computer is which and how to write a letter but I don't know how they work, what they really mean. Jesus, I can drive a car but I can't tell you how everything works in it. But these new guys that are coming through, they've got presentation software, bandwidth, newsgroups, palm pilots, I don't know. The whole language has changed. I know how to talk to customers, find out what they want and sell it to them but now I'm starting to wonder whether the old techniques are all you need anymore. Jesus. So one day, it could happen, I get the call to go upstairs, and there's a bunch of older guys in suits sitting around a table and the guy who has asked you up there, you go back a long way and have gone through the same shit with each other, he's looking at you in a way that he's never looked at you before, there's a thin, gauzy veil between you for the purposes of the meeting, it's not personal, it's purely business, and you know the older guys, some of whom are from outside, have been looking at the spreadsheets and the appraisal reports, they don't know about you, don't care about how experienced you are, how committed you are, what you've put in to the company, how proud your wife has been of your advancement, bottom rung to the top, a little note from the kids slipped into your lunch box, photos on the desk, that whole soft-furnishings world that you crawl into at night and the weekend, the pet names and the reassurances, family holidays and the supermarket run. They're not concerned because they can't allow themselves to be concerned just as you could never allow yourself to be concerned when you called some guy upstairs into the same room with a bunch of older guys in spectacles and grey suits from outside, slipping the glass wall up, sit down Barry/David/Peter, I'll come straight to the point. You can probably guess what this is about. Believe you me, it doesn't give me any pleasure to have to do this but I'm obliged to tell you that the board – gesturing at the men around the table – have recommended some changes to the management structure of the department and that I'm afraid that we're going to have to release you. The anonymous, grey-suited cowards can't even do their own dirty work. Naturally, we will be putting together a package that reflects your contribution to the organisation and your present salary level. These details will be confirmed by the personnel manager but in the meantime it's felt that it would be in everybody's interest if you don't try to return to your desk after this meeting is concluded. Your personal effects will be sent on to you. I am sure that I speak for the board, too, when I say that you have played an extremely valuable role in helping the organisation reach its present level of profitability. From a personal point of view, I will miss you as a colleague and as a friend. Unless you have any questions, we won't go any further. The personnel manager has cleared her diary for the rest of the day and will be able to see you straight away. Thank you. Yes, Gavin – here he took his glasses off and looked me fully and frankly in the eye – I have told other men that the company no longer has a role for them. No longer needed. Not wanted. Not good enough. Nothing that they have is of any use to us. Go away. Get out. Don't try to return to your desk. Can you imagine what it must feel like to be told that? How dirty and furtive must you feel when they tell you not to try to return to your desk? But I want to get the picture of my daughter at her birthday party from the bottom drawer. But I must collect my address book. But I bought a present for my wife at lunchtime. Please. This is hard enough as it is. We insist that you do not try and return to your desk. It isn't your desk any longer, you see. The desk belongs to the company. Your role in the company no longer exists. It's not personal. You have no more reason for going to that desk now than the postman. Perhaps even less reason, for he at least has a dynamic relationship with the organisation. You haven't. The sooner we can sort out the financial and legal aspects of your severance the sooner you can begin to think clearly about the future. But I've always thought of my future as being here. I don't want to think of it outside of this company. I'm afraid that the decision has been made and there's nothing you or I can do about it. I hope that you don't think that I'm being unnecessarily harsh; it's just that this sort of business should be wrapped up as quickly as possible, in the interests of all the participants. Please don't make me leave. If you can, please try to bring your emotions under control. I understand that this is a very difficult time for you; please don't make things worse. But they already are worse. I loved working here. I've done nothing bad, have I? What have I done that's been so wrong? I've always given my best, I've been loyal. My sick record is very good. I've never looked for another job – not even out of casual curiosity. Please don't make me leave. I love working here. I'm sorry, but I'm going to have to terminate this interview if you continue in this vein. This isn't a pleasant task for me either, you know. We are offering an excellent package, including full salary for three months' notice that you won't be required to work. My wife used to be so proud of me. I'm sorry? My wife. She would wave me off every morning and sometimes she'd slip in a little note from one of the kids, hello Daddy, here's a picture of Toby – Toby was a little ginger cat we had, got him from a farm – lots of love from Emma. Emma's going to university next year, we've recently put her horse in new stables. Luke will be able to learn to drive soon. I don't know where the years go. It's bad at night. I look at my wife sleeping beside me, so peaceful and innocent, and I reach out to touch her but it's like she's dissolving in front of me, and I look at my own hand and I can see right through it to the bedroom window. I feel like I'm dissolving too. These warm, feeling human beings that rely on me, they don't want me to dissolve. What can I do? Keep working, blot out the fear. You can't go back, Gavin. Blot out the fear. Better get used to it. Yes, all right Lee, I'll have one more. Here, get some cigars for everyone. I like you, Gavin, you'll fit in well.

'Six months later we're back at the same restaurant. I've fitted in well, like he said I would. I've hit the ground running, know my way round, spend a lot of time north of the border looking after some big clients. We're up in the lounge, the little bald manager has taken our order, we're supping pints of lager, and the waiter comes up to say that the table's ready. All the lads get up but Graham says, hang on Gavin, I want a word with you. Turns out there's been some little query from accounts about an expense claim I submitted. He's gentle at first, giving me the benefit of the doubt. But the problem is I had been a little bit naughty with a couple of receipts for meals out, slipped them through anyway and assumed that the accounts boys would turn a blind eye in the usual way. You know, the forty-miles-in-a-thirty-zone protocol. Turns out the auditors have been in and they've been sniffing around some of the claims Graham's boys have been submitting, he's had a flea in his ear so he's got to find someone to take it out on. Now I know that he knows what I've done, and he knows that I know. But he plays it so low-key at first — must be some mistake in accounts, he's sure there is a simple explanation but he's got to find out what it is. Let's go through it step by step. The receipts went upstairs with the form and you gave a copy to Sheila. Did Sheila initial the receipts? How many receipts did you say there were altogether? Okay, the form goes upstairs with the receipts and Sheila files it away. Is that right? What I don't understand is how the figure that appears in Sheila's summary sheet is different to the one that accounts have if, as you say, you gave Sheila a copy of the form. Naturally, I can get Sheila to pull out a file copy tomorrow. That's not the point, though. I'm trying to get a handle on how this could have happened. Let's go back to the start. You get back from Scotland. The orders docket goes upstairs. You keep hold of the carbons – right? Did you complete the third section? You're not sure. But in any case, Sheila would have picked that up, I know she would, this is routine work for her. No, I'm puzzled about how two completely different figures appear for the same claim. It shouldn't happen. Now, a process of elimination will help me establish how this has happened, but in the meantime you might like to wrack your brains one more time and tell me if there's anything you should have told me that you haven't. He takes his glasses off and looks me full in the face. Because I'm obliged to tell you that this question will be raised at tomorrow's operational planning meeting. Yes, Dennis will want a full report. No I, can't give you any indication as to the outcome, Gavin. My remit only extends so far. You'll just have to wait and see. I'm sorry, Gavin. I run a tight fucking ship. All right? He pats me on the knee. Good lad. Let's go and join the others. Don't let what I've just said spoil your meal. We sit down at the table but it's as much as I can do to finish my starter. Graham's on good form, cracking jokes and getting stuck in with the boys. Afterwards we go to the same basement club but this time I don't sit with him. Proper bastard. I'm thinking, that time when we were drunk and you told me all that stuff about wanting to drive your car off the hill and the fear that ate you up at night, but I won't confront him, of course I won't, he knows that. Graham is unassailable. He could tell me his deepest, dirtiest secrets and I would take them to my grave or until either of us leaves the company, whichever is the sooner, because Graham could pull the rug from under my feet, spit-roast me and hang me out to dry with one little word or gesture. This isn't about the expenses discrepancy. I'll get a bollocking and a written warning from the finance director, that's the worst that can happen, it will blow over quickly, and anyway they've all got their snouts in the trough one way or another, it was just bad timing as far as I was concerned. No, this is because Graham knows that I've listened while he laid all that maudlin crap on me, and didn't flinch. I have to live with the knowledge that Graham is a doubt-ridden paranoiac who will probably top himself (and his family too) one fine day, if a heart attack doesn't get him first, but he knows that I've got a taste for the life too and that I'll hang on to it as tenaciously as he does and one day stand as he does looking at the trapdoor under my feet and wondering when it will open. What he's done is hold up a future-mirror to me. And I will hang on tenaciously. Because when you're selling well and earning good commission, life is tasty. A few good deals sorted out north of the border, long-term bookings and a developing new business base, and suddenly you're buying a quad bike for the weekends, holidays in Italy, ordering from the upper end of the menu. You don't want to drop through that trapdoor into the world of call centres, warehouses and canteens. I've been there. It's not comfortable. Graham's right. Even after the rush has gone and you're grinding away, call after all, visit after visit, new exciting sales opportunity after new exciting sales opportunity, you're always going to hang on to it. Because when you've been in sales that long, there's little else that you can do. And pretty soon, you get to do the same mindfuck yourself on some poor new guy trying to keep up with the pints in the Pig on the Green or the Frottage and Flea or whatever the hell it's called, and you say, I like you, Mr Johnson, you'll fit in, I can tell. Come on, let's join the others.'

Mr Johnson opened his eyes. The courtyard was cooler and gloomier than before. The two Tonys and Mark had already gone back indoors. Gavin ground his last cigarette out on the pebbledash and led Mr Johnson back up the concrete stairwell and down the grey corridor to the sales department.

CHAPTER THREE
JUDY ORION

MARGARET LOOKED UP as they entered. 'That's quite a smoke break for a non smoker,' she said, but she didn't seem cross. 'Luckily for you the phones have only just come back on.'

'I was initiating Mr Johnson into the wonderful world of sales,' said Gavin. 'I think I overran.'

'God help him,' said Margaret. 'I'm sorry to say, Mr Johnson, that we've got phones but still no desk for you. I suppose we can't have everything at once. You'll have to stay with Tony for the time being. No sign of Judy Orion. I'll try Debbie Stevens again.'

Mr Johnson resumed his watch at Tony's side. 'I suppose I should take you through the basics of the sales process,' Tony said. 'You could listen to me on the phone but it might be a good idea to get some background first. There's a training session later on which you're probably going to. Has anyone mentioned that to you?'

'No, but since there seems to be so much confusion about where I should be sitting and what I should be doing, that's not a surprise. At my interview, in-house training opportunities were mentioned. I'll be glad to get some grounding in the theory before I have to address the practice.'

'What sales experience do you have, exactly?' Tony asked.

Mr Johnson explained about the impromptu presentation he had made at his last company and said that he was keen to develop his skills in this area. 'But as I mentioned to you before, I didn't intend to concentrate on sales at the expense of other skills and experiences.'

'I'm sure you didn't. But cynicism aside, a good grounding in sales can give you an insight into most other areas of business, if you're so inclined. I don't want to sound like Judy Orion, but it's true.'

'Can you really be trained to be a good sales person or is it about instinct and innate ability?'

'Yes you can, to an extent. If you think about it, you can pretty much be trained to do anything, within reason. Although much of the training industry is like snake-oil selling, it's possible to pick up some useful tips here and there. Some people don't need training at all. I'm not sure about that – in my experience, most formal training is worthless but I don't think you can learn everything on the job. You'll always get the instinctive sales animal types like

Margaret, but there are fewer of them around these days. The best way to approach sales is to accept that it's a job that you have to do and just get on with it. Pick up whatever advice you can from experienced people, listen to what they say and how they say it, remember the basic techniques. It's a job like any other. We all grouse about it but none of us has made the effort to do anything else. Once you reach a basic level of competence – and provided that what you are selling has some value to somebody somewhere, even if you don't see it – you can get on reasonably well. Then, probably against your better inclinations, you are a salesperson. But nobody has forced your hand. However talented and wonderful you think you are, you are in sales. And why shouldn't you be? If you dislike it so much, go and do something more interesting. That's what I think, all the talk about escape committees and the extended cigarette breaks aside. It's hardly coal mining. On the one hand we detest the job, and on the other we do it to the best of our abilities (sometimes) and with a certain degree of pride. There's no denying that making a sale is immensely satisfying. It's a strange kind of duality, I know. People like Gavin are just the same. He's had more experience than me. Gavin should probably be presenting arts reviews on the television or running a minor dictatorship somewhere but here he is, worrying about his quarterly targets and telling stories about the past like any grizzled old rep. I suspect he'll do that until he retires, or runs amok one day with a machine gun. Probably the latter. I'm no different, or won't be in a few years. Do I worry about this? Yes and no. In the abstract, of course, I'm miserable. But on a day-to-day basis there are enough incentives to keep me at work. Or maybe I'm happy in the abstract and miserable on a day-to-day basis. It's increasingly difficult to tell. Sales is just a job that pays the bills, really – some months more than others, of course.'

'What would you really like to do?'

'Who can say? As you get older, you become less and less confident in your ability to do anything other than what you are doing at that particular time. Ideally, I'd like the job history section on my CV to read "Lover of women" and "Prose stylist" but I don't suppose it's likely to. I don't want to depress you but the longer you stay anywhere, the harder it is to imagine moving on, let alone doing anything about it.'

'Is there much opportunity here for internal promotion or movement?'

'Yes and no. At the moment, as you can probably tell, the company is going through a period of tremendous flux. The whole strategic development thing was an early example of this, and rumours are circulating of bigger changes to come, possibly at the very top. I don't take much notice of that sort of thing myself, but I wouldn't be surprised if plans are being drawn up somewhere to bring in some new overall strategy that will redefine the way in which we all work and describe in new ways existing processes and practices that have served us very well for years but which some developmental team feel need overhauling. I don't mean to sound cynical but that's the way it usually works. It sounds as though you were with a much smaller outfit prior to joining us, so you won't have much experience of major organisational change. You'll soon get used to it here. My advice is to keep your head down and your ears pricked up. What you've got here are the basic problems common to organisations of a certain size – the problems that come with volume and mass, the attempts to clarify and define, the relentless obsession with matter. Perhaps I'm not making myself clear – these are just sense impressions, really. Perhaps the closer you get to the actual strategic decision making processes, the clearer the picture becomes. My role is very specific and my ability to make decisions limited. If I worked in conceptual initialisation, for example, I might feel differently.'

'Margaret, whom I met when I was waiting in the first-floor reception area, mentioned conceptual initialisation. It's a funny-sounding name. What goes on in there?'

'Between you and me, I'm not one hundred percent sure. If you asked our Margaret, she'd tell you that it's a department for people who fancy themselves as commercial hot-shots but who don't want to pick up a telephone. She's always banging on about the bloody concept engineers swanning around telling everybody what to do. That's a bit unfair but when you work in sales you do tend to develop an us-and-them complex. It's basically a sort of marketing function mixed up with product development and ideas-generation. If that sounds vague, it's supposed to. Conceptual initialisation is still a relatively new enterprise and I haven't had the time to find out more about it. I knew a few people who went to work in it but I've sort of lost touch with them.'

'If I'm honest,' said Mr Johnson, 'the little I've heard of conceptual initialisation makes it sound an appealing proposition, something more in line with the job I imagined I'd be doing when I applied for the graduate management programme rather than what the job looks like it might be from my experiences here so far. But isn't it true that conceptual initialisation falls within strategic development along with sales?'

'Yes, and straight marketing, business development, product maintenance and client profiling – the point is, there is so much overlap that it doesn't really do to get hung up on the exact definitions. It all depends on what you do. From my point of view, and without being all parochial about it, sales is the most important function in the company because we bring the money through the door. I'm sounding like Margaret again, but it's true – at least, we try to bring the money through the door. Every company hits a lean period from time to time. But if you asked a concept engineer what was the most important function in the company, they would tell you it was conceptual initialisation and explain it in terms of the primacy of ideas generation and strategic overview. The cleaners have their own particular view as do the accountants and the despatch clerks. It's a normal condition in an organisation of a certain size. As for your own promotional prospects, who can say? Look around you. There are thirty or so people in here at varying levels of experience and competence. Some will get new jobs elsewhere in the sales industry, others different or more senior roles in this or other departments. And some will fossilise slowly over time. I'm afraid that's the most likely route for all of us regardless of our own ambitions and expectations. But that's me being jaded. You seem a motivated character who's keen to learn and eager to acquire new skills. Good luck to you. But first of all you've to get to grips with the telesales question. I've been rambling – you should have told me to shut up and get to the point. We'll go through the basics of the sales presentation and then you can listen to me while I make a few calls.'

Tony had begun to explain to Mr Johnson how they went about canvassing for new business when a woman appeared at Mr Johnson's shoulder and introduced herself as Judy Orion. Mr Johnson stood up and shook hands positively.

'I'm sorry about the mix-up and confusion,' she said warmly. 'I'm sure Tony's been looking after you.' Tony nodded and looked embarrassed. Mr Johnson took his hand out of his pocket where he had put it after shaking Judy's.

'If you'd like to come with me I'll explain your role in more detail and give you your induction programme.'

Mr Johnson followed Judy into an office at the far end of the room. It was furnished with a desk and swivel chair, a low two-seater settee and a pine bookcase packed with what looked like motivational texts.

'Please, sit down. I would have seen you earlier but I was called into a meeting first thing. How are you finding everything so far?'

Mr Johnson sat on the settee. 'I'm just finding my feet, really. I haven't done that much yet. The usual first day – trying to remember names and faces, who does what, that sort of thing. Tony had just started explaining how they canvass for new business.'

'It will all make sense in time. I don't want to overwhelm you with information from the word go but I do like to take the time to get to know my staff personally. Sales is all about building relationships and that starts with the relationship between the salesperson and their manager.'

'I meant to ask you about that,' said Mr Johnson, and got the letter out of his pocket. 'I was told to report to Mr Bannister. Is he my manager or are you?'

'A bit of both,' said Judy. 'Les is responsible for the operational side of things. I deal with personalities. My strength is helping people bring out the best in themselves. I was brought in to do a very specific job. Les has his own way of running things, which I respect, of course, but you'll be seeing much more of me on a day-to-day basis. Les and I run on different but complementary paths. It's a sort of simultaneous management structure, if you like. Does that make sense?'

'Yes, I think so. I'm sure everything will become clearer the longer I spend here.'

Judy leaned back in her chair behind her desk; Mr Johnson leaned forward on the settee.

'What's your background, Mr Johnson?'

Mr Johnson told Judy about his academic record and recent work experiences. She seemed particularly interested in his involvement in sales at his last job. He didn't embellish his account but he was worried that Judy might overestimate his experience in this area.

'What I really want to do is to develop my commercial skills in a creative environment,' he said, trying to steer the conversation in a vaguer direction.

'Excellent,' said Judy. 'You are in exactly the right place. We have a very strong commercial focus – of course. And creativity is always encouraged.'

'How long have you worked here?' Mr Johnson asked her.

Judy raised her eyes to the ceiling. 'Let me see – two-and-a-half, no, it must be over three years now. There's a bit of a story behind it, actually. I was brought in initially on a consultancy basis. The executive director wanted to develop the company's sales profile. I came in to provide one-to-one coaching in sales technique and motivation and ended up staying here. I suppose I must have been doing something right. My present role developed from there.'

'Have you always been in sales?'

'Not at all. I've had quite a varied career and came to sales relatively late on. I've done all sorts of things. For me, sales is what you might call a late vocation. I didn't have any formal training in it. I've been very fortunate. I was at a loose end a few years ago and applied for a telesales job. I'd never thought about sales before. I took to it naturally. I was also lucky enough to have couple of extremely influential mentors, there and in other places – people who were prepared to pass on their wisdom and experience and who took the time to help me develop my skills. But there is no magic secret to sales, Mr Johnson. It's all about self belief and confidence. I firmly believe that. If you have self belief and confidence, you can do anything.' He didn't demur. 'I don't mind telling you that before I joined, this company's sales profile was in a very bad state. Productivity low, morale lower. I'm not blaming individuals – it was a cultural thing. Business was conducted along traditional lines: this is how we do things here, always have done, always will do. Do you know what I mean? I'll never forget what one of my mentors told me when I first worked in the industry: habit is the handmaiden of inertia. Root habit out. But how do you do that?'

Mr Johnson looked thoughtful – he wasn't sure whether he was expected to respond. He wasn't.

'Not the way that some managers would do it – that is to say, by sacking people. One of my colleagues, I won't name names, thinks about staff in terms of a card index. He talks about shuffling people who aren't needed to the back of the box until the time comes to bring them to the front again. That's not my way. You don't have to remove people from post. When I took over this department, I didn't get rid of anybody. Not that there wasn't a good case for doing so, or that I wouldn't have had the full backing of the senior management cluster. But I didn't need to. Do you know what I did? I talked to every member of staff personally, asked them what motivated them, why they came to work, what frustrated them about the job. You see, I had to get to know them as people before I could justify any decision I made about them. And what I found was a lot of dissatisfied employees, Mr Johnson. People with talents that they had never been given the opportunity to develop. People stuck in a rut, coming to work like robots and whiling the day away until it was time to go home. Because nothing was expected of them. No-one was challenging them. My job was to challenge them. How did I do that? Not through major surgery, that's for sure. I tweaked things here and there, picked out certain individuals for particular tasks, changed the structure, introduced new incentives. Motivational meetings every morning. Nothing earth shattering. I called everyone into a meeting room and left the door open. I told them that after listening to what everyone had had to say, there were going to be some changes to the way that the department worked. No-one was going to lose their job – in fact, if everything went according to plan, more staff would be recruited. It wasn't going to be easy – they would have to work harder and be more versatile. I was completely honest with them: I told them that the fortunes of the entire company rested on the sales department improving its productivity. But I knew that they could do it. I knew that they could make themselves proud of what they achieved at work. I've left the door open deliberately, I said. That's my management style. But it is also open so that anybody who doesn't want to stay for the ride can get off and leave right now.'

She leaned across the desk. 'Not one of them left the room. Not one.'

She sat back again. 'That's all it took. I told them that I believed in them and they started to believe in themselves. And I do believe in them. There's no mystery. This job isn't rocket science. It's about listening – that's selling in a nutshell. The 70/30 principle – you'll be familiar with that, I'm sure. Sales people should listen for seventy percent of the time and talk for thirty. That is something I try to practise in all areas of my life. As well as being the art of the possible, sales is the art of persuasion, and once I'd persuaded the sales department that they could do a good job, that they had what it took to be winners, half my job was done. The rest is about keeping motivational levels high and monitoring their performance.'

She paused and turned to drink from a plastic bottle of water so that she was outlined in profile against the window sunshine. Her hair shone in waving bands of gold.

'You've got a very impressive library,' said Mr Johnson.

'I like to keep abreast of the current thinking. Knowledge is power. Needless to say, it is the Americans who are leading the way in these matters.'

She took from the shelves two glossy, colourful volumes, each with a portrait of the same square-faced, evangelical-looking man on the cover.

'Have you ever read Ted Schturm?' she asked. Mr Johnson shook his head. He hadn't heard of Ted Schturm.

'He's extremely influential. I read this book' (she held up a copy of Free Your Mind And Your Profits Will Follow) 'in one sitting. This one' (The Team That Trains Together Stays Together) 'is the seminal work on team building. I like to introduce some of the issues from these books into our daily motivational meetings. Some of my staff have even organised study weekends where they discuss the books in greater depth. It's not just theory – these American writers really know what they're talking about. Ted Schturm, for example, used to be a janitor and now he's CEO of the same organisation. There's a great training video he's produced called From The Basement To The Thirtieth Floor that begins with a shot of his office building from a helicopter and his voice describing how he literally worked his way up from the bottom to the top of the company. It's absolutely true. The US is very different to the UK. They really respect sales people over there. Sales people are treated like gods. In the US, Mr Johnson, selling is regarded as a profession no different in significance to law or medicine. That's our task: to professionalise the sales industry, to ensure that it is given the respect it deserves. Have you ever been to the United States?'

Mr Johnson shook his head. 'No, but I'm very interested in American literature. I studied Transcendentalism as an option in my third year at university.'

'It's a different world,' said Judy. 'I lived in the US for three years. I've seen the way that people go to work there. They are naturally positive. Not like in this country where everybody sits on the bus grumbling and coughing or slumped behind the wheel of their car moaning about the traffic. In America, they look forward to going to work. It's the can-do attitude that makes all the difference. Do you know what the first thing I did when I came here was? I banned the word "can't". It doesn't exist here anymore. I don't want to hear it. The only obstacles to being the best you can be are the ones you erect yourself. Children don't have the same inhibitions. They just ask, "why not?" and keep on asking until you realise, why not indeed?'

Judy pulled a video from the shelf. 'I recommend that you watch this at the earliest opportunity,' she said, handing Mr Johnson a copy of Impossible Ain't A Word I Know by Warren Hootz, a heavy-set man with a drooping moustache and sad eyes.

'I love this video. The team watches it at least once a month. Warren Hootz used to work in the garment industry in New York. The gist of it is that for years everybody in the industry said "nobody sells clothes in July". So nobody did. But Warren Hootz said: "I bet I can sell clothes in July". And he did, and made himself a millionaire in the process. It proves that you should never believe something just because everybody says it's true. His video is great. It begins with him addressing a breakfast convention at a Chicago hotel where he tells the audience to each give him a dollar bill. He's so persuasive that they all do. Then he says: "Look, you have all given me a dollar bill. I'm now $250 dollars richer just from asking you. If only selling was as easy as that." You see, he had confidence and self-belief. But I believe we can all be as confident as Warren Hootz.'

Judy took the video from Mr Johnson and put it back on the shelf.

'I don't mind telling you that sales has been the making of me. I wasn't always like this. When I was younger, about your age, in fact, I wanted to save the whales, give all my possessions away, live in a commune – classic utopian stuff. I worked in an charity shop when I left college, would you believe. I know, it is hard to believe. Then I got married, quite young, had two children, marriage broke up, I drifted a while, not sure what I wanted to do, local government officer, data processing, all sorts of different things, until I got the telesales job I mentioned. I was thirty-four, I'd never sold before and like a lot of people who don't know the business I had many misconceptions. It's the myth of the dodgy double-glazing salesman, I'm afraid. He's done our profession so much harm. But what I discovered was that you don't need experience to be a good salesperson. I firmly believe that anybody can sell. It's going on all around us, all the time. Every day in a million significant and insignificant ways, mankind is engaged in the act of selling. I'm not just talking about the workplace. It's everywhere. The art of persuasion: we practise it at home, in the street, with our husbands, wives, children, parents, friends. We sell each other ideas, arguments, feelings. It's human nature at its most natural. Selling is about people being people. We can all do it. I have a lot of friends in the performing arts and they all agree. Many of them would make first-class salespeople, in fact. Everyone can sing, Mr Johnson. It's just that most of us don't get the opportunity to develop our natural voice. It's the same with selling. We all possess the wherewithal to become successful sales people. Some more so than others, of course – we can't all be Pavarottis. I wonder what your natural sales voice is, Mr Johnson? Are you a light baritone? A tenor, perhaps? There's room for all types of voice in this choir. But I digress. As I was saying, I was fortunate enough in my first sales job to have a very influential mentor. He taught me much of what I know today. There are certain techniques without which all the raw talent in the world is in vain. You'll be familiar with some of these, I'm sure. The art of closing. Features, advantages, benefits. The importance of listening. The benefit sandwich. Open questioning. One thing I insisted on for my staff when I started here was a thorough grounding in sales technique. Do you know, some of them didn't know what an assumptive close was? I know, it is hard to believe, isn't it? I brought in an expert trainer from outside, someone I had worked with before. He has since joined the organisation permanently as in-house sales training provider. He is running a training session this morning, which I'm assuming you are going to attend. He's called Leo Porter, a very good friend of mine. We go back a long way. I firmly believe that you can't go back to basics often enough. We have to keep refreshing the essentials, Mr Johnson, if we are to be the best we can be.'

Judy got up quickly and shut the door.

'I'm going to ask you something I ask every new starter,' she said, positioning herself between him and her desk. 'I want you to answer me honestly. Are you a winner, Mr Johnson? Are you?'

She stared at him unblinking.

'Because this is a winning team. There is no room for passengers. The door is open. If you want to leave, now is the time to do so.'

Mr Johnson blinked and swallowed hard. The air in the office felt heavy and close. Judy's large blue eyes swam in and out of focus.

'Yes,' he said at length, 'yes, I am a winner.'

Judy laughed and clapped her hands.

'Of course you are. We wouldn't have employed you if you weren't. And anyway, I've made people winners before now.'

She sat down behind her desk again.

'There are people out there' – she gestured wildly with her right arm at the office spreading out beyond her windows – 'who used to be too scared to pick up the telephone. I've seen grown men and women grab the handset, put it down, grab it, put it down. They were actually scared of the telephone, the very tool of their trade. One young woman, I won't name names as she is still here, was an habitual thumb-sucker. Couldn't look you in the face when she spoke to you. Now she's a regular monthly top performer and is being considered for promotion. Frequently chairs meetings, makes presentations. Couldn't be more different. Confidence and self belief: the two most powerful weapons in the salesperson's armoury.'

Judy looked suddenly weary and turned away; she seemed cast in shadow. She smoothed her hair back automatically and drank from her bottle again.

'I love sales people,' she said after a moment. 'They're the most honest people in the world. I care about my staff, really care about them.'

She shivered as if fighting back tears.

'Needless to say, if there's anything you need from me, just ask. You are part of the team now. We'll be seeing a lot of each other.'

'There is something, as a matter of fact,' said Mr Johnson.

'Yes?'

'It sounds as though the job is almost entirely sales based. But from the description I thought that there would be more of a marketing angle – the bit about devising market-specific solutions, for example.'

'Which is exactly what sales is,' said Judy.

'Yes, I realise that. But I am keen to develop a broad range of skills. Will I have the opportunity to develop in other areas?'

Judy smiled and sat back.

'You're enthusiastic and ambitious, aren't you? I like that. You remind me of me when I started my sales career. All I will say is that if you prove yourself and do well, I don't see any reason why you shouldn't go in any direction you like. But first, you've got to show us what you can do with a telephone. Believe you me, there is no better way of finding out what a person is made of. Develop new business, hit your targets – the world will be your oyster. It's all down to you. Is that clear?'

'Yes, I think so. One other thing – you mentioned my induction programme.'

'I'm sorry?'

'My induction programme.'

'Yes,' Judy said, riffling through her in-tray, 'actually, no. It doesn't look as though it has been typed up yet. But I'll sort one out for you. To be honest with you, Mr Johnson, if it was up to me there wouldn't be an induction programme at all. I don't mean to sound flippant. There is no substitute for getting into the job straight away and finding things out for yourself – hand in hand with the appropriate training, of course. I'm all for throwing people in at the deep end. As one of my mentors used to say, if you swim in the shallows how will you catch the big fish? But it's a personnel requirement so we'll just have to put up with it. Don't worry about the schedule for now. You can start off with a preliminary sales training session with Leo, which will be time well spent. That will teach you pretty much everything you need to know about working here. You'll find your colleagues willing to help at all times. Anything else, Margaret will sort you out. And my door is always open – though not right at this minute.'

She laughed, got up, shook Mr Johnson's hand and opened the door. 'Now go out and put yourself in danger of making a sale.'

This time they both laughed and Mr Johnson walked across the office to Margaret's desk, where another sales executive had just rung the brass bell.

'Well done, Joanne love, that's the third one today, hello Mr Johnson love, has Judy sorted you out?'

'Yes, it was very interesting. I'm supposed to be doing preliminary sales training with someone called Leo Porter. Do you know where I should go?'

Margaret looked at her watch. 'That's taking place about now. Tony, are you doing this training course with Leo Porter?'

'Yes,' said Tony rising from his desk. 'They want someone with a bit of experience in there,' he said with a wink at Mr Johnson.

They went out through a door at the back of the sales office by the long board, which Mr Johnson now saw was divided according to names. An empty column had been added on the side nearest the door headed 'Mr Johnson'. Someone had been expecting him, at least.

CHAPTER FOUR
SALES TRAINING

Tony led Mr Johnson along a narrow carpeted corridor, up two flights of stairs and through a door marked 'Training Suite'. They entered a small room in which sat two other young men at a round table. Both had pieces of folded card in front of them on which they had written the word 'Andy'. A flip chart stood to one side.

Mr Johnson introduced himself. Tony appeared to know them already.

'Are you two new here too?' Mr Johnson asked.

'Newish,' said the Andy nearest to Mr Johnson.

'Sort of,' said the other. 'I've been here about two months.'

Mr Johnson wrote his name on a piece of blank card and opened a vinyl presentation case that had been placed on the table in front of him along with a small bottle of sparkling mineral water and a plastic cup.

'Is this mine?' he asked Tony.

'The famous starter pack,' said Tony. 'You're honoured.'

Inside the case was a pad of lined paper and a ballpoint pen. Although he didn't let on, Mr Johnson was quite impressed with this. He pledged inwardly to keep a daily record of ideas and thoughts and not to doodle.

'Actually,' said Tony, 'I've forgotten to bring any paper. Could you lend me some?'

Mr Johnson tore a few sheets off for Tony and offered the two Andys some but they both had spiral-bound notebooks with them.

Tony and the Andys began to discuss various clients and sales they had and hadn't made. From their conversation, Mr Johnson gathered that the market was static at the moment and there was a lot of pressure on the sales team to cultivate new business. But the lead generation process wasn't working very well. Apparently, a dedicated lead generator had left over a month ago and hadn't been replaced as yet. This wasn't surprising; the job wasn't very attractive, as it necessitated spending all day trawling through newspapers, magazines and websites for leads and entering them into a database. The other problem was that many leads, even good ones, weren't followed up by the sales reps. Tony said that it was simply a matter of time and that the natural instinct was to rely on your existing client base. Nobody really liked cold calling, even though it was an essential part of the job. One of the Andys said that he didn't mind cold calling but perhaps that was because he was still relatively new. Mr

Johnson didn't say anything; his own limited sales experience wasn't enough to form an opinion on cold calling, or, indeed, any kind of calling, and in any case had come about only because someone had phoned in. He had been pleased with the way he had handled the enquiry but knew that the caller had already had some interest in the company's services. It was hard to imagine picking up the phone and making a presentation to someone who had never heard of him or the company he represented. But he supposed that this and other issues would be dealt with in the training session and that he would become used to it in time.

Leo Porter swept in. He was stocky and tanned with close-cropped grey hair. He wore rimless glasses and a gold watch and looked as though he had just come back from a long holiday.

'Morning gang,' Leo said. 'I know Tony but what about the rest of you? Who are you and what have you been up to?'

The two Andys and Mr Johnson introduced themselves and gave a brief account of their background and experiences to date. Leo asked them what they thought about working in sales. The Andy who had been with the company for two months said that he found the office a stimulating environment because of the number of people who worked in it. At his last company, an IT service provider, he had been closeted away in a cubicle and didn't speak to anyone for days at a time. He found the atmosphere in the office supportive and enjoyed the balance it provided between individual effort and teamworking. The other Andy said that although he had never planned to have a career in sales, he was surprised that he had taken to it as well as he had. He had made his first sale the previous week and felt that he had broken something of a pain barrier. Leo agreed that the first sale was the hardest and said that he must be a natural because he'd started selling even before he'd had any formal training.

Mr Johnson explained that he knew very little about formal sales as such but wanted to find out as much as possible and develop new skills. Since it was his first day and there had been some confusion about where he was supposed to sit, it was too early to say what he thought of his experiences so far. But the more he got to know people, the more confident he would become.

Leo thanked them for their input. 'So not a lot of sales experience as such, except for Tony of course.'

'It's always worth doing a refresher course, Leo,' Tony said.

'Absolutely. You never stop learning in this game. Routine is the handmaiden of complacency, as someone once said. Right, I'm Leo Porter, I'm the in-house training provider. Sounds a bit formal. I've been in sales all my working life – I've done a bit of everything but I'm still learning every day. I came here as a consultant over a year ago – and I haven't left since. Not literally, of course – I do have a home to go to. And a wife. And three kids. And two dogs. Prior to this I worked in Australia for five years. But you don't want to hear my life story.'

He changed the subject as if flicking a switch. 'Why do we need sales people, Mr Johnson?'

Mr Johnson sat up and thought hard for a moment before saying: 'Because they bring the money in?'

'True enough. If nobody's selling, nobody's buying – and we go out of business. Andy? Two Andys, eh? Tell you what, you're Andy One and you're Andy Two. Andy One?'

'To inform customers about products and services.'

'To make sure my mortgage gets paid,' said Andy Two, and they all laughed.

'Spot on,' said Leo. 'Never underestimate the power of individual motivation for self-gratification ends.' He picked up a marker pen and drew a crude pyramid on the flip chart.

'Now, I'm going to throw my own rule book out here. A lot of sales trainers will bombard you with science and psychology. Mumbo jumbo for the most part. Sales shouldn't be that complicated. But this is worth remembering.'

Leo divided the pyramid into five sections and wrote in each one, in ascending order: *Physiological – Safety – Social – Esteem – Self-actualisation*.

Mr Johnson heard Tony mutter under his breath: 'Here we go again.'

'Has anyone come across this before?' Leo asked the room. 'Don't say anything, Tony.'

The two Andys and Mr Johnson drew a blank. 'No? Good. It's called Maslow's Hierarchy of Needs. Maslow was an American psychiatrist...'

'Psychologist,' murmured Tony.

'...who worked out that all human behaviour can be explained according to these categories. What's this got to do with sales? Good question. Surely sales is just about getting someone to part with their money? Good point. But it's not as simple as that. Everyone has their reasons. Maslow's Hierarchy of Needs explains what those reasons are. Each of these categories represents a key motivating factor. At a basic level, we all need food and water. As we develop, we proceed through the various stages until we reach self-actualisation, a condition that can only be arrived at when all the other needs have been met. In career terms, that means a good job, holidays and a pension – and a general sense of well satisfaction. Do you see what I'm driving at?'

'Is this something that applies to the salesperson or the customer?' asked

Andy One.

'Good question,' said Leo. 'The beauty of Maslow is that it applies to both equally. It helps you understand what buttons you should press with your customers and what motivates yourself. We've all got our personal motivations. Now I'm guessing here – I'll leave you out of this Tony, because I know what motivates you by now – but for the sake of argument and from what you've told me about yourselves so far, I'd say that you, Andy One, are primarily motivated by social factors, the need to express yourself in a broad environment. For Andy Two, on the other hand, I suspect that self-fulfilment is very important to you. Am I right?'

Both the Andys nodded solemnly.

'As for you, Mr Johnson, correct me if I'm wrong but I imagine you need a lot of validation and approbation from your peers. You are also very new here. I reckon that you are very strongly in the safety band.'

Mr Johnson wasn't sure what he should say but nodded approvingly nonetheless. It seemed to make a certain amount of basic sense.

'Okay, I'm no psychiatrist, and it's a good job considering the state of my mind, and this isn't an exact science, but I would recommend you have a think about Maslow and see how it applies in your work and in your home life. I don't want to get bogged down in it now but when you're in a live sales situation, you'll find that Maslow is extremely relevant. Any questions? Tony?'

'Yes, Leo, I think I've raised this with you before but wouldn't you agree that there's something overly deterministic and prescriptive, if not proscriptive, about Maslow's methodology, at least in the way that you've represented it? For example, the construction of the hierarchy implies that there is a sequential progress that can be made through its various stages leading finally to self-actualisation at the pinnacle. Yet, as you've suggested, individuals may be motivated by different factors at different times. This, surely, points to a prevailing condition of flux rather than fixity. On the other hand, implicit in what you and other sales trainers say about Maslow is that it is a useful correlative tool for understanding the actual process of, for example, a telesales call. Yet if both parties in the process are proceeding from different starting points, how does Maslow in this case explain, or provide a reliable guide to, the way in which that process should reach a conclusion? In other words, if a person motivated by physiological needs is trying to sell something to a person for whom self-actualisation is a key factor, how on earth will they understand each other? I don't mean to be picky – I'm just thinking aloud really.'

Leo Porter took off his glasses and sat down in front of the flip chart.

'Like I said, Tony, this isn't an exact science. You take from Maslow what you need, that's all. It's useful for identifying what motivates different people. It's just a pointer.'

Mr Johnson looked at his bottle of water. He suddenly realised that he was hungry.

'The other thing,' said Tony, 'and I don't mean to be funny but amongst psychologists, Maslow's Hierarchy of Needs hasn't had any credibility for a long time. I'm not getting at you, Leo, but I sometimes think that Maslow and a whole load of other models that sales trainers wheel out are a slightly more sophisticated version of Chinese whispers. I wonder who the first trainer was to hear about it and think, yes, I can apply that to the world of sales? Do you know what I'm saying? It's just a piece of work from a psychology paper in the 1960s that has been seized on by practitioners in a very different field who are looking for something to support their own notions of how their industry works. Very few people really know what Maslow was getting at and what the real application of his theories was supposed to be. It's just something that has acquired authority through repeated reference over time. In fact, I wouldn't be surprised if it transpired that Maslow was really called Moslow and in fact devised a hexagram rather than a pyramid, and that his name and ideas have been distorted through time. As I say, I'm not being personal. It's just a thought, really. I know we've discussed this before.'

Leo looked hard at Tony, who was doodling on his paper.

'Like I said, Tony, I'm not a psychologist. All I can say is that a lot of experienced people in the industry find Maslow and certain other models very useful. It's certainly helpful for people new to the job like Mr Johnson here. I'm not sure there is much point in getting bogged down in this any further. If anybody – apart from Tony, of course – wants a print-out of Maslow's Hierarchy of Needs, I'll run them a copy off after we've finished. Can we stop discussing it now?'

Mr Johnson stopped copying out the pyramid Leo had drawn on the board and opened his bottle of water. The training seemed to have entered a cul-de-sac. No one spoke for a short while.

'Smart-arse. You're worse than Leonard Bragby,' said Leo at length, only half-joshingly.

'Thanks a lot. I must have gone up in your estimation.'

'Who's Leonard Bragby?' asked Mr Johnson.

Leo and Tony looked at each other. 'Shall I?' said Tony.

Leo looked at his watch. 'If you want to see me tear what's left of my hair out and get the screaming ab-dabs, yes. But I'd rather press on. There's a lot to get through. So, no. Anyway,' he clapped his hands, 'enough theory. Let's look at the practice.'

Leo reached down and pulled out a sheaf of papers from his briefcase and handed each of them a sheet on which was written F. F. F. in large black letters.

'All right then – maybe a little more theory.'

'Here we go again,' muttered Tony. Mr Johnson thought he was sailing very close to the wind.

'Apologies to Tony, who has heard all this before, but I'm going to throw the rule book out again. I've said that sales is simple – which it is. There are no magic formulas. But this is as close to a universal skeleton key as it gets.'

He stood up and smiled. 'Any guesses as to what this means? F. F. F. Don't say anything, Tony.'

The two Andys and Mr Johnson pondered their pieces of paper.

'Anybody?'

'Facts, features and finish?' asked Andy Two.

'Good try, Andy,' said Leo. 'You're probably getting it mixed up with Features, Advantages, Benefits.'

'Judy Orion mentioned that,' said Mr Johnson. 'Is it something to do with closing a sale?'

'Sort of,' Leo said. 'It's the basic structure of the sales proposition. We'll cover it later. Anybody else?'

'Find Features First?' said Andy One.

'Finesse Final Features?'

'Final Financial Focus?'

'Frauds Fakes Finaglers?'

'Okay, you're not getting it.' Leo looked quite pleased about this. 'Tony, what's the biggest problem that sales people encounter?'

'Objections.'

'Exactly. You might be confident that what you are selling is really going to benefit the customer. But he just doesn't get it. And sometimes he'll use any excuse he can to get you off that phone. Anyone know the main objections you'll have to confront?'

'I haven't got any money?'

'Yes, Mr Johnson, good. Any others?'

'You're speaking to someone who isn't the decision maker?'

'Yes, good.'

'You're a fraud,' said Andy Two.

'Sorry, Andy, what do you mean?'

'I mean, the prospective customer doesn't have any faith in your proposition.'

'Yes, I see. Yes, spot on Andy. "I don't believe what you're telling me." "I don't need what you're trying to sell me." "I don't think it will work for me." Okay, I'll hold my hands up – sometimes you just can't get round the money objection, though there are ways of finding out whether it's a smokescreen or not, which we'll cover later. It can also be difficult getting round what we call the gatekeepers, i.e. a receptionist or secretary who is determined not to put you through to the decision maker. We'll look at strategies for dealing with that situation later, too. But what do you do when somebody just isn't convinced about the value of your product or service? Well, it just so happens that there is one foolproof way of countering them.'

Leo faced the flip chart and wrote in big red capital letters: *Feel – Felt – Found*. He turned back to the group with a look of triumph.

'Feel – Felt – Found. The Leo Porter patent remedy for sales objections. This is how it works. We're going to do a little role play. I'm a salesman from an imaginary company. Mr Johnson, I want you to be the customer. Bring your chair up next to mine.'

Mr Johnson moved next to Leo and sat forward with his hands on his knees.

'All right, Mr Johnson, I'm phoning you up and selling to you. I want you to throw some objections back at me.'

'I've never been in a role play before,' said Mr Johnson. 'What do I have to do?'

'Nothing too complicated. Just relax and imagine that you are a busy businessman. I'm sure that won't be too hard. I'll provide you with clues. Right? Right – we're in role – now.'

There was a pause.

'Ring, ring,' suggested Andy One.

'Sorry,' said Mr Johnson. 'Good morning, can I help you?'

'Good morning. I'd like to speak to Mr Johnson, please.'

'Who's calling?'

'It's Leo Porter from Patent Remedies Ltd.'

'Can I ask what your call is in connection with?'

'Yes, it's regarding your company's beverage and comestible flow management system.'

'I'm sorry, Mr Porter, are you trying to sell something? Because Mr Johnson won't be interested.'

The two Andys and Tony laughed.

'All right,' said Leo, clapping his hands, 'let's come out of role for a moment.

Actually, Mr Johnson, that's very good. You're thinking on your feet. Sometimes the hardest part of the call is getting past the receptionist. We'll cover that later. For the sake of argument, though, let's assume that I've got straight through to you. Okay – back in role... now.'

'Ring, ring.'

'Good morning, Mr Johnson speaking.'

'Good morning, Mr Johnson. It's Leo Porter here from Patent Remedies Ltd. Is this a good moment to talk to you? Always check that it's convenient,' Leo said in an aside to the group. 'It shows consideration. Yes, Mr Johnson, Leo Porter here. I hope this call hasn't come completely out of the blue. I should ask you whether you've heard of Patent Remedies Ltd before.'

'I don't think I have,' said Mr Johnson. 'What do you do?'

'I'd be delighted to explain. Patent Remedies provides bespoke business solutions for modern companies in a variety of sectors. I'm interested in finding out about your company, Mr Johnson, to see if we might be able to work together in the future. Is this a convenient time to talk to you?'

'Yes, it's all right. But is this a sales call, Mr Porter?'

'That all depends on you, Mr Johnson,' laughed Leo.

'That sounds ominous.'

'It wasn't meant to. But I'm getting ahead of myself. Am I right in thinking that you are responsible for your organisation's beverage and comestible management infrastructure?'

'Yes, that is correct.'

'Excellent. I wanted to make sure that I was talking to the right person. Would that include responsibility for the purchase of new beverage flow management systems?'

'Yes it would.'

'What systems do you use currently, Mr Johnson? Just make anything up,' he added, seeing the look of incomprehension on Mr Johnson's face.

'At the moment we use the Hi-Grade System provided by Wobtek Ltd.'

'And how long have you been using it?'

'Let me see – about two years,' said Mr Johnson.

'When is the contract up for renewal?'

'In six months' time.'

Leo simulated intensive note taking. 'Always make notes,' he said to the room. 'And how have you found the Hi-Grade System so far?'

'We're very pleased with it. It meets all our beverage and comestible needs.'

'I'd be interested to find out more about your exact requirements. Would you mind telling me about them?'

'Not at all,' said Mr Johnson, leaning back on his chair and placing his arms behind his head. 'What do you want to know?'

'Firstly, how many people work for your company?'

'Approximately 175.'

'And how many vending machines and food preparation utility areas do you have?'

'We have two drinks machines, a snack vending machine and one kitchen area, which contains a sink, a fridge and a microwave.'

'How are the vending machines maintained?'

'Wobtek provide a weekly maintenance service as part of the package.'

'Any other sources of food and drink?'

'Yes, a sandwich company sends a man round every day at 11.00am.'

'I bet he's a popular fellow.'

'Not really – the quality of the sandwiches is very poor. They are a series of variations on egg mayonnaise, including something called Welsh egg mayonnaise, which nobody buys.'

'That sounds unpleasant. Is the sandwich company connected to the Hi-Grade System?'

'No, it's an entirely separate enterprise.'

'That's very interesting. What are the most important things you look for in a beverage and comestible management flow system?'

Mr Johnson looked up at the ceiling, which was made of large, stippled polystyrene tiles. A strip of shaded fluorescent lights marched down the centre of the room. One of the tiles was mottled with damp.

'Well, I suppose value for money is the most important thing. Quality, too, of course.'

'What about the impact on the efficiency of the company? I'm thinking of things like the time employees spend going to and from the machines or to the kitchen areas.'

'Well, as a matter of fact, that is a bit of an issue for us.'

Leo winked at the others and rubbed his hands.

'In what way, Mr Johnson?'

'Sometimes it seems that everybody is away from their desks getting drinks. It can be very annoying at busy times.' He was thinking of the sales office when Margaret had told everyone to get on the phones.

'Have you tried to do something about it?'

'We instituted a maximum number of drinks per employee per day policy but it's a very difficult rule to enforce.'

'I bet it is. That sounds like quite a task you've got there.'

'Yes. Sometimes I wonder where it will all end.'

'If I can just re-cap a moment, Mr Johnson. You've told me that you are currently using the Hi-Grade System provided by Wobtek Ltd. The contract is up for renewal in six months' time. Value for money and quality are very important to you – of course – but you have what sounds like a big issue with the time your company is losing through employees' trips to the machine and kitchen area. Have I missed anything?'

'No, you've covered all the main points,' said Mr Johnson.

'Now this is where I come in. What if were to say to you that I could provide your company with a beverage and comestible flow management system that met all your quality requirements, was extremely competitive on price and solved the problem of employees trekking long distances to and from the vending machines and kitchen areas? What would you think of that?'

'It sounds very interesting in theory. How does it work in practice?'

'Patent Remedies Ltd, Mr Johnson, have developed a free-standing beverage and comestible utility unit that provides hot and cold drinks, hot and cold snacks – including sandwiches, so it's goodbye to Welsh egg mayo – and re-heating facilities. Being free-standing, it doesn't need to be plumbed in to the water mains and so can be situated wherever it is required. Despite providing a comprehensive range of services, the units are surprisingly compact and fit comfortably and discreetly into most office environments. What do you think about that?'

'It sounds too good to be true. Where's the catch?'

'There isn't one.'

'What about maintenance?'

'We provide a daily re-stocking and cleaning service as part of the package.'

'That sounds expensive.'

'It isn't. You haven't told me what you are paying at the moment but I'm confident that the Patent Remedies system will work out extremely economically for you. I'm convinced that we can work with you on this, Mr Johnson. What do you think?'

'I would have to see it first.'

'Of course. I wouldn't expect you to purchase such a sophisticated service unseen. We would be delighted to come in and give you a demonstration. Once you've seen the utility unit, you won't want to let it go, I can assure you. When would be a good time to do that?'

'How about tomorrow?'

'Yes, that would be wonderful.'

Leo paused and looked at Mr Johnson, who smiled back at him. 'Was there anything else?' Leo asked him.

'No,' said Mr Johnson. 'I think you've covered everything. I look forward to seeing you tomorrow.'

Leo clapped his hands. 'Out of role for a moment, please. Mr Johnson, I wish that all customers were like you.' The others laughed. 'You're supposed to throw up objections,' Leo said softly.

'I'm sorry,' said Mr Johnson. 'I was carried away with what you were telling me about the utility unit. It sounded ideal.'

'Try not to think about the utility unit too much. Object! All right – one, two, three: back in role now.'

'Actually, looking at my diary, tomorrow isn't convenient after all.'

'When would be convenient, Mr Johnson?'

'I don't know. I'll have to call you back. I'm very busy at the moment.'

'Is there anything that I haven't explained properly?'

'No you covered all the main points. Goodbye.'

Leo stared at him.

'It's just that I'm not convinced about what you're offering,' Mr Johnson added quickly.

'What are you not convinced about, Mr Johnson?'

'Well, it all sounds very impressive and everything, but you would say that, wouldn't you? I just don't think that the Patent Remedies system will work for me.'

'Finally,' whispered Tony. A sensation of imminent climax built up in the little room. Leo Porter leaned forward and spread his arms out. The two Andys held their pens ready above their spiral notebooks.

'Mr Johnson, I can understand why you feel like that. A lot of other people have felt the same way. But they've all found that once they've tried the Patent Remedies free-standing beverage and comestible utility unit they won't use anything else. Ever. Again.'

Leo sat back, his palms held upwards. 'You see?'

Mr Johnson had the sense of having arrived by way of a circuitous mountain path to an impossibly high plateau of great clarity, reason and illumination. He saw.

'You see? It really is as simple as that. I understand why you feel – confirmation of empathy, shows you've been listening. A lot of other people have felt – acknowledgement that the customer isn't wrong to think in this way. But they've found – the unarguable evidence of mass experience and the suggestion of a commercial track record. Thank you, Mr Johnson – we got there in the end. You were a rottweiler to start with and then turned into a lap dog. But you got your snarl back eventually.'

Mr Johnson moved his chair back to its original position, sat down, and poured a cup of water. The others were staring at their notebooks. Mr Johnson saw that Tony had covered the sheet Leo had handed out with doodle. He had also added a U, a C and a K after each F.

'Right gang,' said Leo. 'End of part one. With a bit of luck, lunch should have arrived.'

He stepped out of the room and returned with two heavy-duty foil platters piled with sandwiches and cocktail snacks covered in clingfilm.

'Doesn't look like they've sent any drinks up,' said Leo. 'Will you manage with the water?'

They all nodded and Tony uncovered the food. Leo handed round paper plates and serviettes and they dug in.

'I bet this doesn't happen everyday,' said Mr Johnson to no-one in particular. He picked up a tuna mayonnaise sandwich and a mini onion bhaji which he dipped into a plastic pot of yoghurt and mint sauce.

'No – so don't get used to it,' said Leo.

'Looks like Mr Johnson is getting the special treatment – a presentation case and a sandwich lunch all in one day,' said Andy One.

'It's a good job,' said Mr Johnson through a pulpy mouthful of bread and tuna mayonnaise. 'I didn't bring any lunch with me. What do people usually do here?'

'Depends,' said Tony. 'When there's a lot of work on, which is most of the time nowadays, people usually eat at their desks. There are a couple of sandwich shops close by but nowhere in particular to eat. There isn't a pub nearby, either, which is a shame.'

'Do people go out much after work?'

'Not as often as they used to. I haven't done so for ages. It's been so hectic recently that there hasn't been the time.'

Mr Johnson took a mini samosa from the platter and dipped it into the sauce. The sauce was watery and ran thinly off the samosa. A freshet of minty yoghurt trickled down his chin. He dabbed at it with the serviette. No-one else seemed to care for the Indian mini-snacks. Mr Johnson was conscious of not wanting to appear greedy but at the same time was keen to do justice to the buffet, which seemed to have been over-catered. He left a discreet interval before helping himself to another sandwich – beef and onion on sliced brown bread.

'So it's your first day, Mr Johnson,' said Leo, who had stood up and wasn't eating. 'How are you finding things so far?'

'All right. There's a lot to learn but it's all been very interesting.'

Tony looked at him and pulled a face. 'I don't think we've given Mr Johnson a very good impression so far. He sat around for ages in reception and there wasn't a desk for him when he came upstairs. Then the phones went on the blink. And he's still deskless. I'll be amazed if he comes back.'

'Join the club,' said Andy Two from across the table. 'I'm still waiting to get connected to the computer network.'

'Have you spoken to the systems manager?' asked Leo.

Andy raised his eyes to the ceiling. 'I would if I knew where to find him,' he said. 'I've left messages on his phone, even sent him a letter through the internal mail. Nothing. It's very frustrating.'

'Hasn't he got any assistants who could help?' asked Mr Johnson.

'I wouldn't bother with them,' said Tony. 'They know as much about computer systems as I do. All they do is hit your monitor and turn it on and off.'

'I'll see what I can do,' said Leo. 'Mind you, it shouldn't stop you getting on the phone. In my day we didn't need computer systems. We used card indexes then.'

'And your phones were probably steam-powered, too,' said Tony.

'Watch it. I'm not that old. What exactly did you do in your last job again, Mr Johnson?'

'I was a research manager at an information research company. It was interesting work but I wanted to broaden my horizons. That's why I applied here.'

'You'll certainly get your horizons broadened. There are a lot of opportunities for talented sales people in this organisation.'

Mr Johnson felt Tony shift in his chair. He felt compelled to explain himself further.

'I hadn't planned to move into straight sales as such but I can see how it will be useful for my longer-term ambitions.'

'Which are?'

Mr Johnson felt self-conscious. They were all staring at him.

'Well, I'm looking to move into a more strategic role, possibly in a product development capacity. I would like to have more direct dealings with clients and I want to develop my commercial skills and work in a creative environment.'

'You mean marketing?' asked Andy One.

'Yes, with an element of marketing. It's difficult to say. I did a combined honours degree at university which didn't really set me up to enter a particular career area but did equip me with a lot of important transferable skills which I hope to be able to bring to bear in this job. I realise that I'll need a lot of training.'

A mobile phone rang. It was Leo's.

'Excuse me a moment,' he said, and left the room.

Andy One leant towards Mr Johnson. 'Let me guess: your academic experiences and extra-curricular activities helped you develop effective communication and analytical skills, whilst writing your final-year dissertation taught you valuable time-management skills. Your degree has made you a well-rounded and versatile person able to adapt to any business culture.'

'Yes, something like that.'

'Snap!' said Andy Two and Tony. They all laughed again.

'We've all been there,' said Andy Two. 'Good luck to you, anyway. Let us know how you get on.'

Mr Johnson felt foolish and his face reddened but looking at the others he realised there was no malice intended and he reached for another bhaji.

'We're all frustrated product development executives, marketing managers, stand-up comedians and novelists,' said Tony. 'I've talked to Mr Johnson about all this already. I've been plotting my escape route for years. But I'm also here for the duration. The thing about sales is, it drains you. Your mind wants to get out but your body isn't capable. Or maybe it's the other way round – I can never remember. I'm that tired. I need a long holiday.'

'You're putting Mr Johnson off,' said Andy Two.

'I reckon Mr Johnson knows his own mind, eh Mr Johnson?'

Mr Johnson pulled a concurring face and took another beef and onion sandwich.

'Good God,' said Andy One, 'you can put it away.'

'I only had two pieces of toast for breakfast,' said Mr Johnson, spilling crumbs onto the table. He felt embarrassed again. Tony showed moral support by taking another sandwich himself. Leo came back into the room.

'Sorry about this gang. I've got a domestic crisis on my hands. We're going to have to do the next part of the training another time. Hope that's okay.'

No-one objected. Mr Johnson stopped eating and put the notes into his presentation case.

'Thanks for your contribution, Mr Johnson,' Leo said as they left the training room. 'You were very good in the role play. I look forward to seeing you on the other side of the counter, so to speak.'

Mr Johnson wasn't sure what to say so he shook Leo's hand and thanked him before following the others back to the strategic development department. When he arrived there he asked Margaret what he should do next and whether a desk had been found for him. She didn't know what the next stage of his induction programme was and, no, a desk hadn't been found. They were still chock-a-block.

'It's muck and bullets in here, love,' said Margaret, chewing her lip. 'You'll have to work-shadow some more. Sorry about that. You'll be smoking again in no time at this rate.'

Mr Johnson smiled. 'Judy Orion was going to run me off a copy of my induction programme. I don't know whether she's had the time.'

'I've no idea, love. She's in a meeting for the rest of the day, anyway.'

'Is Debbie Stevens around? I don't think I've met her yet.'

'Your guess is as good as mine, love. Haven't seen her all day. It's not going too well for you, is it? Are you sure you don't want a cigarette? I'm going for one in a minute.'

'No, really, I'm fine. If I start I won't stop. I'll go and sit with Tony again.'

'Tell you what, love. You can go and see Bob Hobbleton. Everybody gets to see Bob on their induction. You might as well get it over with now.'

'Bob Hobbleton? I haven't heard of him yet. What does he do?'

Margaret smiled slyly. 'You'll find out soon enough. Follow me.'

As Margaret got up from her desk, Joanne came up and rang the bell again.

'Well done, Joanne love. Is that target now?'

'Yes,' said Joanne. 'I'm 4% over.'

'And well ahead of time, too. Joanne's hit target,' Margaret said to the office at large. A quiet ripple of applause followed this announcement. 'Can you all get on the phones, please?' she added.

CHAPTER FIVE

ORGANISATIONAL THEORY

Margaret led Mr Johnson across the office to a small anteroom in which a thin man with lank grey hair and a salt-and-pepper beard sat at a desk poring over what looked like a text book.

'Bob? Can you spare five minutes? This is Mr Johnson. He's a new starter in the strategic development department and he needs an induction.'

Bob got up and stretched out a hand to Mr Johnson. 'Yes, Bob Hobbleton, pleased to meet you. Do sit down.'

'If you could just give him an overview of the organisation, Bob, help him get a handle on the important stuff. All right Mr Johnson, love? If you need anything else you know where to find me.'

Margaret winked at him as she left the room. Bob asked Mr Johnson a little about his background and experiences while he worried at the metal clips of a ring binder.

'Can't seem to get them to align,' he said. 'Sorry about that. Yes, all ears. You'll be working for Les Bannister, then? Yes, good. Excellent department. Heart of the company. Have you met Judy Orion yet? Yes, really turned things around here.'

'What's your role?' Mr Johnson asked.

'Sort of consultant, information professional, advice and guidance, marketing generalist, that sort of thing. Work from home quite often. Common business practice these days. What course are you doing?'

'Course?'

'Yes, further training, life-long learning, career development programme, that sort of thing. Everyone seems to be doing one at the moment.'

'I don't know. No-one's told me about that yet.'

'Do you have any formal qualifications?'

'Yes, I've got a combined honours degree in humanities. I did my final-year dissertation on the American transcendentalists.'

'No, I mean professional qualifications, that sort of thing. Membership of institutes, diplomas and the like.'

'Not as such. I've only ever learned on the job. My role at my last company was very specific. I've just been in a preliminary sales training session with Leo Porter, which was interesting, so all being well I will build on that. My transferable and so-called soft skills are very strong, however, particularly communication and time-management.'

'I recommend you have a word with personnel asap. Get booked on to a few courses. I can help you out. I run a few in-house training sessions. In my other life I do a bit of teaching at a local college. Obviously we get a lot of outside people in too but very often it's the in-house expertise that is the most relevant. The biggest problem we encounter is the gulf between theory and practice. I often think that the whole of an organisation's activities can be characterised as the attempt to marry business theory with business practice, to span the abyss that lies between rhetoric and reality.'

Bob immediately became more focused.

'This place is no exception. You may be aware that classic organisational theory holds that there have been a number of great periods in the modern history of corporate development. The first, lasting roughly for the decade immediately after the end of World War Two, was the age of production. The business of business in those days was the production of goods. That was the principal functional imperative of successful businesses – perhaps an inevitable legacy of the recent war. In the 1960s, the focus shifted to finance. The most important department in the organisation was the accounts department. That is what major companies thought of themselves as first and foremost being about. If you looked into the background of most executive directors in those days, you would find that the majority by far were drawn from financial functions. This place was no exception. Again, the focus changed. The 1970s was the decade of sales, to be replaced in the 1980s by marketing, which as far as we can see is still the prevalent characteristic of most companies. It certainly is here. In my view – and you'll say that I'm biased but I think that by any objective measurement it's the case – marketing owes its longevity as a fundamental cohering business principle to its essential adaptability, its protean quality. In many respects, every organisational function is to do with marketing, whether it is an innately inward- or outward-looking function. We'll talk more about internal marketing later. But I wouldn't want you to think, Mr Johnson' – here he leant forward – 'that this emphasis on certain core functions enjoying a primacy at any given time implies in any way that they exist to the exclusion of all others. Marketing, for example, was a critical feature of the business landscape in the 1950s. It was just that senior managers hadn't grasped its full significance. When I say that at that time production was the function by which business defined itself, what I mean is the rhythm and tempo of organisational life kept time with the exigencies of the company's production activities. Of course that is still true to a certain extent, although things have changed enormously since companies like this one embraced the challenge thrown up by the emergence of new technologies and began to address their customer service profile. Yet in a strange way, marketing has informed the activities of so many other functions that it is no longer recognisable as marketing as it once was, if you see what I mean. In many respects, sales is now what marketing was, because the fundamental precepts of marketing – market intelligence, customer service, identifying client needs and so on – have utterly transformed the profile of the sales function here and elsewhere. But I'm getting ahead of myself. Let's break here and have a coffee. Can I get you one?'

Mr Johnson said yes and Bob Hobbleton went out. Mr Johnson guessed that the room wasn't actually Bob's office as there was no sign of the typical paraphernalia associated with a work area, although a laptop was open on the desk and a stack of books lay close by: Principles of Organisational Theory; Corporate Psychology for Managers; Towards the Wormhole: New Readings in Quantum Economics.

Margaret put her head in. 'Are you all right, love? Is Bob explaining everything?'

'I think so,' Mr Johnson replied. 'It's mainly background information at the moment. He's very thorough.'

'Yes, our Bob's certainly thorough,' said Margaret, and winked at him again as she walked away.

A moment or two later Bob came back in holding two cups of coffee gingerly by the rims. 'Oooch,' he let out, putting them down on the desk. A small quantity spilled over from each cup and splashed onto the desk.

'I used to have a couple of cup holders,' Bob revealed as he fished in his pockets for tissues and mopped up the coffee. 'Don't know what happened to them. Made life a lot simpler. Always curse myself for losing them. Anyway' – he got up to shut the door – 'let's press on. There's a lot get through. By the way, you might want to take notes at this point as I'm going to get on to the general history of this place and some of the key developments that you need to be aware of. You'll probably hear a lot of the same stuff from other people but I make no apology for that. The thing with me is that I'm in a very good position to give you a broad overview. They say that the devil is in the detail but at the same time I firmly believe that you shouldn't lose sight of the big picture. It's all about finding where you belong in the great scheme of things. With a company this size, it can sometimes be difficult for the individual to put down a firm anchor. That's why we have a mission statement, for example – as an anchoring device. Everyone should be able to find themselves somewhere in the mission statement. That's the beauty of it. The mission statement is a pithy condensation of everything this organisation is about and yet it is flexible enough to embrace every function and every individual. But I'm getting ahead of myself – I'm sure you'll be getting some mission statement training in due course. You'll find people are very up on it here, and not just the senior managers. Let's press on. I've got to distil a lot of hard information into some unforgiving time parameters. Are you taking notes?'

Mr Johnson opened his vinyl presentation case and loosened his tie.

'I've worked for this organisation for over three decades and needless to say I've seen a great many changes in that time. Staff have come and gone, management cultures altered out of all recognition and extensions and annexes flourished like mushrooms after rain. Everything changes. I can remember vividly my first day here. I was younger then, of course. I worked in a small team that gathered market information and made recommendations to the company's strategic planning process, among various other responsibilities. In many ways, we were a precursor of what we now call cross-functional teams. And we were quite a team. Now there are only me and Bob Savage, who you probably haven't met yet, left. Everything seemed more containable then. I might be guilty of being nostalgic but I'm sure that everyone knew everybody else and there were fewer distinctions between individuals and departments. I remember that you could pop up to see the executive director for a chat about this and that without having to book an appointment weeks in advance. She's still here, of course, but her role has also changed out of all recognition. Now I don't see her for months at a time. I suppose that email has made a difference – whereas once you would have to make the effort to talk to someone directly, today you can fire off a quick message even when they live next door.'

Bob paused and looked wistfully at his ring binder.

'I would be guilty of dishonesty if I said that things weren't simpler in the old days. The company was smaller, then, of course, and a man knew exactly where he fitted into the scheme of things. Now I sometimes think that I have only the mission statement to orient me. But we must all change with the times, Mr Johnson, and I'm no exception. It always gladdens my heart when I see young blood coming into the organisation. The old need the young to keep them on their toes and the young need the old to impart their experience. I have worked on some of the most significant projects in the company's history over the years, each one of them very different but all of them characterised by one consistent factor – quality and standards. That's two factors, then. In a way, I see my role here now, aside from providing a general educational service to new starters like your good self, as a beacon of consistency in a sea of commercial change. I don't need to tell you how much business practice has changed in recent years, not the least of these changes being wrought by the striking and sudden-seeming leaps in technological advancement which have affected all of us in our working and indeed our private lives.'

Mr Johnson noted key words from Bob's talk on his pad. The room was stuffy and he wished he'd brought some water in with him. He was tired.

'The internet, of course, in the main. I don't need to tell you what an impact that has had here and elsewhere. Needless to say, I was born and brought up in a generation that had never heard of internets, emails and mobile phones. When I first started work here we used an extensive system of card indexes and suspension files. Indeed, one of the first major projects I worked on was concerned with the company-wide systematising of disparate card-indexing cultures. I always say that the key to understanding an organisation's culture is the analysis of its indexing and information systems processes. You look surprised. I know that such a view is no longer fashionable in these hard-nosed, commercial times. That's partly why I made the conscious decision to develop marketing generalist skills so as not to get left behind as the tides of business change swept this organisation and elsewhere. But my first and real love is information systems. I firmly believe that the distinctive life of an organisation can be properly understood only with reference to its information gathering and storage activities. There's so much information nowadays.'

He suddenly swept his arms into the air.

'Where does it begin? Where does it end? Where does it even exist? I refer of course to the rise and rise of electronic information. We live in a world, Mr Johnson, where we are surrounded by information that we can't touch and perceive only through a window, as it were. Are you with me?'

Mr Johnson nodded and added some more notes to his pad. He had already filled one side of A4, though he wasn't sure that the notes would make a great deal of sense after the session.

'Information that has a secret life of its own, information that can reform itself quietly out of sight, information that can even destroy itself without human intervention. Documents that exist in a multitude of versions. Where is the original statement of fact? What is the ur-information? Who records all the changes? If I were to audit the organisation now, if I were to try and take a snapshot and freeze-frame its activities, what would the picture tell me? It would be only a partial picture. Because so much remains hidden and so much changes even as the frame is being frozen. When you consider this in tandem with the ever-increasing commercial pressures that this and other modern business organisations find themselves under you have nothing less than a recipe for total chaos – potentially at least.'

Bob got up and began pacing up and down behind his desk.

'My own role here has changed out of all recognition. My work is increasingly concerned with bringing to bear upon the present the accumulated experiences of the past. Perhaps this is inevitable, almost a natural physical law, if you will. There is almost an abstruse, recondite quality to the projects I undertake these days. But I don't want you to think that I'm somehow out of the main current. Far from it, in fact. Each to their own: set against the banks of busy commercial beavers out there' – he gestured at the sales office – 'there must always be people who take the considered, longer-term view. I haven't worked here for so long without both adapting and consolidating. You might want to make a note of that: adaptation and consolidation; the twin imperatives of organic organisational cultures.'

He stopped pacing and sat down again.

'But needless to say, everything changed when Judy Orion started.'

Bob worried at the ring binder again; Mr Johnson said nothing. He had already filled half of the second side of the paper. They passed a minute or two in this way. Finally, Mr Johnson said: 'Do you actually work in the sales department?'

'No, I don't. I report to the conceptual initialisation manager currently.'

'I've heard of conceptual initialisation already but nobody seems sure what it is. What happens there? It does sound very interesting, certainly as far as my own ambitions are concerned.'

'It's difficult to describe in a straightforward way. Conceptual initialisation is connected to marketing, product development and sales, though not explicitly.' Bob warmed up again. 'I must admit to a personal interest here. Some time ago I was entrusted with the responsibility for producing a report on the future development of the company's marketing activities. I audited the existing functions and made recommendations for a major restructuring.' Bob reached picked up an attaché case from beside his chair and took out a heavy document with a plastic front page and spiral binding.

'Here,' he said, pointing to a page entitled: A New Way Forward: Conceptual Initialisation. 'I came up with the title and the thinking behind it. My recommendations were largely acted upon and a new department was born. It was perhaps the most significant project I have ever worked on here. It represented quite a daring feat of imaginative construction, even if I say so myself. In a company of this size, capturing and harnessing creativity is at a premium. I'm not certain whether this holds water scientifically – perhaps you know better than I do – but I am convinced that there is an inverse relationship between the proliferation of organisational matter and the quality and durability of business focus. Do you understand what I'm driving at? But here's the paradox – just as the likelihood of achieving a consistent level of focus lessens under such circumstances, so it becomes more desirable. You'll be familiar, I'm sure, with the term "project creep". That is to say, the inevitable and inexorable moving forward through dimensions of the conceptual and material aspects of a project beyond its original time and resource parameters. Some people prefer to refer to this as the "snowball effect". Projects are hungry; they devour all matter they encounter. Definitions shift and change. Multiply this effect hundreds of times across an organisation, especially one as large and complex as this, and you have nothing less than a recipe for anarchy. Are you with me? Yes? Therefore, co-ordination and overarching control mechanisms must be deployed. Yet the conditions necessary for their development and implementation are axiomatically unfavourable. Thousands of organic conceptual and material project entities perforce insist upon a multiplicity of structures and processes. All that information with a life of its own. To put it crudely, left hand and right hand. Yes? To refine, to bring together these disparate strands is the imperative task at hand. In the case of this organisation, the field was left to grow rampant and wild, if you will. Good people stood back helplessly as projects and activities proliferated uncontrollably. Yes, of course, strategic planning mechanisms have always existed here. It's just that they were unable to provide an adequate degree of control over multifarious processes and activities. The situation couldn't persist infinitely. Critical mass was reached. That's where I came in. I was charged with identifying the pinch points in the present process and activity structure and recommending an organisation-wide solution. No mean task, you might say – and you would be right. I won't go into too much detail now. Suffice it to say, I embarked upon a lengthy consultation process and audited the primary functions. I didn't do this alone. I was given access to staff in key areas and chaired a project team.'

Bob paused and smiled.

'It was almost like the old days, for a while. I drew inspiration from the generally younger members of the project team and I like to think that they benefited from my knowledge and wisdom acquired over three decades. I say that I like to think that they did; I know that they did. I instituted a formal feedback procedure designed to assess their views. I asked them to be candid. They were. For many of them, it was their first experience of working on a cross-functional team.'

'I don't think I've ever worked on a cross-functional team,' said Mr Johnson.

'I've heard a little about them before. I don't suppose that the sales department could be regarded as a cross-functional team.'

'Not as such, although as with all functions, the sales department has begun to embrace some of the principles of cross-functionality, especially in respect of fluidity and flexibility. Fluidity and flexibility – the twin underscoring principles of cross-functionalism. That sounds good – I'll make a note of it.'

Mr Johnson did the same.

'You can only imagine the gratification that I derived from seeing my ideas permeate the organisation. I say my ideas – I didn't invent cross-functional team-working, of course. But I like to think that I acted as an apostle, an evangelist, if you will. The conditions were fertile, as I've already outlined to you. What was needed was a single-minded focus, the vision to take the raw material of ideas and fashion a concrete organisational structure from them. I didn't do that alone but I did provide the impetus for the implementation of the ideas. I'm sorry, I am talking at length. You are new here, I know. But I am convinced of the centrality of conceptual initialisation to the forward development and organic good health of the organisation. And if you are to understand how things work round here, you'll do well to acquaint yourself with its first principles.'

'It certainly sounds interesting and makes considerable conceptual sense, even at this early stage. I'm particularly struck by what you said about drawing together disparate elements and providing a focus for activities. I didn't have a clear understanding of the company's structure when I applied for the job. The original position was a general graduate training programme and I suppose that I imagined it would involve me in the sort of area you've described. But they told me that there were no vacancies on the programme and offered me what seems to be a sales role instead, which I suppose will be very different.'

'It certainly wouldn't be the same thing as working in conceptual initialisation, although as I've said, organisational structures across the board are less rigid than they once were. The sales department itself has its own sub-structure of activity teams, functional task-groups and tactical focus-units. I wouldn't imagine that you'd find it too static and restrictive in there.'

'I hope not. But I am keen to develop certain skills I acquired in my last job. As much as anything else, I'd like to be exposed to as many of the company's activities as possible.'

'I'm sure you will in time. From our brief talk, it is clear that you have an enquiring mind and a thirst for knowledge. But I wouldn't say that sales is the wrong place to start. It is part of a larger department after all – I mean, strategic development. And there is no substitute for a solid grounding in commercial principles, which is certainly what you'll get in sales. I sometimes wonder whether I wouldn't have benefited from such a grounding myself. But I suspect it's too late for me. Fortunately, there is still plenty to do. I keep abreast of the current developments and endeavour to make sure my colleagues are apprised of the latest thinking. And there may be other projects to work on – perhaps not as significant as that which gave birth to the conceptual initialisation department, though who knows? Things change so quickly round here.'

Bob paused again and Mr Johnson looked at his pad on which he'd written and underlined 'Conceptual Initialisation'. Bob put the document back into the attaché case.

'If you're ever interested, I could give you a copy to read. I had more than one made up.'

'I'd like that. I am interested to know how conceptual initialisation works in practice.'

'You don't need a book to tell you that,' said Bob. 'It's actually quite straightforward. Needless to say, my work on the project didn't end with presenting my findings and making a set of recommendations. I actually provided a rational superstructure for the forward development of the new department. I identified five synergetic elements – you'll certainly need to make a note of them if you're interested in how the department works – which inform the essential relationship between conceptual initialisation and its cognate functions – namely ideas gathering, conceptual analysis, rationalisation, harmonisation, and concept-to-concrete fulfilment. In practice, this means that the work of the staff in the conceptual initialisation department – they are known as concept engineers, another term I devised – embraces every stage in the life of a new business idea, right through from conception to the point at which it is handed over to the department or team responsible for giving it tangible life. That's it in a nutshell, although I should add that there is an important difference between what my report originally envisaged and what has actually happened. I recommended the establishment of what you might call a virtual department, more of a loosely-associated cross-functional team drawn from disparate organisational strands which formed and disbanded according to immediate business imperatives, with a senior and experienced figure assuming an overall steering role in relation to its activities. I envisaged a strong electronic structure for it. However, a formally constituted department was set up and a new manager brought in from outside to run it. Later it was all brought under the strategic development umbrella.'

Bob paused again and looked away from Mr Johnson.

'But there is a time for leading ideas and a time for stepping back and seeing the fruits of your labours carried forward by others. I have learned that through long experience. You, of course, as a salesperson, will be concerned very closely, though not necessarily explicitly, with the work of the conceptual initialisation department. One of the most important areas of their work is the feeding through of new ideas for the effective operation of the sales function.'

'As I said, conceptual initialisation sounds very much like the sort of area I'd like to get involved in. I don't suppose I should say this but from what I've seen of sales so far, I'm not sure I would want to stay in it for too long.'

'There is no reason why you shouldn't move on in time. The very essence of my report related to the cultivation of a fluid creative environment that would encourage the company-wide sharing of ideas through cross-functional team-building and transparent information systems. Sir Colin himself acknowledged as much. Talented people have crossed departments before now; one or two – Leonard Bragby, for example – have even moved from sales into conceptual initialisation. There isn't a formal career ladder as such here but the company's structure, particularly in these times of great change, certainly admits a degree of latitude and provides occasional opportunities.'

'I've heard of Leonard Bragby already but who's Sir Colin? I don't think anyone has mentioned him yet. Is he in charge here?'

'Yes and no. The day-to-day management of the company is the responsibility of the senior management cluster which reports to the executive director. She in turn reports directly to Sir Colin, who has what you might say a non-executive figurehead role in relation to the organisation at large. Sir Colin has been here almost for ever, so you could say he has acquired a lot of implied authority in addition to his formal status in the hierarchy.'

'Will I get to see him?'

'I'm not sure. Perhaps towards the end of your induction period. Sir Colin is something of a remote figure. His day-to-day involvement in the life of the organisation is negligible. We don't see a great deal of him but he does keep an office here. He's usually out and about somewhere representing the company's interests before its key stakeholders and interested parties, signing high-level agreements, that sort of thing. I don't suppose you'll have a great deal to do with him, but you never know.'

'What about the executive director?'

'She's been with us almost as long as I have and has presided over considerable organisational change. As I've said, I see less of her than I used to, although I continue to keep her updated by email. She sees more of Sir

Colin than anyone else. They have a weekly meeting.'

'It sounds like the relationship between the Prime Minister and the Queen,' said Mr Johnson.

'As a matter of fact, it is,' said Bob, and wrote something down on a piece of paper. 'That's a very good analogy. I'll use that in my book, if you don't mind. My latest project, you may be interested to know, is the writing of a history of the company from its early beginnings to the present day.'

'Well, I don't mind as long as you give me a share of the royalties,' said Mr Johnson.

'This is an interesting conversation,' said Bob. 'I'll go and get some more coffees. Hello again, Margaret.'

Margaret's form filled the doorway. She was chewing her lip violently and smelled strongly of cigarettes.

'I'm sorry to interrupt, Bob, but there's an important call for Mr Johnson.'

'A call for me? Who is it?'

'Not sure, love, they didn't give a name.'

Mr Johnson looked from Margaret to Bob and back again. 'Shall I?'

Bob smiled blankly back. 'Yes, we might as well call it a day now. I expect you will have other inductions to attend. But you're welcome to come back at any time.'

'Yes, Mr Johnson has got a very busy schedule,' said Margaret.

'I'll come back later,' said Mr Johnson. Bob said nothing, but as Margaret led Mr Johnson back to his desk she gently suggested that he defer seeing Bob again until all his other inductions had been completed. She also told him that there hadn't really been a call for him but that since he had already been in Bob's office for over an hour and a half, she thought it would be better for everyone if she brought their interview to a premature close. Apparently it was customary for the sales department to do this if one their number was caught by Bob; he had rather a reputation for prolixity. (Margaret preferred to call this 'going on with himself'.)

'Bob had a lot of interesting things to say and seems to have been involved in a number of important projects but I'm not exactly sure what it is he does here,' said Mr Johnson.

'You're not the only one to wonder, love. He's one of those people who have been here since the year dot and nobody knows what to do with.'

'He seems very knowledgeable, though,' said Mr Johnson. 'He knows a lot about organisational theory and the history of the company. He said he's writing a book about it.'

'Oh, he's knowledgeable all right,' said Margaret and went on to mutter something about £30,000-plus a year for a bloody archivist.

'I don't suppose they've found a desk for me yet?'

'What do you think? Debbie Stevens hasn't turned up either and the phone system went on the blink again for twenty minutes. It's bloody chaos in here. Do you mind sitting with Tony for a bit longer?'

Mr Johnson sat down at Tony's desk again. It seemed that the question of his seating arrangements wouldn't be resolved immediately, however many inductions he undertook in the meantime.

CHAPTER SIX
LEONARD BRAGBY

TONY WAS REACHING A CONCLUSION with a sales call. He had a very relaxed style and seemed to know his stuff. Tony talked about levels of service provision and improved product features but not in a pushy way. It sounded as though the person at the other end of the phone was interested and even about to buy something.

'So, then,' finished Tony, 'I'll pop a brochure in the post for you and perhaps call you back in a week or so. Thank you for your time, goodbye.'

'That sounded like it went well,' said Mr Johnson when Tony had replaced the handset.

'I've no idea,' Tony said. 'I don't think she listened to a word I said.'

'What will happen when you phone her back next week?'

'I'm not going to phone her back next week.'

'Are you going to send her a brochure?'

'We don't have any brochures. We just say that to get off the phone if the call doesn't sound promising.'

'Is there any promotional material available to send out?'

'Not any more. Judy Orion put a stop to it when she started. She says that if you can't make a sale through the power of your own voice, it's not worth selling. Actually, I hate to say this, but she's got a point – we did used to spend a small fortune on glossy marketing stuff that just got chucked in the bin at the other end. Anyway, we're supposed to be a paperless office – can't you tell?'

Mr Johnson looked around him. Tony's desk was quite clear but most of the rest of the team seemed to be working round teetering piles of newspapers, folders and boxes.

'Where have you been, anyway?'

'I've just had an induction session with Bob Hobbleton.'

Tony whistled. 'I hope Margaret rescued you in time. I had a four-hour induction with him when I started.'

'He's very knowledgeable, though.'

'Oh yes, he's knowledgeable all right. I bet he told you just how knowledgeable he is. What did you think of the sales training?'

'It wasn't easy being put on the spot in the role-play but it was a useful experience, considering I know very little about sales. But I suppose the practice is very different to the theory.'

'It depends on the theory. There's no harm in reminding yourself of the structured sales call from time to time, even if they rarely proceed along such rational lines. It's the trotting out of half-baked psychological theories that I can't stand. Feel – Felt – Found is extremely simplistic but it's actually more relevant than Maslow, Mundfeld, Hertzbergen and all the rest of them put together.'

'If you don't mind me saying, you did give Leo a bit of a hard time in there.'

Tony laughed. 'Serves him right. Leo's okay but he should know better than to make reference to scientific models he doesn't really understand. He got off lightly on this occasion. I'm afraid I like to argue for the sport of it. Every time I go into a training session I pledge not to say anything but sometimes it's all too provocative. Then you hear your mouth getting the better of you and it's too late. It's worse when there are more of us – if you think I was hard on Leo, you should hear Gavin. And as Leo said, Leonard Bragby was the hardest of all. Leo's not the worst offender by a long chalk. But these people ask for it, frankly. I remember doing a principles of leadership training course once. We were discussing what made a good leader and the trainer said that he thought Hitler was an effective leader, despite all the negative stuff, because he ruled a powerful country and was able to get people to follow his ideas. He seemed to admire Hitler's charismatic qualities. Bragby went for him. It was the trainer's smugness that did it for him – as if a world war and genocide could be put in the balance with charismatic personal qualities applicable to the modern business environment and somehow be found wanting. Bragby said that in any case, by any objective measurement Hitler wasn't a good leader since his policies led to the destruction of Germany, which in business terms would clearly not be a good thing. It would be like a bullish and forceful personality seizing control of an organisation in a state of flux staffed by uncertain and susceptible employees and driving it into the ground in a few short years. Then he walked out, saying that force of personality should never be confused with effective leadership and why didn't the trainer hold Pol Pot up as an example the next time he ran a training course? He also called the trainer a fraud. Bragby had a point, of course. Now, we have an understanding amongst us that trainers are not allowed to get away with lazy allusions and half-baked theorising. It's harsh but they need to be told. They earn enough, after all. The principle is important and anyway, it helps pass the time until the buffet lunch. I hope I didn't put you off. You seemed to enjoy the role-play, anyway.'

'No, it was fine. I've never had that sort of training before and all this theory is still new to me. I suppose I can expect to hear about Maslow again before I'm through.'

'Yes, with the inevitability of a bad penny turning up, I'm afraid. Just remember – get the trainer to explain themselves properly when they refer to pseudo-scientific theories. Nine times out of ten they will get flustered and defensive. You might even make them cry. It's all good sport. Do you want to listen in while I make a call?'

'Yes please.'

Tony connected a small ear-piece on a wire to the back of his telephone and handed it to Mr Johnson who fixed it into his left ear.

'I'm calling back someone I spoke to last week. He's what we call a medium-to-hot prospect. Listen and learn.'

Tony dialled a number on his keypad and Mr Johnson heard a ringing tone. Someone picked it up at the other end but Mr Johnson couldn't detect what they were saying. The line was obscured by a cloud of hiss.

'Hello?' said Tony. 'Hello?' He pressed a button and dialled again. This time the phone rang twice before cutting out altogether.

'The bloody phones,' shouted Margaret, rising from behind her desk. She stormed out of the room, presumably in the direction of the systems manager. The whole office seemed to relax. Tony pushed his chair back. 'Cigarette?'

'It's tempting but I'd better not. If I start again, I won't stop. I think I'll get another coffee, though. Is there a machine nearby?'

Tony directed him to a landing outside the sales office where a large vending machine stood. He pondered the options and chose a strong white coffee without sugar. An amiable-looking bearded man wearing a brown jumper appeared at his side.

'You look like a new starter. What's your name?'

'Mr Johnson,' said Mr Johnson, extending his right hand.

'Bob Savage. What do you do?'

'I'm a market intelligence consultant in the strategic development department. It's my first day.'

'That's sales, then, is it?'

'It's a generalist role but it certainly looks like it's going to have a strong sales aspect,' said Mr Johnson, putting his coffee down on a shelf next to the machine. 'What's your role?'

'Bit of everything, really. Information processing for the most part.'

'Are you in strategic development?'

'Good lord, no. Statistical and financial management. I'm responsible for electronic desk research, internal market information distribution, that sort of thing. My role is primarily concerned with providing internal information management systems with accurate information from external sources.' He got himself a drink. 'So you'll be one of these new commercial high-fliers we're always hearing about?'

'I don't know about that. I'm still developing my commercial skills. To be honest with you, I'm trying to work out who does what and how everything fits together.'

'Join the club. If you ever find out, let me know. I've been here longer than most and I'm still trying to work out what's what. It's been worse than ever recently.'

'I haven't even got my own desk yet, but I suppose it is my first day. Things should get sorted out in time.'

Bob Savage raised his eyes to the ceiling.

'That doesn't surprise me. My computer exploded last year and I had to wait four months for a replacement. Have you seen Bob Hobbleton yet?'

'Yes, I had an induction with him earlier. It was very interesting. He mentioned your name, as a matter of fact. Didn't you used to work together?'

'Yes, we started at around the same time. It was a very different organisation in those days, of course. He's an extremely knowledgeable man, Bob. Not many like him round here anymore. He's one of the thinkers. I'll tell you something for nothing,' Bob said, beckoning Mr Johnson even closer. 'If you want to progress here, listen to the words.'

'I'm sorry?' said Mr Johnson, startled by the sudden change in the tone of Bob's voice. 'What do you mean?'

'It's all about language,' said Bob. 'Language is all. Bob Hobbleton would probably tell you the same thing. He or she who controls the linguistic and metaphorical high ground controls the organisation. It's a pet theory of mine, if you will. Aside from the conjuring up of ever more outlandish metaphors to describe standard business practices, it's their capacity to turn verbs into nouns that lies behind it. It's a modern malaise. You hear so many new and extraordinary formations. Are you with me? Like when US generals speak of the intercept being successfully launched or sports commentators speak of assists. Or the other way round.' His voice dropped to a whisper. 'This morning, for example, I was given permission to bespoke a report that had been written for the senior management information collation sub-group. I'm not sure when I'll get the time to do it as I'm extremely busy finessing the third quarter's budget for the financial controller. But how on earth do you bespoke a report? And here's another thing. Have you ever had a piece of information back-stabbed? You look puzzled. It entered our vocabulary only recently. To back-stab a piece of information means to pass on a piece of news that carries an implicit derogation of its subject without the conveyor appearing cognisant of this derogation. Not terribly subtle and certainly not a new phenomenon but I think the fact that it has acquired a distinctive appellation is significant. It indicates that…'

Here he was interrupted by Gavin.

'Is he boring you to death? Hey, Dr Johnson, are you boring him to death?'

Mr Johnson was confused for a moment. 'Do you mean me? I don't have a doctorate, although I did register for a MPhil shortly after I finished my undergraduate studies. I didn't complete it, though.'

'No,' Gavin laughed, 'we call Bob Dr Johnson because he sounds like he's swallowed a dictionary.'

Bob Savage looked embarrassed and edged away from the coffee machine.

'Perhaps I'll see you later,' he said to Mr Johnson. 'A few of us have an email group on which we discuss some of the ideas I was referring to.'

'Yes, I'd be interested in that,' said Mr Johnson. Gavin smirked and looked the other way. 'Once I've been connected to the network, of course.'

'Of course.' Bob smiled sadly into his coffee and ambled away down the corridor.

'You got away lightly there, Mr Johnson,' said Gavin. 'Bob could bore for England.'

'He seems a nice man, though.'

'Nice has got nothing to do with it. Every time I go to the coffee machine he pops up. I think he's lonely. If you let him think you're interested in his ideas he won't leave you alone. He thinks he is the company theoretician. Whatever you do, don't join his email group. It's just him and Bob Hobbleton.'

They walked with their drinks back to the sales office. The phone system was still down and Margaret hadn't reappeared. Tony was outside with his cigarettes. Mr Johnson sat down in the chair at Tony's desk and took the notes he'd made with Bob Hobbleton from his presentation folder. He couldn't extract a lot of sense from them, although the Five Synergetic Elements were clearly enumerated. He wrote them out again on a new piece of paper in diagrammatic form with sturdy arrows connecting one from the other. In the top left and right corners he wrote 'marketing/product development?' and 'sales?' and at the top of the page 'Strategic Development Department'. He was blocking in the last of the arrowheads when Tony returned.

'Keeping busy?'

'I'm trying to write up my notes from the induction with Bob Hobbleton,' Mr Johnson said, putting the papers into his presentation folder. 'I want to get to grips with the structures.'

'Let me guess – Bob explained about the Five Synergetic Elements?'

'Yes. Are you familiar with them?'

'I've heard of them but to be honest, I have as little to do with that sort of thing as possible. It's really a conceptual initialisation matter. I've got my call times to worry about, anyway.'

'What call times?'

'It's the sales office standard – three hours on the phone a day at least. Doesn't sound a lot but it's not always easy.' He picked up his handset and listened. 'Still nothing. Needless to say, it all goes out the window when the phones are down.'

'I'm not sure that I'd be able to talk to people on the phone for three hours a day.'

'You will when you get used to it. They won't expect you to at first, anyway.'

'What happens if you don't do three hours a day?'

'In theory, you get a written warning after a certain period. Doesn't often happen in practice. It's the same with targets – if you miss three on the trot you can get the sack. Three strikes and you're out, that sort of thing.'

'Has anyone been sacked for missing their targets?'

'Not recently. Because we haven't been doing that well lately, they'd have to sack everyone at some point. Someone got sacked a while ago for fiddling their call times, though. Turned out that they were filling most of their three hours by calling an information line number at a local leisure park. The same number kept coming up on the telephone bill. Stupid, really. It's actually easier to phone customers, even if you don't sell to them properly. At the very least you get a bit of aimless chat.'

When Tony mentioned targets, Mr Johnson had a fleeting vision of himself labouring in vain against a dark, oppressive and immovable object. It hadn't occurred to him that he would be expected to work to set financial targets or that his job security would depend on his doing so.

'I've never had to hit targets before,' he said. 'As you know, I haven't really done sales as such. In my last job, we worked to deadlines but there was no direct financial connection to performance.'

'Don't worry, you'll get used to it. A lot of people in this office were in the same position that you're in now. I'd worked in sales before and Gavin's got a lot of experience, one or two others too, but that's about it. You'll be fine. Don't worry about the call times, either – if you're making the sales, they'll leave you alone. Leonard Bragby used to do no more than twenty minutes a day on the phone but nobody bothered about it because he did more in twenty minutes than most people did in a week.'

'Did you know him well?'

'Yes, pretty well. We used to sit together when I first came here. He hadn't been here too long himself. This was before Judy Orion started – there was less pressure then. She never trusted him and was instrumental in moving him to the conceptual initialisation department almost as soon as it was set up.'

'Why didn't she trust him?'

'Lots of reasons. He didn't need managing, for one thing, which is something few managers can abide. He also used to write funny stuff for the staff newsletter but they thought he was laughing at them. Which he was.'

Tony reached into his drawer and took out a four-page newsletter printed in black and white.

'Have a look at this,' he said, drawing Mr Johnson's attention to an article on the back page. It was entitled 'Word Mine Drama Latest' and credited to 'Bernard Lagby'.

Reports have reached us of the discovery of a new and profitable seam of pure business gibberish in a remote corner of the company. Employees had been hacking away fruitlessly at a stubborn wall of mundane business-speak for several hours when they suddenly broke through into a hitherto uncharted seam. This is good news for the organisation since supplies of tiresome buzzwords, incomprehensible jargon and absurd metaphors have been running low in recent months. Terms such as 'cascade', 'tranche', and 'raft' have long-since lost their freshness, more and more employees are electing to get back inside the box, and few if any feel comfortable anymore with running standards up their poles in order to elicit the appropriate response. As for blue skies, these days we see nothing but heavy black clouds, thus affording few opportunities for helicopter views. And where have all the poppies gone, tall or small? Perhaps they've been lopped by the helicopter blades. Indeed, the crisis has been so severe that for a while it seemed as though the company's metaphorical engine would seize up from the lack of fresh terminological lubrication. Happily, the opening of this new seam will keep the metaphor mill, mixed or otherwise, running for many months to come.

The discovery has unearthed many new and wonderful word formations. But surely pride of place must go to 'let's TWOC a hot one and ram-raid the shop of ideas'. Not only does this resonate with topical, street-derived energy, it provides a vivid metaphorical description of the process by which ideas are generated and makes a sly reference to the often plagiaristic character of this process. Other words and expressions we can confidently expect to be bandied around the company with alacrity in the forthcoming weeks are:

Imaginarium – the place where concept engineers generate original thinking.

Dreadline – an imminent target that is likely to be missed.

Cascading up – a playful inversion of the stalwart term. Also an impossibility since cascading is axiomatically a downward motion.

Rat in the well situation – a set of circumstances whereby a company has grown complacent through earning easy profits over too long a period, the term deriving from the notion of making repeated visits to a well that provides an apparently limitless supply of fresh water only to draw up in the bucket one day a dead rat, implicit in the metaphor being the assumption that no work has been done in the meantime on maintaining the water table or prospecting for new wells. A strain of ambiguity runs through this one since it isn't clear whether the rat drowned before the well ran dry or died of thirst afterwards – or indeed, whether the well is actually dry at all. Business philosophers frequently discuss its deeper meanings – put simply, this is a variation on the ant and the grasshopper fable.

'You can't drink a dead rat' – characteristic of the type of language that would be employed in tandem with the bullish management style that would perforce emerge during the circumstances prevailing after the rat has been found in the well – presupposing, of course, that the well is in fact dry.

Company lexicographers are already hard at work updating the approved word lists. Expect to hear these and other terms cascading into your ears in the near future.

'That's very good,' said Mr Johnson, handing the newsletter back to Tony. He'd never read anything like it before. Although there was an easy-going atmosphere at his last office, no one displayed an irreverent attitude to the job. 'Have you got anything else?'

'No. I used to but I had a big clear out. He wrote a lot of pieces like that. That was one of his earliest efforts. Some of the later stuff was a bit nearer the knuckle. He wrote something about a marketing professional who read about the seven Ps upside down and spent his career worrying about the seven Ds. That was after he'd moved to conceptual initialisation, which didn't endear him to his new manager since he came from a marketing background himself. That's why Bragby didn't stay long in that department. Eventually, they wouldn't let him publish anything in the staff newsletter, which was a pity because his stuff was the only thing worth reading in it. There is also less time nowadays to spend on satirical writing during working hours – more's the pity. Now the newsletter contains bland information about new starters, charity activities, first aid networks and the Christmas do. They will probably ask you for a potted biography at some point. There's a questionnaire they get you to do. That was another thing Bragby wrote for the newsletter once – an alternative questionnaire. Instead of the usual questions about the car you drive, when and where you were happiest, your favourite drink and so on, he put in questions such as "What in your life are you most ashamed of?" and "If you could murder somebody and be sure of getting away with it, who would that person be?". It was divided into two parts – work and out-of-work. That went down well. We used to have a good laugh when we sat together, before things took a turn for the worse. You know – routines, silly voices, that sort of thing. We had this running gag about an underground railroad that would rescue sales people from their miserable jobs and take them to safety over the border, like slaves escaping or spies defecting – set them up in a new flat, give them a whole new identity, forged papers and so on. Bring them out one by one until there was no one left in the office. It's still an appealing prospect.'

'Well, whenever you're ready to tell me about the escape committee, I'll be happy to join. I don't mind admitting that I am still quite apprehensive about beginning a sales job, even after the training and work-shadowing. It does seem as though you frequently have to expose yourself and lay yourself open to the risk of being rejected. How do you get used to that?'

'You don't, really. But in a strange way it doesn't matter after a while. You see, the secret is, although I, like most of the people here, detest the job, I also rather enjoy it. I think I've said this to you already. It's a purely intellectual process, perhaps, a conceit, if you will, but one which provides an almost physical satisfaction. To engage in selling requires you to leave yourself vulnerable and naked, to risk ridicule and opprobrium being heaped upon you. You could ask: how do I work under such constraints? But I like to look at it the other way. I don't think in terms of being constrained. The risk is a challenge, a stimulant. At times you actually relish the exposure, rejoice in your nakedness, yearn for ridicule. I know it sounds ridiculous but I'm not being entirely unserious. It's a strange duality. And after all, there are greater hazards in the world. The slights and scorns you may encounter working in the sales industry hardly correspond to the daily dangers faced by sewage workers or coastguards. I should emphasise the word "may". Frequently, our customers, or, indeed, the cold leads, are pleased to hear from us. Many of them enjoy the cut and thrust of the structured sales call, when we can be bothered to deliver it – they respond to its essential rhythms and pulses, they perceive the hidden beauty in its form. And I feel it too, in spite of myself. I think even Bragby might have felt the same way about it. You probably will in time, too.'

'All the same,' said Mr Johnson, 'I do worry for myself. It seems as though you are very much left to your own devices in this job. I don't want to be melodramatic but it appears to be a solitary and lonely existence, particularly when all your work is done over the telephone, and in spite of the fact that you are in a large room full of people. I know that right now, nobody is working as such and there is a good level of communication between individuals, but fundamentally, you all have to be on the phones on your own if you are to survive. It sounds very primal.'

'Yes, it can be something of a lonely communion. I used to feel that very strongly. And I can see why you feel that way right now. It seems like such a long time ago now but I was once new to all this myself. I didn't mean to end up in sales. It just sort of happened. I remember very well the first sales call I ever made. I left university, drifted for a few years, couldn't or wouldn't apply for traditional graduate jobs, didn't want to teach, travelled for a bit – the usual thing. Then I ran out of time and answered a small ad in a local newspaper – dynamic, committed self-starters required for market-leading business-to-business solutions provider. OTE £30K plus benefits – you know the sort of thing. The reality, needless to say, was very different. The company was a small, shabby outfit that sold ad space in worthless business directories in a variety of sectors. They operated out of a small, shabby office on the edge of an industrial estate. It was a real hole-in-the-wall affair, not at all like this place, though not quite a portakabin. Scuffed lino in the entrance area, worn carpet, a dirty old drinks machine. No computers – it's going back some years, though for all I know they still don't have computers. They'd only just got a fax machine, in fact. The job was rudimentary, crude. There was no training or induction. Again, the contrast is striking. On my first day there, I was given a skeletal introduction to the nature of the work. It was extremely basic. Twenty or so of us lined both sides of a long room. It was an exclusively male environment, and save for me and a couple of others, inhabited by men in their fifties at least. The place had the yellow smell of bankruptcy, divorce and failure. It also smelled of cigarettes. Everyone smoked at their desks. I wasn't a smoker when I joined the company but I was on twenty a day after one week there. The work was basic, repetitive. Leads came from sections of the telephone directory. Depending upon where we were selling business-to-business solutions, we would work methodically the relevant local directories. Leads were allocated according to alphabetical sections. Some directories were known to be "better" than others and were ascribed almost magical properties. Tales would be told of pots of gold buried deep in the Cardiff, Brighton or Thetford books. Place names were uttered with the reverence normally accorded to battles or military campaigns. Rumours would circulate: "I've heard it's Northampton; they say we will be getting Carlisle next week." I remember that I used to do very well with the Highlands and Islands. Exeter, on the other hand, was always a wash-out.

'But how intimately acquainted you become with a city or a district when you pick through the bones of its business listings. And the visualising! You knew for certain that when you rang B&J Motors on Mill Street in Doncaster, a man in oily blue overalls would shamble into an untidy office in a corner of the workshop and rummage for the phone beneath a pile for invoices and parts catalogues. B&J Motors never wanted to hear from me, but neither did Allott and Finch, Solicitors in their restored Georgian townhouse in the old quarter of Bridgwater, nor McTucker's breakfast bar near the bus station in Lincoln. Not at first, anyway; not until the patter came.

'I detest the word but it is absolutely the right one. Quite simply, if you can stick at the job long enough and you can string more than a few words together, the patter comes. It's like the point at which you discover you can drive properly, the moment when your feet and hands know what they are doing with the controls independently of your conscious agency and you no longer have to think ponderously through every stage in the process. Or when you can whistle in tune or ride a bike with both your hands off the handlebar. Well, maybe not those last two – they come as revelatory moments, not incremental improvements. With the patter, you realise when you have it but aren't sure when you got it. It's a slow process, slower with some than with others, a gradual acculturation. But once it comes, you're away. Yes, the same anxieties beset you and you are never immune to the despondency that comes with repeated setbacks. But you know that there is a switched on part of you that gets right into the current, even steers the current. You catch yourself engaging in familiar banter with strangers, modifying your voice, selecting your words carefully depending on the customer – most of all, you have become a passionate advocate of the product or service you are selling, even if, as is most likely, you have in real life no faith in it whatsoever.' He fell silent for a moment. 'I don't mean to bend your ear. I'm confused about the whole business myself. I'm just thinking aloud. All I can say is that it's like being taught Bulgarian against your will and then finding that you can't stop speaking it and even miss it if you don't for a day or so. But I suppose that's the institutionalisation aspect of it all. What I really need is a good long spell away from work, a holiday or early retirement. I've probably put you off now.'

'Not at all,' said Mr Johnson. 'I can see that the job does raise some important philosophical questions. But I still think that I'll join your escape committee.'

Tony laughed. 'Not that it's going anywhere fast. But you're very welcome. What did you think of Judy Orion?'

'I don't know really. She seems very keen. What's all this about weekend discussion groups?'

'God knows. It's something she keeps suggesting but I don't know anyone who's stupid enough to go on one. Sounds like wishful thinking to me. My advice is to stay from her as far as much as you can. We've all got our own ways of dealing with and rationalising the job but Judy is so fanatical that if you let her get her hooks in you she'll never let you go. She fancies herself as a motivational psychologist – she's also in league with Leo Porter. Not that she hasn't done some good things here. To be honest, if you keep busy enough, or even just look like you are keeping busy, they will all leave you alone. Watch your call times and keep making the sales. Don't bother with her ridiculous videos, either. The morning motivational meetings will probably be as much as you can bear. There, I'm being negative again.'

'It's all right,' said Mr Johnson. 'I need to know who to watch out for. It doesn't sound like I'll be reporting much to her, anyway. What about Mr Bannister?'

'God knows. I haven't seen him for weeks. He's either off at a conference or in bed at home trying to work out how to run his department. Not even Les is clear about how everything fits together anymore. He used to have a lot more direct say in things but that all changed when Judy Orion started.'

A series of red lights flashed on and off on his phone. 'Looks like we're on again.' Margaret returned to her desk, still scowling and chewing her lip. 'Can you all get back on the phones, please?' she said to the office at large. Tony was about to resume Mr Johnson's initiation into the mysteries of the sales call when a woman appeared and introduced herself as Debbie Stevens.

'Finally,' said Debbie, as they shook hands.

CHAPTER SEVEN
THE CONCEPTUAL INITIALISATION DEPARTMENT

DEBBIE Stevens wore a black business suit and looked like a younger version of Judy Orion. 'I can only apologise for all the confusion,' she said. 'Has Tony been looking after you?'

Tony looked embarrassed and turned away.

'I've had plenty to do,' said Mr Johnson. 'It hasn't been a problem. Have they found me a desk yet?'

Debbie grimaced. 'Yes and no. It's chock-a-block in here at the moment, as you know, but I've found you a space in the conceptual initialisation department for the time being. It's not ideal, I'm afraid, but it will have to do for your induction period at least. Hope that's all right with you.'

'That's absolutely fine. I'm actually very interested to find out more about conceptual initialisation, anyway.' Tony smirked. Mr Johnson shook Tony's hand and thanked him for his help, picked up his presentation case and followed Debbie out of the sales office. As they passed through the door he had gone through earlier on the way to the training suite, they ran into Bob Hobbleton. He was carrying his ring binder.

'Hello again, Mr Johnson. I've just bumped into Bob Savage. He mentioned you. Have a look at that email group when you get the chance. It's an interesting discussion forum. Where are you off to now?'

'We've found Mr Johnson a temporary desk in conceptual initialisation,' said Debbie. 'He has been sent from pillar to post, I'm afraid.'

At the mention of conceptual initialisation, Bob raised his eyebrows. 'Looks like you are moving on sooner that I thought. Don't forget – the Five Synergetic Elements.'

'Good old Bob,' said Debbie as they walked along the corridor. 'What would we do without characters like him? Did he tell you what he actually does?'

'Not as such but he had a lot of interesting things to say.'

'Oh, Bob's interesting all right. If you ever find out what his job is, please let me know.'

They passed by the stairs that led to the training suite and went on through a set of double doors and into a bright and broad corridor.

'This looks newer than the other part of the building,' said Mr Johnson.

'It's not that new but it is more modern than the sales office area.'

'There are so many stairs, landings, corridors and offices that I could do with a map.'

'I know, you could get lost here very easily. Here we are.'

They turned into a long, white office. Debbie introduced Mr Johnson to a smartly-dressed young woman called Joanne, who was the conceptual initialisation department administrator.

'Look after Mr Johnson,' said Debbie. 'He's had a rough time so far. See you later, Mr Johnson. I'll let you know when the desk situation is resolved.'

She disappeared from the office. Joanne showed Mr Johnson to a desk at the far end of the room. Apart from Joanne and Mr Johnson, the office was deserted.

'Where is everybody?' Mr Johnson asked.

'The concept engineers are in their weekly brainstorming meeting. Here's your home for the moment. Make yourself comfortable. The coffee machine is outside, just down the corridor. I'm afraid your computer isn't connected to the network at the moment but you can use the basic applications if you need to. We'll sort a phone out for you as soon as we can. There's a stationery cupboard behind my desk – if you need anything from it, please ask first.'

'Have you any idea how long I'll be sitting here?'

'Your guess is as good as mine. At least until the end of your induction period – whenever that is. I don't suppose it matters where you sit until you actually start on the phones. You can always pop back in to work-shadow.'

'That reminds me – I still don't have an induction programme. I forgot to ask Debbie Stevens when I saw her. Could I ring her?'

'I'll sort it out for you. Do you know what you should be doing now?'

'I've no idea, I'm afraid. I could do with typing some notes up on the computer.'

Joanne switched on the monitor and typed in a password.

'I was going to say that you could find out more about the company and some of its procedures on the intranet but of course you're not connected to the network yet.'

'Have you any idea how long that will take?'

'Not long, I shouldn't think. I'll try and track down the systems manager.'

'He sounds a difficult man to get hold of.'

'You can say that again. In the meantime, if there is anything you need, just come and ask me. Especially if it's stationery.'

Joanne went back to her desk and Mr Johnson took out the notes from the presentation case. He opened a document on the computer and began to transcribe his notes. The atmosphere felt conducive to concentrated work.

Although the office was presently empty, Mr Johnson could tell that it housed a very different set of activities to the sales office. It felt cooler and more thoughtful. In the place of the motivational posters of dolphins, icebergs and the earth from space and the target board that adorned the wall in sales, the conceptual initialisation department was decorated with reproductions of abstract expressionist paintings and tasteful black and white prints of old movie actors. There were no external windows. There were fifteen other desks in the office; behind and to the left of Mr Johnson was a partitioned office with windows that he presumed belonged to the conceptual initialisation manager Bob Hobbleton had referred to. He had spent about five minutes transcribing his notes when the concept engineers entered the office. They were mostly in their late twenties and early thirties and were more casually dressed than their colleagues in sales. To a man and woman, they sat down at their desks and got to work without any fuss or bother. No-one seemed particularly interested in Mr Johnson; he said hello to a young man who sat at the desk nearest to him who said hello back and smiled and immediately attended to his work. Mr Johnson got up to go to the coffee machine and offered his neighbour a cup; he politely declined.

When Mr Johnson came back from the coffee machine he found that his computer had crashed and his work was lost. He had forgotten to save it. He couldn't get the machine to start up again. He mentioned this to Joanne, who said she would add it to her list of things to discuss with the systems manager. She had some good news, however – a telephone had been found for him and would be set up shortly. Mr Johnson sat down again and resumed the manual interpretation of his notes from Bob Hobbleton's induction. He tore up the first diagrammatic version of the Five Synergetic Elements he had produced in the sales office and sketched out a new one following a different structure. This one also he tore up; he decided that he should wait until he had a fuller understanding of the relationship the conceptual initialisation department had with its cognate functions before he attempted a definitive visual schema. In any case, he thought, since he was to be working at least initially in sales, he should work out his understanding of the organisation's structure from the point of view of that department rather than conceptual initialisation. He wondered whether there was a similar synergetic process that applied to the sales department and, indeed, to all the company's other functions.

Mr Johnson turned instead to the notes he'd made during his sales training with Leo Porter. In truth, he hadn't made many comments since he'd spent much of the session in role-play. They were skeletal, though more explicit, than those he'd made with Bob Hobbleton. He wrote on another clean sheet of paper: 'Feel – Felt – Found' and beneath that: 'Dealing with receptionists? Features – Advantages – Benefits?'. He also wrote down the word 'Bragby' and underlined it twice.

It was strange being separated so soon from his new department and he wondered how he would be able to continue with his specific sales training. He supposed that Debbie Stevens would provide him with everything he needed. He also wondered how long he would have to stay in conceptual initialisation. Not that he was complaining; he was already quite at ease in his new surroundings. Joanne came over with a telephone which she plugged into a socket under Mr Johnson's desk. She told him that for the time being it was only good for internal calls but that the technical team would connect him to the outside world at the earliest opportunity. Apparently responsibility for the company's telephone network fell within the ambit of the systems manager; when Joanne told him this, Mr Johnson raised his eyebrows in mock horror, which seemed to be the appropriate thing to do. He continued with the transcription of his notes and was interrupted shortly afterwards by the telephone ringing – his first proper call at the company. It was Debbie Stevens. She apologised once again for all the confusion and promised to send through his induction programme asap. The seating situation might take longer to resolve. There were company-wide issues with resource allocation at the moment and the technical team were currently looking at the resource allocation spreadsheets with the express intention of back-filling key areas. This too fell within the range of responsibilities of the systems manager. Needless to say, none of this would be of any consolation to Mr Johnson but she asked him to bear with them for a little longer. At least he had a desk, even if it wasn't in the right department; in certain departments, employees had been forced to hot-desk and others sat down on a first-come-first-served basis. If it looked like the technical team were dragging their feet, Debbie suggested that Mr Johnson contact Judy Orion, who had more authority to get things moving than she did. Judy, however, was likely to be unavailable for the rest of the day, so he'd have to grin and bear it for the time being. Debbie apologised for all the confusion once again. Mr Johnson asked her what he should do next for his induction in the absence of a formal programme. Debbie suggested he familiarise himself with the company's formal culture and processes on the intranet or do some desk research on competitors and general market intelligence. Mr Johnson explained that he wasn't connected to the computer network. Debbie was frankly stumped and recommended he lobby Joanne to get the situation rectified as soon as possible. In the meantime, he should enjoy the quiet time while he could since he certainly wouldn't have much in the future. They both laughed at this and Debbie put the phone down quickly, though not before she told him not to hesitate to contact her should he have any other requirements. Mr Johnson decided to finish the transcription of his induction notes and any other thoughts that had occurred to him so far and then speak to Joanne about other work he could usefully perform before he immersed himself in the sales role. He reckoned that this would show proactivity on his part as well as insinuate him, even if only in a mild way, into the life of the conceptual initialisation department.

There was little more he could do in the way of development with the notes from Bob Hobbleton's induction and the training session so he set himself at recording his impressions of the organisation so far, key areas for personal development, and the ways in which he could use his experiences to enhance his CV.

As far as he could tell, the company had a multiplicity of functions and departments and areas of responsibility seemed to overlap one area to another. It was at once looser and more structured than his previous place of work. From what he had seen of the sales office, there were at least three figures with managerial responsibility, if Les Bannister, who had overall responsibility for strategic development, were entered into the equation. Mr Johnson made a mental note to find out exactly how his role impacted on the work of the conceptual initialisation department, which gave every impression of enjoying considerable freedom from outside forces. From what Bob Hobbleton had told him, the very essence of conceptual initialisation was to inform thinking and practices in other areas of activity, which, Mr Johnson guessed, implied that it should possess some autonomy. He worked this into a diagram on a new sheet of paper which showed a series of concentric circles with 'sales' at the core and 'conceptual initialisation?' running around the perimeter. So far, he had been exposed to just two core functions and yet they themselves seemed to be composed of numerous levels and many overlapping areas of responsibility. He noted down the key people he had met so far and meditated on their relationship with one another. It was quite clear that Judy Orion sat at the heart of the sales enterprise, although Margaret obviously had much more of a direct involvement in the operational running of the department. She was responsible for the sales canvassers, whereas Tony had implied that there were other members of the team, himself included, who reported more or less directly to Judy Orion. Judy hadn't referred much to Margaret and Margaret hadn't referred much to Judy. Perhaps they didn't have a good relationship or maybe, because of her involvement in management-level activities, Judy found it more appropriate to deal with her immediate deputies through Debbie

Stevens and Margaret was simply preoccupied with call times and targets. Mr Johnson hadn't met Les Bannister, although as far as he could tell he would have little day-to-day involvement with him – if he appeared at all. He couldn't begin to imagine how conceptual initialisation fitted into the picture. If it was part of the same overall departmental family as sales, it certainly seemed to keep its distance. But since he hadn't had the conceptual initialisation function explained to him by anyone who actually worked in it – Bob's conception was clearly rooted in theory rather than practice, Tony's in vague acquaintance – it was perhaps too early to try and guess what its exact relationship with its neighbour was. Although they were reasonably close geographically, the conceptual initialisation and sales departments might as well have been in separate buildings, so different were their respective atmospheres. Mr Johnson decided to think about the Five Synergetic Elements with reference to the little he had perceived so far of the distinctive quality of the conceptual initialisation office. When Bob Hobbleton had described them to him, Mr Johnson had visualised the Five Synergetic Elements as a mercurial core of movement, an endlessly mobile system of ideas existing independently in a silvery space beyond the physical environment of the organisation as a whole; this, at least, is what he came up with when he thought about the impression Bob had given him at the time. This picture seemed to correspond closely with the actual condition of the conceptual initialisation office, which appeared to have been designed to encourage quiet creative thinking and focused strategic development, although this impression might have had more to do with the fact that the concept engineers were preoccupied with the outcome of their weekly brainstorming session. Perhaps it was noisier at other times. Mr Johnson revised his diagram to place the Five Synergetic Elements at the centre and sales and marketing at the periphery. Over these two he wrote 'strategic development' and added a series of arrows leading from the Five Synergetic Elements to a single point at which he wrote 'other functions – need to find out how relate to FSE'.

He was deep in his work when a voice at his left shoulder said: 'You must be Mr Johnson.' Mr Johnson looked up and saw a small, bright-looking man smiling at him. He was wearing a yellow shirt unbuttoned at the collar beneath a tan suit. 'Mark Mitchell,' the man said, and offered his hand. 'I manage the conceptual initialisation department.' Mark's handshake was light but confidently firm. 'Have you got five minutes?' He motioned Mr Johnson into the office at the back of the room.

'Sounds like you've had quite a time of it so far,' said Mark as they sat down, Mark behind his light wooden desk and Mr Johnson on a black leather easy chair in front of him. 'Joanne was explaining that you're supposed to be in sales but they can't find room for you. Sorry if you've been mucked about.'

Mr Johnson shrugged. 'I expected things to be a little chaotic to begin with. I've had plenty to do so far.'

'Have you been given an induction programme yet?'

'No, but I'm hoping to have one as soon as possible. I've had a number of inductions but no programme as such, if you know what I mean.'

'Yes, I'm afraid I do. Have you any sales-related work you can be getting along with while you're sitting in here?'

'I've been transcribing some notes from one of the induction sessions but I'll be finished before long. I don't think sales can provide me with anything until my seating situation is sorted out. Is there anything I can do here?'

'Aside from sitting around listening to people telling you how important their jobs are?' laughed Mark. 'Yes, there is, as a matter of fact. We're always happy to have an extra pair of hands, so to speak. Do you know much about the work of the conceptual initialisation department?'

'Bob Hobbleton explained to me how it was set up, so I think I've got a basic understanding.'

'So you've seen Bob, have you? Did you get out in under two hours?'

'It wasn't as bad as that. He did seem to know a lot about the history of the company.'

'Oh, Bob knows a lot about history all right. I suppose he told you that the conceptual initialisation department was all his idea. Yes?' Mark stood up and closed the door. 'That's only partly true. Bob was part of a team that looked into the organisation's structure. He came up with the name and not much else. I was brought in to actually get it under way.'

'He seemed very keen on the Five Synergetic Elements. Didn't he devise those either? They're one of the things I've been making notes on.'

'Well, maybe he was responsible for one or two of them. The team came up with a very detailed background report with numerous recommendations, some of which were acted upon. I don't believe in getting bogged down in history, however. We should be looking forward at all times. What matters now is the conceptual initialisation department's current complexion. Mr Johnson, everybody that you meet during your induction period will tell you that their role or function is the most important in the company, that without them, the whole organisation would fall apart. Well, I have to say that in the case of the conceptual initialisation department, that is absolutely the case. Anything that happens in the company happens more or less directly as a consequence of work undertaken in this department.'

Mr Johnson wondered whether he should have brought his notepad in with him. Mark was warming to his theme and Mr Johnson decided it would be rude to break his flow. Outside the office he could see the heads of the concept engineers bent intently over their work. Occasionally ideas would be shared between desks. A man entered the office at the far end and handed something to Joanne. An atmosphere of earnest dedication prevailed. The environment in conceptual initialisation seemed to encourage calm and rational thought. It felt an altogether more appropriate setting for Mr Johnson to advance his career than the sales office; indeed, from the little he had been able to gather so far, the conceptual initialisation department was not dissimilar to the office he had worked in at his previous company, though this one was larger, brighter and more concerned with higher-level matters. It occurred to him that he might be able to involve himself in the life of the department and make himself, even in a modest way, indispensable to its smooth functioning. He wasn't sure how long it would take to do this; it was more than likely that he would be called back into sales before he had the chance to make a good impression. On the other hand, it did seem that there were serious resourcing issues within the company, so there was every reason to suppose that his desk-less state would persist for more than a few days. The notion that he could point blank refuse to go back to sales also crossed his mind, albeit fleetingly. However it would pan out, it was clear to Mr Johnson that he had been given an unusual opportunity early on to take his career in a different direction. He knew that he had much to learn but actually felt that he was at less of a disadvantage starting at the foot of the ladder in conceptual initialisation than he would be in sales. A market intelligence consultant, after all, could work in many different areas. His communication skills were sufficiently developed to enable him to adapt readily to new challenges and he was confident that the broad scope of his degree actually put him at an advantage when it came to quickly acquiring new skills and assimilating complex information. If he continued to pay attention and make notes of the key issues there was no reason why he shouldn't get to grips very quickly with the work of the conceptual initialisation department. After that there was no knowing what might happen. He wished he'd brought his pad in with him.

'But there's no question that the strategic focus of the entire organisation has sharpened as a result,' said Mark. 'I'm sorry, Mr Johnson. Have I lost you?'

'No, that's all perfectly clear. But I would like to know what sort of work I'll be involved in while I'm sitting in here.'

'I'm not exactly sure at the moment. We're currently concentrating our energies on a major developmental project that will have an enormous impact on the entire organisation. It's nothing less than an attempt to calibrate every set of activities in the company with the commercial imperatives that govern the working rhythms of the sales department and hence the primary commercial objectives of the organisation as a whole. This is extremely important – it's nothing short of a total integration of all aspects of the company's work according to a strong commercially-focused governing principle. I'm not exaggerating when I say that the future of the company rests on the success or failure of this project. That's one of the reasons why I really do believe that the conceptual initialisation department is the true heart of the organisation.'

'What you're describing fits in with what Bob Hobbleton told me,' said Mr Johnson. 'But how does it all work in practice?'

Mark took an unruled sheet of paper from a pad on his desk and beckoned Mr Johnson closer.

'Imagine that the conceptual initialisation department is the hub of a wheel,' Mark said, drawing a crude circle in the centre of the page. Mr Johnson was pleased – this was more or less what he had represented on his notepad before Mark had spoken to him. 'Within the wheel you have the eternally renewing circle of the Five Synergetic Elements.' Here he drew and numbered five curved arrows chasing each other around the interior of the circle. 'This is the generating motor of the organisation. Into the hub run the spokes of the company's functions, bringing in their own business requirements and commercial imperatives. The hub revolves, endlessly reshaping and re-envisioning the organisation's disparate and discrete activities. Are you following me? Business energy created in the hub flows back up the spokes to the wheel rim, which represents' (here he added in the final spokes and with a flourish drew a wheel around the diagram) 'the forward momentum of the company as far as its external audiences perceive it. Yes, endless revolution. But the conceptual initialisation department is a neutral hub, Mr Johnson, if such a thing exists. Its outward concerns and inward focus are shaped by para-departmental informative factors. The conceptual initialisation department doesn't have an ideology or a platform. Our purpose, our raison d'être, if you will, is to provide an objective environment for the rational development of innovative concepts for the organisation at large. Imagine a dynamic glue binding together multiple disparate elements and you'll be halfway to grasping the essential nature of the conceptual initialisation department.'

At that moment, Mark was interrupted by a telephone call. It was from Joanne. Shortly after he had finished the call, Joanne stepped in and handed

Mark an internal post envelope. Apparently it contained Mr Johnson's CV. Someone from the sales office had brought it through.

'That's quite strange,' said Mr Johnson, 'because they didn't seem to be expecting me there – I can't imagine why they would have my CV. Mind you, they had put my name on the target board, and there was a presentation case waiting for me in the training suite.'

'No, it does seem a very odd situation,' agreed Mark. 'To be honest with you, the administration side of things here isn't all it could be. It wouldn't surprise me in the least to discover that sales were simultaneously not expecting you to turn up for work and in possession of your CV. But since it's found its way in here and you're going to be with us for a short while, I might as well have a look.' Mark cast his eye over the document. 'Yes, it looks like you've acquired a broad set of experiences in some general areas and a general set of experiences in some broad areas but I'm not sure exactly why you've decided to go into the sales side of things.'

'I didn't as such. The job I applied for in the first place was a general graduate management training scheme. But when I was interviewed it turned out that the only vacancies they had were for market intelligence consultants in the strategic development department.'

'Which sounds like another way of saying sales.'

'Yes, so it seems. I don't mind a strong sales element to the job because I'm keen to develop my commercial skills but I would like a bit of variety. That's why I was so interested when I heard about the conceptual initialisation department. It's much more my sort of thing.'

'Looking at your CV, I would have to agree with you. I can clearly see that you possess well-developed conceptual skills and an enthusiasm for fresh challenges. I'd go as far to say that you'd probably be wasted in the sales department but would be much more suited to the role of concept engineer. That's all well and good on paper, however – you may be very different in practice.'

'Possibly, though it's too early for me to say. I must admit that when I sat down in this office I immediately felt more at home. But I suppose that sooner or later space will be found for me back in sales.'

'Maybe. In the meantime, as I said, we can find something for you to do. I like original thinkers and self-starters. I'm not making any promises but if you impress me I might be inclined to put in a word in your favour if and when the question of where you work should arise. I can't be any more explicit than that, you understand – the decision wouldn't necessarily be in my hands.'

Mr Johnson's heart leapt at these remarks and he nodded vigorously. He'd had the same thoughts himself. He knew that he couldn't rely on entering conceptual initialisation by what was essentially the back door but at least he had the sympathetic ear of its manager. He resolved again to apply all possible diligence and attention to any work he undertook within the department.

'It's not as though there isn't plenty to do. The sales-related project we're currently engaged on is called the Big Sell. It's been several months in the offing and we're approaching the final phases. I won't say that everything has gone according to plan – projects of this scale and scope rarely do – but if it helps, you could say that we're now at the harmonisation stage of the Five Synergetic Elements model that Bob Hobbleton outlined to you. The next step, of course, will be concrete-to-concrete fulfilment, at which point the Big Sell will be rolled out across the organisation and implemented.'

'The Big Sell – that's a serious-sounding title,' said Mr Johnson. 'It conveys very strongly the sense that the entire company is getting behind the sales effort and thinking commercially.'

'Yes, that's the idea and I'm pleased you've spotted it. In many ways, the Big Sell is the fulfilment of all the changes that have been taking place here recently. I don't want to get bogged down in unnecessary detail but apart from any other reason, conceptual initialisation was established with the express purpose of sharpening the company's commercial focus. The idea behind all this is that everyone, whether they are involved in sales or not, should put their hands to the same pump. From the despatch clerks to the senior management cluster, all work should be directed towards supporting and encouraging the sales effort. It's not an original idea, of course, but it's one that many organisations overlook – frequently at their peril. But without the conceptual initialisation department, the Big Sell would never be more than a good idea. Ideas don't magically transform themselves into practice. The post room isn't going to decide one day off its own bat to sharpen its commercial focus and lend a hand to the sales drive. Why should it? All functions are driven by their own immediate imperatives – even, or perhaps especially, the sales function. Concept engineers are the only people in the company who can deal independently with all other functions and draw together the multiple disparate threads of the organisation's activities into a coherent pattern. They are also the only people who are charged with the responsibility for thinking constantly, thinking about their own ideas and the ideas of others. That is the very essence of the concept engineer role – to think constantly. A concept engineer cannot stop thinking. Imagine a snooker player lining up his shots – forever. Or think of it in these terms – you can assemble all the parts required to make an engine but without fuel it won't do anything. Again, that's the job of the conceptual initialisation department – to provide the fuel, the organisational petroleum, if you will, for the corporate machine. It's all grist to the greater mill.'

'The more you tell me about conceptual initialisation, the more interested I am,' said Mr Johnson. 'Formally speaking, what qualifications do you need to become a concept engineer?'

'It's difficult to say. We recruit from such a diverse set of backgrounds and experiences. There are certain basic building blocks such as a good first degree, appropriate work experience, useful skill sets – the usual sorts of things. But as much as anything else, we look for lively and creative personalities, the sort of people who can bring a fresh eye to existing issues, develop new ideas and who are unafraid to propose unorthodox solutions. As a manager, I thrive on the creativity of my team. My door is always open – not now, obviously, but usually both literally and metaphorically – and I always say to the team: don't bring me problems for solution, bring me solutions for approval. Do you see what I'm getting at? I know that other departments have a more traditional approach to staff-management relations but in here the team enjoys considerable latitude. The dress code, for example, is a little more relaxed than elsewhere. I like people to look smart but feel comfortable. We're not a red braces office, if you know what I mean. While you're sitting in here, for however long it may be, I want you to feel that you can come and go as you please, within reason of course. Break times are flexible, get as many coffees as you want, that sort of thing. I also like to get all the staff together at least once a week, off- or on-site, for a brainstorming session. We find that this is where the best ideas are often generated. Anywhere that we get together as a team to formulate new thinking we call the Imaginarium. I came up with that term myself – the thinking behind it is that you can gather like-minded people together in any situation and, provided you follow the rules of brainstorming, share your thoughts freely and without fear of judgement or ridicule. The Imaginarium is wherever a quorum of concept engineers is, just as the White House is always where the US President is. Sometimes we all stop what we're doing and visit a leisure park for the day or go ten-pin bowling, though we've had fewer opportunities to do that sort of thing recently because we've been so busy. I hope that gives you some idea of the culture in here. We do work hard but I like to think we work hard in a relaxing and nurturing environment. I like to know what my team are doing but I'm not on their backs all the time. They're grown men and women with minds of their own; I'm not going to insult their intelligence by treating them like children who need constant monitoring. Without naming names, I know that this view doesn't prevail across all departments; I can only do my best to provide a pleasant, creative and supportive environment in here.

'But in terms of formal training, it's pretty much done on the job. It also depends on the exact role people have in the department. Although the general job title is concept engineer, there are three roles within that. We've got conceptual outriders who are dedicated to catching ideas from within and without the company for conceptual engineering. Then we have knowledge management experts who analyse various media and information sources. Finally, project captains manage the formal processes by which ideas are turned to concrete realities. This means that we have a demand for different skills in different areas, all of which are informed by the imperatives of the Five Synergetic Elements. Some of the team have got marketing qualifications, some general business diplomas, others none of these things. Some of the team have prior product- or people-management experience, others none. We have a mixture of internal and external recruits. I come from a marketing generalist background myself; we've had one or two people in the past who've come through the sales route.'

'I've heard about someone called Leonard Bragby who was in sales and then came into the conceptual initialisation department.'

'Who mentioned Leonard Bragby to you?'

'A few people, actually. They talked about him in the sales training session I attended and Bob Hobbleton mentioned him too. His name seems to keep cropping up.'

'Yes, and no wonder. He worked in here for a while but it was a bit of a mixed experience all round. I really can't go into any detail. He tended to move from department to department. I'm not sure what he's up to now. But I'd rather not look back. We're all focused on the Big Sell now, and you're going to play a part in it, at least for the immediate future. It's a bit irregular but there's no point in sitting around twiddling your thumbs, is there?'

'What would you like me to do exactly?'

'I'm still not one hundred per cent sure. I think, to get you started, you could have a look at an aspect of some work that's been done on the distribution tangents; that is to say, the area of the Big Sell that deals with the relationship between the dynamic imperatives of the distribution function and the objectives of the Big Sell itself. It's a crucial element in the project and one where we're likely to encounter the stiffest resistance when it comes to the concrete-to-concrete fulfilment stage of the process. Of all the functions in the organisation, the despatch area is the most change-resistant. Sickness records are poor, there's little willingness to embrace the challenges thrown up by new technologies, commitment to customer service, both internal and external, is low – the usual sort of thing. They are hardly likely, therefore, to be natural enthusiasts for a strategy that directs their efforts apparently in a direction that ostensibly is for the benefit of another department – and requires them to work harder. Our challenge is to persuade them of the benefits of incorporating the demands of the Big Sell into their normal working practices without alienating them. Needless to say, a lot of preparatory work has gone into the question of the distribution tangents. Once we have formulated an action plan, it will feed into the overall strategy we'll be presenting shortly to key internal stakeholders. As far as your involvement in the short-term goes, I think I'll get you to have a look at some third-quarter spreadsheets that provide a breakdown of the recent inputs, throughputs and outputs of the despatch function. It's not the most exciting work in the world but I should say that the life of the concept engineer isn't just thinking, thinking, thinking. Don't feel under any great pressure. I simply want to test your durability and give you something constructive to do. As I've said, it's a critical element of the overall project but you'll be looking at just a small part of it. I won't set you a deadline for the time being. You may find it a little boring; I make no apologies for that.'

'That's fine by me because I do enjoy close analytical work,' said Mr Johnson. 'In my last job I had to do a lot of research and analyse quite complex data so this won't be a problem. I'm used to working to project deadlines and I also know that creativity is ten per cent inspiration and ninety per cent perspiration.'

'You're not wrong there,' laughed Mark. 'You'll be sweating buckets for the good of the company before you know it.'

'The only thing that worries me is that I'm not connected to the network yet. Joanne has promised to chase the systems manager for me but I'm not confident that I'll be sorted out sooner rather than later. Will this be a problem in terms of the work on the distribution tangents?'

'It shouldn't be. There's nothing that I can't give you on a disk for the time being. It is a nuisance your not being connected to the network yet but I'm sure Joanne will do everything she can to help. As I said before, organisation isn't this organisation's strong point, if you know what I mean. To be fair, the technical team are under unprecedented pressure at the moment, what with all the changes that have been taking place and the continued expansion of the company's electronic profile. I don't understand a lot of the terminology myself but when someone from the systems manager's office tells me that he can't look at my monitor until Monday because they're all occupied on updating server memory for the back-office functions, I have to take his word for it. So don't worry about it for the moment.'

Mark took a disk from his drawer and put it into his computer. He clicked about a bit, took the disk out and handed it to Mr Johnson.

'Right, have a look at that. There's just the one spreadsheet on there. Any problems, let me know.'

'What exactly do you want me to come up with?'

'For the moment, I want you to just have a good look at it and see what you think. There's a lot of data on there and I don't expect you to make sense of all of it at once. The ultimate object of the exercise is to refine the working practices of the despatch area and align them with the imperatives that govern the Big Sell project. Imagine a vast garden filled with millions of vegetables and flowers. You are tilling a quiet corner, absorbed in your own work. Perhaps you'll never see the whole garden or be aware of the inter-relatedness of all its elements. But your tilling is as important to the overall organic health of the garden as the work of the man with the watering can, the woman sowing the seeds or the head gardener himself. This disk is your first piece of work; till it gently and don't worry yet about the garden at large. Is that clear?'

'Yes, I think so – as long as you don't mind me asking you for help if I get stuck.'

'Not at all – anything you're not sure about, please do not hesitate to ask. There's nothing worse than sitting on your own in state of confusion simply because you're too scared or too proud to ask for help. You'll find that your colleagues will be happy to help, too. People tend to get on quietly with their work in here – unless we're in the Imaginarium, of course – but they're a helpful bunch.'

Mark got up and opened the door and Mr Johnson returned to his desk. The concept engineers were still hard at their brainwork. Mr Johnson's neighbour looked up and smiled as Mr Johnson sat down but resumed his work immediately.

But he had forgotten that his computer had crashed. He knocked on Mark's door and explained that he wouldn't be able to access the disk. Mark came out and fiddled around at the back of the computer. Apparently a lead had worked loose, nothing more complicated than that. Mr Johnson apologised and said that he wasn't very good at the technical side of things. Mark admitted that he wasn't either but said that since he employed concept engineers, not computer engineers, he wasn't going to worry too much – each to their own area of specialisation. He checked that Mr Johnson understood what he was expected to do, and Mr Johnson said he did. Mark went as far as to put the disk into

Mr Johnson's computer and open up the spreadsheet.

'All you need to know is on here,' he said. Rows of figures marched up and down the spreadsheet. In the column on the left-hand side was a row of initials, denoting, Mr Johnson supposed, members of staff in the despatch function. It appeared comprehensive enough. Mr Johnson thanked Mark for his help and turned his attention to the task at hand. He was merely tilling a small corner of a large garden. From tiny acorns, great oaks might grow. A promising career lay in sunlit relief before him. All that was required was for him to pay attention, absorb new ideas and develop new skills. He wasn't such unpromising raw material, after all. A thorough job on the spreadsheet would make a favourable impression on Mark. He began to look at the figures in earnest.

CHAPTER EIGHT
THE DISTRIBUTION TANGENTS

But after Mark Mitchell had gone back to his office, Mr Johnson felt quite alone and the confidence in his ability that Mark had engendered in him through the agency of gently motivational words diminished rapidly. Not only could he not imagine completing the project, he had no idea how he would actually begin it. He dredged his mind for inspiration from his previous job. There were few pointers; the work there had somehow seemed more achievable and containable. This may have had something to do with the comparative size and cohesiveness of that company. For one thing, the work was undertaken in one small office. It was located in an old commercial building in a sleepy quarter of the town that everyone knew would one day be subjected to the attentions of urban improvers and regenerators; that day, however, had not come for as long as Mr Johnson had gone to work in the district. His thoughts strayed back to the gloomy, green entrance lobby that was reached from the street by a short flight of worn, stone steps, the edges eroded over time by the shoes of thousands of clerks, storemen and porters; eighty-two years, in fact, if the foundation stone by the front door were to be believed. An ancient concierge dozed in a wooden and glass cubicle immediately to the right as you entered. A large black pin-board told the tale of the companies that occupied the building. The lift was rickety and unreliable. Mr Johnson, for his health's sake as much as a concern for his personal safety, always walked up the echoing stone staircase to the fourth floor which was home to his small research development company. Although he worked there for just fourteen months, the oak-panelled office with the cracked linoleum and sturdy metal filing cabinets was as an ineffable and elemental aspect of his consciousness as the house in which he had been brought up or the white stone farmhouse in north Wales in which his family spent a week every August until he was eleven years old. His route to work was predictable and secure, his days were spent in the pursuit of realistic and quantifiable objectives. Tea and coffee could be made at any time in a dedicated kitchen area in a corner of the office. Lunch was eaten in a dim canteen in the basement that served the whole building. The food was basic – pie, chips and beans, pasta variations – but Mr Johnson always looked forward to lunch, especially on Fridays when fried liver and onions was served. Mr Johnson was aware of the existence of other companies in the building but rarely spoke to anyone outside of his own enterprise. Even at lunchtime, each company kept to itself. He knew that some of the tenants had been mouldering quietly on the upper floors for decades – theatrical outfitters, import and export agencies and civil engineering consultancies, for the most part – but he rarely, if ever, strayed far from the same stairs and corridors that led to his own office. While he worked there he had the sense of having found a safe and warm corner in a mysterious, though not minatory, labyrinth. Others had shared the feeling. On winter afternoons when the rain lashed and the wind rattled the old, green-framed sash windows, Mr Johnson and his colleagues used to tell each other that they were in the cosiest place in the world. No-one ever admitted that it might in fact have been too cosy. At first, Mr Johnson had wondered whether going to work should really be such a pleasant experience. Not that he didn't work hard. The company was engaged upon a series of complex research projects that required serious attention to detail and a comprehensive knowledge of the relevant industrial, commercial and academic sectors that provided the contracts. Mr Johnson and his colleagues spent their working days tracking down information on the internet or thumbing through business directories and abstracts of recondite academic papers. Reports were submitted and recommendations made. This process could often take days or weeks. There was no pressure to take short-cuts or skimp on detail, save the pressure that came from the company's commitment to meeting deadlines specified by the clients, a commitment that was felt instinctively by everyone who worked there and which never wavered. No, he had worked hard, and yet, thinking back, it somehow hadn't felt like proper work, whatever that was. He well remembered one of his colleagues telling him that few people ever left the company, what with it being so congenial and everything, and that the longer you stayed there, the more comfortable you became, the incentives to look for other jobs fewer. Benign institutionalisation, he had called it. Mr Johnson had felt the same way when he was at university; it was in order to remain in the warm, secure world of departmental corridors and libraries that he had registered on an MPhil programme once he had graduated, and the same compunction about being absorbed into a too familiar, and possibly in the longer term, unchallenging, environment had driven him to abandon his academic studies and apply for the job with the research company.

'I need fresh challenges,' he had told his manager when he tendered his resignation. 'I think I'm in danger of getting stuck in a rut.' His manager had looked at him curiously, told him that he was very sorry to hear that Mr Johnson wanted to leave because his work had been extremely impressive even in the short time that he had been with them, and that he was of course much liked personally by everyone who worked there, himself included, it went without saying. 'Your eye for detail and your meticulousness are quite exceptional in someone so young,' he had told Mr Johnson. 'What sort of challenges exactly are you hoping to encounter?'

'I'm not sure, really. It's not that I'm unhappy in my work here – far from it. It's just that I feel I need to test myself on a broader canvas.' Some weeks before this conversation Mr Johnson had sought some careers advice from his old university. He had used a computer programme that matched his skills and qualities with possible career areas and a careers adviser had encouraged him to audit his work, academic and social experiences and think about how he could use them to develop a career plan. The list had been quite impressive and the careers adviser had suggested to Mr Johnson that he would be suitable for a wide range of roles in the business world. 'Many companies recruit graduates from all sorts of disciplines, including the traditionally academic,' she had told him. 'Although you don't possess any vocational qualifications as such, your skills profile would make you a very attractive proposition in commercial terms. People with your academic background no longer need to think solely in terms of becoming teachers, lecturers or retraining to be accountants. You could equally see yourself as a marketeer, a sales manager or an entrepreneur. After all, the more progressive businesses will provide you with tailored training or encourage you to undertake an appropriate professional career development programme.'

These words had given great encouragement to Mr Johnson. Just prior to this interview, he had dipped a tentative toe into commercial waters when he had taken a call from someone who was interested, in theory, at least, in the company's services. Mr Johnson had given what was effectively an impromptu sales presentation which concluded with the enquirer confirming that he would indeed be interested in doing business with the company, a commitment which was subsequently formalised by Mr Johnson's manager and which developed into a three-year contract for six large research projects with a strong international profile. This single incident gave rise to Mr Johnson's reputation with his colleagues as a commercially-minded man and his manager promised to reward his unsuspected business acumen with a modest enhancement to his salary and more involvement in the company's new business generation activities in the future. But Mr Johnson knew that there was little likelihood of this becoming a more significant element in his job; the company's small size militated against their taking on more than a few contracts at a time and the order book was full for the next sixteen months.

Having made one important contribution to the future commercial success of the company, Mr Johnson wanted to do it again and again. He was confident that he could develop his commercial skills in tandem with an ever-improving commitment to high standards and information integrity, and when he saw the advertisement for the graduate management position, he knew that it was time to move on. At the interview in the hotel, Howard and Debbie Jackson had talked a great deal about the importance the company placed on commercial awareness and flexibility. They had looked at Mr Johnson's skill set with great interest and agreed that with the appropriate training in specific business techniques, there was every reason to expect that he would do very well in the job. Of course, they couldn't make any promises at the interview but by the way they shook his hand on the way out, Mr Johnson felt certain that they would be writing shortly with good news. The fact that if he were successful he wouldn't be on the graduate management programme as such – they had made this clear at the very beginning of the interview – but would instead be a market intelligence consultant in the strategic development department had concerned Mr Johnson a little at first but once Howard and Debbie had outlined clearly what the job entailed, he realised that it represented a significant move into an area of work that would provide ample opportunity to develop his commercial awareness and acquire marketable skills, and he decided that he would take it up if offered. Three days letter an offer letter arrived and the next day he spoke to his manager. His manager made no attempt to hide his disappointment and made a point of saying how sorry he was to see Mr Johnson leave, for professional and personal reasons. In response to Mr Johnson saying that he wanted to develop his commercial focus, his manager acknowledged that the company wasn't exactly a cutting-edge enterprise but that commercial focus came in many guises and that all he would say to Mr Johnson was that he should remember that being commercially minded, or, indeed, commercially successful, wasn't achieved merely by working in an office staffed by identikit employees in blue suits and being in possession of a palm pilot. Mr Johnson had smiled at this, though it crossed his mind now that that was exactly what the sales office he had joined was like, although he hadn't in fairness seen any palm pilots yet, which was a good job since he had no idea how to use one. A slim pocket diary had always sufficed.

'And nobody works here to become a millionaire,' his manager went on. 'I acknowledge that.' Mr Johnson, needless to say, hadn't mentioned the salary question but it was an important factor in his decision to move on. Quite simply, he could see no promotional route there. He began as a research assistant and after eight months became a research manager. Above this level was the general manager, who owned and ran the company. No one ever got rich in research, his manager had said. 'Not even me.' This was true – his manager often wore the same old jumper to work for weeks at a time and lived in a housing association flat in the north of the city. He seemed genuinely concerned about the welfare of his employees and employed enough people to ensure that jobs were done to the correct standards and in the requisite depth rather than cheese-paring resources in order to pay himself a bigger wage. Mr Johnson's new job, on the other hand, offered immediately a better basic salary and extremely attractive on-target earnings. A pension and other perks had been mentioned. Mr Johnson had liked the idea of being rewarded for good performance. He often stayed late into the night to complete a task and had even worked in the public library or at home at the weekend. He hadn't received overtime, and didn't expect any, although his boss was generous with time off in lieu. Not that Mr Johnson was often able to take advantage of this; he genuinely believed that if work needed to be done, it should be done. They were all in the same boat, after all. But he had begun to think that he might be better advised putting this commitment and energy into an enterprise that provided commensurate professional and financial rewards for such diligence and effort.

'It's not really about the money,' Mr Johnson had lied. He wondered what he would do if his manager made him an improved offer.

'Normally it's against my principles to offer an inducement to an employee to stay,' his manager said. 'And in practice, it's not possible to anyway. But I'd like to go on record and say that in your case, I would make an exception – if I could.'

'Thank you,' said Mr Johnson. 'That means a lot to me.'

'Good luck – not that you'll need it. I'm sure you will be a great asset to your new company.'

His colleagues, when Mr Johnson told them that he was leaving, were equally complimentary. 'There's no keeping a high-flier,' one of them said. 'You'll be a captain of industry before you know it.'

On his last day, after working a month's notice which his manager had kindly offered to waive and Mr Johnson magnanimously insisted on observing, they all went to the pub at lunchtime and in the afternoon drank warm white wine from paper cups in the office. At four o'clock a violent summer storm broke. The rain rattled and the wind lashed the windows and lightning flickered above the slick slate pitched roofs and hulking water tanks of the surrounding offices and warehouses. Mr Johnson and his colleagues shook hands and they presented him with a tasteful metal pen and a plastic novelty clock to mark his fourteen months' continuous service. He made a little speech and left the office for the last time, almost slipping on the greasy stone steps at the front. That seemed an omen – whether for good or ill he didn't know. In the streets the crowds of office workers shouldered their way to the bus stops and railway stations. The city was summer storm dark and the bus smelled of warm wool and wet dog. He rewarded himself with a bottle of red wine and spent the evening quietly at home. The next day was Saturday. Mr Johnson bought his first suit, a blue one, a new shirt and tie and brushed up on his transferable skills. He also stopped smoking. It seemed a significant thing to do. He scrubbed away the orange stains from the second and third fingers of his right hand with a nail brush and bought a tube of smokers' toothpaste with added whitening agents. First impressions were very important. On Sunday he did a reconnaissance trip in order to get the timings right for Monday, factored in contingency time for increased volume of traffic, and attempted to get a good night's sleep. But he never slept well on Sundays, a hangover from school days. His body was tired and his mind afire. The night was humid and close. He opened his bedroom window, at which point a burglar alarm went off nearby. Dogs joined the cacophony. At 2.00am he switched on the light and tried to read himself to sleep. Normally this was proof against insomnia, but not on this occasion. Mr Johnson became engrossed in his book and the clock radio soon showed 4.15am. Unable to sleep, he went downstairs and made a milky drink which he drank on the settee. Fine granular grey light showed through the thin curtains and the birds started up. He must have dropped off to sleep because he sat up with a start when the milkman made his delivery. Mr Johnson turned on the radio. It was 6.45am and past the time when he could safely go back to sleep. He made a pot of tea and two rounds of toast which he consumed on the settee whilst browsing through the remains of the Sunday paper. He had saved the quick crossword but completed less than half of it before it was time for a bath. He considered and rejected fishing from the kitchen waste bin the pouch of rolling tobacco he had proudly thrown away on Saturday. The new shirt and tie had been ironed the day before. Mr Johnson left the house at 7.50am and walked the short distance to the local railway station. The bottle of milk remained on the step. The sky was bright blue and cloudless, the day warm even at eight o'clock. The letter confirming his appointment was folded in the inside breast pocket of his suit jacket. Two carriages hoved into view. There was standing room only. The carriage was dirty, airless and muggy. For the first time in his life, Mr Johnson felt like a proper commuter. He realised that he hadn't brought his new pen with him. Neither had he brought a bag, which might pose a problem if he had to bring home any documentation at the end of the day. On the other hand, there was something quite appropriate about embarking on a new career with no encumbrances. He felt as though he had turned over a new leaf and was standing at the head of the first blank page of the book. In which case, he had opened a new volume rather than turned over a new leaf. Mr Johnson thought about what turning over a new leaf might entail in his new company. The act implied correcting one's behaviour in order to effect an improvement in one's performance. In his case, he was entering a new enterprise with no negative indicators. The idea of opening a new volume seemed to make more sense in this context after all. He would work his way down to the bottom of the first, clean white page. If things went well for him, turning over a new leaf would merely constitute making a rational progression through the necessary pages of career development rather than drawing a line beneath a previous set of dissatisfactory experiences. And if things didn't always go according to plan? There was no reason why everything shouldn't go swimmingly. He fully expected to be on a learning curve, a steep one, no doubt, to begin with. But unless he did spectacularly badly, turning the pages of the book would represent a positive and progressive act, the negative indicators, such as they were (for he was prepared to acquire some in the normal course of events) perhaps recorded as footnotes or mentioned in the index, unless the book were a work of fiction. Or a concordance. The rattling train was packed and although his mind was active, Mr Johnson's eyes were heavy and gritty. He patted the folded letter in his pocket for reassurance. He almost missed his stop in the crush. On the platform his head felt clearer. It didn't do to worry too much about the trajectory his career might take. He would take things steadily in small and manageable chunks, one day at a time. It was a short walk from the station to his new office. Even without the formal structure of a graduate management programme, Mr Johnson was sure that he was about to enter a rational and organised environment which would offer him the opportunity to develop his existing skills and acquire new ones. The very term 'strategic development' and the description of the role provided by Howard and Debbie Jackson suggested this. No pen, no bag, no watch. Mr Johnson asked a passer-by for the time. It was 8.58am. He was approximately two minutes away. The timings were excellent; the reconnaissance had certainly been worth doing. He walked across a narrow car park, already full at nine o'clock, and through a set of double doors with horizontal metal handles at hand height. The doors swung to behind him and he found himself in a small, tidy reception area. A desk, unoccupied, faced him. Staircases ran off to the left and right of the wall before which the desk sat. On one side of the reception were two low vinyl chairs, on the other a cheese plant. Sunshine warmed the vinyl floor. Mr Johnson took the letter from his pocket. A security guard wearing a blue uniform emerged from an ante-room.

'Are you lost?' he asked

'My name is Mr Johnson,' Mr Johnson said. 'It's my first day here. I'm looking for Mr Bannister in the strategic development department.'

The security guard scratched his head. 'I don't think I've come across that one before but that doesn't mean a great deal. There are so many new departments and functions that it's hard to keep up with what's what.'

This wasn't an encouraging start. The security guard beamed at Mr Johnson.

'Is there someone else I could see for directions?'

The security guard yawned. 'I'm sorry. I've been on since midnight. Ted will be here any time now. He'll have more idea than me. I don't want to tell you to go in one direction when you really should be going in another. Have a seat for a moment until Ted turns up.'

Mr Johnson sat down on one of the low vinyl seats and the security guard retired to the ante-room. Employees entered singly, in pairs and in small groups through the front door and headed up the stairs to the left and right of the reception desk. Aside from the desk, the chairs and the plant, the reception area was quite bare. It was altogether unlike the lobby in Mr Johnson's last office building, which was devoid of natural light and oppressively weighted by heavy, dark panelling and old iron fittings. Bright light streamed through the doors and broad windows. The security guard reappeared.

'It looks like Ted's running a little late. I don't want you to have to sit around here all day but by the same token I don't want to be responsible for sending you up to the wrong section. There's no point in getting your career here off on the wrong footing, so to speak.'

'That's all right,' Mr Johnson said. 'I don't mind waiting.'

'I'd phone up for you but as I said, I'm not sure what or where the strategic development department is. If you were in straight sales or one of the marketing functions, I'd be on surer ground. In any case, there seems to be a problem with the internal phone network. Normally, I could try and track down this Mr Bannister who you need to see from the telephone directory, but not today, I'm afraid. At least, not right at this moment. I've got a feeling that there's more than one Mr Bannister here, too, though I could be wrong. Between you and me, I'm fairly new here myself and I'm still putting names to faces. The last place I worked was a very different affair. I'd been there for over twenty-five years, for one thing, and knew what went on in every last corner. There were fewer employees to get to know there. This place is much less predictable, though I'm sure I'll get used to it in time. Usually, there are a couple of ladies on reception, but one is on holiday and goodness knows where the other one has got to. But Ted will be able to sort you out. He's an old hand.'

Just then another security guard in a blue uniform entered the reception area through the front door.

'Yes, morning Ted,' said the first security guard. 'I'm glad you've arrived. I have a new starter here. Mr Johnson, isn't it?' Ted shook Mr Johnson's hand. 'Now then,' said the first security guard, 'Mr Johnson has been told to report to the strategic development department but for the life of me I don't know where or what it is.'

'Strategic development, you say?' said Ted, and took a pencil from his pocket and scratched his ear with it.

'I did explain to Mr Johnson that I'm still quite new here myself and haven't got used to all the names and departments yet. And I don't think I was giving away any trade secrets when I told him that things change here all the time.'

Ted laughed and put the pencil back in his pocket. 'You can say that again. I've been here longer than most but even I have difficulty in keeping up with all the departments and functions. And don't get me started on the cross-functional teams.'

'Cross-functional teams?' said Mr Johnson.

'Don't ask,' said Ted. 'It's some fancy new way of describing something that everybody does as a matter of course, for all I know. It used to be so much simpler in the old days. Strategic development, you say? Sounds like it might be something to do with sales and marketing.'

'That's what I thought,' said the first security guard. 'The thing is, I didn't want to send Mr Johnson in the wrong direction on his first day.'

'You did the right thing,' Ted said. The first security guard looked pleased with this. 'Can I have a look at your letter?' Ted asked Mr Johnson. 'Mr L Bannister, it says. I think the best thing you could do would be to call up to him.'

'I thought of that,' said the first security guard, 'but the internal phone system is on the blink again.'

'Not again?' said Ted. He stood in thought for a moment. 'Well, under the circumstances, I suggest you go up to the first-floor reception area and ask for advice. We normally send new starters in sales and marketing there.'

'That had crossed my mind,' said the first security guard, 'but I wanted to wait for your input.'

'You did the right thing,' Ted said. 'No point in sending Mr Johnson on a wild goose chase. But if you go up to the first-floor reception, I think you'll be all right.

'Up those stairs?' Mr Johnson asked, pointing to the left of the reception desk.

'No,' said Ted, 'the stairs to the right. It's just a short flight. You go past a mezzanine landing to the first floor and a little way further you'll see some double doors with glass portholes at head height on your right. Go through the doors and somebody should be at the reception desk. I suggest you take it from there. You'll have to take the stairs, I'm afraid, because the lift doesn't reach the ground floor. Yes, I know, it is a bit strange. One of the quirks of the building's design.'

'That's all right – I like walking,' said Mr Johnson, and shook both their hands.

'No, not that way,' said Ted, as Mr Johnson headed to the stairs to the left of the reception desk. He clapped his hand to his forehead. 'Looks like I'm getting lost already,' he laughed, and re-crossed the reception area to the stairs to the right of the desk. He passed the mezzanine level and opened the double doors to the right on the first floor as Ted had directed. He entered a smaller reception area. Behind the desk sat a well-dressed woman in her fifties or thereabouts who was murmuring into a telephone. The fault with the network must have been rectified. She raised her eyebrows when Mr Johnson entered and he stood for some time at a little distance from her desk until she had finished her conversation. Her murmuring voice was warm and reassuring. Mr Johnson felt that he had arrived at a significant stage in his journey. The security guards had been as helpful as they could be but they didn't seem to be closely connected to the active life of the company. In this reception area, however, Mr Johnson felt that the lines of communication would be clearer. It seemed more closely connected to the rest of the company. Clarity was all important. He was at the head of a blank page, after all. There was important work to be done. It was time to make a clean start and meet fresh challenges. He was carrying no baggage. Once he was given a template, he was certain he would make a good impression. If he worked hard and paid attention, there was no telling what he would be able to achieve. He believed that the harnessing of diligence, conscientiousness and attention to detail to a focused commercial imperative would enable him to gain experience in a broad variety of business roles and lead to a successful career here, and, perhaps, elsewhere.

There were no guarantees, of course. But he did possess nascent commercial skills that were ripe for development. If he applied himself properly he ought in time be able to tackle any project, however apparently complex. That's why he'd applied for the job in the first place. This particular task was a case in point. Although he had no prior knowledge of the despatch function, logic dictated that he should be able to come to some sound conclusions given a little effort and familiarisation with the terminology. The spreadsheet was clear enough, after all. There was nothing that couldn't be deduced by reference to first principles and sound theory. There was no mystery to any of it. Everything could be deduced with a little application. How did anybody else start out? Mr Johnson had the overall conception. He was merely required to fit micro details into a larger schema. If he made the right impression in conceptual initialisation, Mark Mitchell might see his way to offering him a permanent role. He'd admitted as much. There were no guarantees, of course. But serendipity was a wonderful thing. Hard work married to commercial acumen plus creative instincts. That was why he had applied for the job in the first place. Taken as a unit of work, the question of the distribution tangents should have presented no greater problem than any project he had undertaken at his last company. It was simply a question of becoming familiar with the terminology and the work culture. Although Mark Mitchell hadn't said as much, Mr Johnson suspected that he had been given this task precisely because it required him to apply research-oriented skills he already possessed. In fact, there wasn't an awful lot of research to the task. It was rather a case of making logical deductions from the evidence available. There were no tricks or traps. Everything that he needed to know about the current state of the despatch function was contained in the spreadsheet in front of him. There was no need to bring to bear even the modest IT skills he had acquired in his last job and had mentioned on his CV. There was no mystery. He looked again at the figures. Without knowing what was the quantifiable base level of expectation that applied to the despatch function, he ought to be able to assess its relative level of effectiveness. Mr Johnson turned to the notes he had made on the overall conception of the Big Sell. He decided to return to first principles. The sales function drove the organisation. All the other activities within the organisation must be calibrated to achieve congruency with the imperatives of the sales function. He guessed, though it wasn't exactly clear from the figures in front of him, that the despatch function operated according to the practices of habit and custom, that it was driven, if it were driven at all, by the need to fulfil its own operational imperatives rather than working with reference to the wider commercial objectives of the organisation, whether defined in terms of the Big Sell or just ordinarily. Of course it was. That was the reason for the development of the Big Sell in the first place. Having reaffirmed this to himself, Mr Johnson sat back and considered the issue anew. A thought struck him. Since the question of improving the effectiveness and efficiency of the despatch function was central to incorporating that function into the overall conception of the Big Sell, surely the key to implementing the strategy in this respect was to address cultural and qualitative phenomena at least to the extent to which quantifiable questions were being addressed? This was not an argument for neglecting close figure work – far from it – but it ought surely to be the route to improvements in effectiveness and efficiency that the overall strategy demanded. Mr Johnson summarised this thought on his pad.

'Any weak spots?' said a voice at his shoulder. Mr Johnson looked up and saw Mark Mitchell smiling down at him.

'No obvious ones,' said Mr Johnson. 'But I was thinking that it might be taken as read that the entire despatch function is axiomatically deficient in operational terms if set against the tactical requirements and strategic expectations of the Big Sell when considered as a whole.'

Mark Mitchell nodded. 'I see that you are already thinking several stages ahead. Yes, you're quite right. Nevertheless, it's important that we establish in micro detail where the pinch points are likely to be. In many respects, the work you're doing is something of a foregone conclusion. But we mustn't run before we walk, Mr Johnson. Think about what I said about snooker players lining up their shots one after the other. You're already looking for the tasty long pots. That's the overall picture. In the matter of the small, vital details, however, it's essential that we don't fluff the apparently easy reds and send the white ball skewing into the pocket. Do you follow me?'

'Yes, I think so. You need to see that the basic building-block work has been done.'

'Exactly. Are you all right to carry on?'

'Yes, but before you go, would I be right in thinking that the Five Synergetic Elements should come into play at some point?'

'To a certain extent. The Five Synergetic Elements should be in the background always in everything you do. They effectively describe the operational life of the conceptual initialisation department. But they are also helpful guides in micro-planning and development activities. I suggest you refer to them at difficult points and build them into your overall conception of the task. At all events, they ought to shine, albeit suggestively, from your conclusions. Is that clear? And one more little secret that I'll let you into: I don't wish to teach you to suck eggs but make sure that any recommendations you make are Smart – that is to say, Specific, Measurable, Achievable, Relevant, and Timed. That sounds simple enough but you'd be surprised how often it gets overlooked in the haste to complete work. It's a standard mechanism in our business for assessing the effectiveness of any plan or objective. Keep that in mind along with the governing imperatives of the Five Synergetic Elements and you will be fine. If there's anything else you need to know, just ask.'

Mark returned to his office. This time Mr Johnson could see a clearer route to accomplishing the task he had been set. He quickly noted down the Smart principle, which he was glad Mark had mentioned since it would be a useful quality control check on any recommendations he might make. Mr Johnson realised that it was impossible to second-guess what Mark really wanted him to come up with because Mark was testing his adaptability as much as expecting him to reach a definitive conclusion. He decided to trust to his instincts and assume that the general trust Mark had placed in him could be taken as a tacit endorsement of whichever path he chose to follow in respect of the question of the distribution tangents. That he lacked basic knowledge of the activities and structure of this function was sufficient reason to approach the matter cautiously; on the other hand, Mark's confidence in his abilities and the modest skills he already possessed ought to compensate for any deficiencies in his knowledge base. Mr Johnson was coming to the conclusion that generalist skills could be applied to almost any aspect of an organisation's activities. He was fully aware that he was at the bottom of the ladder in terms of possessing such skills; those that he had he was conscious of deploying only tentatively. Others would be deployed in time. But he was a quick learner and there might be an opening for him in the conceptual initialisation department sooner than would normally be expected – Mark Mitchell had intimated as much. A simple spreadsheet was hardly the Rosetta Stone, after all. The figures in their little cells looked back at him. Some cells housed three figure numbers, some four, some five. Some had decimal points. In a way, it was a pity that the first project Mark had engaged him in was figure work, albeit of a modest type. Figures had never been his strong point. Mr Johnson hadn't passed his Maths O' level and had successfully avoided numbers at his last job. He knew his way round a spreadsheet, although he had tended to use them for rudimentary schedules rather than as calculating tools. But the underlying principles of the Five Synergetic Elements ought to be enough. They swam to the forefront of his consciousness, radiant, golden and spherical. He saw, as it were, the eternally renewing cycle of conceptual initialisation in the motional relationship between each element. It really was a very good way of explaining the dynamic energy creative thinking engendered within the organisation. Without the existence of the Elements, Mr Johnson supposed, the pervasive flux and chaos Bob Hobbleton had alluded to would by now have been endemic. From his point of view, a solid conceptual anchor was very welcome. It was hard enough working out what everybody did and how all the departments fitted together; he couldn't begin to imagine how he'd fare if there were no sound theoretical principles to guide him. He looked at the figures again. It was evident that the despatch function was underperforming in some areas and achieving base levels of expectation in others. Which areas were which wasn't entirely clear; what was certain was that nowhere was the despatch function exceeding expectations. Overall, the figures communicated a strong sense of inconsistency. Mr Johnson made a note of this on his pad. Of course the figures would communicate inconsistency; the despatch function presently lay outside of the remit of the Big Sell. In this sense, it would soon be embraced by the principles of the Five Synergetic Elements, which themselves had given birth to the Big Sell. This time, Mr Johnson saw the Elements as a celestial mother producing forth the Big Sell in the form of a starchild. It was all so simple, yet so profound. The Big Sell was evidently the ultimate working out of the Five Synergetic Elements, the rationale for their existence, perhaps, although Bob Hobbleton hadn't mentioned the Big Sell at all. Perhaps he hadn't been privy to the consultation and development that precipitated its introduction. Given that this process was still in progress, this wasn't a surprise. And from what Mark had told him, Bob was keen to claim greater ownership over the development of the conceptual initialisation department than his efforts had perhaps deserved. Not that this was to be wondered at – anyone who had played a role, however modest, in the generation of the department was entitled to feel proud about it, even to overstate the extent of their involvement. It was such a persuasive superstructure, after all. Even spreadsheets were explicable with reference to it.

'Any more thoughts?' said Mark at Mr Johnson's shoulder.

Mr Johnson looked up at him. 'I think I'm getting there. It seems that there is considerable inconsistency in performance levels across the function. Would I be right in thinking that?'

'Yes, to a great extent. I don't think I'm betraying any trade secrets when I tell you that the entire despatch function has been lying fallow for years. It bears some relation to the conditions that apparently prevailed in the sales department until fairly recently – morale low, productivity lower, that sort of thing.'

'The situation in sales certainly seems to have been turned round, from what I could tell,' said Mr Johnson. 'It felt quite energetic in there, although in fairness it was hard to form an accurate picture because the phones were rarely working. But everyone seemed to know what they were doing, and Judy Orion was highly motivated. Maybe that's just a perception.'

'No, Judy's motivated all right. I suppose she told you how she single-handedly revolutionised the sales function?'

'Something like that, yes. Is that not really the case?'

'Not exactly. Of course, she has made an important contribution since she began here, but from what I've been told, anybody with half an eye for a commercial opportunity could have turned round the sales department at that time. It was very fertile ground. Motivational meetings, the introduction of targets, regular performance reviews – they're hardly radical initiatives. And I should say that the benefits to the organisation brought about by the spread of creativity through the formation of the conceptual initialisation department have been felt in sales at least as much as anywhere else. It's been something of a domino effect, if you will. But it doesn't do to get too wrapped up in the doings of other functions, however closely our fortunes are tied. That may sound paradoxical to you, Mr Johnson, since we are presently engaged in a process that seeks to place the imperatives of the sales function at the heart of the life of the organisation. Perhaps it is a paradox – the business world is as riddled with them as anywhere else. But we must continue to work as we do, in relative isolation, drawing information for analysis from elsewhere before throwing it into the crucible of creative thinking and presenting our findings to the rest of the organisation. That's how conceptual initialisation works – a simultaneously inward- and outward-looking activity. Conceptual initialisation is effectively neutral. It has no agenda save the relentless improvement of the company's commercial and organisational wellbeing through sound creative thinking. We do our job and step back once we have completed it. Others must do with our recommendations as they see fit. So it is with the Big Sell. We will shortly be presenting our findings and making the case for forward development at a presentation which will be attended by key internal stakeholders. I can't promise anything but you may have a part to play in this, Mr Johnson. At the very least, the work you're doing now will feed into the overall strategy. Before that, there will be a brainstorming session for senior members of the project team, myself included, to put the finishing touches to the concluding phase of the exploratory and developmental stage. I may well ask you to attend, depending on your progress with the distribution tangents work, of course. It will be a good experience for you and you may have something to contribute. Don't look alarmed – there's nothing mysterious about brainstorming, and I won't drop you in at the deep end. I don't believe in doing that. But in the meantime, carry on with the spreadsheet work. It seems as though you are on the right track.'

'Before you go, can I ask you something?'

'You can ask me anything you like.'

'There are many things that I'm still not sure about,' said Mr Johnson, 'but I expect I'll find out more in time. I realise that I have to find my own way round the distribution tangents question, although I know you'll guide me along the way.' Mark nodded at this. 'But one thing in particular does concern me, and that's the question of authority. I'd like to understand where the real source of power lies in the company. I realise that there is an identifiable hierarchical structure with the executive director at the top and the senior management cluster immediately beneath her, but there also seem to be other, less explicit sources. For example, I've been told that Sir Colin is actually over everybody else, yet by all accounts he reports to a non-executive management board. As far as I can tell, they have no direct involvement in the active business of the company but the executive director must take their views into account, through Sir Colin, of course. Bob Hobbleton outlined the shape of this relationship but I still haven't seen any physical manifestation of it. And all the departments that I've encountered so far seem to enjoy a considerable degree of autonomy and appear to have very little to do with each other. This one is no exception; I realise that it exists primarily to provide creative impetus for other departments' activities, particularly with the development of the Big Sell, but it doesn't seem to have much physical contact with the outside world, as it were. It was the same in the sales department, as far as I could discern from my brief exposure to it. Everybody seems to be preoccupied with their own particular branch of work, even when it has wider applications, as is certainly the case in sales and in here. I'm not sure that I'm making a great deal of sense. I suppose that what I'm trying to do is get a grasp of the overarching structures and see where I fit in. But perhaps it's too early to do this.'

Mark looked at him kindly. 'No, you're not wrong to try and pin this down. Many people work here for years without fully understanding how they fit into the greater scheme of things. Generally, they find their own level eventually. You've raised an interesting point, as a matter of fact – there is a distinction between hierarchical structures and sources of power. I prefer not to get too fixated on structures and titles. That's partly to do with my own management style – I don't wish to blow my own trumpet but I don't think that my team see me as a remote authority figure. I like to think that I can engage with them on their own terms. They need to see that I'm action as well as words. In many respects, I'm just a concept engineer like anyone else. Of course, it is necessary for me to have greater overall grasp of certain issues and to maintain a positive and supportive managerial authority within the department. But the point is, in here ideas are everything. I possess no secret knowledge. The theoretical underpinnings of conceptual initialisation are in the public domain, as it were. Ideas empower people, not managers. Everyone in this department enjoys considerable autonomy in terms of project remit. They know that I'm not going to be on their backs all the time. But they also know that I'll support them come what may. They trust me and they know that I'll never let them down. Personal politics don't interest me – I've never wanted to climb the greasy pole and I don't bend with the prevailing wind. I suppose what I'm saying is that in here the culture is as liberal as it's possible to be and that there's relatively little distinction between management and the managed. But I'm not sure that is the case in every department.'

'I certainly don't think that it was like that in the sales department,' said Mr Johnson, 'although that might have had more to do with the nature of the work than with the personal qualities of the management level.'

'How do you mean?'

'It's the solitariness of the sales role – that was my perception, anyway. I imagine that it would be difficult for a manager to play an active role in the working life of the salesperson and so they would seem removed from the actual working processes. All the motivational meetings in the world couldn't change that. It's different in here, as far as I can tell. Although people get on with their work quietly, there seems to be a shared sense of collective objectives and group meetings appear to stimulate greater cohesion even when the outcomes are individualistic. I don't know, they're just first impressions.'

'I must say, Mr Johnson, you are demonstrating a very sophisticated understanding of the key issues.'

'Do you really think so? I do feel that although there is still so much to learn, I am beginning to see something of the overall shape of things.'

Although he didn't feel particularly confident about the distribution tangents question, there was no question that he was thinking constructively about the wider issues. The extent to which he was willing and able to articulate these thoughts surprised him. There was no doubt that Mark Mitchell helped him feel confident enough to express himself.

'But I suspect that being in a more congenial environment helps,' said Mark, as if divining Mr Johnson's thoughts.

'Yes, I suppose it does.'

'I'll cut to the chase, Mr Johnson. You don't want to go back to the sales department, do you?'

'No, I don't. The more I think about it, the more I realise that my appointment was essentially a mistake. From what I've seen and heard, I don't think I am cut out to be a sales person. But of course, I will do whatever I have to do. At the very least, I will have acquired some valuable experiences, and, with luck, some new skills in the meantime.'

Mark winked at him. 'Since it is still the meantime, crack on with those distribution tangents. It sounds as though you are heading in the right direction with them. Try not to worry too much about the sales department. For as long as you are in here, you will be given opportunities commensurate with your talent and ability. Which as far as I am concerned are becoming more and more impressive by the minute. Don't hesitate to ask if you need any help. I'll be in my office.'

Mr Johnson turned to the screen. A minute later, Mark appeared again. 'I don't want to put any pressure on you, Mr Johnson, but you should know that events were galloping apace even as we spoke. A message has been left with me to the effect that major hierarchical changes are imminent. This has given added impetus to the company-wide application of the Big Sell, which may now happen sooner rather than later.'

'What sort of hierarchical changes?'

'I'm not sure. There have been rumblings about change high up in the company for some time. Now it seems that change is going to happen at last, although I don't know what exactly is planned. But on a more immediate level, I can tell you that it doesn't look like Les Bannister will be returning any day soon.'

'What's happened to him?'

'I'm not exactly sure but apparently he's off for twelve months for reasons as yet unspecified.'

'Will that have any bearing on me? I think he was ultimately my boss, although Judy Orion suggested that they shared responsibility for the department. But wasn't he your boss as well? Doesn't strategic development embrace sales, conceptual initialisation as well as certain marketing functions?'

'That's what Les liked to think,' said Mark. 'I certainly didn't report to him. His biggest concern was negotiating his way round Judy Orion. I don't think his departure, temporary or permanent, will have much effect on you. It certainly won't on me. But it will have an impact on the general organisational structure in terms of potentially creating favourable conditions for the early implementation of company-wide strategies such as the Big Sell. But I'm talking at you while you have important work to do. From what you've told me, you are really getting to grips with this question. All I would say is concentrate a little more on the finer details. Your overall conceptual grasp of the underlying principles is very sound. Attend fully to the facts and you will achieve a harmonious balance of theory and practice. You're nearly there – if you have any problems or queries, you know where I am. Is that all right?'

'Yes, I think so. I have felt a growing confidence in my conceptual grasp. Do you think it's fair to say that if I keep the principles to the foreground I'll have a sound framework for understanding the broad detail?'

'Absolutely. And spoken like a true concept engineer, if I may say so. Keep up the good work.'

Mark returned to his office. Evidently Mr Johnson was on the right track. The more he understood the underlying principles, the more durable the foreground framework would become. The numbers would take care of themselves. Mark had said that he had spoken like a true concept engineer. Mr Johnson didn't know what a true concept engineer sounded like – he had exchanged no more than a few desultory words with his immediate neighbour and whilst he and Mark had been talking, everybody else in the office, Joanne included, had kept their heads down – but he liked the idea that he sounded like one. It represented one more small step away from the sales office. Mark's words had become more and more encouraging in this respect. Each time he spoke to Mr Johnson, he laid more emphasis on his involvement in future projects and less on his probable return to sales. Mr Johnson expelled the thought immediately, but it struck him that 'probable' may now have become 'possible' and may be soon, he hardly dared contemplate it, 'unlikely'. But first there was the question of the spreadsheet to attend to. For some reason, it looked different since Mark had last spoken to him. The numbers seemed less remote and forbidding. A sound conceptual underpinning was clearly the way forward. Mark had also mentioned a brainstorming session. As far as he was aware, Mr Johnson had never participated in a brainstorming session before, although at his last company he and his colleagues had often shared ideas informally across their desks. His manager had encouraged this and sometimes used to join in. This usually occurred on a Friday afternoon, after the team had returned from the local pub. Presumably brainstorming here would be a more formal, or certainly formalised, activity. Mr Johnson had enjoyed the group discussions that took place at his last company. Sometimes they drew useful and pertinent business conclusions from their discussions. Sometimes they simply enjoyed a good old chat with each other. That would be something he would have to get used to doing without here. Everybody was wrapped up tightly in their own work. There was certainly plenty to talk about but much of it was concerned with the practicalities of work matters. At his last company, Mr Johnson and his colleagues often discussed work matters but also found the time to take in current affairs, literature, football, films, history, comedy – a range of subjects that ostensibly had little connection with the business at hand but which didn't distract Mr Johnson and his colleagues from the work they were paid to do. Indeed, the team were frequently able to talk and work at the same time. Even his manager, whilst maintaining a necessary professional distance from the team, was known to perch on the end of a desk and initiate a conversation about real ale or French cinema.

'How are things progressing?' Mr Johnson looked up into Mark's smiling face.

'Quite well, I think. I'm getting close to achieving the harmonious balance you referred to.'

'Excellent. I don't want to put you under unnecessary pressure but as I mentioned, things are hotting up. It's been confirmed that Les Bannister has left the company and that the anticipated changes may have implications at the very top of the organisation.'

'Do you mean the executive director or Sir Colin?'

'I don't know for sure – somebody is playing their cards very close to their chest – but I wouldn't rule anything out. We'll have to wait and see. In the meantime, all our efforts are being channelled into achieving the early approval and implementation of the Big Sell. You can see how intent everyone is on achieving this objective.'

This was true. The concept engineers still had their heads bent over their work but if anything they emanated an even stronger sense of collective purpose allied to individual endeavour. The room vibrated with their intense mental effort. Some of them had even switched on their desk lamps.

'Each concept engineer is a strong team player as well as a keen and capable individualist,' said Mark, gesturing at the room. 'You can tell that simply by looking at them at work.'

Mr Johnson's neighbour looked up, smiled across at Mark, and returned to his work under a pool of light.

'Thanks to their dedication, we have every reason to be confident that we can deliver the Big Sell proposal ahead of the original deadline. Do you know, Mr Johnson, I didn't need to browbeat or coerce any one of them into stepping up their efforts. A simple email sufficed. "Dear Team," I wrote, "the time parameters have shifted and we have the opportunity to implement the

Big Sell sooner rather than later. All hands to the pump! Mark." Needless to say, no one replied with any queries or complaints. They all quietly and uncomplainingly got on with their work. I see the same commitment and attention to detail in you, Mr Johnson. I don't need to be on your back all the time. Keep up the good work. If you need anything, you know where I am.'

Mark returned to his office and Mr Johnson attended to the spreadsheet once more. It was quite clear that the despatch function was characterised by a high degree of inconsistency, if not outright flux and chaos. It was difficult to see how the situation could be resolved short of a total overhaul of every area of its activities. Presumably the imposition of organisation-wide standards and a focus on a strong centralising conceptual imperative would improve matters. If the spreadsheet were to be analysed in a few months' time, it might tell a very different story. It was no surprise that the disparate elements of the despatch function were at such variance with one another. The whole department appeared to be pulling in many different directions. It was about to embark on the same journey in terms of departmental change and organisational restructuring the sales department had embarked upon a year or two before. It was probably not a moment too soon. Presumably the Big Sell would bring the same rigorous focus to other departments that presently lacked it. Perhaps that was what the other concept engineers were engaged on at that moment. Soon the entire organisation would be calibrated according to clear and agreed commercial principles. The figures shone brightly in their cells. Mr Johnson clicked the highlighter on and off repeatedly so that the cells seemed to wink at him. He summarised his thoughts so far on his pad, to the effect that: the despatch function was performing inconsistently; it lacked rigorous focus; the principles of the Five Synergetic Elements as revealed through the strategic dynamism of the Big Sell would bring order and discipline to the activities of the despatch function and a harmonious convergence with its associated functions would be realised. He had just begun to represent this in diagrammatic form when Mark appeared again.

'Any firm conclusions?'

'Yes, I'm summarising my thoughts now. I thought I'd do a text and a diagrammatic version.'

'That's an excellent approach. Pop them into my office when you're ready.' He disappeared again. Mr Johnson concluded his drawing and sat back to contemplate his work. Read through as a piece, his written conclusions gave the impression of a strong grasp of the conceptual underpinnings but were perhaps a little sparse when it came to the fine details. He felt that he had achieved a harmonic balance but this didn't come across in print. The diagrammatic representation was better, although Mr Johnson suspected that it was easier to cover up for deficiencies in knowledge in pictorial form. He closed his eyes so as to order his thoughts. Every time he tried to return to first principles, the principles shifted. His conception of the Five Synergetic Elements was just as mutable. That, presumably, was quite natural, and even positive; it represented a progressive movement in terms of his grasp of the theoretical basis of his work and his place within the organisational superstructure. His eyes smarted when he opened them. The room was white hot and bright. There were no windows and the computers, lights and lamps gave off waves of heat. Mr Johnson got up from his desk and walked out of the office to the coffee machine. No-one looked up as he passed. He selected a strong white coffee without sugar. A friendly voice said: 'Here you are again.' It was Bob Savage.

'Hello,' said Mr Johnson. 'Do you work round here?'

'Not as such. I fancied a bit of a stroll. How are you getting on?'

'All right, I think. I'm sitting in the conceptual initialisation department at the moment while they sort out my resource allocation.'

'I know, Bob Hobbleton told me. Looks like you really are one of those high fliers we're always hearing about. Have you had any information back-stabbed your way yet?'

'Not that I'm aware of, although I have had to take a lot on board. There is certainly plenty to get my teeth into.'

'Yes, there's no shortage of material. Have you had a chance to look at that email group I mentioned?'

'No, because I'm not on the network yet.'

'Still off the network? I shouldn't be surprised. I've been off myself often enough.'

'I've also had a lot of work on, even though I'm not actually a formal member of the conceptual initialisation department. This is the first coffee I've had for ages.'

'Yes, you do look as though you've been working hard. Your eyes are tired.'

'Are they? I haven't been aware of it, but then again I haven't looked in a mirror for a long time. There has simply been so much to do.'

Bob Savage looked up and down the long corridor. 'Why don't you have a break? There's a staff lounge quite near here where we could take our coffees and have a nice sit down and a chat. You look like you could do with a break.'

'You're probably right but I'm close to finishing a piece of work for Mark Mitchell that will have a bearing on the implementation of the Big Sell strategy. It's particularly pressing since certain organisational changes may lead to its early adoption.'

'The Big Sell, you say? I don't think I've come across that one before.'

'The project aims to calibrate the activities of the entire organisation with the commercial imperatives that underpin the sales function.'

'You mean it's another attempt to bring order to chaos?'

'Yes, I suppose that's one way of looking at it. I've been involved only peripherally so far. I'm addressing the question of the distribution tangents in the despatch function.'

'Very impressive. I suppose this is one of Mark Mitchell's initiatives.'

'I'm not sure. He certainly seems to be playing a key role in the project. As its name implies, the Big Sell is a major undertaking. I'm surprised you haven't heard about it before.'

'Oh, I'm sure I will in good time. It wouldn't be the first such enterprise. Good luck with it. Are you sure I can't interest you in a little break? You do look tired.'

'Thanks, but no thanks. If I pause now, I'll lose my thread altogether. Apparently, I might be asked to go into a brainstorming session at any moment.'

'That's quite right, Mr Johnson,' said a voice at his shoulder. It was Mark Mitchell. 'In fact, we're ready to go any minute now.'

Mark and Bob nodded at each other but didn't exchange words.

'I'll go for that sit down, then,' said Bob, and ambled off down the corridor with his coffee.

'Looks like I arrived in the nick of time,' said Mark. 'There's no getting away from him. Whenever I go to the coffee machine, he pops up. I think he's bored.'

'He seems a nice man, though. Is there really a brainstorming session right now or did you come to rescue me?'

'Yes there is. I'd like you to take part, assuming you've completed the work I set you.' Mark got himself a black coffee and they walked together back to the conceptual initialisation department.

'I think I'm almost there with it. I felt as though I had achieved the balance you referred to but when I looked at my findings in black and white, I wasn't so sure. I'd like you to cast your eye over them.'

'I will, if I get the chance. I've got a couple of things to sort out in my office and the brainstorming begins in five minutes.'

Mark went into his office and shut the door. Mr Johnson sat down and looked again at the spreadsheet with reference to the notes he had made on his pad. If anything, they seemed more at variance with each other than before he had gone to the coffee machine. The brainstorming would have to wait. He wished that he had taken up Bob Savage's offer of a break in the staff lounge. Heat and light bounced from the walls. The coffee sat untouched. Mr Johnson closed his eyes, opened them, closed them again. All the concept engineers had their lamps on. He sought to resolve his thinking on the question of the distribution tangents. There were sound reasons for believing that the entire despatch function could be brought into congruent tandem with the principles underpinning the Big Sell strategy and hence the organisation as a whole. In his mind the relationship between the theoretical background and the practical foreground was represented as a flux of golden arrows and spheres. The processes were renewing themselves eternally, bringing the liquid light of organisational logic to the murk of departmental inertia and chaos, or something like that. They were just sense impressions, after all. His eyes smarted in the glare. The spreadsheet had given the barest clues to the state of the despatch function and its relationship with its associated departments, yet Mr Johnson had deduced that it was fit and ready to be embraced by the conceptual rigour of the Big Sell. From that point of understanding, practical recommendations could be made as to the forward development of the function and its integration with the operational imperatives of the Big Sell. That wasn't his job. Others could do with his findings as they wished. If his summary demonstrated an innate understanding of the conceptual underpinnings, it had done its job adequately. Mark Mitchell appeared and blotted out the white glare.

'It's time now. Are you ready?'

'Ready?'

'Yes, for the brainstorming. It's time now.'

'I don't know. I'm not sure how far I've really got with the question of the distribution tangents. For a while back there it felt as though I'd cracked it but on reflection I don't think that I have. I'd be grateful if you could look over my work before we go.'

'There's no time for that, Mr Johnson,' said Mark to the office at large. For the first time, all the concept engineers were looking at Mr Johnson with expressions of mild curiosity.

'What do you think, team? Should Mr Johnson go to the brainstorming session?'

The team yielded a mild susurrus of approbation.

'I have every confidence in you, Mr Johnson. From what you told me on the occasions I came to check on your progress, you had demonstrated a subtle grasp of the central issues and were close to drawing a set of sound conclusions, if not making concrete recommendations. It's a yes, then,' he said to the room again, and everyone applauded quietly.

'The other thing is, I'm actually extremely tired,' Mr Johnson said as an aside to Mark, as he was ushered towards the door. 'It's just come over me like a wave. I'm not sure how much use I'll be.'

'We are all tired, Mr Johnson. Some of the team have been working flat out for months on this project. If you want to be a concept engineer, you'll have to get used to being tired. There will be plenty of time for rest later on. I've forwarded my calls to your extension, Joanne,' Mark said as they passed the administrator's desk. Joanne gave Mr Johnson a mock salute as they left the room. He stuffed his notes into the presentation case and let his reluctant feet follow Mark through a maze of corridors and down several flights of stairs into a white-painted room with a narrow band of windows just below ceiling height on one side. Three men were waiting around a rectangular table. Mr Johnson recognised none of them from the conceptual initialisation department. He really was tired.

CHAPTER NINE
BRAINSTORMING

Mark Mitchell made the introductions. 'Mr Johnson, this is Steve, our marketing services manager, this is Mike, our business development manager, here's another Mark – Mark's involved in managing key aspects of the despatch function.'

All three nodded and smiled at Mr Johnson, who sat down next to Mark Mitchell at the end of the table. 'Mr Johnson has just come on board. There's nothing like jumping in at the deep end, is there? Mike has overall responsibility for the Big Sell. Mr Johnson comes highly recommended, gentlemen. He's been getting to grips with the question of the distribution tangents. Very impressive so far, and he's still, formally speaking, a sales person.' Steve, Mike and the other Mark nodded approvingly.

'With the exception of Mr Johnson, we've all experienced brainstorming conditions before but there's no harm in revisiting first principles. As most of us know, the only rule in brainstorming is that everybody gets the chance to speak and that no idea is too ridiculous to put forward. So that's two rules, then. The two fundamental premises of brainstorming. It's not predicated on anything complex. You simply need a pen and paper – and your brain, of course. Some people call it a thought shower nowadays, which isn't the pleasantest expression on the market, I must admit. And, of course, we'll need a facilitator. Someone to keep things moving, to manage the cut and thrust. But it's your opportunity. That's you, Mr Johnson, and all of you. I don't want anyone to be backward about coming forward. Any questions?'

They all shook their heads. Sheets of sun rolled through the upper windows. They seemed to be aimed directly at Mr Johnson's head. The room was very hot. Mark Mitchell was still talking.

'There are two fundamental premises to brainstorming. Any idea, however preposterous, is legitimate. There are precedents for this in commercial history…'

'Which instances?' asked Mr Johnson, suddenly sitting forward and manipulating his pen.

'…where the development of a profitable business idea has arisen from a serendipitous, chance or even off-hand remark offered under classical brainstorming conditions that has improved the fortunes of a major business organisation. A pen and paper. Bring your brains. Don't leave them at the door. Keep them with you at all times. The thinking should never stop. Yes, the outcomes of the brainstorming session will feed into the activity overview plan which in turn will inform the decisions taken by the strategic implementation team with regard to the new three-year plan in which the Big Sell will be executed. Then there's the imminent stakeholder presentation, of course. As you know, the time parameters have shifted in our favour. Are you with me?'

They all nodded again.

'That's the revised three-year plan as set out by the strategy directive review last month. Not the old five-year corporate statement. Nobody refers to that anymore. Yes, the relevant documentation has been removed from the intranet. Ready? We need a facilitator. Mr Johnson, perhaps. Nothing like jumping in at the deep end. Don't worry, there's nothing to it. You can sit here as you are. I'm conscious of the time parameters. Use these big sheets of paper and these marker pens.'

'I'm ready if you are.'

'We're in brainstorming mode... now.'

'I suggest we begin with the objectives of the Big Sell and work backwards from there. There's no harm in revisiting first principles.'

'All well and good but do we actually have a clear understanding of those objectives? If you recall, they were set well before preparatory and exploratory work was done on the conditions to which the objectives actually refer. What with the time shifts, surely everything has changed? Expression putting the cart before the horse comes to mind.'

'Or shutting the stable door after the horse has bolted.'

'Or spoiling the ship for a ha'porth of tar.'

'Focus please.'

'So much work has been done on the micro elements of the strategy that perhaps we should be working up from the bottom.'

'Cascade upwards if you will.'

'I will.'

'Mr Johnson, have you taken everything down so far?'

Mr Johnson traced arrows and boxes on the paper, nodded attentively. The sheet was marked in red, black and green. Heat washed in waves through the windows. He needed a drink of water.

'This is one such idea that might normally seem untenable. I can hardly utter it for fear of public humiliations but here goes anyway. What about removing the task-specific operational responsibilities from the strategic development review team and empowering the cross-functional activation groups to make direct recommendations to the corporate climatic bar?'

'That bit again?'

'Removing the operationally-specific task roles from the cross-functional procedure team and aligning the strategic implementation groups with the requirements of the third-quarter corporate review.'

'I think that the billings action aspect of it is crucial.'

'The billings?'

Mr Johnson entered 'billings' into a thickly outlined black box and under the heading 'Crucial Elements' wrote 'outside the box – new thinking and innovation'.

'Yes, among certain others. I suggest a reorientation of the cross-functional objectives for the third quarter. Why don't we add the marketing dimension to this aspect of the process?'

Mr Johnson thickly circling the paper in imperishable markings, collecting annotations.

'In a sense, however, the marketing dimension informs every aspect of the project, which is ironic given the circumstances, I know.'

'Because of the overarching sales focus?'

'Quite.'

On the sheet entered 'essential dichotomy – cf 5SE – marketing primacy – hobbleton?'

'If I may add some flavour to Steve's last comment.'

The newness of the faces aroused confusion in Mr Johnson and he looked unblinkingly at Mark Mitchell for anchorage. The other Mark was talking in the glare.

'Instigate an upper-level re-orientation and reallocate the slackage. That way we can back-fill the post-production requirements without netting. In time.'

'How this can even be contemplated under the current climate eludes me. The resource allocation, back-filling you say, and yes, but from where and how all this? Particularly back-filling despatch area in current circumstances. The systems are stretched as it is.'

'Which is exactly what Mr Johnson has been looking into. Isn't that right Mr Johnson?' Again, vigorous nodding. He was analysing the resource allocation question among other things. He was getting to grips with the tangents. He was facilitating.

'That is indeed.'

'So in that case, a broader analysis required. Cannot, repeat, cannot rely on other functions to iron out resource allocation creases on their own terms.

Term organisational glue springs to mind.'

'Agree in entirety. Tangents question broader than single function, which yes, of course, all know, realise, aware of, but has time been devoted? Surely same degree of attention required?'

'Couldn't agree more.'

'Got that?'

'Yes, I think so.'

He marked the paper once more, this time in a bold stroke of green. The available space had quickly filled up. The thickly scored whiteness spiralling greens and reds and blacks. Mr Johnson blinked at Mark for reassurance. In turn, committed the names and faces to memory. Steves, Marks and Mikes. He was facilitating. The urgency seemed to have vanished.

'Bring it back to the process. Ideas spiralling. Please remember focus – brainstorming, not inter-departmental assassination.'

The heat rising in sheets and waves, the thirst, the imperishable markings. Got that? Yes, got that so far. Red, black and green ink scoring the page. Someone was still talking.

'Some good thinking. Like creativity. Process is the key to everything. When you sit in this room green and blue pressing against the glass, dim hot afternoon. Almost tropical, aquatic. The process must be agreed.'

'Must not forget not is critical.'

'When you, Mr Johnson, the dimness of this room mid-season, blue, hot. Hot as a plate pressed to your brow. The reports upon which hinge. Some tangentially, others opaque. No great distinction. Central to the company's fortunes, our own no doubt withstanding. Blue and black.'

'The sky as dead as a plate.'

'The process, yes. Hinge on this, no?'

'Key appointments across functions. Make net the focus. White bones and grass. The net of all activity. No wonder all the business and the time departing. All the slippage. This and which mustn't be overlooked.'

'The alternatives. This and others.'

'The alternatives which we all know.'

'A seed of doubt, running before we walk springs to mind. Suggest we stick to our knitting, this sure am all aware.'

'Ideas spiralling. Bring it back to the originals. Are you getting it?'

'As wet as a buggy.'

'What?'

'In marching time you'll raise it, I'm sure. Hot as juggy.'

'Bringing out the sub-strata, strands, some other aspects to focus on. Don't want to spanner but as for a sheep, as for a lamb. Literally.'

'Literally this and others.'

'The team awaiting, departmental confirmation. Send them in all directions. Netting the focus in reorientation. Mr Johnson, your steam brow this afternoon. The room now steam-plated, blue afternoon. Grass and green black brow in subaquatic plate room.'

'I'm shuggy?'

'You in the buggy climate and arching point made men of this. Heard the confusions, gathered, parted. You running the show now.'

'See, info tankard and back again. You washing up against the boards, saline and withered, this in time and throughout. If we bring it back into focus, clarity restored.'

'Yes, throughout this and others. Hilarity applaud. The red and black climbing the wall, interior, exterior, dim press-plate brow this afternoon.'

'Only if certain may not. Up against wall of hard. Considered, yes and blue buggy. These in it, for some, sure.'

'I have him vote if no others. See how on board they become. Feeling of heart, the blue pressing, an iron, green and black.'

'Dim, bright room. I am of the under-pinnioned champion.'

'Which is of the requirement.'

'All the team.'

'Shall progress.'

'All clear? Yes, away. Each one of us work up respective outcome documentation. Mr Johnson, the distribution tangents particularly important – that's axiomatic in your case. Got that?'

The room returned with a snap. 'Distribution tangents, yes, I've got it. Who do I need to see about this?'

'You can see me later,' said Mark Mitchell. 'Write up what you have put on your paper and circulate the notes. You can stay in here if you need some peace and quiet. Is that all clear?'

'Yes, I think so.'

The brainstorming was over and Mark Mitchell, Mike, Steve and the other Mark walked out of the room leaving Mr Johnson on his own with the big sheets of paper.

CHAPTER TEN

BILFRED

Mr Johnson attended to the notes he had made. They whirled and swirled in curlicues and filigrees of green and red and black. He had filled up three sides. He took the A4 pad from his presentation case and tore off a clean sheet. He wasn't sure whether Mark had meant for him to work up the notes from the whole brainstorm or just the information relevant to the distribution tangents. He decided that he ought to do both. It was clear that the work he had already done on the subject needed developing into a more comprehensive proposition. Mark and his colleagues had closed the door on their way out. In addition to the high-level windows, the room was lit by fluorescent strips and was altogether very bright, though less hot than it had been during the brainstorming. Mr Johnson switched the lights off, which immediately made the room dimmer and cooler, though there was adequate light to work from. His eyes felt gritty and sore and his head ached. He regretted not bringing any water into the room. There was a lot of work to be done. On the other hand, he had facilitated his first brainstorming session and it had seemed to go well. He made a mental note to ask Mark Mitchell for feedback later on and another to add the experience to his CV as evidence of his broad range of business skills. With these positive thoughts, he drove the tiredness from his mind and focused on the papers. He decided to work up the notes on the overall brainstorm first and extract the distribution tangents from them. At the top of the blank sheet he wrote: 'The Big Sell'; and beneath that: 'Objective: To identify and implement the dynamic functions of the Big Sell.'

He paused and sat back. The notes he had made during the brainstorm, taken as a whole, seemed disjointed and disconnected. Mr Johnson realised that conceptually speaking, he was working from the top down and decided to look at the notes relating to each activity as a set of discrete phenomena before attempting to devise an overall superstructure. He screwed up the page headed 'The Big Sell' and tore off seven separate sheets and at the top of each one wrote the letter D and the numbers one to seven. He remembered that there were seven Ds in marketing and was sure that his notes could be fitted somehow into the categories. Mr Johnson began to work through his notes with the intention of categorising them under the relevant D category and then making strong sequential connections between each category. Then he realised – it was obvious, really – that until he learned what each D stood for, he was guessing as to the appropriateness of the respective categories. Distribution was no doubt one of them but he had no idea what the remaining six might be. Mr Johnson gave up on the Ds and tore a new piece of paper from the pad and entitled it 'Sequential Stages'. But he realised that he had to all intents and purposes outlined these stages already on the original notes he'd made in red and black and green marker pens. He also saw how the process of crossing out text had obscured the legend for the diagrammatic element of the notes, so he painstakingly went back over them and re-wrote the words above the crossings out. From this he began to wonder whether it wouldn't be better to merely duplicate the notes in tidier form rather than break them down into their component elements. There were spare sheets of A3 paper at the end of the table. He took three and laid them side by side. He needed to attach them together. There wasn't a stationery cupboard in the room so he went outside and looked up and down the corridor. It was deserted in either direction. He walked in one direction without encountering a soul or, indeed, a room. He turned round when the corridor ran into a stairwell and walked back past the brainstorm room for a little way. Finally he came to a door on the left. He knocked. There was no response. He pushed the door open gently. Inside a man sat with his feet on the desk and his eyes closed. Headphone wires trailed from his ears and ran into a computer. When the man realised someone else was in his room he gave a start and clicked his mouse and took the plug from his ears.

'What do you want?' he asked.

'Hello. I was wondering whether you had any sellotape. I'm working in a room down the corridor and need to attach some large sheets of paper together.'

'Not sure if I do. Have I seen you before?'

'I don't think so. I'm Mr Johnson. I'm new here.'

'I'm Lionel Bilfred,' said the man, getting up and offering his hand. 'You gave me a bit of a shock. I'm not used to visitors. Which department do you work in?'

'Strictly speaking sales but I've become attached to the conceptual initialisation department for the purposes of my induction. I've just facilitated a brainstorming session on the distribution tangents and other key issues with Mark Mitchell, who I'm sort of working for at the moment, and the business development manager. There's a major strategic project in the offing called the Big Sell, which seeks to calibrate the entire organisation according to the commercial imperatives that underpin the sales function. What do you do?'

'As little as possible,' said Lionel. 'Actually, that's not strictly true. I keep an eye out for changes and developments, have a look at the processes, that sort of thing.'

'Is this your office? Most people here seem to work in an open plan environment.'

'Yes, and don't tell anybody about it. I was overlooked the last time they reorganised the working environment and as far as I'm concerned I can stay overlooked. I'm quite happy with my music, my kettle and my closed door. So don't mention the fact that you've seen me to anybody.'

'No, of course I won't.'

'Because there's no way in the world that I'm going to work in an open plan office.' He rummaged in a draw. 'No, nothing doing, I'm afraid. I don't have much need for stationery items. I've never been in a brainstorming session, myself. What goes on there?'

'It's difficult to say. A lot of people talk about different things and then they try and reach a definitive conclusion. Brainstorming is underpinned by the notion that you can say anything within its context without fear of ridicule or censure. It was interesting, although I'm not sure that I got down all the relevant information. It was also very warm in the room and I'm rather tired.'

'What department did you say you were in? Conceptual imaging?'

'Conceptual initialisation. It's a relatively new function.'

'Can't say I've ever heard of it. What does it do?'

'It's hard to say exactly. Conceptual initialisation embraces aspects of marketing and product development but exists primarily to ensure that company-wide ideas generation has a strategic and operational focus. It works closely with all departments, especially sales. At the moment they are informing the development of an activities strategy for the Big Sell. I'm working on a project closely tied to its formal application.'

'Sorry, I haven't heard of the Big Sell either,' said Lionel, 'although it sounds quite important. I'm just glad I've got my own office.'

'Which department are you in?' asked Mr Johnson.

'I'm not. The last time they had a departmental reorganisation, I got overlooked.'

'So who's your line manager?'

'Don't have one. I know, it is a bit strange. But they still pay me – touch wood. At the very least, I've got somewhere warm to come during the day and access to electrical services. I make sure that I send the odd judicious email to certain bodies – enough communication to maintain a vague sense of my value as far as the organisation is concerned but not enough to start people thinking about me particularly. Forgive me, I'm being flippant. I don't know what you're going to do about the sellotape. I'm sorry, I'm not thinking. Pull that chair up and sit down – like I said, I don't get many visitors.'

Mr Johnson sat in front of Lionel's desk. On the computer screen, which was at an angle, he saw lines of dense-looking codes and encryptions.

'One of the processes,' said Lionel. 'It probably looks like a load of gobbledegook to you. But not to the trained eye. I follow shifts and changes in the organisational culture as revealed through the agency of information code.'

'You've certainly found a quiet place to work.'

'Yes, I suppose you could say that I have found myself a comfortable niche. I am somewhat unassailable – so long as I stay in here, of course. This peace and quiet has certainly given me time to think.'

'What do you think about?'

Lionel eased back his chair and clasped his hands on his lap. He seemed pleased to have been given the opportunity to talk. 'Lots of things. Work, mainly, which is a bit strange since I am rather cut off from the main currents of activity. Or at least my relationship to the rest of the organisation. Before you came in, for example, I was ruminating on the possible existence of a fourth sphere of existence to add to home, work, and home-work. I had some downtime between process monitoring, you see. I was getting close to defining it when you arrived. No, don't apologise. I still have the thread of the idea. It was to do with the amalgamation of the existing three spaces through the agency of constructive anonymity. Does that make any sense? I'm not sure that it does to me now. I think I was concerned to arrive at a condition of acceptance of one's place within the organisation entirely on one's own terms. This condition would be achieved by retreating into one's environment and quite simply not worrying about what is going on elsewhere. Do you follow?' Lionel got up to close the door. 'For example, here we are now in my room. Does anybody else know that we are here? Probably not. I don't have a line manager and you've been left to work on an important project on your own. So far so good. But let's extend this train of thought into the next category. Does Mr Johnson know what Mark Mitchell – that was his name, wasn't it? – is doing right now? Are Mr Johnson and his project at the forefront of Mark Mitchell's mind? Almost certainly not. You see, what seems an urgent priority to us is of negligible concern to the next man. Just because your line manager has given you a job to do doesn't mean that he is sitting waiting for you to complete it without any other thoughts in his mind. Quite the opposite. I would have thought that someone in Mark Mitchell's position would have a million other things to think about it. A project such as yours, with all due respect to you, Mr Johnson, will be a trifling concern to him. In fact, he probably only gave you the project so that you could have something to do. I hope I'm not personalising the matter – the principle applies across the organisation. Most tasks, especially those delegated by higher levels of authority, are generally devoid of meaning and exist merely to fulfil a delegating requirement. I am convinced of this, and the more time I spend away from the main currents of activity, the more convinced I am. This is true in an individual and collective sense. Even the Big Sell will be like this to an extent, despite its overarching relevance to the organisation at large, although I only know the little you have revealed to me so far. But it's all about perception, isn't it? Do you know, Mr Johnson, sometimes I like to imagine that I am in a little cabin in a great ship. I love to let the low hum of the engines lull me. Above, below and around me the ship is alive with activity and purpose. I neither have a place within this purpose nor exist without reference to it. I am poised between action and inaction. I think and yet my thoughts concern themselves with a condition of not thinking. It is quiet in here, in the heart of the ship.'

Mr Johnson thought about the ship's cabin. The office was lulled by a softly pervasive vibrating thrum of electricity and motors. They could have been far out at sea for all he knew.

'Imagine all that invisible discourse taking place, the billions of atomised, fragmented pieces of information hurtling though the networks and systems, and me, sitting quietly at the heart of it all watching the processes for subtle shifts and changes. There is something almost existentially poetic about it all, don't you think? But I've been talking incessantly about myself. What about you? I'm not used to visitors and when I do receive them I feel compelled to explain myself. There is no formal pressure on me to do this, of course. But what about your relationship to the rest of the organisation? What do you think of when you think of yourself in relation to work?'

Mr Johnson outlined his work experience to date and his ambitions for the future. 'It's too early for me to say for sure how I feel about my relationship with this organisation. I am very willing to learn and like to think that I possess good communication skills. But there is an awful lot to take in. I have to accept that I'm on a very steep learning curve. On the one hand, the size and complexity of the organisation mean that it is difficult for a relative newcomer to get a clear understanding of how things work. On the other, there do seem to be more opportunities here for developing or changing roles than in a smaller organisation. I've already sort of moved from one department to another. All I can say is that if I work hard and take advantage of any opportunities that come my way, I would hope that I stand as good a chance as anyone else of advancing. To begin with, I've been getting to grips with the theory and trying to see how it works in practice.'

He was conscious that this sounded a bit flat and empty. Certainly in contrast to Lionel, it hardly constituted a theory about work. Lionel must have guessed that Mr Johnson was thinking this because he said that that was a quite natural feeling and that he too had felt the same way when he was at Mr Johnson's stage. Over time, however, he'd found that he gradually lost his faith in a rational structure underpinned by a corporate culture that rewarded individual effort in an objective context.

'I prefer a more occult reading of the situation,' he said. 'You talk about your enthusiasm and your willingness to learn. But are these things enough in themselves? You may find in time that your career development will be determined at least as much by the phases of the moon, the height of the tides, the whims and caprices of others and the imperatives of ancient central-European folklore as it is by the refinement of your skill set, your attendance on training programmes and the prompt execution of tasks handed down by your line manager. Well, is that really so ridiculous? Take your communication skills, for example. What proof will they offer against the company going bankrupt next week or sweeping changes taking place to the management culture which may lead to your losing your job at a stroke? Again, I don't wish to personalise the situation. It's just a thought. And what, exactly, are communication skills? It's merely a term that describes myriad mysterious processes that resist human quantification. Just think of the billions of impressions, subjective responses, instincts and feelings that constitute human discourse. How on earth can all this be described in terms of a skill set? Suppose that you and I became good friends. How would that happen? Should we analyse it? Would it not devalue our relationship to see it in terms of a process, or, worse, to acknowledge that one or other of us had deployed a strategy to persuade the other of our fitness for friendship? It's all a question of how we look at things. For example, people employed in the sales industry say that every area of one's life can be understood by reference to the sales process. I have heard this said, that every day, in a million overt and covert ways, humans are engaged in the act of selling. Now, what the proponents of such a theory are suggesting is that there is an organic condition in the natural world that makes human beings naturally pre-disposed to work in the sales industry. This in turn legitimises their work function. Can you see how cunning these people have become? By suggesting that selling is somehow as natural as breathing, all reasonable objections to being engaged in the act of selling are removed, since to be in opposition to sales is to be in opposition to life itself. Yet I prefer to look through the other end of the telescope, to reverse the perspective flow, if you will. Instead of drawing its inspiration – and hence its legitimacy – from life, I would argue that work actually sits in a state of negative opposition to life and that work environments and cultures are merely grotesque distortions of it. Rather than being the ultimate fulfilment of organic natural conditions, work is an entire world of anti-life. For otherwise – extending the argument into a related area – we should be forced to conclude that millennia of human evolution and social development have been but the preparation for the advent of Homo Consumus – shopping man and woman. Do you see what I'm getting at? Perhaps you don't. I'm sorry, I haven't had the opportunity for a good old chat for such a long time. I get so few visitors down here. Put crudely, what I suppose I'm saying is that we must resist the notion that work is everything and we are somehow obliged to prostrate ourselves before it, be conquered by it. I know that this isn't strictly speaking part of your induction; you've probably been bombarded with information you can barely grasp, nor reasonably be expected to remember. I do go on with myself, I know. As far as my own position is concerned, I yield. I seek a rapturous absorption into the fabric of the organisation. I have abrogated my rights to a social personality and have retreated into a quiet, dark corner of myself. In respect of my relationship with my immediate environment, I barely exist at all. My requirements are few; my impact on the world around me negligible. I take what I need according to my needs. Does this sound unscrupulous to you, Mr Johnson? Perhaps I am unscrupulous. I wasn't always like this. Once I was engaged, committed, involved. Like you, I had ambitions and could see a logical and traversable path before me. At one time I was responsible for managing a team of people. I had middle-level management duties. I discharged my duties to the best of my ability. I reached a peak of achievement – I was going to say plateau but, looked at in even modest macro-time, I enjoyed no such stroll across a broad and level higher plain. Then, gradually, though rapidly enough, my ability diminished. Jobs and tasks went unperformed, key staff left. I lost whatever grip I once had on the schedules and procedures. People began to talk. Word spread. Each day I laboured beneath a dead weight of unanswered correspondence, half-completed projects and unpaid invoices. I diminished in myself. Bit by bit work was taken away from me and responsibilities reduced. I've no idea how this happened, nor, more pertinently, when. It's like the point at which a person's face changes or their body mass increases. Day-by-day the alterations are imperceptible but looked at over broad time a startling transformation has taken place. But would you detect that transformation if you were to study photographs of yourself taken every day from your birth to the present and laid out in a line? Perhaps. Needless to say, I awoke one fine day to find myself without a department or a specific role. But they didn't sack me. Oh no. I was left to moulder – a worse fate, you might say. I knew then that I had passed through a door and would never be able to make the return journey. When you lose that sharpness, Mr Johnson, that sense of being a man in control of his own destiny, you never regain it. Not in a modern business organisation, at any rate. It goes for ever. I knew that there was no point in trying to rebuild my position. I wasn't sharp enough anymore. As far as my old job was concerned, a trainee I had managed – whom I had even recruited and trained up, if you don't mind – was running the department. Well, she was welcome to it. She was, in fairness, sharper, and I'd never enjoyed the job anyway. Instead, I descended, I shed whatever residual responsibilities I had and let the tides of organisational activity flow around me. Soon – sooner than I could have dared expect – I was to all intents and purposes a solitary island in the midst of a broad river of oblivious activity. I quickly became part of the landscape, neither obtrusive enough to be over-visited nor hidden away enough to be discovered. I became both a fixture and a fitting, an immutable element in the office environment. I asked for nothing from anybody and no-one asked for anything from me. Departments came and went, functions altered, new processes emerged. Gradually, I slowly sank from view. It has been both a literal and a metaphorical journey. I am now physically some floors down from my own office. As you can see, this is a small room with no natural light. But it isn't quite rock-bottom. From here I can expect to move finally into a cupboard somewhere, at which point my career will be over and my journey ended. There is little else to add. My work now is routine, predictable. I monitor the processes. What does this mean? Not a great deal, in practice. I look out for alterations and adaptations. This code that you see on the screen now denotes a series of changes that are being made to the deeper systems. The endless reconfigurations, the almost infinite sequence of permutations, the subtle shifts and sideways shuffles of data – all of this I keep a weather eye on. You could say that I have an innate sympathy for this kind of work – certainly more for this than for managing a department. I don't expect anyone else to share my enthusiasm; I certainly don't report on it. My requirements are simple. I have a kettle, music and access to electrical services. There is no natural light in here but my room is warm when I need to be warm and cool when I need to be cool. I like to think that I have achieved a harmonic balance between my need to remain in gainful employment and my desire to distance myself from the onerous demands of working life. Yes, I can see how that might be interpreted as being unscrupulous. But as I hope that I've explained clearly to you, I have not been in control of the journey that has led me to this place. But I like to think that I have pioneered a trend. For who could honestly say at the end of their career that they were in a worse position with respect to their job and actually knew less than when they started? That's certainly likely to be the case for me. I'm not particularly proud of this. I had no desire at the start of my career to turn negation into a way of life. But it has been an honest retreat, at least. I merely conceded in the face of insuperable odds. My time had come and I stepped down gracefully. I have mouldered, but on my own terms. I am happy here. I have everything I need here. My needs are minimal. I don't receive many visitors. You are the first person I have seen for a long time. Does any of this make any sense to you? I'm not even sure myself. My thoughts are faint dabs, timid impressions, upon the canvas of existence. I can only speak for myself. I have so much time on my hands down here. I try to set down my thoughts as often as I can remember to but when I do they seem over-impressionistic and rather rambling. Sometimes it doesn't do to categorise and formalise our thoughts and feelings. If my experience has taught me anything, it is that we are all to a greater and lesser extent passive creatures to whom things happen. And to return to my original point, I too like to think that I possess excellent communication skills. Once I gave presentations, led meetings, ran training sessions, although I couldn't claim to have facilitated a brainstorm. I'm still personable. I like to talk, although I rarely get the opportunity to do so. And yet, here I am – alone, with my music and my technology. What price my communication skills? Yes, it's been a queer sort of trajectory, all in all.

'I know that I do go on. But I feel that I am close to really knowing my mind on these questions. And work is so much in our lives even for people like me for whom it isn't. What does it mean to be an employee? What are we supposed to think and feel about ourselves? For some, actualisation is achieved through work. That's the same as the sales principle I outlined earlier, where work is an agency for the fulfilment of natural, organic conditions. For others, work is an endurance and an artificial constraint upon natural happiness. I think that really, we just need to belong somewhere and feel safe. An interesting question is the extent to which people domesticise their working environments – you will, no doubt, have seen desks with galleries of family photographs and quirky objets d'art. Yet far from representing the domestication of the workplace, such behavioural culture in fact represents the imposition of work culture on a domestic sensibility – quite the reverse of what people think they are engaging in. In my case, you could argue that I am as guilty as anyone who pins up pictures of their children or the last Christmas do next to their computer, for what is this little room if not a semi-domestic space? But my situation is different, if you look at it more closely. This office resolutely refuses to conform to the accepted definitions of either domestic or working environments. It is a neutral space – an embodiment of the principles of the fourth space, in fact – and as close an approximation to my diminished mental state as it is possible for a room to be. I have my kettle, my music and my computer; that is all. Remove these facilities and an archaeologist stumbling upon this room five hundred years from now would be hard-pressed to tell you exactly what use it had been put to. Do you follow me? Does any of this make any sense? I get so few visitors down here. I have no desire to turn my room into a cosy corner. That's simply not possible in a modern business environment. A company such as this doesn't admit the possibility of cosy, organic space. It's true that I am as guilty as the next man of a nostalgic folk-yearning for a warm and secure working environment. Imagine the warmth of a laundrette on a cold winter's day. A simple low bench, the newspapers, cigarettes, good, easy chat with colleagues and customers, the warmth from the machines steaming up the plate glass windows and people coming in from outside stamping their feet and blowing on their hands. Or a workman's hut, sitting around a brazier washing down mugs of strong, sweet tea. Imagine the black-metal, wind-blown security of the engine driver's cab or the after-hours camaraderie of a restaurant kitchen. Here, we enjoy no such comforts. I can't say that this office is cosy, although it feels reasonably secure. In our line of work, Mr Johnson, peaceful, easy freedom is only manifested mentally. Physically, the light is always too bright, the background chatter and hub-hub too disturbing, the demands of the job too complex and confusing. We are engaged in a mental fight for the supremacy of our own minds. Work fills up all the head-space available to it with worry about work, and worry about work diminishes you. Finally, you can yield to the tide or swim against the current. Or make an island of your remaining piece of brain and let it all flow past you. I'm not sure where this is going, but do you know what I mean?'

All through this, Mr Johnson had been watching Lionel's face intently, which changed expression startlingly with every phase of his argument – now wistful, now impassioned, now resigned. Once he had stopped talking, his features assumed a blank cast. He appeared, for the moment, to have talked himself out.

'But what do you think, Mr Johnson? You've said very little so far. What does work really feel like for you? How do you regard the boundaries between private and public space? Do you in fact see any distinction between them? Or do you live according to strong rules of compartmentalisation? I dare say that my own situation is unusual – you could tell me a very different story.'

'I don't know. It's still too early to say. I've never worked for such a large organisation before and at the moment I'm still collecting impressions and trying to find my way around. I can see how it might be possible to occupy a particular niche here but it will be a long time before I can think about finding one. There's a lot to learn and I'd like to advance my career as far as possible before I settle comfortably into a role. My last job was very different. It was a smaller company with an informal culture. I felt very comfortable there but after a while I got restless and craved new challenges. It must be very different if you've worked somewhere for a long time.'

'I can't even remember when I started here, and that's the truth. After a while you become a part of the furniture, whether you want to or not. Some are large, handsome dressers, others scuffed vinyl chairs; it all depends upon your personal trajectory. I fancy I am a scuffed chair, myself. When you first start in a job, you are conscious of wanting to remember every detail and record every impression you receive. For a while, each day stands distinctive in crystalline relief. Time is charged and memorable. Then, very slowly, weeks start to pass unnoticed, you begin to clock up anniversaries, working habits change before your eyes, new people start, become experienced members of staff, and leave before you've even said hello to them. Sometimes the first you hear of them is when you drop your standard pound into their leaving collection. Important projects you've worked on, key projects which have helped to make your name and reputation, are rapidly forgotten about, even by those who worked on them with you. Then one day you wake up and realise that you have spent years sitting at the same desk, routinely working away at tasks which have less and less meaning to you or the organisation as a whole. You become a dull automaton engaged in rote work for which you receive neither recognition or reward. Do I sound pessimistic? I don't mean to. You are at the beginning of your career here, and from what you've told me you have already enjoyed some significant achievements. When I was your age, we didn't have brainstorms but if we had I doubt very much whether I would have been asked to facilitate one so soon. Your star seems to be very much in the ascendant, Mr Johnson, and I suspect it will be a long time before it wanes. Mine waned a long time ago. Soon, perhaps, it will finally gutter and expire. I shan't be sorry. My present tasks are manageable; I have everything I need here.'

Lionel's face assumed its blankness once again. He sat silently for some time staring at his hands which he had clasped together on the desk. At length, he said: 'Oh, I don't know, Mr Johnson. We are all of us just trying to get by. I'm not a bad man. I don't want you to go away with the wrong impression of me. I was like you once. I don't know where it all went wrong. I wish I could remember the moment and go back in time. I'd do it all differently, whatever it was. Sometimes I think that I stopped concentrating for a minute on a Tuesday seven years ago and missed a critical instruction or a valuable piece of information. While my eyes were closed briefly, the entire organisation wheeled about and set off in a different direction, and when I opened them again I was outside the main body forever.'

He leant across the desk and stared at Mr Johnson.

'I didn't want that to happen. Who would? But once you are cut off from the flow you can't rejoin it. You can leap back into the current but it's not your water anymore. I chose a slow subsiding, a yielding to the prevailing climate and a gradual disappearing from sight. But the tiredness is the worst thing.'

'I'm sorry?' said Mr Johnson, opening his eyes.

'Did you nod off for a moment?'

'I'm not sure. Perhaps. I was thinking about the ship.'

'I said that the tiredness is the worst thing. Even though my job is relatively undemanding, I'm tired to my bones. It's a very particular form of weariness. I think of it as structural tiredness, a fundamental condition of mind and spirit utterly immune to the palliative effects of early nights and reduced caffeine or nicotine intake. I've come to accept that now my normal state is tiredness. Rather than regarding tiredness as something to be countered in order to be more wakeful, I feel that wakefulness is a condition to be countered in order to be more tired. I default to tiredness, if you will. How has this come about? Work has brought this about. In my case, increased responsibilities brought with them intense mental pressure which pressed on every level of my consciousness, even sleep. Soon, especially sleep. Dreams about working blended effortlessly into the waking working day. In time I couldn't distinguish one from the other. I would make remarks to colleagues about meetings that had apparently never taken place and write reports on projects that had never been undertaken. Does this sound strange to you? More disturbing still, I would take work into my dreams and discuss real issues and concerns with figmentary workmates. Yet after a while dream work seemed more tangible and solid somehow than real work. I did my best work in my sleep. I was on top of the job, eager for promotion, full of ideas. I wasn't aware of any incongruity – the only person who wasn't. Around this time everything began to unravel. Schedules went awry, jobs uncompleted, invoices unpaid. Gradually I became isolated from the main current of activity. Staff I had trained and developed rapidly outstripped me. I lost my sharpness. I slipped away quietly from sight. I have no regrets. I have everything I need here. This structural tiredness will never be dismantled.'

'Structural tiredness. Yes, I can relate to that.'

'You must be tired too. You were dropping off again. Have you been working too hard?'

'I don't know. Yes. There's so much to learn and I don't want to miss anything. I've got to keep going. I'm working on an important project with company-wide implications.'

'I used to think like that. I kept going for as long as I could. Then I just stopped. It's the same with career development. You, now, are keen to develop key business skills and bring the positive experiences you acquired in your previous job to your new role, whatever that may be. I was just the same. I was an effective communicator, a good time manager, an enthusiastic proponent of innovative thinking. I worked well under my own initiative and as part of a team. Now, I don't have the slightest interest in learning anything and the only skill, if it can be called a skill, I care to develop is the refinement of my condition of anonymity. I hope I don't sound too cynical, Mr Johnson. I'm actually not in the least bit cynical. I believe in truth, justice, decency and dignity. But no-one is going to provide us with these virtues on a plate and free of charge. If leading a good life in a modern business organisation necessitates a retreat into a windowless little room off a forgotten corridor, so be it. I make no pretence. And I'll let you into another little secret, Mr Johnson. I'm not on the network. Yes, I know, it is hard to believe. I haven't been on it since I moved in here. The page of code you see on my screen is from an old file that exists only in my computer. I have a few others I look at from time to time.'

'But I thought that you were engaged in the monitoring of processes and observing changes to the organisational culture?' said Mr Johnson.

'Strictly speaking, I am,' said Lionel. 'It is possible to deduce from a page of static code the developments that are taking place in the wider organisation. Think of it this way: the whole of Hamlet is hidden away in a string of 26 letters. Every time you look at your computer keyboard, you are reading Hamlet. You can write anything you want from the 26 letters of the alphabet, and so it is with my codes. There are billions of possible configurations and relationships on this screen. The potential for the eternal movement of information and instructions is contained in this one file. By looking at it for long enough I can extrapolate enough knowledge to make an educated guess as to the current situation in any function in the company. Does that make sense?'

'A little, yes. I feel less concerned about not being on the network myself yet, though I'll certainly be happier when I am. But you mentioned when I first came in here that you periodically send out emails updating people on your progress. How do you do that if you're not on the network?'

'With some difficulty, of course. I do actually compose and send emails but they all sit in a folder on my own computer. There must be hundreds waiting to go out. But if for any reason someone came down here and decided to look at my files, they would find evidence of my efforts going back years. It's a useful precaution to take, if nothing else. Needless to say, I hope that day never comes. You are the first visitor I've had for a long time. When I said before that I don't get many visitors, what I should have said was that I don't get any visitors. And that's the way I want it to stay, so I'll remind you what I asked you earlier: don't tell anyone about me. I hope I can trust you?'

'Yes, of course you can.'

'In that case, you can have some sellotape after all,' said Lionel, opening the bottom drawer of his desk and handing Mr Johnson a roll of broad, transparent tape. 'Now that we've become friends and I trust you, you are welcome to my stationery. I don't have much use for it. You can keep it if you like.'

They seemed to have run out of things to say to each other. Mr Johnson moved to go and Lionel reminded him not tell anyone about his office and put his earphones back in place and his feet on the desk. Mr Johnson closed the door behind him and returned to the brainstorming room. He began to copy clearly the original visual schema for the processes onto the new sheets of paper. This seemed to him a much more logical approach, one which would ensure that the ideas generated in the brainstorming session were replicated as closely as possible in the session's report. Mr Johnson made a separate note on a new piece of paper to talk to Mark Mitchell about ensuring the full and accurate rendering of brainstorming ideas in follow-up papers and wrote 'tape recording?' at the end. For his own part, he felt that if he were to facilitate a brainstorm again in the future, he would like to have a more proactive role in proceedings. He was pleased with his performance but had a suspicion that he had acted more in a secretarial capacity than he would have preferred. But he was still new; his induction period hadn't even been completed and he was already taking a lead role in important projects. They could hardly expect him to contribute to the extent an experienced employee would. All in all it had been a very satisfactory experience. These positive thoughts gave him renewed enthusiasm and he worked quickly and effectively on the transcription of the processes and their categorisation into sequentially-related stages. They were coming together with greater clarity than before and Mr Johnson was conscious of the presence of the Five Synergetic Elements in all that he set down. Effectively he was providing a detailed model for each element of the Big Sell, as he had perceived it in the brainstorm. It was quite possible, he thought, that no other such envisioning of the project existed. When he had finished the diagrams to his satisfaction, he turned his attention to the question of the distribution tangents. Using as a guide the model he had set down relating to the management of the synergetic relationship between specific functional imperatives and the objectives of the Big Sell itself, Mr Johnson listed on one side of a piece of notepaper the key issues relating to the distribution tangents question and on the other the proposed solutions as devised in the brainstorm. Now that he had the schema for the overarching processes under his belt, he was much more confident about working up the distribution tangents material. He felt that he had laid secure foundations and was now merely adding a capstone to a sturdy edifice. Conceptually speaking, he had never felt more in control of his work. Mr Johnson wondered briefly at this but accepted quickly that he was now more and more acquainted with the business imperatives of the conceptual initialisation department and, however new he was, had already acquired considerable experience on a significant project. Lionel Bilfred's words had also had an effect. He was more determined than ever that he would keep on top of his work and not miss important information or instructions. Although Lionel enjoyed considerable autonomy and even had his own office, Mr Johnson didn't envy the extent to which he was cut off from the main currents of organisational activity. He wondered what effect if any the Big Sell would have on Lionel's work. Ideas spiralled onto the page. A distribution tangents strategy gradually took shape. All the theories and ideas to which he had been exposed so far coalesced into a logical pattern of discrete yet concretely connected principles with a strong operational relevance. Mr Johnson felt a surge of pride. Although he had relied on the contributions of others, particularly during the brainstorm, this really was a piece of work to which he could put his name. He was just considering how Mark Mitchell would receive it when a breathless woman whom he recognised from the conceptual initialisation department appeared at the door and said: 'Mr Johnson? Yes? Yes, you've got to come right away. Mark Mitchell and the senior concept engineers are all going into a presentation. You're presence is required.'

'My presence? But I'm not a senior concept engineer. I'm not any kind of concept engineer.'

mouth at the site of this cleverly manufactured beauty. He hadn't been in this part of the building before. It was probably one of the newer sections. Staggering sense impressions assailed him. But his colleagues were either impervious to the wonders of their surroundings or blasé about them, for to a man and woman they pressed on, heads bowed, some scribbling notes into their presentation folders, others tapping insistently at the keypads on their pagers.

At the head of the group strode Mark Mitchell. At points he would turn to his team and offer an encouraging word or glance that would help carry them that extra step up a long sloping passageway or through a series of strong doors. The journey seemed to go on and on. They went through an older section once more, passing innumerable offices on either side, meeting rooms, quiet areas, long rows of shelving filled with magazines, directories, bundles of computer cable, catering tins of coffee, dockets, and box files. They passed managerial suites, creative labs, secretarial centres, training rooms, entertainment lounges, lecture rooms and kitchenettes set in deep recesses in the walls. They climbed flights of stairs that turned back on themselves, rode three different elevators and, without breaking their stride, entered an ancient paternoster and exited it three floors later on the other side. Finally, they turned a corner into a blaze of afternoon sunshine and were ushered by an anxious-looking young executive into a long room in which sat more than a dozen men and women in blue and black suits around a rectangular beech wood table thoughtfully laid with note pads and pens and a tumbler and bottle of water at every place.

When they were all inside, the executive who had ushered them in closed the door, looked at his watch and made a little signal to two women who stood at the end of the table in front of a white fold-out notice board. Mr Johnson found himself sitting next to a stocky man in his forties wearing a blue suit on the one hand, and Mark Mitchell on the other. They were about half way down the table, and facing a wide window at the edge of the building against which the sun threw itself relentlessly.

Mr Johnson whispered, 'I'm Mr Johnson, what's your name?' and the man in the blue suit replied, so that everyone could hear, 'Mike Morrison, but of course I know your name, Mr Johnson, from our meeting earlier,' and smiled at the people around him, who all smiled back. Then Mr Johnson realised that he had been in the brainstorm with him. It felt like a long time ago.

'I'm sorry that I didn't know your name,' he said, covering up for himself. 'I didn't catch it earlier. I've met so many people recently and I haven't been here very long. But of course I recognised you from the brainstorm.'

Again, Mike Morrison addressed the immediate environment: 'I sometimes think, Mr Johnson, that we should all wear name tags now that this organisation has grown so large,' and laughed, and again Mr Johnson's neighbours to the side and opposite nodded and smiled broadly.

Feeling a little bit foolish, Mr Johnson was about to say to Mike that he didn't want to draw too much attention to himself so early on in his career when he was overtaken by the desire to sneeze. He got his right hand up in time and managed to keep most of it back but the internal force of the action singed his nasal membrane and made the roof of his mouth smart.

'Don't suppress your sneezes in future, Mr Johnson,' said Mike. 'There's nothing worse than trying to suppress a violent sneeze for politeness' sake. You merely succeed in turning the violence back on itself and making an undignified snorting noise that is actually more embarrassing than an honest-to-goodness blast into a handkerchief.'

Across the table a solid youth with red hair nodded vigorously. 'Don't suppress it, that's the key. Don't suppress it.'

Mr Johnson smiled weakly and held his pen ready over his notepad, head inclined towards the top of the table. But the after-effects of the sneeze had still to play their part and when he poured a glass of water and took a sip, the gas made the raw parts of his mouth smart anew. Worse than this, he noticed that a viscous string of nasal discharge had attached itself to the bottle, presumably from his right hand. Fumbling in his pocket, he removed a tattered pink serviette and hurriedly wiped the bottle clean.

He returned the serviette to his pocket and saw with some dismay two shiny globs on the hem. Out came the serviette again and, feeling for a dry spot on it, he discreetly dabbed at the hem and then scrunched the serviette up. As far as he could tell, nobody had spotted anything unusual in his behaviour. The two women were already deep into their presentation. He did notice, however, that the nasal discharge had left two faint spots on the hem that caught the light when he shifted position in the chair, which was often given the heat in the room and the proximity of his neighbours, particularly Mark Mitchell, so he pulled over the bottle of mineral water, unscrewed the cap and carefully splashed a quantity of water over the affected area. He still hadn't explained to Mark about the brainstorming notes. It didn't feel the most opportune time to do so and in any case he supposed that had Mark needed them there and then, he would have said something. It was inconceivable that he would be called upon to give a presentation. Mark presumably wanted him there for the experience.

Mr Johnson was giving his wet patches a quick, vigorous rub with his elbow when he heard Mark say, 'and this is where Mr Johnson, who is new to the department, comes into play'.

Mr Johnson wheeled round in astonishment and in so doing slopped a quantity of water over Mark's lap, like a priest incensing a congregation.

'I'm so sorry,' he said, and instinctively pulled the serviette from his pocket again and began to dab furiously at Mark's tan suit-trousers.

'Mr Johnson, it appears that some nasal discharge has been transferred from your soiled serviette to my trousers,' Mark said, though not unkindly. Quietly, he added, 'I've just given you your cue. This is the right moment to mention the distribution tangents you have been working on.'

'But I'm not prepared to give a presentation,' he whispered back. 'I haven't had the opportunity to go over my conclusions with you yet.'

'Don't worry about that Mr Johnson. You've done a lot of work on the subject and I've got every confidence in you. Nothing like jumping in at the deep end. Up you get.'

Mr Johnson's head felt hot and red and he saw that his colleagues across the table and the people who were already in the room, were staring at him. The two women at the head of the table sat down and a presentation pointer was passed to him. He felt his body get up from the chair and walk to the display board. Reluctantly he followed it. He opened his presentation case but there was nothing in it except save several sheets of ruled paper on which were a series of semi-coherent messages and figures. They looked familiar – they could have been a version of the notes he'd made in Bob Hobbleton's office. His report on the distribution tangents was nowhere to be seen. Neither were the notes he had transcribed on the brainstorming meeting. He must have picked up the wrong ones when he left the meeting room.

Mr Johnson saw that his audience was settling down. Glasses of water were poured, shirt sleeves rolled up, hair unpinned. Mark Mitchell was beaming proudly at him and the anxious-looking man at the door was busy finding extra seats for a new body of executives in blue suits who had just entered. By the sound of it others were massing in the corridor outside. Mr Johnson sneezed again, boldly this time, and the red-headed youth applauded him.

'Thank you,' Mr Johnson heard himself say and, catching a little thread of self-confidence, added, 'I'll refrain from pulling out my serviette this time,' which occasioned a natural and gratifying ripple of laughter.

He took a deep breath. 'Yes, as Mark mentioned to me, this is a very opportune moment to mention the matter of the distribution tangents and their place within the overall strategy that has been outlined in considerable detail by our colleagues here' – he nodded at the two women who had conducted the presentation, who nodded back at him – 'which of course is a very important issue given the particulars of the project and the long-term objectives which we are all working towards, particularly since new resource alignments are envisaged and additional back-factoring sought. Pass me a glass of water please, think you, I'm sorry, I mean thank you.'

Mr Johnson looked at the illegible notes. 'If we agree that a sound overarching strategy underpins any given departmental and corporate objective, then we must also agree that a micro-understanding of the precise activities that in turn underpin that strategy is the only point from which a full understanding of the macro situation can be achieved. In other words, we must address the question of where things go and how.'

That more or less summarised his latest thinking on the question. Mr Johnson put the notes on to the table. They would be of no help at all. His confidence swelling modestly, Mr Johnson paced back and forth before the board. 'No activity, however small, should escape strategic objectification. In other words, it should be Smart – that is to say, Specific, Measurable, Achievable, Relevant and Timed.' His audience yielded a sussurus of approbation and Mark smiled at him again. 'The distribution element in the overall strategy is most certainly Smart. It dovetails with other core elements yet retains a discrete identity to a degree sufficient to ensure independent auditing.'

Mr Johnson picked up a red marker pen and swiftly outlined the shape of the distribution tangents strategy as far as he could reconstruct it from memory on the board.

'This is a simple rendition but it should give you an idea of how the distribution question is being tackled. As you can see, the crux of the issue is the manner in which the inter-dependent elements of the strategy relate to the strategic goal. I'm still new to the conceptual initialisation department – in fact, I'm not formally speaking a member of it – but I have taken the liberty of modelling the distribution tangents strategy on the principle of the Five Synergetic Elements which underpins the function of the department.' Mark nodded and some of the others made notes. 'At the initial stage in the process, we gather together the raw materials, which is analogous to the ideas gathering stage of the Five Synergetic Elements. Having been gathered, the materials are then analysed. Next, they are organised; that is to say, rationalised. Thus a harmonic relationship between the materials and the requirements of the objective is achieved. Finally, the act of distribution itself is implemented, so completing the process through the concrete-to-concrete fulfilment stage.'

Mr Johnson looked his audience up and down. They looked back at him attentively. As far as he was able to tell, the presentation was going well. He glanced at Mark Mitchell for confirmation of this but he was whispering something to the business development manager and didn't catch Mr Johnson's eye. Now that he had explained how the structure of the distribution tangents strategy was based on the principle of the Five Synergetic Elements, there was little more to say. 'There are glaring inconsistencies in the relative levels of performance in the despatch function. We can assume that the problem will be rectified when the function is brought within the remit of the Big Sell strategy. There isn't much more to say on the subject at this stage other than that I recommend a close monitoring schedule through the first three-quarters and the formation of an integrated, cross-functional policy team as soon as possible. Thank you for listening. Perhaps you'd like to add something, Mark?'

'Yes,' Mark said to the group. 'I'd just like to emphasise the cost-saving benefits to this approach and if you need any further illumination, please do not hesitate to contact Mr Johnson in conceptual initialisation. He's the man with the plan on this one.'

Overcome with relief, and not a little pride, Mr Johnson hurried back to his seat with his presentation case. He forgot to pick up the notes from the table.

Across the table, Mr Johnson's colleagues beamed at him and when he asked Mark how he thought it went, Mark said 'wonderfully' and patted him on the knee.

'Yes, I think they'll buy it. We're in business.'

Mr Johnson was in such a state of exhilaration he hardly noticed his colleagues' contributions to the meeting, and soon the team was heading back to the conceptual initialisation department. But it was a carefree party that made the return journey, with Mr Johnson at its head. There was much joshing and horseplay – his colleagues carried him like a rolled up carpet into the paternoster and they rode it all the way to the top of the shaft and tumbled shrieking as it rolled over and went down the other side – and when they arrived home, in addition to the promised coffee and sandwiches, glasses of red and white wine and a jug of fresh orange juice awaited them. Mr Johnson's performance had impressed his colleagues. A group of junior concept engineers exchanged anecdotes in low, impressed whispers – 'just dabbed at Mark Mitchell's trousers cool as you like' – and Joanne assured him that he was welcome to help himself to any stationery items he wished at any time, without fear of judgement or rancour.

When the congratulatory speeches had finished and the last drop of wine drained from his plastic cup, Mr Johnson returned to his desk. The message button on his telephone was flashing. It was someone in the systems manager's office saying that Mr Johnson's network access would be sorted out 'very soon indeed, a matter of a few short days'.

Mr Johnson sat down and turned round slowly in his chair. Normal service was being resumed in the office. At the back of the room, young men in sleeveless shirts huddled in informal creative synergy. The conceptual outriders were busy at their work stations drafting memoranda, making recommendations and sending tendril feelers into the marketplace. The knowledge management experts were casting their expert eyes about the daily press, both in print and electronically, and despatching their succinct summaries around the organisation, mainly electronically but on paper too if appropriate. Through it all, Mark Mitchell walked from desk to desk offering a kindly word here, an encouraging pat on the back there. Finally, he stopped by Mr Johnson's desk.

'Well,' he said, 'now that all the excitement's died down, I think we should have a little chat about your immediate, medium- and long-term future. Clearly, recent events have thrown some of my original plans into disarray – a very happy dilemma, of course. Come into my office – there's something I want to discuss with you.'

Mr Johnson followed Mark in.

'Sit down, please. How's your cold now? Nothing worse, is there, than a tickly nose at a delicate time? But I think that once you had accepted that you should give into the force of it and not suppress it out of some misplaced sense of propriety, you were home and dry – not literally, of course,' he added, patting his trousers which were still damp-looking. 'You were probably quite nervous, not knowing whether or not you would have to address the room. But you did extremely well – extremely well indeed. You truly jumped in at the deep end and caught the big fish. But I digress. Sit down, sit down,' he said, motioning Mr Johnson into a black leather chair and turning the yellow Venetian blinds on the windows that looked out into the office at large to a discreet angle. 'There's something I want to show you.'

CHAPTER TWELVE
MR JOHNSON'S PROJECT

Mark opened his desk drawer and took out a small bundle of cards secured by a rubber band.

'These are for you, Mr Johnson. Welcome aboard.'

They were Mr Johnson's business cards. His job title read: 'Concept Engineer'. He didn't know what to say.

'Now that you are formally part of the team, I'd like you to get your teeth into your first major project. I want you to develop the outline work you've already done and build it up into something with a universal application. How do you feel about that?'

Mr Johnson put his arms behind his head and stretched his legs.

'I feel very good about that, but I'd like to know what exactly is expected of me.'

'Of course. I'm looking to develop the work that has already been done on the distribution tangents, Mr Johnson, and I think that you're the man to do it. Your performance just now dispelled any doubts I may have had about you. I want you to apply the methodology you employed when you looked at the spreadsheet and apply it to the work of all the other functions in the organisation in tandem with the roll out of the Big Sell. How does that sound?'

'Ideal. But how will it work in practice?'

'That's a very good question. You will be given a dedicated conceptual initialisation department project budget and empowered to set up a cross-functional task team to explore the financial and practical hinterland before reporting back to the senior management cluster at a date in the future that we will agree between ourselves. It's classic conceptual initialisation procedure, of course. You gave me the idea during the course of your presentation, as a matter of fact, when you mentioned the formation of an integrated cross-functional policy team.'

'Will the project be driven with reference to the Five Synergetic Elements?'

Mark winked at him. 'You don't need me to answer that, Mr Johnson. You are a very quick learner and already have a very good grasp of the theoretical underpinnings. As you know, everything we do here is driven with reference to the Five Synergetic Elements. I think this department is going to benefit from your input. You've already made a valuable contribution to a key aspect of the

Big Sell. Now is the time to test yourself in a broader arena.'

'A broader arena? That sounds like a very serious responsibility. But if you think I'm up to it, I couldn't turn it down. I must say that this represents exactly the sort of break I was hoping to get. Thank you very much for giving me the opportunity.'

'You're very welcome. But it is an opportunity you have made for yourself through your hard work and your instinctive grasp of business essentials. You should be thanking yourself as much as me.'

'I suppose this means that there's no danger of my returning to the sales department?'

'None whatsoever. Your new business card is testimony to that. Consider yourself a fully paid-up member of the team, Mr Johnson. Once again, welcome aboard.'

'It's a pleasure to be aboard. So, where do I begin?'

Mark pondered for a moment. 'I'm not exactly sure. Needless to say, there are some formal procedures we need to go through in order to formalise the structure of the cross-functional team and the release of your budget. But it shouldn't take too long. For the moment, I suggest that you make initial contact with some people I would recommend as key team members. There's nothing like getting the people angle sorted out first. Your phone is now working, I believe?'

'Yes, it is, although I'm still not connected to the computer network. Someone from the system manager's office left a message to say that the connection would be sorted out very soon but I think I ought to chase him up.'

'You certainly should. I'll get the number for you. In the meantime, give the following people a ring and explain that I've recommended you contact them with a view to joining a cross-functional team to work up a practical proposal to extend the findings relating to the despatch function into an organisation-wide strategy within the remit of the Big Sell as agreed at the stakeholder presentation. Is that clear?'

'Yes, I think so – to begin with, at least. What should I do after that?'

'Once you have secured broad agreement, you need to draw up a schedule of activities and draft a project outline for discussion at the first project team meeting – whenever that is. It's your project, so you should assume that you will enjoy a generous degree of implied authority. On the other hand, in conceptual initialisation we pride ourselves on a collaborative decision-making process, so the true nature and scope of the project should be revealed only after the requisite norming stage has been experienced. Beyond that, it's your creation. I'll be on hand to guide you when you need me. But I suspect that you'll be proceeding under your own steam soon enough.'

Mark handed Mr Johnson a piece of paper on which he had written six names with department details and extension numbers next to them, plus the system manager's extension.

'Off you go, then. You know where I am if you need me. And once again – congratulations.'

Mr Johnson left the office and sat down at his desk. The rest of the room was deeply absorbed in creative and analytical activity. Someone, presumably the woman who had fetched him from the Imaginarium, had placed the notes he had made in there on the desk. He pulled out his conclusions on the distribution tangents work and was pleased to find that he had done the subject greater justice with his note-less presentation. Then he attended to the matter at hand. Mr Johnson hadn't come across any of the names on the list before. Mark's handwriting was none too legible but with a little effort, Mr Johnson could make out the details: Henry Woodward, marketing communications, 215; Barbara Forrest, accounts, 261; Michael Fielding, supply, 251; Anna Woodman, marketing communications, 216; Tony Parkman, processing, 256; Jill Woodford, administrative liaison, 265. It was odd that there was no one from conceptual initialisation on the list, but then the nature of cross-functionalism insisted on a broad range of representation on the team. Mr Johnson moved to dial the first name on the list but pulled his finger back. It would be better to make a list of objectives first. He wrote down a quick summary of the project and thought about how he would present it to the putative team members. This was probably the closest he would come to making a sales call. Mark hadn't told him whether the contacts would be familiar with the principles, or even the existence, of the Big Sell, so to all intents and purposes he was making a series of cold calls. But he felt sufficiently confident in his own understanding of the strategy to communicate it clearly to the uninitiated. This must be where all major projects began, he thought. To be given ownership of such an important project so early in his career, and so early in the life of the project, was extremely gratifying, but he pledged not to become complacent and expelled such thoughts from his mind in order to focus on the business at hand. He finished the notes and dialled Henry Woodward's extension. The phone rang six times before Mr Johnson heard a click and the ring tone change subtly. A woman's voice answered.

'Hello, general administration, Margaret speaking, may I help you?'

Mr Johnson recognised the creamy and insinuating voice immediately.

'Hello Margaret, it's Mr Johnson here. How are you?'

'Mr Johnson?'

'Yes, we met when I first came in. I was supposed to report to Mr Bannister in strategic development but there was some confusion about where I should go. You kindly provided me with tea and biscuits. I'm now a fully paid-up concept engineer.'

'I'm sorry, Mr Johnson, there must be some mistake. I really don't recall meeting you. In any case, Mr Bannister has left the organisation.'

'I'm sorry. Are you not Margaret on first floor reception?'

'No, no, I'm Margaret in general administration. You must have the wrong Margaret. I'm one of the other ones. I can see how the mistake has arisen.'

'You do sound very similar to Margaret on first floor reception.'

'Yes, we've often been mistaken for sisters. Can I help you?'

'I was trying to contact Henry Woodward in marketing communications. He's extension 215. Perhaps I misdialled.'

'Possibly, although when no one answers the phone in marketing communications the calls usually come through to me. I'll check the internal phone directory for you, though. Let me see: Woodman, A; Woodman T; Woodford J; Woodward H. That'll be the one: 215. That's marketing communications all right. He must be away from his desk.'

'I'll try him later. Thanks for your help.'

'You're very welcome.'

Mr Johnson made a note to call Henry Woodward later on and tried the next contact on his list. This time he went straight through to Barbara Forrest's voicemail, which told him that she was on annual leave. He started to leave a message but the time elapsed before he got round to explaining himself adequately and he decided to leave it until she returned. As he was making a note against Barbara Forrest's name, Mark Mitchell breezed past him with his briefcase. Mr Johnson turned round and saw that Mark's office was in darkness with the door shut. He felt relieved to be left to his own devices at last. Michael Fielding's number rang out but when he dialled Anna Woodman's number, a friendly voice said: 'Hi, Anna speaking, can I help?'

'Yes, hello Anna, my name's Mr Johnson. I'm calling from the conceptual initialisation department. I've been asked to speak to you by my manager, Mark Mitchell, about a new cross-functional team I'm setting up. Have you got a minute?'

'Of course I have. What's it all about?'

Mr Johnson briefly explained the project remit with reference to the outcomes of the Big Sell presentation.

'I haven't heard of the Big Sell before but it sounds like an important project.'

'It is. It's nothing less than an attempt to calibrate the entire organisation according to the commercial imperatives that underpin the activities of the sales department.'

Anna let out a low whistle. 'That sounds very important. I'm glad I just work in marketing communications. But you can count me in. I've had some experience of cross-functional teamwork and it sounds like I need to get my head round this one. What do you need me to do?'

'For the moment nothing except wait for further instructions. I'll be sending out a schedule of activities and a draft agenda for an initial meeting in due course.'

'Could you email me a summary of what you've told me so far?'

'I'd love to but I'm still waiting to get on the network. I don't have email access at the moment.'

'You poor thing. Have you spoken to the systems manager?'

'Someone from his office left me a message to say I'd be sorted out soon. But I know they're very busy in there.'

'They always are, I'm afraid. I'd recommend you keep trying to see exactly when they expect to connect you.'

Mr Johnson tried the systems manager's office. Predictably, he went straight through to voicemail. 'It's Mr Johnson in conceptual initialisation,' he said. 'I understand you are very busy but I'd appreciate it if you would contact me to discuss my network connection. I have some important project work to do.'

Then he dialled Henry Woodward's number but got through to Margaret again. When he looked up from his desk, he saw that the concept engineers had disappeared. Perhaps they'd followed Mark after an interval. There might be another meeting in the Imaginarium, or any Imaginarium. Since he was now a fully paid-up member of the team, there should have been no reason why Mr Johnson shouldn't have joined them, but in truth he was all brainstormed and presentationed out and glad of the quiet time to focus on his new project. His mind strayed again to happy thoughts about his rapid entry into the conceptual initialisation department, but once more he banished them. There would be time enough for modest self-congratulation later. The very essence – or at least one of its essences – of conceptual initialisation was diligent focus on the task at hand. Some of the concept engineers had been working flat out on their projects for months on end. Now that the Big Sell had received the necessary degree of approval required to take it to implementation stage, the department would have a new set of tasks to deal with. The concept engineers had certainly showed no signs of slacking. The office was pleasantly quiet but still fiendishly hot. Some of the desks had little electric fans clipped to the edge. Mr Johnson's didn't. Rivulets of sweat ran from his forehead and stung his eyes. He couldn't take off his suit jacket because he knew that he had large sweat disks under each armpit. Someone could come back in at any minute. Joanne appeared in the doorway at the other end of the office. She said something in Mr Johnson's direction but he couldn't hear her. He got up from his desk and moved towards the door but saw that Joanne was in fact pointing something out to a young man in a blue suit who nodded approvingly and disappeared, followed by Joanne. The young man looked as though he had come for an interview. Mark hadn't mentioned anything about formal vacancies or new starters. Mr Johnson felt a sharp prickle of worry but remembered his business card. He took the top one from the pile and read it: Mr Johnson, Concept Engineer. Ext 456. He tucked it into his inside breast pocket, next to his letter of appointment. The fact of the business card was incontrovertible. There was no need to worry. He tried Tony Parkman's extension, which also went straight to voicemail. He read the notes again and tried to arrange the other papers into some sort of order. First he organised them by time of writing, which was difficult since it wasn't always possible to ascertain exactly what he'd written and under which circumstances. Then he attempted a conceptual arrangement. This wasn't much easier as there was so much overlap in terms of theory and meaning. Finally he placed the papers in size order, A3 on the bottom. A thorough rewriting of all the notes he had made would have to be undertaken. This could develop into something resembling a process manual, which may or may not exist presently. Mr Johnson made a note to speak to Mark Mitchell about this at the earliest opportunity. He tried Jill Woodford's extension but he must have misdialled because he went through to Tony Parkman's extension again. When he dialled the correct extension, he went through to Jill Woodford's voicemail. It was clearly going to take some time to put this project team together. Mr Johnson summarised his actions so far in advance of Mark asking him for a progress check. It would be so much easier if he could use the email system. At this stage in the process it was just about possible to get by with the telephone, notepaper and his own computer, but in time the requirements of the project would demand constant access to other members of the team. On the off chance he tried the systems manager's office again. This time someone picked up the phone.

'Hello? It's Mr Johnson...' but immediately the line was obscured by hiss and went dead. Perhaps the phones were on the blink again. He tried Jill

Woodford's extension once more and got through to her voicemail. Then he rang the systems manager's office and also went through to voicemail. Mr Johnson sighed and wheeled his chair back. He put his feet on the desk and his arms behind his head. Presumably all projects began with such unpromising experiences. The Big Sell must have been merely an unuttered idea before it took concrete shape. Even the Five Synergetic Elements, too. He admitted to himself that that the more he got bogged down in the hard detail of project team building, the less close at hand the Five Synergetic Elements seemed, though he hesitated to add 'relevant' to this. It was time to revisit first principles. Mr Johnson searched his pile of papers for the notes he'd made following his conversation with Bob Hobbleton. He couldn't find the originals but he pulled out a later transcription. Evidently, he was in the ideas-gathering stage, if indeed that far on. Which suggested there ought to be an elemental stage preceding the extant first one. Or perhaps such activities formed a loose glue that bound the conceptual elements together, the practical ghosts in the theoretical machine. He attempted to summarise this thought on a new piece of paper but the result was unsatisfactory. Beyond a bald statement of their existence, perhaps it wasn't possible to formalise the Elements on paper. Maybe they were stated in more detail somewhere on the intranet. In any case, they seemed to owe their durability to purely conceptual qualities. Mr Johnson visualised them as revolving golden spheres or fluid arrows. Others may have had their own private pictures. It didn't do to get bogged down in the fine detail too much, and yet projects such as this could only acquire concrete shape, both conceptually and practically, after the necessary detail work had been undertaken. A concept engineer, after all, a successful and effective concept engineer, owed his or her durability to the subtle and harmonious balance of ideas work and a close eye for detail. It was ninety per cent effort, which in that case implied an imbalance in the direction of detail and effort over pure conceptual inspiration, unless effort could be taken to mean an expenditure in the direction of mental and physical – though not necessarily manual – work. Mr Johnson made a half-hearted attempt to notate these thoughts but dropped his pen on the desk. The room filled up again. Joanne reappeared with another young man in a suit and left again. A conversation was struck up three desks away and quickly subsided. The pen lay untouched on the desk. Heat rose in swathes from the machines and lights and wrapped Mr Johnson's forehead in a crown of white light. He so wanted to concentrate. Mark passed his desk. Mr Johnson nodded and moved to say something but Mark went straight into his office. He reappeared moments later and breezed out of the office again. Four concept engineers followed him.

Joanne returned to her desk. The room emptied. Mr Johnson's telephone rang six times and stopped. The notes lay untouched on the desk. It was all very quiet. Mr Johnson closed his eyes and tried to visualise his first project team meeting. He had no experience in such matters and wondered whether he should sit at the head of the table, unless it were a round table, which would be more in keeping with the democratic culture of the conceptual initialisation department, unless the cross-functional composition of the team implied a suspension of normal conceptual initialisation practices, it was pointless speculating. He also wondered how he would maintain order. Anna at least would be on his side. She had sounded very positive when he had outlined the scope of the project. Presumably marketing people could be relied upon to show willing and embrace new concepts. However difficult putting the team together would be, this was exactly the kind of work Mr Johnson had envisaged doing when he applied for the job in the first place. He was pleased that Mark had identified early promise in him. Leadership skills were very important nowadays. You couldn't put a price on them in CV terms. Presumably his successful facilitation of the brainstorming session had helped Mark make up his mind, although Mr Johnson suspected that this success owed more to luck than judgement. There was no substitute for being thrown in at the deep end, after all. He was already proceeding under his own steam and demonstrating the capacity to work under his own initiative as well as part of a team. There was nothing to be afraid of. He'd made a successful presentation at a key stakeholder meeting, and without the aid of his notes. He was pleased that he hadn't taken them to the presentation. Although comprehensive, they were somewhat rudimentary and might have impeded the free flow of creative thought he'd demonstrated to the audience, although it hadn't felt like that at the time. There was nothing like standing up in front of a room full of people to cure stage fright. Even the business with the serviette and water seemed less important in retrospect. He allowed himself a wry smile and patted the serviette, which was still in his pocket. It was silly of him to have been so nervous. Mark was a good-natured manager and clearly trusted him. They would laugh about the incident in the future, possibly over a drink. All the anxiety Mr Johnson had felt prior to the presentation had gone. A hurdle had been cleared – no, a series of hurdles – and if the finishing line was not yet in sight, it was at least several laps nearer. There was nothing like having a supportive manager. Instinctive ability allied to acquired business experience multiplied by an empowering line manager equalled a progressive working culture and the prospect of career success, to the benefit of the employee and the employer. This thought he summarised in equation form.

There was no telling where any of this would end. With a successful project under his belt, Mr Johnson could expect to move rapidly through the ranks of conceptual initialisation. He saw himself one day introducing a new recruit to the rest of the team, exchanging easy banter and knowing winks with his colleagues and making presentations to key stakeholders, internal and external. Inwardly reprimanding himself, he turned his thoughts to the matter at hand. He called through the list again but this time everyone's phone went straight to voicemail, even Anna's, whom he had wanted to update on his progress so far. Mark hadn't returned but the room filled up with concept engineers again. Desklamps were switched on, switched off. The heat was white and relentless. Mr Johnson adjusted his feet and put his hands in his trouser pockets. There was time enough for team-building, even given the unforgiving time parameters the department evidently worked within. The business card said it all. Mr Johnson patted his breast pocket for reassurance. Great things often came to those who were prepared to wait and work hard. In time the words would come in a creamy smooth ribbon flow. It was all a question of acculturation in tandem with sound conceptual underpinning.

'Mr Johnson.'

'Yes, I'm relatively new here.' There was time enough for everything. He thought he heard the telephone ringing and adjusted his feet on the desk.

'Yes, Mr Johnson.'

He sat up quickly. It was his neighbour. The rest of the concept engineers were heading towards the door. There was no sign of Mark.

'Can I help you?'

'You'd better come with me. There's a big announcement about to be made in the presentation atrium. It's been confirmed at last: there has been a change at the very top of the company.'

CHAPTER THIRTEEN
ALL CHANGE AT THE TOP

Mr Johnson picked up his notes and stuffed them in his presentation case but his colleague said that he wouldn't need them. 'Shouldn't take too long. We'll be back at our desks and in the swing of our project work again before we know it. Come on – we're missing the action.'

They left the office and turned right down the corridor, then left, right again, then right again. They entered a long, straight corridor. Mr Johnson's colleague was setting a good pace and soon disappeared into the distance. A great clamour of cheering and whooping could be heard. Driving his tired limbs on, Mr Johnson emerged onto a broad landing and ran up panting behind a large group that had gathered at the balcony, which was already three-deep. He couldn't see any of his colleagues nearby.

'What's happening?' he asked a tall, skinny youth with floppy hair and thick glasses.

'Don't you know? It's all change at the top again. They brought in a new executive director this morning. The new man has already made some sweeping changes. I think that he's just finished a lengthy handover session with his predecessor. It was all confirmed at a breakfast meeting first thing. The technical boys are busy putting the minutes onto the intranet as we speak. They will be worth a look.'

'I've heard that changes were imminent but I won't be able get to look at the intranet. I'm not on the system yet.'

'Not on the system?' said the other incredulously, lifting up his spectacles as if he were looking at Mr Johnson for the first time. 'How long have you been here, for goodness sake?'

'I don't know. Not long. Maybe longer. I started in sales but have recently joined the conceptual initialisation department. There was a resource allocation problem when I arrived. I've never been on the network. The systems manager is looking into it. Apparently there has been a problem with the backfilling of certain task areas and they've got to take another look at the logistics spreadsheets.'

A sympathetic look passed across the skinny youth's face but his attention was drawn away by a flurry of noise from the atrium below.

'What's happening now?' Mr Johnson asked as he tried to peer over the shoulders of the employees pressed up against the gallery balustrade.

'It's the retiring executive director. She's about to give a goodbye speech.'

Hard as he tried, Mr Johnson couldn't catch much of what the executive director said, although he gathered that it was very funny because every so often the crowd in the atrium would laugh collectively in a way that sounded like the sea sighing.

'What is she saying now?'

'I'm not one hundred per cent sure but I think she is giving an account of her own application for a job at the company all those years ago, embellished with little exaggerations in the interests of a cohesive narrative, and building to a tidy conclusion that will enable her to contrast the working culture of 1974 with that of the present day and so segue effortlessly into the final part of her address which will require her to acknowledge that although she is looking forward to retirement and all the opportunities it will afford for the resumption of old interests and the eager cultivation of new ones, she is sorry to be leaving such a marvellous group of people – yet she knows in her heart that if at the point of her departure the organisation is in an even better state than when she found it, this is due primarily to the quality of its employees (respect being paid here to the staff, to her predecessor and also, with just the appropriate degree of self-effacement, to herself) and that she is certain that her successor, although he will, no doubt, have very particular views on how the organisation's business should be taken forward, couldn't wish to take up the reins of a more productive and expert set of employees. She will then graciously receive a number of tasteful presents paid for from the proceeds of an impromptu collection around the departments, a card and a large bouquet of flowers. Then we'll all go back to work. That's my interpretation, at any rate – it's hard to catch what she's saying.'

A conclusive salvo of laughter was followed by a prolonged bout of applause. The crowd on the gallery began to disperse and Mr Johnson finally got to the balustrade and looked down into the atrium. A diminutive woman, almost obliterated by an enormous bouquet was being escorted through a set of double-doors by a pair of kindly but firm security guards. 'Goodbye,' she cried, 'goodbye.' One final, faint 'goodbye' was heard, the double-doors shut behind her, and she was gone.

Immediately she disappeared, another set of double doors opened across the atrium and in strode a pugnacious looking fellow, considerably younger than the departing executive director, brandishing a sheaf of papers and pointing significantly at his watch. The band of senior and middle-managers who had fluttered and bobbed around the departing executive director as she was led from the atrium wheeled round as one and swept over to her successor. He issued a curt series of orders and one by one they went north, south, east and west with straight backs and purpose etched on their brows.

The skinny youth, who was still standing next to Mr Johnson, sighed.

'So it begins, then. The great repositioning.'

'What do you think will happen now?'

'No-one can tell for sure, but it's extraordinary how a change at the top of an organisation can affect every fine thread of its culture, even in an organisation as complex and diverse as this one.'

'That sounds ominous.'

'It's not meant to but there's no harm in being wary.'

'Wary? Of what?'

'Of sweeping changes, multi-level realignments, a revisiting of the corporate steer, a change to the numbers. New words, new ways of describing the organisational zeitgeist. What's your name, by the way? Mr Johnson? I'm Joe Napier. No, Mr Johnson, we are entering a period of primal flux. I don't know how much you've read on the theory of organisational biorhythms but you can expect to notice, in a relatively short period of time, some essential changes to the spirit of the company, both in terms of the big picture and the small details. Colleagues that you could rely upon yesterday to say certain things or behave in a particular way, tomorrow will be doing and saying quite the opposite. You are new so you may not be alive to all the nuances and shades of difference. I, however, have been with the company for what, three, three-and-a-half, no, in fact over four years, and I have worked in three different departments for at least four different line managers. I've seen many changes in that time, and yet I believe that my eyes will witness stranger sights still after this change at the top.'

'But I have only just become familiar with the raw essentials of my immediate environment. My induction period isn't over yet and I have had at least two different jobs already. I'm only just getting to grips with the conceptual initialisation function. What will all this mean for me?'

'Oh, I shouldn't worry about it. For most of us, life will go on pretty much as before. I'm often struck by the capacity of Homo Sapiens to adapt to new environments. We'll muddle through somehow, don't you worry. Anyway, from what I have heard, you've already made quite a name for yourself. I'm guessing you're the Mr Johnson who made that speech at the presentation. Yes, news does spread very quickly round here. They are probably talking about you upstairs already. No, I wouldn't worry about the changes, they will happen anyway, but you seem at least as well equipped as anybody else to ride them out.'

'Well, it's nice to be so well thought of but I feel very inexperienced despite my initial successes, and in any case I'm not on the network yet and that worries me since of all the departments in the organisation, conceptual initialisation needs to be in constant communication with the rest of the company. It's a matter of principle with them.'

'Oh yes, I forgot. Not on the network yet. Did you say that you've seen the systems manager about it?'

'Not face to face. I'm not sure where his office is. Someone from his office left me a message on my phone but I haven't heard from him since. I've tried him myself but I just keep going through to voicemail. I'll have to get my manager to sort it out.'

'Who is your manager?'

'Mark Mitchell, he's head of conceptual initialisation. Do you know him?'

'I think I've heard of him, yes. To be honest with you, there seem to be so many managers and departments and divisions and cross-functional teams and innovation task forces here nowadays that I've given up trying to work out who is over what and who is responsible to whom. My advice is keep a clear eye on the corporate steer and everything else will follow.'

'What's the corporate steer? I haven't heard of it before. Is it the same as the mission statement?'

'No it's not, although obviously they refer to one another conceptually. The mission statement summarises the whole essence of the company's existence and provides an orientation point for its staff and customers. The corporate steer, on the other hand, is an overarching expression, usually numerical, of the organisation's short-, medium- and long-term business objectives as set by the senior management cluster and agreed upon by the non-executive board. Aside from minor modifications, and unless the organisation undergoes a cataclysmic sea-change in direction, the mission statement will remain unaltered for long periods, although it is always worth referring to in order to remind oneself of the company's core values, and one's place within the greater scheme of things. Every employee should be able to find themselves somewhere in the mission statement. The corporate steer, on the other hand, is very much a creature of a particular financial period and is susceptible to frequent revisions as a consequence of fluctuating conditions in the market, legislation, human resource variables, and the price of sugar.'

'The price of sugar?'

'Yes, in the canteens and kitchen areas. Have you any idea how much an organisation like this gets through in a typical year? I'm merely illustrating the extent to which apparently insignificant areas of expenditure impact upon the macro-economic picture.'

'I don't take sugar myself in tea or in coffee. Anyway, I usually use the coffee machine'

'Very laudable. You'll fit in very well round here. Apparently, a cross-functional team was set up a few weeks ago dedicated to getting employees to cut down on or eliminate the stuff from their drinks altogether. They anticipate financial and health benefits. You might want to get involved with them.'

'I don't know. I've still got so much to learn and I have a project of my own to develop, which has barely got off the ground. My time's pretty much accounted for for the indefinite future. But getting back to the question of the network, what do you think I should do? The situation is getting beyond a joke and it sounds more important than ever that I have access to the standard currents of information. Should I go and see the systems manager in person? Where is his office?'

'As far as I know, it's over that way somewhere.' Joe gestured airily with his right arm at a bank of smoked glass windows two floors up on the opposite side of the atrium and to the left, from where Mr Johnson was standing, of the double doors through which the retiring executive director had disappeared.

'What, where those windows are?'

'No, not exactly. Those offices are part of the new project development suite. It's through there and across a bit, down some stairs – I'm guessing now. In truth, I don't have the foggiest notion where the systems manager's office is. I've never seen him face to face. The best thing you can do is keep telephoning him.'

'I've tried that but I only ever get his voicemail. And I can't email him, obviously.'

'The problem, as I understand it, is that he's got number recognition up there. My computer crashes sometimes, and I often think that when I ring him up and there's no answer and I go though to his voicemail that he's there all right, he knows who it is, but wilfully won't pick up the telephone. Worse than that, it's rumoured' – here his voice dropped to a whisper and he looked up and down the gallery, although few people remained on it – 'that he sometimes knocks people off the network just for the sport of it. Now, I'm not saying that I believe that myself but sometimes I've noticed that one or two people in a local network have crashed but their neighbours haven't and it's not always mere mechanical or program failure. I'm no technical expert but I know most of the obvious reasons for computer failure. But sometimes you get the oddest messages on the screen. Not the usual fatal exception or illegal operation alerts but rather gnomic statements or injunctions: 'morbidity slack low' or 'advance replica showbox', that sort of thing. I've no idea what they mean, although sometimes the messages seem tailored for individual users. Not that they include your name or anything obvious like that – rather, they may refer to something with which you are familiar in your daily routine or to a thought that occurred to you in a meeting but which you were certain you didn't reveal to anybody else. Or they may allude in an opaque way to a dream you have had. For example, if you have dreamt of a particular arrangement of household objects or woken up with a strange emotional sense connected with a sub-conscious encounter you had while sleeping, you may receive a message that refers to such phenomena but in an indirect way and purely metaphorically. But directly enough to make you think, yes, that's just like the dream I had, or, yes, very similar to a feeling I remember having had about Norfolk last Tuesday. There's no room for irrational superstition in a modern, multimedia organisation but I sometimes think that the systems manager can read men's souls. That's my suspicion, anyway. I wouldn't go to the stake for it and other people can take it or leave it as they wish.'

Their conversation was interrupted by the arrival of Mark Mitchell, who appeared to be in a state of some agitation.

'Hello again,' Mr Johnson said. 'Joe, this is my immediate line manager, Mark Mitchell. Mark, Joe. I came to see the leaving presentation,' he added for Mark's benefit.

'Never mind that now,' Mark said hotly. 'What I really want to know is the meaning of the notes you left in the presentation suite.'

'Which notes?'

'You know very well which notes I mean. The ones you left on the table. They found their way back to my office. Imagine my horror when I saw that instead of being a clear and unambiguous guide to the distribution tangents, they were nothing but a few scrappy sheets of paper filled with unintelligible nonsense, none of which appeared to have any relevance to any of the issues that we discussed in the brainstorm nor to the presentation you made. And the colleague who fetched you from the Imaginarium and put the rest of the notes on your desk took the liberty of keeping back a sample and passing them on to me. It's quite plain that you went to that presentation totally ill-equipped and unprepared and merely trotted out a series of meaningless truisms about project planning and strategic development without a thought for the sensibilities of your colleagues or indeed for me, who has shown you so much consideration. Thanks to you, the credibility of the entire Big Sell strategy has been thrown into question. I'd also like to have a good look at the work you claimed to have done on the spreadsheet I gave you. I trusted you enough to take you at your word when you said you had arrived at some sound conclusions. Clearly, that trust was misplaced. In the meantime, consider yourself off the project. I dread to think what you've been doing – or, more likely, not doing – in that direction. You've been nothing but trouble since the day you started, hanging round the conceptual initialisation department like a bad smell, worming your way into its practices. Just because you didn't have the guts to carve out a career for yourself in sales doesn't mean you can go bothering other departments. And another thing – you never listen. This isn't the time or the place to go over everything now but I insist on seeing you later for a frank and full conversation.'

Mr Johnson's mouth popped open and closed like a goldfish. 'Is there a problem? I thought I was doing well.'

'Is there a problem? Where would you like me to start? Of course there is a problem, but as I said, this isn't the most opportune moment to discuss the matter. Perhaps you'd like to spend some time reflecting on your recent performance before you come and see me.'

Mark's voice rose to a high pitch as he finished his address, and as he turned on his heel and marched away across the landing, Mr Johnson saw for the first time that the new executive director was watching, his hands on his hips and his head at an angle of acute interest. Mr Johnson attempted a rueful smile at the new executive director but he didn't get one in return and when Mark vanished into the stairwell, the new man followed him with some purpose.

'You see,' sighed Joe, 'it is as I said. The middle-level management stratum has begun jockeying for position. It appears that the new regime will be characterised by a highly personalised political dynamic rather than the almost statist, bureaucratic imperative that governed the company's organisational development for the past two decades or so. I'm not sure how familiar you are with organisational tectonics theory – I looked at it as part of a career development programme I undertook last year – but you may expect to see the almost literally eruptive consequences of the chafing of two distinctive and antagonistic organisational principles in the coming weeks. It's Year Zero for all of us, I'm afraid. All we can do is keep our heads down and hope the clouds of change sweep over our heads without engulfing us entirely.'

'It is all very well for you to talk about organisational tectonics but I've got the small matter of an appointment with my manager to look forward to. He sounded really angry yet everything seemed to be going so well. I hadn't deliberately not made a success of things in the sales department. There was simply a resource allocation problem. I didn't get the chance to do any work there. Since then, I've been working closely with Mark on a key strategic project that concerns the whole company and as far as I knew he was happy with my performance. I thought that the presentation went very well considering that I wasn't expecting to do it. I was given more development work to do as a consequence and he made me a formal concept engineer. I was also, and still am, extremely tired. I've worked as hard as I can, flat out, in fact. I can't understand what's happened. What on earth shall I say to him?'

'Under the circumstances, I don't think there's much you can say. Evidently you have not gone out of your way to cause trouble. The problem as far as I see it is that you can longer rely on the good offices of your line manager. This sort of thing is likely to be a problem for all of us in the weeks and months to come. If I were being unkind, I might say that you perhaps put too much faith in your relationship with him in the first place. It's an easy mistake to make – I've done it myself. The problem with these people is that they bend like the wind. All your manager is concerned about now is impressing his new boss, regardless of all the brave words he's probably uttered to you about the importance of career development, supportiveness and trust. That stocky fellow who was standing behind him won't be interested in your relationship with Mark Mitchell. He simply wants to stamp the company with his own imprint, and that starts with the level of managers immediately below him. It will all settle down in time but my advice, for what it's worth, is: stick to the facts, keep your emotions in check, make a clean breast of whatever it is you've done or not done, make sure you've got as much documentary evidence as possible and use your forthcoming appraisal as an opportunity to find common ground. Personnel are the people to talk to in the first instance.'

'My appraisal? But I haven't been here long enough to be appraised.'

'Everybody's getting appraised at the moment, old staff and new. Apparently, they are introducing a radical new performance and development review process, which promises to be a great improvement on the previous system as it will assess employee performance according to a set of commonly-agreed competency clusters rather than the arbitrary benchmarks that fell out of subjective objective setting. I'm naturally sceptical but I have to agree that the new system should provide an altogether fairer structure for rewarding hard working employees – and, of course, not rewarding lazy employees.'

'But what am I to be assessed on? I haven't really done anything yet.'

'Oh, I wouldn't say that. There's your presentation, for one thing. You've quite clearly made an impression on Mark Mitchell, for better or worse. You never know, by the time of your appraisal he might have stopped being angry with you. And you mentioned the work you've done on this special project.

That's bound to count for something, whatever your manager thinks. No-one goes through their career without acquiring any negative indicators. Try not to see this situation in personal terms. The thing to remember is that the new appraisal process will seek to achieve congruity across functions at an optimal point, which is why the organisation is being recalibrated en masse to bring everybody into the same appraisal period. If you take the personal element out of it, you might feel comforted to know that you are part of a larger process that is only really concerned with standardising HR practices. All these things get sorted out in time.'

The atrium was deserted now.

'As I said, personnel are the best people to help you. I suggest you go there as soon as you can. Your brief career here has obviously reached something of a crisis point and you probably need some sound objective advice, not the least on how to manage your next encounter with Mark Mitchell.'

'That makes a lot of sense. I don't think I could face going back to conceptual initialisation straight away. I can see that I have to sort a few things out first. For all I know, Mark has probably cleared my desk. Where is the personnel office? Is it near here?'

'You're practically underneath it now. They have got their own lift. I'll show you.'

Mr Johnson followed Joe a short way along the gallery. They stopped at a pair of steel lift doors and Joe pressed the button. Almost immediately the doors opened.

'It's just two floors up. Turn right when you get out and walk along the corridor through a set of double doors. You'll find the personnel office on your left. I've got to get back to my desk. Lots of work to do. Goodbye for now – and good luck.'

CHAPTER FOURTEEN
THE PERSONNEL MANAGER

The floor on which the personnel office was situated was deserted. Mr Johnson went into a reception area and was about to go out again when a pleasant-looking, bespectacled middle-aged woman appeared from an anteroom and asked if she could help him.

'I'm Mr Johnson. I need to talk to somebody about my forthcoming appraisal and a number of other matters.'

'You can talk to me,' said the woman. 'Come into my office.'

He followed her and she offered him a chair in front of her desk, which was in front of a window.

'Are you Margaret Cletheridge? I think you wrote to me confirming my appointment.'

'No, I'm the personnel manager,' the woman said. 'Margaret works for me. She's not here today. Mr Johnson you say?'

The personnel manager went through a pile of papers on her desk. 'Yes, Mr Johnson. I wondered when you'd show up. I've heard about you already.'

She opened an internal envelope and removed several rough sheets of jottings which looked like the notes he'd taken out of his case at the presentation.

'Mark Mitchell sent these up with a note asking me for my comments. He's your immediate line manager, isn't he? Mark wanted my opinion. He refers to "a screed of offensive gibberish and a number of other offences against good taste and good business practice". He's concerned about your performance in a certain presentation. Apparently there are other notes in his possession which he's equally exercised about. He's not a very happy manager at the moment. Did you know that he had sent these notes to me?'

'No, but I knew he had seen them. He's asked me to see him for a frank and free discussion. I was very surprised because I had been given no indication that there was anything wrong with my performance. All this sounds very serious. Am I in trouble?'

'That all depends upon what you have to tell me,' said the personnel manager. 'Do you deny making these notes?'

'No, of course not.'

'This is your handwriting?'

'Yes.'

'When did you make them?'

'I'm not sure. It might have been during my induction with Bob Hobbleton. But I've made notes on other matters too, and in several versions.'

'You saw Bob Hobbleton, did you? Can you remember why you thought you should make notes when you were with him?'

'Well, for one thing he kept asking me to do so. I was trying to keep pace with what he was telling me about organisational theory and the history of the company. It was very interesting but hard to keep up with at times.'

'That's all well and good but how did the notes come to appear in the presentation suite?'

'I kept them in my case after the induction with Bob and took them out in the presentation suite thinking that they were the notes I'd made on the distribution tangents. That was the initial project Mark had set me to work on. I'd left a lot of papers in the Imaginarium. I must have put the notes on the desk and forgotten to pick them up them when I'd finished my presentation.'

'What happened to the notes you'd made on the distribution tangents?'

'As I said, I left them in the Imaginarium. Someone brought them back to conceptual initialisation for me.'

'So you made a presentation on the question of the distribution tangents without recourse to your notes. That's very impressive but not a little reckless. That seems to be the crux of Mark Mitchell's objection.'

'I know. But I had done a lot of work on the subject and it all came back to me in the presentation – at least, I thought it did. Since then, Mark has asked me to develop my findings into a more comprehensive strategy. He has made me a fully paid-up concept engineer on the strength of the work I did and how I performed in the presentation. I've got a business card that says as much. Everyone seemed very happy with what I said in the presentation.'

'I've no doubt that you made a great success of the presentation, although it does sound as though you were flying by the skin of your teeth. But that's not really the point. There are right ways of going about things and there are wrong ways. I'd like to find out some more background information. You say that the pieces of paper in question remained in the presentation case from the time you were being inducted by Bob Hobbleton until you attended the presentation session and gave your little address. Is that correct?'

'Yes, I think so. Sometimes they would have been out of the folder and on whatever desk I was working at while I transcribed them, including the time I spent in the Imaginarium.'

'Do you think that Bob Hobbleton would be able to remember seeing the notes?'

'Perhaps. I don't know. These might even not be the notes I made when I saw Bob Hobbleton. It could have been somebody else.'

'Do you mean someone else when it should have been Bob Hobbleton or someone in another setting altogether?'

'I don't know. I've seen so many different people since I started here, it's hard to remember who does what. I haven't even had a proper induction programme so I don't know whether or not I was supposed to be seeing Bob when I did. Margaret suggested I talk to him.'

'Margaret Cletheridge?'

'No, Margaret in sales.'

'Leaving aside the question of whether or not it was in Bob Hobbleton's office that you made the notes, or what version they are, can you recall the nature of the information you wrote on to the paper?'

'I'm sure that it related to what I was being told, which, as I have said, was principally concerned with organisational theory and the history of the company, but I remember feeling very hot and thirsty at the time. Bob talked about a lot of different subjects, so it's difficult to be sure. I have made notes and drawn diagrams on a series of questions so it is difficult to remember exactly which notes I made where and which version is which. I have updated a number of key points and thrown old notes away.'

'You say you felt hot. Were you sitting close to the window?'

'Possibly. Some of the rooms I have been in had windows, I remember. Others relied on artificial light. I am afraid that I can't be more precise. I am fairly sure Bob Hobbleton's room had no natural light. It did feel quite gloomy. But the conceptual initialisation office had no natural light either yet felt airy and bright. That is the best I can do.'

'Thank you for your candour but it is quite important that we establish the nature of the papers and the reason for their remaining in your case until the presentation. Again, I must ask you what it was you wrote down and why.'

'Well, I think it must have been to do with a process that it was necessary for me to familiarise myself with. Bob talked a lot about the way the company works and changes in its business practices over time. Perhaps it was something to do with that.'

'That's good. Go on.'

'I imagine – no, I'm sure – that I was making an effort to transcribe a staged sequence of events into a simple notated form.'

'Did you capitalise key words and indent the text at appropriate points to indicate sub-stages in the overall process?'

'Yes, I suppose I must have done.'

'And when you stood up to address the audience at the presentation, did your notes serve as an aide memoire, to the extent that although they were not concerned directly with the subject matter of the moment they nevertheless provided a rational superstructure for the clear and unambiguous treatment of the question of the distribution tangents?'

'No,' said Mr Johnson, 'because as I have told you, the notes I had made for the presentation were not in the case. All I found were the notes you have in front of you.' He had the feeling that the personnel manager was trying to catch him out. Then it came to him. 'Yes, yes, I remember now. I was attempting to set out the principle of the Five Synergetic Elements that inform the structure of the conceptual initialisation department. How could I forget? I have spent so much time thinking about them recently that I quite overlooked them. Bob Hobbleton explained how important they were and I used them as a model for the distribution tangents strategy in the presentation, although I hadn't intended to. I suppose that in that respect I could have used the notes as an aide memoire for the presentation, though not in the way I would have planned. But I think that it went down well. Since the Five Synergetic Elements were devised with the conceptual initialisation department in mind, it didn't seem inappropriate to refer to them in relation to the question of the distribution tangents. Mark Mitchell even complimented me on it at the time. I also mentioned Smart objectives, which Mark had told me were extremely important. Yes, that was it. The Five Synergetic Elements. I can't pretend that I understood them fully when Bob Hobbleton first outlined them to me but as time has gone by I have been able to see more and more how the theory works in practice. It seems to be a useful cohering principle. I have been exposed to so many new people and so many new ideas since I started here that I have needed to orient myself round clear and unambiguous theoretical models. I hope I haven't gone too far down this route. Bob Hobbleton also said that the biggest question a modern business organisation faces is bridging the gap between theory and practice. Of all the theories I have encountered, the Five Synergetic Elements has seemed to have the greatest degree of practical relevance. They have certainly informed the work I have done in the conceptual initialisation department, particularly in interpreting the spreadsheet Mark gave me. I suppose I should also say that I was keen to absorb knowledge that would help me make the transition from sales to a more product development-related role. But in any case, that would explain what was on the notes.'

All through this the personnel manager said nothing. When Mr Johnson had finished, she sat back in her chair and considered him from behind her spectacles. The sun poured thickly into the room and Mr Johnson felt tired again. He wasn't sure whether this was an immediate tiredness or was a consequence of the tiredness he had tried to remember feeling in Bob's office where he had made the notes or from the conceptual initialisation office where he'd made the notes on the distribution tangents, or indeed whether he had only just thought that he had felt tired because of the sunshine on that previous occasion because of the sunshine now. He yawned wildly and raised his hand to stifle it. The personnel manager stared at him. On the notice board behind her and to the left of the window were pinned health and safety bulletins, cartoons and a list of important telephone numbers. The sunshine filled the whole room with golden promise. Mr Johnson fixed his eyes on a poster showing the correct procedures for the manual handling of heavy goods. A little man in silhouette appeared in many poses – on his haunches, arms raised, bending over (this picture had a thick black cross through it), carrying the box.

The personnel manager said: 'Mr Johnson, it really would be much better for all of us if you attempted to answer my questions in a straightforward manner.'

She waved the notes at him. 'I am afraid there is a discrepancy between your account and what we might be forgiven for calling the prime exhibit. You see, I have had a good look at the notes and I've taken the liberty of circulating them among my colleagues for their comments. You have just explained to me the nature of the notes you made. You were very persuasive and had I not been in possession of the material evidence, I would have had no hesitation in believing your version of events. However, this tells a very different story.'

The personnel manager pulled her chair right up to the desk and beckoned Mr Johnson forward. When she moved the sun was blotted out.

'Would you agree that the Five Synergetic Elements that underpin the activities of the conceptual initialisation department could be described as a core functional activity as well as a theory of organisational structure?' Mr Johnson nodded. 'Would you also, therefore, agree that any rendering of this process in notated or diagrammatic form would only be comprehensible if a clear and unambiguous structure were deployed?' Again Mr Johnson nodded. 'That's all well and good in theory. But the reality is rather different.' She held up one of the sheets to Mr Johnson. 'See here' – she pointed at a faint blue sentence against which notes in a number of different hands had been added – 'and here, for example. There is quite a divergence in terms of what exactly you are saying but one thing is for sure: these notes do not in any way form the skeletal outlines of a process or the summary of a core functional activity. Do they?'

Mr Johnson took the sheet and looked it up and down and from side to side. He could distinguish certain of his words but taken as a whole, the notes were devoid of any sense whatsoever.

'No, they don't seem to,' he admitted. 'They do look rather impressionistic. It's strange, however, because I feel that I understand the theoretical underpinnings of the Five Synergetic Elements model and grasp its practical application. But it is true that you wouldn't know that from these notes. I should say, though, that I have made numerous revisions and attempted to refine my understanding of this and other ideas over time. I couldn't say for sure that these notes represent my definitive understanding of the Five Synergetic Elements.'

'The next stage, of course,' continued the personnel manager, ignoring him, 'is to try and decoct a definitive meaning from them and work our way towards the moment that you stood up in front of the audience at the presentation and gave your little speech, regardless of whether these were the notes you intended to use there or whether they related to your induction session with Bob Hobbleton or indeed anybody else. I suggest that we look at the text from a number of interpretative perspectives, beginning with my own understanding, so far as I have one. Let's see – to me, the first sentence is a sort of manifesto. It seems to be communicating a strong purpose, which I find a little odd given that it was apparently written in the context of an induction session, which to all intents and purposes is a show-and-tell platform for the inductor and a listen-and-learn opportunity for the inductee. Yet as far as I can make out, you have written "Mandarin pathways secrete" – not sure about this next word but it looks something like "incorrigible" – "secrete incorrigible mindlessness for the frail". That's the best I can come up with.

'Next, you have written what looks like "yearn return, the warm locks. Bitter unbending skylights cancel themselves out". There follows a sequence of boxes and whorls that bear no resemblance to letters at all. You go on to say that "stumps may rocket box back. Blind Devonian, 23 instances" and finish off with a warning to the "Dutchman" not to "overstate" his case. That is my interpretation at any rate. As I say, other people suggest a different meaning altogether. One of my colleagues has offered a more transparent reading. She believes that you have merely given an account of your journey in to work on your first day and that the boxes and whorls indicate the fare stages you progressed through on the way. Did you come in to work by bus on that day?'

'No I didn't, I'm afraid. I caught a train for some of the way and walked the rest of it.'

'That's a pity. I had thought that a rather persuasive interpretation. Now, my immediate superior, the new executive director, who took this piece of paper away with him for over an hour, concluded that it is in fact a story about a little dragon and a pot of gold in a barrel. Does that sound familiar?'

'I'm sorry, but I'm none the wiser,' Mr Johnson said.

The personnel manager sighed and moved her chair back to its original position. After she had moved the sunshine landed on Mr Johnson with its original force.

'Well, we haven't progressed very far and we have still got the question of your core competencies to address and the identification of six stepped objectives for the next review period. I think we should park the question of the notes for the time being. But we might as well get everything else sorted out while you are here.'

'Does that mean that you are going to appraise me rather than Mark?'

'To an extent, yes. I don't think you are quite ready to go back to the conceptual initialisation department just yet.' She checked her watch and looked in her diary. 'Happily, the best practice in recruitment training module that was scheduled for this afternoon has moved to next week, so we can have a good clear run. You've caught me at a good time.'

'I've never looked at my core competencies before,' said Mr Johnson, keen to steer the conversation away from the question of his performance in the conceptual initialisation department. 'I am not sure what they are. How do they work and what do I need to do?'

'The company's new core competency framework is structured according to the Stringhof-Blaskwell model. I don't suppose it's something you're familiar with. I wrote a paper on it for my part-four psychometric analysis examinations three years ago. Essentially, the framework is derived from personal assessment review sessions which are designed to identify employees' critical skills and attributes. It conflates the competency framework with the objective-setting and performance-review processes. Put simply, Stringhof and Blaskwell's argument is that since the context in which the development review assessment session (it emphasises an "ideal state" dialogue process) is conducted is determined entirely by what the participants bring to it and yet is held to have something of the sanctity of the confessional about it, moderating extra-physical factors need to be removed from the equation when the summary document is prepared and an actions and objectives schedule agreed upon. In practice, it means that the conclusions reached during the course of the review cannot be considered "outside" without reference to the particular circumstances of time and fortune that gave rise to the conclusions in the first place, or something like that. I might be confusing it with the Frunk-Parsons "box" template, it all seems so long ago now. Is that clear?'

'A little. I have to say, it does seem to be somewhat early in my career for a full appraisal. I am still relatively new, although it feels as though I have been here a long time. Do you know, I've really no idea how long I have been here.'

'It is never to early for an appraisal, Mr Johnson. In any case, the entire organisation is being reappraised according to a new objective steer that the new executive director decided upon immediately after taking up the reins of the organisation. This means that several different review periods have to be unified under a new process structure, some short-term objectives turned into long-term objectives and some long-term objectives turned into short-term objectives. Usually, your line manager would appraise you but I think that might not be appropriate under the circumstances. Let's look at this as a gentle introduction to performance reviews, competencies and objective-setting. You may find that we have to set some temporary objectives now and review them the next time a new cohort of appraisees is filtered into the main body. But don't worry. The process should balance out and congruity achieved within three months. In any case, this talk is entirely academic until we've agreed upon a core competency framework for you. You must be thirsty – I'll fetch some water. You may be in here for some time.'

The personnel manager left her office briefly and returned with two plastic cups of water. She took a manila folder from a cupboard behind her desk and pulled out her chair so that she sat at Mr Johnson's left side. He drank the water down in one go, splashing a small quantity on his right leg.

'You've spilt some,' said the personnel manager gently. 'Are you nervous?'

'A little, I suppose. This is the first time I have ever had to look at my core competencies or devise objectives. I don't know where to start.'

'Don't worry,' said the personnel manager, and smiled at him. 'That's why I am here. We'll take it very slowly and sequentially. I am sorry if I was a little sharp with you back there. It's part of my job, I'm afraid. You never know when you are going to be called upon to intervene in a disciplinary matter. But I don't think we need take the question of the notes any further for the moment. Everyone is allowed one indiscretion at the beginning of their career. I'm sure that Mark Mitchell will come round in time. Let's forget all about it for the moment. Why don't you look after the notes until further notice?'

Mr Johnson took the papers, folded them and put them in his trouser pocket. He felt immediately more secure being in possession of the prime exhibit.

'Now to begin,' she said, 'and to begin properly we must go back to the very beginning, starting with your CV and letter of application which formed the basis of your initial interview with us. I know very little about you personally and I would not want to form an opinion of you merely on Mark Mitchell's perceptions. And there is never any harm in revisiting first principles.'

She removed three A4 sheets from the manila folder and laid them on her lap. The room began to feel pleasantly close and the personnel manager's perfume smelt warmly of flowers and spice.

'So far, so good,' she said. 'A standard, well-presented covering letter that communicates very strongly your interest in the company and your suitability for the role, and a well-constructed CV on no more than two sides of A4 that states clearly your employment and education histories in descending order, emphasises your key skills and qualities and deals briefly, but not peremptorily, with your social and private interests, thus building an impression of a well-qualified and well-rounded individual.'

The personnel manager turned to Mr Johnson and smiled at him. 'It's quite obvious why they wanted to interview you.'

'Thank you,' said Mr Johnson. 'I had an interview with a careers adviser at my old university shortly before applying and I also did some research into letter- and CV-writing. I was conscious that you get one shot with an application. I have heard so many horror stories from well-qualified candidates who never got a chance to be interviewed simply though carelessness on their CVs.'

'Well, there is certainly nothing careless about yours,' said the personnel manager. 'In fact, it's almost a model example. Clear, to the point, and you have even spelt liaise properly.' They both laughed at this.

'I must admit, I did double-check that one in the dictionary.'

'Because the spell-check on your computer threw it back?'

'Exactly.'

'But we digress. I am going to throw out the rule book here and start with your personal details instead of your academic qualifications and work experience. I always think that you should examine the private man in order to establish his public credentials. Did you talk much about this aspect of your CV in your interview?'

'Not really. They were mainly interested in my employment history. They didn't even seem particularly interested in my academic achievements.'

'Did you give as much thought to the detailing of your social and private interests as you did to the rest of your CV? Be honest here.'

'I don't suppose I did. They didn't seem as important as the employment and educational aspects.'

'Do you mean you lied about them?'

'No, of course not,' said Mr Johnson, taken aback.

'So you are an enthusiastic chess player, enjoy watching and participating in a variety of sports, attend frequently the cinema and theatre, and you are a keen rambler who enjoys visiting the countryside as often as time allows. When did you last enjoy a ramble in the countryside?'

'Let me see. Not recently, if I'm honest. I went camping in the Peak District last summer but nothing since. I don't seem to have had much spare time lately.'

'But you would maintain that the statement was true when you wrote your CV and came for an interview?'

'Yes, absolutely. The intention is always there.'

The personnel manager wrote something in the margin on Mr Johnson's CV.

'And when did you first develop a taste for country walking?'

'When I was very young, just a boy.'

'Who stimulated this interest? Your mother and father?'

'Actually, no. It was as a consequence of a school trip to a youth hostel in Northumberland. In the late 1980s.'

'What did you enjoy about the trip?'

'Everything. The sights and smells of the country and the historical sites. The old youth hostel on the edge of a wood. The way the sun and clouds played hide and seek above Housesteads Fort.'

'How long did the journey to Northumberland take?'

'It seemed to last for days but I suppose it was just a few hours.'

'Was the day hot?'

'Yes.'

'Where did you sit on the bus?'

'In the middle but nearer the front.'

'Near or off side?'

'I don't remember.'

'Try.'

'I think it was the near side.'

'Aisle or window?'

'Aisle. The day was hot and the window seat would have been uncomfortable.'

'Who did you sit next to?'

'I don't think I sat next to anybody.'

'You sat all on your own for a long coach journey to Northumberland? Did you choose not to sit next to anybody?'

'I suppose so. I'm not sure. I think it just happened that way.'

'Let's go back to before you boarded the coach. Where did you all meet?'

'Outside the school gates. It was a Saturday morning in August.'

'Who brought you to the school gates?'

'My mother.'

'Did she wave you off?'

'Yes.'

'Did she see that you sat on your own on the coach?'

'I'm not sure.'

'But you wouldn't have wanted her to know that, would you?'

'No, I suppose not.'

'What do you think she would have thought had she known that no-one wanted to sit next to you on the coach?'

'I didn't say that no one wanted to sit next to me.'

'But they didn't, did they Mr Johnson? You milled awkwardly at the school gates keeping a sufficiently dignified distance from your mother but unable to enter into the conversations the other children were having. You felt shy and clumsy and although you were looking forward to the trip to Northumberland you were simultaneously dreading it because you knew that it would entail prolonged bouts of anxious solitude for you, beginning with the journey on the hot coach. Is that not right?'

Mr Johnson looked down at his shoes and said nothing. The personnel manager leaned across and gently touched his forearm.

'Is that not right, Mr Johnson?'

'Yes,' he said after a moment, 'yes, that is right.'

The air hung soft and still in the bright office. 'Tell me about the sandwiches,' the personnel manager said after a short while.

'How do you know about the sandwiches?' asked Mr Johnson in amazement.

The personnel manager smiled at across at him. 'Mr Johnson, I've been in the human resources business for many years. One learns to deduce situations from what is unsaid. One gains profound insights into people's lives. You didn't deny it when I asked about the sandwiches, did you?'

'No.'

'Then tell me all about them. In your own time.'

'We must have been about an hour-and-a-half into the journey,' said Mr

Johnson at last. 'We were on the motorway, I'm not sure where exactly. Perhaps it was Yorkshire. I was hungry.'

'Had you eaten breakfast?'

'Yes, a little. But it felt like a long time ago. I had a packet of sandwiches in my knapsack and some cold bread and butter pudding, a couple of apples and a carton of juice. My mother had packed it up. I took out the packet of sandwiches and opened them. They were wrapped in greaseproof paper.'

'What was in the sandwiches?'

'Cheese and pickle, my favourite.'

'How many rounds?'

'Two, I think.'

'What happened next?'

'It's difficult to describe. An arm reached over from behind me and grabbed the packet. The next thing is, the sandwiches were being thrown around the back of the coach. I got up to try and get them back but then another boy emptied the knapsack and chucked the rest of the contents about.'

'What did the teachers do?'

'One of them got up from the front of the coach and restored order. But it was too late by then. My packed lunch was ruined. The worst thing was the bread and butter pudding. No-one had ever heard of anyone being sent on a school trip with cold bread and butter pudding before. Even the teacher was laughing about it.'

Mr Johnson paused and took a deep breath. 'After that, for the whole trip everyone called me Mr Bread and Butter Pudding Boy.' In spite of himself, Mr Johnson felt his eyes prickling with tears at the memory. 'They used to say it in a grotesque southern American accent,' he added in a hoarse whisper.

Instinctively, the personnel manager took his hand held and held it. 'Children can be very cruel,' she said.

'And teachers,' said Mr Johnson.

'Yes, and teachers. But it didn't ruin your trip, did it? If nothing else, you came back from Northumberland with an abiding love of country walking, didn't you?'

'I suppose so,' said Mr Johnson. 'But it came at a price. Even now, I regard country pursuits as essentially solitary activities.'

'Would you agree that this experience has informed your essentially solitary approach to workplace matters?'

'I don't know. I've never thought about it. I don't think that I have a problem associating with people at work.'

'I'm not saying it is a problem as such. And I didn't mean it as a criticism.

On your covering letter you say that you work well as part of a team and under your own initiative. That is on the whole true. I think your record here bears that out but it would be fair to say that in your case the individualistic approach usually prevails at the expense of the collective. That certainly is the feedback I have had, from Mark Mitchell and others. Your successes here have been largely connected to projects which have required periods of intense, solitary activity before being brought into the glare of public scrutiny. I am talking principally of the question of the distribution tangents and your approach to the presentation. Needless to say, your failures have been on the whole due to your almost pathological insistence on maintaining a resolutely individualistic attitude to matters which are by any objective measurement only understood properly with reference to corporate imperatives. Here I refer, of course, to the gnomic quality of your induction notes. And Leo Porter identified you as being someone for whom safety is very important. This motivates you above all else, even at the risk of isolating you from the main currents of activity. You want to be liked and you want to feel safe. Leo Porter had a very clear idea about where you fit into Maslow's hierarchy. Yes, I have heard all about that. Again, I don't mean any of this as criticism per se — not unconstructive criticism, at any rate. I must admit, Mr Johnson, that you remind me of nobody so much as Leonard Bragby. I don't think I am breaching confidentiality when I say that I once had a very similar conversation with him.'

'I have heard a lot about Leonard Bragby. Why does everyone keep mentioning him? What was he like?'

'To describe him fully would require more time than we have available today. Let's just say that of all the young men and women in the strategic development cross-functional area he was the one most likely to become President of the United States — or be hanged for treason.'

'They talked about him a lot in the sales and conceptual initialisation departments. It sounded as though he was too much for people to handle.'

'There is some truth in that. Leonard Bragby could do anything he put his mind to, which wasn't often, it should be said. Everything came too easily to him. The problem was that he could do sales work standing on his head but always wanted to let you know that he had much better things waiting for him. He was the same when he moved into conceptual initialisation. He always put himself outside the main currents of organisational activity. There was also the question of his satirical writing. He upset a lot of people. The situation could not persist indefinitely.'

'What happened to him? No-one seems to be sure.'

'At first we moved him into different areas. We always try to develop and encourage real talent. We thought that if we gave him more responsibility he would buckle down and behave himself. But it only made things worse. To be brutally frank, the longer he was here, the more people he infected with his maverick pessimism. He ended up running a small team of concept engineers. Needless to say, he was immensely competent. Competent – but lazy. His team quickly became a dark engine of negativity working ceaselessly against the strategic interests of the organisation as a whole. Good people went bad under his jurisdiction. Mark Mitchell used to despair. Finally, we had to strip him of all the vestiges of authority and give him a routine job in a quiet department. I've rather lost track of him, to be honest. He certainly doesn't cause the trouble he used to cause. But it took us a long time to repair the damage in the conceptual initialisation department.'

'Couldn't you just have sacked him?'

'Sacked him? Goodness me, no. He would have had us up before a tribunal in no time. He was too clever to sack. No, it was easier – and cheaper – to absorb him into the wider life of the organisation.'

'It seems a shame that someone so talented should go off the rails like that. Perhaps he never found the right role for himself.'

'That is probably true. But I'll be honest with you, Mr Johnson – I did have a lot of time for Leonard Bragby. This is strictly between ourselves, of course. He had a strong personality and could always give you a run for your money. He was stimulating company. I shouldn't really say this, but you could do worse than speak to him yourself. Your careers do have some curious parallels. It might help you prepare for your meeting with Mark Mitchell. At the very least, you could learn which paths not to take.'

'Do you really think I am like him? From what I have heard, he was something of a troublemaker. But I have never gone consciously against the interests of the organisation. I have always worked hard and tried to learn how to be an effective employee.'

The personnel manager smiled and squeezed his hand.

'Of course you have. Let's just say that a little nipping in the bud now will be proof against bad things happening in the future. It is all a question of keeping on top of your negative indicators. You would have to go a long way to emulate the worst antics of Leonard Bragby. Since his time we have all had to be more vigilant. My job is to ensure that good people don't go to the bad.'

'Am I a good person? Am I an effective employee?'

The personnel manager laughed and let go of his hand.

'You don't need me to answer that, Mr Johnson. We have identified a lot of promise in you. I wouldn't be talking to you now if that weren't the case. Look at this interview as an investment in your future. Do you want to work here?'

'Yes, of course I do.'

'Do you honestly think that you make a valuable contribution to the long-term health of the organisation?'

'I hope so. I want to. But there is so much to learn. Sometimes I don't know what I should be giving my attention to. Also, my job has changed so much since I started here.'

'That is quite normal. You are on a very steep learning-curve. We all are. In many ways, your induction period will never end. That's the way of things in the modern business organisation. But it is plain that you possess a strong skill-set and an enquiring mind. Your ambition to develop your commercial focus in a creative environment is very laudable and I suspect that you have had the opportunity to do that already. You are also diligent and conscientious, even when you are putting your energies in the wrong direction. Nobody carves out a successful career without acquiring a number of negative indicators along the way. But I think that even given the present situation with Mark Mitchell and the ambiguity that surrounds your note-taking practices, you are squarely on the credit side of the balance. Try not to worry too much. Of course you will make mistakes. We all do.'

'Even you?'

'You don't need me to answer that, Mr Johnson,' she said, and smiled and took his hand again. 'You look tired.'

'Yes, I am tired. I have been working hard lately. Everybody has, I know. But I am very tired.'

He was overwhelmed finally by the warmth of the room and the floral spice of the personnel manager's scent. She drew him closer to her side and he laid his head on her breast.

'Don't worry, Mr Johnson,' she said. 'It's time to turn over a new leaf. A good sleep will sort you out. It usually does.'

'Did Bragby sleep much?' he heard himself asking as warm waves of sleep lapped his head.

'I don't think Bragby ever slept,' she said quietly. He felt her hand stroking his hair softly. He nestled closer to her breast. He couldn't imagine how he would ever get up again. Sleepy perfume and silk wound softly around his soul. All was quiet and still.

'I'm expecting a visitor any time soon,' said the personnel manager. 'You are going to have to leave the office.'

Mr Johnson sat up with a start and rubbed his eyes. 'Was I asleep long?' he asked. 'It feels as though I was. I hope I didn't shout.'

'No,' laughed the personnel manager as she stood up and straightened her blouse, 'you were as quiet as the proverbial.'

'I'm not sure that I really feel like going back to work but I know I should.'

'I tell you what – why don't you have a sit down in the little room behind you? It's nice and private and I can wake you up later on if you go back to sleep. It seems a shame to send you back to your desk just now.'

Mr Johnson turned round and saw a door he hadn't noticed when he came into the office. He got up and the personnel manager led him into a little ante-room furnished with a low vinyl two-seater settee and a glass-topped table strewn with personnel management magazines. On the floor behind the settee stood a grey cupboard.

'Is my appraisal over? Have we sorted out my competencies and objectives?'

'To an extent. I think we've established that you are competent. And I think we both know what your objective is, don't we?'

The personnel manager winked at him as she shut and locked the door. A few minutes later Mr Johnson heard a man's voice in the office and a low-toned conversation begin. Mr Johnson wasn't sure exactly what the objective was the personnel manager had referred to but he knew he wouldn't be able to return to the conceptual initialisation department for the time being. The idea of speaking to Leonard Bragby about his experiences acquired significance. Bragby might be able to offer some pointers for his future career development or at least, as the personnel manager had said, provide an object lesson in how not to do things. In any case, it would be interesting to talk to someone about whom everyone seemed to have an opinion, for better or worse. And their careers did seem to have some remarkable parallels, even given the relatively short period of time Mr Johnson had been with the company. They had both been in the same departments, for one thing. It would do as an objective in the short term, at least. He yawned, curled his legs under himself and lay down. He had no inhibitions about falling asleep again so soon, nor about abandoning for the moment his work on the development of the distribution tangents strategy. There was time enough for that later. In any case, the question of the notes hadn't been resolved from Mark Mitchell's point of view and he couldn't be sure that there was in fact a desk for him in the department anymore. He felt certain, however, that the personnel manager would represent him fairly in this matter, and his head lolled against the edge of the settee and his arm flopped to the floor. Time would resolve this and other issues. He dreamt of nothing and woke quickly. There were louder voices on the other side of the door but he could not detect what they were saying. His head felt full of lead and marshmallows and it fell down onto his eyes again and sent him swooning back to sleep. He could have stayed there all day. It was surprising how comfortable a piece of modern office furniture could be. The sleep really was doing him good. He needed sleep.

'He needs his sleep,' said a voice, which he recognised as the personnel manager's. 'Leave him be.'

'Well, we all can be tired if we like,' said the man's voice. It sounded like Mark Mitchell's, and it grew closer. 'Don't think you can go swanning back down to conceptual initialisation just because you think you're ready, oh no,' he shouted and hammered on the door. 'You need to sort yourself out. I'll give you the seven Ds. Turn over a new leaf? You need to turn over a whole library.'

The personnel manager must have coaxed him away because his voice grew fainter and fainter, but not before he heard Mark shout 'tumbling bloody monkey' or something that sounded like that, it was hard to tell.

Silence returned. Mr Johnson sat on the edge of the settee and waited for the personnel manager to open the door but she didn't and as time passed he settled down gradually into the settee and fell asleep again.

CHAPTER FIFTEEN
NIKOLAI

When Mr Johnson awoke he was conscious of an extra level of silence. The overhead light seemed to have dimmed and the room was considerably colder. His head felt clearer and lighter. The sleep had done him good. He turned the handle of the door but it was still locked.

'Hello?' he said softly and knelt down to look through the keyhole. It was dark on the other side. A fine shaft of cool air penetrated the hole. He rattled the door handle but no one came. 'Hello?' he said again.

The light in the little room grew fainter and fainter. He opened the cupboard doors behind him hoping that he would find a spare bulb. There was nothing in there, not even a panel at the back. The cupboard gave onto another room, which he climbed into. This room was slightly larger than the first, though wholly unfurnished. It was older and shabbier, too. The carpet was thin and worn and the walls covered in a pale brown emulsion. It was lit by a pair of shaded and tasselled sidelights fixed halfway up the wall on the left-hand side. There were no windows.

A brown door stood opposite Mr Johnson. He approached it with a heavy heart but to his surprise the door opened and he found himself standing on a long, broad and dimly-lit landing. It was clear that he was in a part of the building that hadn't been refurbished for many years. Mr Johnson walked along the landing until it tapered and became a narrow, carpeted staircase that climbed steeply between walls lined with peeling red flock wallpaper.

Mr Johnson went up the stairs to another, smaller landing lit by a tall standard lamp. At this point, the staircase turned back on itself and carried Mr Johnson over his shoulder towards a small yellow door at the top of the flight that drew gradually closer as the staircase continued upwards, increasingly precipitously, past dusty recesses housing filthy old stuffed animals such as ferrets and moles, and dim inlaid light bulbs at intervals. When Mr Johnson reached the top step he found the door locked. He rattled the handle vigorously and pressed his face close to a frosted glass panel marked 'Hawarden' but the room beyond seemed shadowy and vague, although he thought that a fire had been lit in there because he could detect a faint orange glow away to the right. Sighing, he turned away and began to descend the stairs. After a while, he found that the wall to his left had disappeared. He hadn't noticed this on his right on the way up. He also hadn't heard the insistent brassy music that poured out of the space, a narrow, sloping cavity with a levelled-off platform mid point upon which were positioned a table bearing an angle-poise lamp and, on the floor, a chair upon which a man sat and a filing cabinet upon which a ginger cat slept and a dansette record player from which flew wildly the stomping bass and parping horns of a mid-1960s Jamaican ska cut. Mr Johnson peered in and caught the man's attention.

'Come inside, come inside,' gestured the man at the desk abstractedly. Mr Johnson eased himself into the entrance to the cavity, which he found widened as it receded so that he could more or less stand up straight in front of the desk.

'My name is Mr Johnson,' he began, but the man seemed to be preoccupied and didn't wait for him to finish.

'I have your notes here somewhere, or on a disk, one or the other. You must be down here somewhere. I am drowning under a sea of memos and files. I only say: Thank God this is a paperless office! When the network goes down, I often say: Whatever did we do before computers? But in an odd way, they seem to have generated even more paperwork. It's interesting, isn't it, that despite the invisible, seemingly infinite storage capacity of the computer, we nonetheless reproduce on paper every email, every file, every letter. Crazy doubling up! And yet, I sometimes wonder whether we will ever feel so confident in our computers that we won't require the comforting tangible evidence of a paper document. What do you think? Um, uh-uh, what's that? Yes, yes, quite, I do so agree.'

As he spoke, the man busied himself with his piles of paper and worried his keyboard furiously. 'Yes, yes, I'm sure that is quite right. This wretched machine has seized up again. It's the network, of course. It always goes down around this time. Yet I often wonder whether it affects everybody in the organisation simultaneously. It's curious, isn't it, how quickly we have lost the capacity for individual communication independent of the computer. When I fall off the network, even for a short time, it is like losing a limb, I imagine. I feel bereft of colleagues, friends. Do you know' – he leaned forward in his seat and jabbed a finger at Mr Johnson – 'I sometimes think that the systems manager doesn't pick up the telephone when I call him. They have number recognition down there, you see. I imagine him sitting in the network room, drinking fresh coffee and smiling when he sees my number flash up on the console. Smiling to himself in a deep, satisfied way and enjoying his coffee. They have fresh coffee facilities down there, you see. Sometimes, I'm offline for days and he doesn't answer the telephone and I'm up here, just me and Alan' – here he gestured towards the sleeping ginger cat on the filing cabinet –

'watching the screen anxiously for signs of movement, sifting through my hard copies, listening to the Skatalites over and over. I don't know what I would do without my records. So long as you have got music to work by, you are all right, don't you agree? I am a vinyl man at heart, of course. CDs never reproduce that warm, electric sound, don't you agree? Just listen to this for a moment. It's got a full ska orchestra with Lloyd Knibb on drums. If you see the systems manager, put in a word for me, won't you, there's a good fellow? I really wonder whatever we did before computers. As soon as I get back online I can complete the third-quarter spreadsheets and get everything back on track before the end of the month. I am immobilised without network access. Don't forget now, will you? There's so much to do. Goodbye. Goodbye. Watch the stairs on your way down. Goodbye.'

There didn't seem any point in asking the man about Leonard Bragby and Mr Johnson climbed out of the cavity. At the foot of the staircase, he turned right into another corridor and followed it through ever-deepening gloom towards another dim yellow light. This time the corridor didn't twist or turn back on itself but continued more or less levelly until it reached another frosted glass door, with the words 'Back Hawarden' etched onto the glass. He tried the handle, which felt looser than the last door but still wouldn't yield. He rattled and jiggled away at it and knocked repeatedly. 'Bragby,' he cried, 'Bragby, are you in there?'

'I'm sorry, are you looking for someone?' said a voice at his shoulder. Mr Johnson turned and found himself staring into a keen little face beneath a mop of thick black hair – a casually-dressed fellow of Mr Johnson's age (but considerably smaller) possessing a mature, good humoured disposition.

'Yes,' said Mr Johnson, 'I am looking for Leonard Bragby. Have you seen him?'

The younger man stroked his chin thoughtfully. 'Bragby, you say? Can't say the name rings a bell. What's his job title? Which section does he work in?'

Mr Johnson had to think about this for a moment because he realised that at no point had anyone mentioned which department Bragby had moved to since he had left conceptual initialisation. The personnel manager had mentioned a quiet department and nothing more.

'I'm not entirely sure. I'm in conceptual initialisation myself, which was where Bragby used to work. I don't known where he went to after that or what his current job title is. I need to talk to him but no-one seems to know where he is.'

'Conceptual initialisation, you say? Haven't come across that one before. Are you a new department?'

'It's relatively new, by all accounts. I am still quite new here myself. I was made a formal concept engineer only recently. By the way, I'm Mr Johnson,' he added extending his right hand.

'Nikolai Brand,' said the other and they shook warmly. 'Come in, anyway. I was just emptying some old files. We try to keep the door locked most of the time. I'll make you a cup of tea and you can tell me all about life on the other floors.'

'What do you mean? Don't you know what happens on the other floors?'

'Not really, and that's the way we like it in here, I have to say. But it is useful to know what's what in the organisation at large. Forewarned is forearmed, as they say.'

They entered a shabby but snug living room that was home to an old horsehair settee and a matching armchair, a little sink with a geyser above it, and four battered old chairs and a battered old table which was cluttered with tea cups and plates.

'Please excuse the mess,' Nikolai said. 'This room doubles as my private office and a staff lounge. They don't use it much as a rule, but it only takes a few cups left unwashed and a scattering of biscuit crumbs to make a place look seedy. Have a seat. I'm sure it is very different in your department. Probably all ergonomically-designed furniture and individual work stations. Or have you embraced the principle of hot-desking? That was the big new thing when I was last up there. Conceptual initialisation, is it? I hope you didn't think I was being rude a moment ago when I said that I hadn't heard of it before but things change so quickly here that whole new sections flourish like mushrooms after rain and are gone the next day. Ever since I was appointed to lead this section seven, was it eight, maybe even nine months ago, I have had very little contact with the outside world. My job is so absorbing and obviously carries a considerable degree of responsibility for a staff of sixty or so souls. There you go – "outside world". Isn't it strange how quickly you become lost in your own micro-environment? Tell me all about yourself, your job and what's going on in your immediate section. And who is this Bragby character and why are you looking for him?'

Mr Johnson patiently outlined his tale, from his arrival in Margaret's reception area, the confusion in the sales office, through his transfer to conceptual initialisation, his sneezing fit at the strategy presentation, the project work, his fall from grace with Mark Mitchell, the interview with the personnel manager, his interest in tracking down Bragby, and his journey to the top of the stairs.

'I tried another door with "Hawarden" written on it but it was locked and nobody came when I called.'

Nikolai put a cup of tea in front of him. 'Yes, that's old Front Hawarden, which hasn't been occupied for a long, long time. We don't go up there very much.'

Mr Johnson mentioned the man in the cavity with the ska records and the ginger cat. Nikolai raised a quizzical eyebrow at this but didn't say anything.

'Oh, and by the way,' added Mr Johnson, 'I think – I can't be positive but I'm fairly sure – that a fire had been lit in the room, as if someone had been in there recently. I pressed my face close to the frosted glass, you see, and thought that I detected an orange glow away to the right.'

Nikolai looked at him curiously. 'A fire, eh? Yet the door locked and barred. And to the best of my knowledge, I possess the only key. It's high time that I took another look at old Front Hawarden. We won't worry about it now. If Juniper is up to his old tricks, well that's another question. But I can't be sure. These are such uncertain times.'

'Who's Juniper? Would he be the man I saw in the cavity on the stairs?' Mr Johnson asked, but Nikolai was busy clearing the table of crockery and began clattering away at the sink, making sensible conversation impossible.

'I expect you have had so much to take in lately that your head feels like hot rice pudding,' Nikolai cried above the fury of the geyser.

'What was that? Do I like rice pudding?'

'Yes, your head.' Nikolai turned the tap off and patted his foamy hands dry on a tea towel. 'I remember my first week. The sea of faces, hours spent in induction training, memorising the acronyms and abbreviations, getting familiar with the nomenclature. And then one day, you realise that you have a quantity of background that you never expected to have and the foreground appears less precipitous. Soon you are striding across a broad and level plain with the sun at your back and an ocean of breath in your lungs. You feel invincible, indomitable, and work is no longer an accretion of tasks and chores but a natural, instinctive process. You become the artist, the paint and the canvas in a never-ending, eternally-renewing creation. That is what happened to me, at any rate, and I am sure that given time and a few breaks, you will feel the same way. If you have had enough tea, I would be delighted to show you around my section. Please forgive the hyperbole of a moment ago. I am still pinching myself. Most of my peers who started at my level are still despatch handlers and liaison clerks. Wonderful men and women some of them. But my trajectory is different. Should I feel guilty about this? I don't as a matter of fact. I still feel warmly about the chaps with whom I shared my induction week. And it goes without saying that I love my staff. No, Mr Johnson, I am not a callous man. But I will tell you something: sometimes I feel tired unto death. It is the weight of responsibility, you see. You will excuse me if after our tour I stretch out on the settee for half an hour?'

Mr Johnson got up and smoothed out the creases from his suit. Nikolai stifled a yawn and checked his watch.

'If we go now we will catch the staff before the next big meeting. Now then, you should know that this part of the company is simultaneously the same as and yet different from the rest of the organisation in certain important ways.'

Nikolai led Mr Johnson through a green-painted door at the back of the sitting room and into a small antechamber.

'Before we enter the main body of the section, I should tell you that we don't get many visitors down here and that some of the staff might be startled when they see you coming. Do not be alarmed. I have never worked with such a gentle group of men, they pose no threat. But please respect their traditions and proprieties – they have their own particular ways. Follow me now.'

Nikolai opened the door of the antechamber and they stepped into a gloomy space. At first Mr Johnson could discern no shape or pattern to it but as his eyes gradually became accustomed to the heavy, grainy light, he saw that they stood at the head of a long room, which was, in dimension, more like a very broad corridor. Green iron filing cabinets of the old fashioned type lined the walls and appeared to cross the room itself in the near distance. In the centre of the floor were heavy-looking, dark wooden tables at which sat dozens of elderly men, some with wispy tufts of hair spouting from their crowns, others completely bald. Most of them wore spectacles. Many of them had cardigans on and some wore clips to keep their shirt sleeves rolled up. Such illumination as existed was provided by erratically placed low-wattage, unshaded bulbs. Moths fluttered restlessly in the gloom. There were no windows.

It wasn't until Nikolai and Mr Johnson passed the first table that the men noticed them. A tiny old fellow jerked his head up in alarm and let out a wheezy cry, which was taken up by his neighbour and quickly spread around the immediate environment.

'It's all right,' said Nikolai, making a conciliatory gesture with his hands. 'This is a friend. This is Mr Johnson. Mr Johnson is from upstairs.'

The men shrank back in their seats at this and one of them emitted a low, frightened whistle.

'Are you sure it's upstairs?' Mr Johnson said to Nikolai. 'This building is so large and complicated that I'm not sure whether I've come from upstairs, downstairs or on the same level all along.'

'It doesn't matter,' Nikolai answered in a whisper. 'To these men, everything outside this section is upstairs. It's all right,' he continued, 'Mr Johnson is with me. I'm just showing him around. Please get back to your work and try not to worry.'

One by one, the men resumed their scrutiny of their ledgers and piles of foolscap, their bald and tufted heads moving slowly in methodical metronomy.

The floor of the office was strewn with yellowed documents and Mr Johnson noticed that some of the tea cups on the tables were furred thickly with mould. He also saw that many of them were smoking while they worked.

'But what do your staff do exactly?' he asked Nikolai.

'Gather and process information, primarily,' Nikolai answered. 'And have meetings. Lots of those. A typical day will start around 9.30am with a meeting of the general steering sub-committee which is charged with making appointments to the full working committees which between them determine the day's tasks for ultimate approval at an umbrella committee meeting. This last committee meets on every other Tuesday, except when that Tuesday follows a Bank Holiday – but not Whitsun, of course. Or May Day. Unless it falls on an even date or when it occurs in a Leap Year.'

'That's a lot of committees.'

'Yes,' said Nikolai, 'and it doesn't take into account the Big Committee upstairs. Everything that is decided by the umbrella committee may be countermanded by order of the Big Committee.'

'Is that the same as the Executive Management Cluster?'

'Yes and no. The Big Committee is formed from elements within the Executive Management Cluster and its remit falls out of the EMC's overall sphere of strategic responsibility. At an operational level, however, it enjoys a considerable degree of independence and has rubberstamping or prohibiting powers over the business of some of the non-core functions.'

'Is this one of the non-core functions?' asked Mr Johnson.

'Yes and no. It all depends on who is looking, where they're looking from, and what the Golden Clock says.'

'The Golden Clock? I haven't heard about that yet.'

'Really? I am surprised. The Golden Clock is the only reliable guide to the state of the organisation at any one time and the relative status of an individual and his department.'

'Is it the same as the corporate steer?'

'In some ways it is and in some ways it isn't. Yes, as with the corporate steer, the Golden Clock expresses a distilled truth about our corporate health at a given moment in time. Like the corporate steer, it offers a succinct guide to our short-, medium-, and, to a certain extent, long-term future. But unlike the corporate steer, the Golden Clock provides a much more personal perspective for any individual who looks at it. The answer I get to a question I address to the Golden Clock will be very different to the one Mr Sandbach or Mr Arley over there will get, even if they ask the question in exactly the same way. Colours, shapes, sounds and sensibilities inform the Golden Clock's function. It is a subtle and infinitely adaptable benchmark. I don't know if that explanation does it justice. Think of something that configures an almost infinite series of relationships between a multiplicity of disparate phenomena and you will be halfway to understanding it. In business terms, the Golden Clock is the closest thing to a unified model of theory and practice it is possible to get.'

'Where is the Golden Clock? I would like to have a look at it. I have spent a lot of time here familiarising myself with various business theories and models so I ought to spend some time getting acquainted with it. Perhaps it will help me track down Bragby.'

'It is not immediately to hand. Juniper keeps it. But I'll ring him and try to get it out for you before you go.'

Mr Johnson was about to ask again whether Juniper was the man with the ginger cat in the cavity but he stopped short, for they had reached the point on the horizon where the filing cabinets appeared to march across the room, which indeed they did, and Nikolai helped Mr Johnson up a wooden ladder, over the top of the cabinets and down another ladder on the other side.

More filing cabinets and desks rolled away into the dim distance. Again, the men in this part of the room whimpered and fretted until Nikolai soothed them with the right words. But one wrinkled gaffer wouldn't be stilled and clung desperately to Nikolai's arm.

'Systems manager... systems manager,' he gasped.

'No,' Nikolai said, 'it's not the systems manager, it's Mr Johnson, a friend of mine from upstairs.'

'Systems manager... systems manager,' he repeated, and Nikolai had to stroke his old head for some time until he was reassured and returned to his desk, although not without a final fearful glance over his shoulder as Nikolai led Mr Johnson on.

'That's very strange,' said Mr Johnson. 'The notion that I was the systems manager seemed to fill that old fellow with horror, yet I can't help but notice that this entire section is bereft of computer technology and that even the telephones don't have any obvious connections either to each other or to the world at large.'

This was true. The only visible equipment were hole punchers and paper knives, while the thick rope cables that sprouted from the backs of the vintage, dusty Bakelite telephones terminated abruptly in mid-air at the side of the tables.

Nikolai stroked his chin thoughtfully. 'Yes, it is odd isn't it? I have often wondered about that myself. Yet make no mistake, the systems manager is as real and serious a presence down here as he is upstairs. I consider myself to be a very forceful personality when put to it and fully in command of my section, but I can assure you that I will move heaven and earth to ensure that I remain on the good side of the systems manager. Because if he is displeased, well, poosh.'

'But what can he do? As far as I can see, you are not connected to the network. I would be surprised if he even knew you were here. It seems like such a quiet little backwater.'

At this, Nikolai grabbed Mr Johnson's forearm. 'Don't say things like that. The systems manager knows we are here all right. Don't make him angry. I had problems with him earlier and have had to take considerable pains to placate him. Please be discreet in this matter. If we are not careful he will crash the system, and then where will we be?'

'But,' said Mr Johnson extremely quietly, 'you are not on the system.'

'Everyone is on the system,' said Nikolai, with a look of such liquid-eyed innocence that Mr Johnson didn't push the point.

'What did you have to do to placate the systems manager?' he whispered.

'He demands tributes in the form of consumer goods and food. Come over here and look.'

Nikolai led Mr Johnson to a large recess in the wall in which was fitted a low metal table laden with cheeses, tins of cooked meat, dried fruit, chocolate cake, handy electrical gadgets, napery and the like. At the back of the recess was a hatch. Mr Johnson leant forward over the tributes and pushed the flap back. Although he could see nothing, he knew that he was peering into a deep shaft. Eddies of warm air coiled and rose from some distant, subterranean furnace.

'Did you see anything?' Nikolai asked when he stood up in the room again. 'I have often peered through the hatch myself but I've no idea where the shaft leads to or rises from. Even a torch isn't much help – the darkness seems to swallow up any light you try to cast upon it.'

'No, I couldn't see anything.'

'And yet, whenever we leave tributes in the form of food and goods for the systems manager, they are gone by morning. I imagine he does it with the aid of ladders and agile agents. My staff, of course, won't go near the hatch. They say it is bad luck.'

They pressed on, but for some time Mr Johnson cast a cautious glance back over his shoulder towards the recess, as if expecting to see a malign hand emerge from it and gather up the cheeses and tinned meats.

At last the rows of tables ended and Nikolai and Mr Johnson turned round and went back the way they had come. On the return leg, however, the old men kept their heads bowed and their hands busy scribbling and scratching. The food and goods still sat on the table in the recess. Moths fluttered restlessly in the gloom. Nikolai yawned. Wearily they ascended the ladder, crawled over the top of the cabinets, and climbed down the other side.

In the distance, above the ranks of bald and tufted heads, Mr Johnson could just about discern the door to the antechamber which had led from Nikolai's office and now led back to it. Something of the geography of this section of the organisation was taking shape in Mr Johnson's mind, and even a little of its relation to other sections, although he was still shaky when it came to the bigger picture.

They paused at an empty desk to catch their breath. The air was hot and heavy. Quite suddenly, Mr Johnson asked: 'How big is the company?'

Nikolai leaned back against the table. 'I am not sure that there is a definitive answer to that question. You could probably measure its physical dimensions if you were so inclined, though it would take you long enough – there are so many sections and wings and annexes and extensions that it is hard to keep on top of all the changes as they happen. For example, you are in one of the oldest parts of the building now, not just because we have admittedly antiquated storage systems and vintage telephones but because of the age of the brick and the woodwork, yet even I, who is in charge of this whole section and has been in old Front Hawarden more than most, couldn't tell you how many rooms there are down here or where all the passages and corridors lead to or come from. I am sure I speak for many other employees when I say that one becomes so preoccupied with one's immediate work concerns that one quite forgets about the existence of other departments and functions. And that is another thing – the perceived size of an organisation is also a consequence of the number of departments, functions and teams it has. As I say, one's own immediate working environment, physical and conceptual, tends to assume primacy in terms of one's conception of the organisation at large. But this state of mind is not entirely a consequence of absorption in a demanding workload. Physical changes to the office environment also play their part. For example, they keep changing the entrances and exits. When I started here eighteen months, maybe even two years ago now, the main entrance to everything was on the south side, yet now I believe it is on the north. But you may tell me a different story.'

'I am not sure,' said Mr Johnson. 'Thinking about it, it was probably on the east because I remember coming to work on my first day with the sun still behind me.'

'There you are, they've moved it again. I keep asking the systems manager for a map but he never gives me one. It is a good job I don't need to go home, I would never find my way back in again.'

'What, don't you go home at all?'

'I haven't for a long time – certainly not since I started down here. Quite simply, there's too much to do. Have you been home recently?'

'Funnily enough, I don't think I have, no. In fact, I haven't been home since I started here, which was, well, some days ago at least, although it is difficult to know for sure. I had put that down the inevitable weight of information that comes with the induction period and my absorption in project work, but I see now that it is a trend that has set in more or less for good.'

'Have you been sleeping well?'

'Not badly, considering. I snatch sleep whenever I can.'

'These fellows tend to nod off for spells at their desks, or in committee meetings, if they are long enough. I think the pace of work in this section suits their temperaments and metabolisms more than the upstairs culture.'

'Yes, it certainly seems less pressured. But that perception may be more to do with the environment and the age of the fittings rather than something intrinsic to the nature of the work itself, which I think is what you were getting at.'

'What do you mean?'

'Well, there are offices elsewhere in the organisation that are furnished to a high standard with up-to-the-mark equipment and are full of sharp-looking young executives familiar with all the latest techniques. But the more I go on here, the less convinced I am that that is any indication that they are engaged in more taxing or productive work. It is just a superficial impression, perhaps.'

'I am sure you are right, and yet I am afraid that you share a minority view. It breaks my heart to say so, but my poor scriveners may not be long for this world. It is only a matter of time before someone on the Big Committee shines a torch down here and decides that they should be trimmed, cut back and rationalised. And, perhaps, that day will not be a day too soon. Yes, I know that sounds unfeeling, but ultimately, unproductive sections of the organisation must be pruned in order to guarantee the long-term health of the organism as a whole.'

'But are they so unproductive?'

'Who knows? You could produce a spreadsheet that said yes, I could produce one that said no. There are bound to be inconsistencies. In the end, that doesn't matter. What counts is the perception. We are going through some very significant changes at the moment and we must be prepared to move with those changes or die. Does that sound harsh? Perhaps I am harsh. Perhaps management experience has made me harsh. Or maybe just realistic. Don't get me wrong – I will do my utmost to keep the Big Committee from scrutinising us too closely. The doors to Front and Back Hawarden will remain locked and I shall continue to provide the systems manager with tributes in the form of goods and food for as long as I have the resources.'

Realising that they had been talking rather loudly, Nikolai looked round at the desks in the immediate environment but none of the old fellows appeared to have heard anything.

'I don't want to upset them unnecessarily,' he went on softly. 'It is going to be difficult enough when the time comes, and it will come one day. Well, I've got my breath. How about you? Good. Let's press on, then.'

In a short while they had passed back through the antechamber and were in Nikolai's office once more. As he had promised, Nikolai stretched out on the settee and had forty winks, though not before he offered Mr Johnson an armchair and draped a tartan blanket over his knees. Mr Johnson soon went to sleep himself. He woke when he heard Nikolai moving about and running water for the kettle.

'Have I been asleep long?' Mr Johnson asked. 'I hope I didn't shout.'

'You may well have done but don't worry, I was out for the count myself. I have only just woken up. Did you have a good sleep?'

'I suppose so, though I could do with more.'

'Me too. I'll try and get my head down again in an hour or two.'

'Do you think you will be able to go home at all in the near future?'

Nikolai looked sadly at him and shook his head. 'You saw my department, Mr Johnson. There is so much work going through at the moment that to take time off, even a few hours, would be almost criminally irresponsible. Besides, I could hardly in all conscience go skipping airily out of here every evening leaving those poor men bent over their desks in the gloom.'

'What? You mean that your staff don't go home either?'

'That's right. Some of the more senior men have been here continuously for over twenty years. A manager must set an example. Best practice must always come from the top down. If they are here, so am I.'

'It is a peculiar situation,' said Mr Johnson, as Nikolai handed him a mug of tea and a plate of biscuits. 'I am no stranger to hard work but I think I would be hard pressed to work solidly for twenty years without ever going home.'

'Yes, that is just what I thought when I started in this section. I vowed that whatever happened, I would keep aside time for myself. I had so many good ideas then, Mr Johnson. The first thing I did was devise a holiday roster for my men. I remember the patient, kindly look in their eyes when I presented it to them. They knew, you see. Other managers had done the same thing before me. Needless to say, not a single holiday was taken. I don't like to look at the roster anymore, though I haven't thrown it away. One day it may be possible to implement it. My men, of course, are stoics, and they don't think any worse of me just because they never go home. They understand the wider business imperatives of the organisation and their role in achieving corporate objectives, even at the expense of a private life.'

Mr Johnson sipped his tea and munched on the biscuits. Nikolai sat across from him on the settee cupping his mug in both hands.

'Yes, the thought is sometimes unbearable. Of course I would love to go home more often. But there is so much to do here. The time slipping through fingers like sand. There are so many other things I would like to do if I could only leave work for long enough. I would like, I don't know, to visit a garden centre, say, and look at the shrubs and fencing. I think of all those steady lives lived out in comfortable stone houses, Glasgow southside, for example, or certain towns in Yorkshire, warm orange and red rooms glimpsed from the pavement. Just to spend an evening in one of those rooms watching television in front of the fire, cat on your lap, wild autumn outside. Make time stop. Just the one evening. Digestive biscuits with butter and Red Leicester and a pot of strong tea. A constant, gentle topping up. Cream ribbon evening. What do I mean by that? An unbroken smoothness for the stomach and the head. No uncomfortable spots on the settee sort of thing. Not like the tatty old chairs in here. I can see that you understand. Perhaps the two of us will treat ourselves one day. My home isn't fashioned from comfortable stone but my living room is snug enough and we could easily get a good fug up. We don't have to watch anything too profound on the television. Snooker would do me. Or a well-made police drama. I could buy some fancy biscuits – not everybody likes digestives with cheese. What do you think?'

'It sounds very tempting.'

'Or what about this? A cold Saturday afternoon up on an allotment on a hill above the town but we're toasty inside a potting shed, heat provided by a three-bar electric fire, eating bacon sandwiches and listening to the football commentary on the radio. Nobody will bother us and time is fixed forever at twenty-five-to-four. I'll let you in on a little secret.'

Nikolai stood up and leaned towards Mr Johnson.

'I have an allotment. Yes, I have. It is a little neglected, I'm afraid, but there is a shed and nobody goes there much.'

He went over to a chest of drawers in the corner of his room and drew from the top drawer a heavy black key.

'This is the key to the shed. I would like it very much if you would go there with me. There are two canvas chairs in the shed, quite comfortable. I have an old radio we could take up there and a Primus stove to cook the bacon on. What do you think? We don't even have to do any gardening. Do you like the idea?'

'I've always wanted an allotment,' said Mr Johnson eagerly. 'There is nothing like good, hard physical work to take your mind off things.'

'Or I know, I know, listen to this. We have adjoining houses in a gentle fold of a quiet valley in a green, fertile, rain-washed country, a land of small, independent producers bound together in a co-operative commonwealth of shared endeavour. Our labours over for the day, you stroll over to my house where we sit on the porch and share a bottle of Irish whiskey while we watch the sun say goodnight. The air is soon filled with sweet night fragrances and sheep bleat softly on distant hills. It is cooler now and I bring out blankets against the chill, though the whiskey does its warming work well. We talk companionably of many things until it is time for you to return to your own house, where we sit the following night, and so alternating through the year until the winter comes and we turn our backs on our porches and bank our fires high. Oh, I can almost taste those nights. And we could find such a place, Mr Johnson. I have work to finish here but afterwards I will be able to take some time off, even a few days, someone can cover for me in my absence, we could go away together or just stay at my house. It's not a stone affair but it is comfortable enough if you are not accustomed to grandeur. I love my job and I do take my responsibilities seriously but there comes a time in a man's career when he must step back from the fray and regroup. I need to forget about the cares of management, if only for a short while. We are tired, Mr Johnson. We need a holiday. We could take that holiday together.'

'Yes, you are right. My induction period is barely over but already I feel that I need a good break. Perhaps when I have found Bragby and you have completed the immediate tasks at hand and arranged for temporary cover, we will go away together.'

'I only hope that we don't wobble along the way. The soupy heat doesn't help. Sometimes I feel so hot I dream of cool green conservatories and soft whirring fans, or imagine myself sliding off hot rocks into cold mountain pools. I think of real winters, wrapped up in a greatcoat, scarf and hat, crunching across tram lines in the snow in a northern European capital on a bright January morning, the air so clean and high it catches your throat like a razor. These thoughts are unbearable.'

They had both finished their tea. Nikolai asked Mr Johnson if he wanted any more. He didn't. The thoughts were unbearable and Nikolai was right about the heat. They sat cupping their empty mugs for a while in companionable silence.

'I suppose that I had better get back to work,' Nikolai said sadly. 'I have very much enjoyed meeting and talking with you, Mr Johnson. In fact, a thought has just occurred to me. We are always in need of able and imaginative people down here. Why don't you join the team?'

'That is a very kind offer but I am not sure how well it would go down in conceptual initialisation. I have only recently become a concept engineer and I would like to prove myself in that area before I think about moving departments. I have got a project to complete, for a start. Things had taken a sudden turn for the worse for me there and I am not sure that my manager would consider letting me go. And I am not sure that I want to. Besides, I really should keep looking for Bragby. I need to talk to him before I do anything else. But thank you very much for the offer. I do appreciate it.'

Nikolai looked crestfallen at this. 'I understand,' he said. 'I don't suppose that I can offer you anything as glamorous as the role of concept engineer. But won't you at least think about it? Maybe in a few months' time you will feel differently.'

'Of course I will think about it. I am keen to get as rounded a set of experiences as possible. And I'm serious about our holiday. I promise I won't forget.'

At this he stood up and they shook hands. Mr Johnson was about to continue his journey when there appeared at the door from the antechamber a band of Nikolai's men. One by one they shuffled into the office, their heads cast down. One of them whispered something to Nikolai, who nodded and smiled.

'Mr Johnson, perhaps you would like to sit down again for a moment. The men have asked if they can sing to you before you go.'

'Well, I am honoured. Of course I'll sit down.'

Nikolai perched on the arm of the chair at Mr Johnson's side. 'They are going to sing you a song of home they have written specially for the occasion,' he whispered.

The men – there were seven of them altogether – assembled themselves into a line and slowly took up the strains of a song. Its meaning and structure were at first difficult to ascertain. The elderly employees wheezed and rasped like clotted plumbing and muffled bagpipes. But gradually a melody emerged, a wistful, rheumy air that spoke longingly of home comforts and peaceful days of leisure. Tears filled the men's eyes as they reached the climax of the song – a long, drawn out emphasis on the word 'home' – and dropped their heads once more. Mr Johnson felt his own eyes watering and heard Nikolai blowing his nose loudly. The men shuffled out of the office and the door to the antechamber closed behind them.

When they had composed themselves, Nikolai said: 'Well, if you must be going, you had better go now. But don't forget my offer.'

'I won't,' said Mr Johnson. 'Thank you for everything. There is just one more thing – you said something earlier about contacting Juniper about the Golden Clock.'

'What?'

'The Golden Clock – that business information system you mentioned.'

'Yes, of course – I'd quite forgotten. I'll ring him now.'

Nikolai went to a cupboard above and to the left of the sink and took out an old Bakelite telephone like the ones in the scriveners' office. He put it on the battered old table and methodically dialled a number. He stood for some moments listening intently into the earpiece before replacing the handset.

He shook his head solemnly. 'No, nothing.'

'Is Juniper not available?'

'There was no answer, I'm afraid.'

Mr Johnson saw that this telephone, like the ones in the office, wasn't connected to anything. A tuft of frayed wires protruded for an inch or so from its rear. He decided against mentioning this to Nikolai, who had put the telephone back in the cupboard.

'Is there another way of finding Juniper?'

'Not that I am aware of. I suggest you keep your eyes open while you are looking for this Bragby chap you have mentioned. I am not one hundred per cent sure which section Juniper works in. In any case, he is a very flexible character who is always on the move. He contacts us as when he needs to and usually through an intermediary. The Golden Clock takes up most of his time these days and that is something with a relevance to more than one department or function. I can hardly begin to tell you how things have changed since the introduction of the Golden Clock – it has altered working practices beyond all recognition. But you don't need me to do any more talking. It is time you went on your way.'

They shook hands at the threshold of Nikolai's office. Mr Johnson asked him which way he should go. Nikolai ruffled his hair in thought for a moment.

'Since you didn't come across Bragby on your way here, I suggest you go in the opposite direction and take a stairwell that will open up on your left a little way back down these stairs and follow that for some way until it bottoms out and runs on a level for a while past some other doors and stairwells. In truth, I am not really sure since I have been so absorbed here recently and things are changing all the time. But it is the best I can offer. You will come across something at some point. For the last time, goodbye.'

Mr Johnson left the office and the frosted door marked 'Back Hawarden' closed behind him. He walked back down the corridor, turning left at the bottom as Nikolai had suggested. Sure enough, a stairwell opened up. He followed this down for half-a-dozen flights and exited at the bottom through another door. He walked along a long, low passage lit by dim fluorescent strip bulbs. The floor was of rough concrete, the walls and ceiling clad in a hotchpotch of ceramic and polystyrene tiles. Mr Johnson pushed open the bars of a set of metal doors that blocked his progress two hundred yards or so along the passage. The doors slammed to instantly behind him. There were no handles on his side. Even if he didn't know for sure which direction he should go, one route at least had been cut off.

CHAPTER SIXTEEN
THE CLEANING FUNCTION

M<small>R</small> Johnson took a deep breath and walked away from the double doors. This section of the corridor was very warm and Mr Johnson had a feeling that he must be close to the heart of the building. There was a stillness in the air; not the stillness of inertia but a peaceful sense of resolution and certainty. He could hear the distant whirring of machinery and a fine, barely perceptible hum and drone of electricity cables.

It had become very hot indeed. Mr Johnson paused to catch his breath. After a few moments he felt better but he was thirsty. He supposed that this was the effect of Nikolai's biscuits, which were the last things he had eaten.

A little way ahead on the left of the corridor was a door bearing the sign, 'Cleaner's cupboard: Keep out'. He hoped that there would be a sink and a tap in the cupboard.

The door pushed open uncomplainingly. Inside it was pitch black. Mr Johnson felt along the wall for a light switch but could not detect one. The further in he went the less the light from the corridor followed him.

There was an overwhelming smell in the air of impregnated cloths and disinfectant; not altogether unpleasant but a little disconcerting in the dense gloom. It also served to make him even thirstier.

Conscious of avoiding buckets and mops, Mr Johnson edged gingerly deeper into the cupboard. Glancing over his shoulder, he saw that the door had swung to slowly so that there was now just the finest slither of light showing.

He was about to turn round and go back before the door closed completely (for all he knew it might operate according to the same principles as a fridge door and only open from the outside) when a voice (it was a man's) said: 'I suppose it's a sink you're after?'

'Yes, it is. Who are you?'

'Who are you?'

'My name is Mr Johnson. What's your name?'

'What is your business down here?' said the voice, ignoring him.

'I'm looking for Leonard Bragby. Has he been here?'

Again the voice chose not to answer him directly.

'I suppose you will be wanting a drink of water.'

'Yes, I was hoping to find a sink.'

'Then it's a good job I am here. You wouldn't want to drink from this sink, even if you managed to find it, which would be difficult without a light.'

'I wondered whether I had missed the light switch.'

'Oh no. There's no light switch in here. Not in this cupboard.'

'I'm sorry, I didn't get your name,' said Mr Johnson, extending his hand into the pitch.

'I know. I haven't told you what it is yet,' the voice came back. 'The water. Not fit to drink. Acqua non potabile.'

'Then can you tell me where I can get a drink? Water, a fizzy drink, anything. Is there a vending machine nearby?'

At this the voice laughed thinly. 'Not down here, I'm afraid. No drinking water. No windows. No lights.'

'But there were lights on in the corridor.'

'Oh yes. Lights on in the corridor all right.' The voice laughed again. 'But not in here.'

'Then I had better go back. I absolutely must get a drink.'

The voice altered, becoming strangely softer, even imploring.

'Don't go yet. I have a drink. Share my drink. Iced tea. My wife made it for me. Have you had iced tea? It's tea in the American style, with lemon juice and sugar. Delicious. Please try some.'

Mr Johnson heard a strong zip being unfastened followed by rustling sounds. A sharp pop indicated a metal cap being unscrewed from a glass bottle; then a sloshing of liquid into a cup.

'Here. Take this.'

Feeling his way into the space in front of him, Mr Johnson's fingers closed around a tin cup; not before they had touched the fingertips of the other's hand, however, which was hurriedly withdrawn.

Mr Johnson sipped quickly from the cup. The tea was indeed delicious. It was tangy, cool and refreshing, and the taste of it carried Mr Johnson, deep in the dark cleaner's cupboard, away across wide grey seas to distant strands, to a frame-house on a broad, sea-nibbled plot, a strong, weathered house set amidst a tangle of bleached, marginal scrub that looked out over the turbulent ocean and back inland to ordered fields and little towns breathing quietly in the gloaming. Wearing deck shoes, cotton trousers and a heavy sweater against the early evening cool, he sat hand in hand with his girl on battered old chairs on the porch watching tankers inching across the horizon, and sipped from a mug of iced tea, American style. He needed a holiday. For a moment, the thought was unbearable.

A heavy silence settled on the cupboard. 'Would you like some more?'

whispered the voice.

'Yes please,' Mr Johnson sniffed, and held the cup out into the darkness. He was trying his hardest not to cry. In a smooth movement the cup was taken from him, filled and returned; again, the other's hand was retracted hurriedly.

This time, Mr Johnson sipped more thoughtfully. He was beginning to feel revived.

'I don't suppose you've got anything to eat, have you?' he asked at length. 'All I have had recently are some biscuits. I've still got a long way to go.'

He thought he heard the other snort and he immediately regretted having asked. He was about to apologise when to his amazement another voice said: 'For heaven's sake, Bernard, give the man a sandwich. He must be famished.' It was unmistakably the voice of a woman.

'All right, all right,' said Bernard.

'I'm very sorry. You must think I'm a terrible hostess,' the woman said. 'You greedy beggar,' she shouted suddenly. 'You'd sit there on your pile of sandwiches and let this poor man starve to death in front of you. I am sorry,' she said, addressing her remarks to Mr Johnson once more. 'I always make him more than he needs, anyway. I'm soft like that. Half the time I end up throwing them away at the end of the day. What did you say your name was? Mr Johnson? I'm very sorry, Mr Johnson. That's it, Bernard, you give Mr Johnson a sandwich now.'

A soft, fat sandwich materialised in his right hand. He fell upon it gratefully. It was extremely tasty – cheese and pickle.

'Is that better, Mr Johnson?' He spluttered an acknowledgement. 'Honestly, Bernard, you ought to be ashamed of yourself,' she said, but her voice was more tender than before. 'And why are we still in the dark? We might not have any electric lights but we've got plenty of candles. Light some candles, Bernard. I'm not having Mr Johnson standing around in the dark a minute longer.'

Bernard muttered and commenced a rummaging activity. After a few moments a single tiny candle tongue flared up; then another and another. Slowly the red, warm light brought forth the suggestion of shapes, at first shadowy and vague, then brighter and bolder. Finally, Mr Johnson was able to see that shelves lined the walls on either side, that the ceiling was quite high for a cupboard and that his interlocutors were a man and a woman in their fifties both wearing peaked caps, blue overalls and industrial footwear. They were seated on plastic office chairs; a few feet behind them was the rear wall in which was another door. At Bernard's feet was a scuffed vinyl sports bag from which, presumably, he had brought forth the bottle of iced tea.

'Now, that's much cosier,' said the woman. Although he wasn't sure whether it was still appropriate to do so, Mr Johnson stepped forward and extended his right hand.

'As I said, Mr Johnson.'

'Jackie, pleased to meet you,' said the woman, who had a strong grip. Bernard nodded but didn't offer his hand. 'What am I thinking of? Bernard, give Mr Johnson your chair.'

Muttering again, Bernard got up and shuffled towards the door in the rear wall.

'It's no trouble, I don't mind standing,' said Mr Johnson. 'I really should be getting along soon, anyway.' But Jackie wouldn't hear of it, and Mr Johnson pulled Bernard's chair forward and sat down facing Jackie. Bernard shuffled back with a low stool for himself.

'So. Mr Johnson. Relatively new here. Which department do you work in, Mr Johnson?'

'Conceptual initialisation. It's a new function, as a matter of fact. I am relatively new here, too.'

'I see. And what is your job exactly?'

'I am a concept engineer.'

'A concept engineer? That sounds very important. And what does a concept engineer do?'

Although Jackie's style was rather interrogative, it was underpinned by an essential warmth and humanity and Mr Johnson found himself relaxing in her company. Bernard had fallen quiet but he had stopped scowling, at least, and Mr Johnson embarked on an account of his career to date, including his experiences in the presentation suite, the project development work on the Big Sell, the drama over the induction notes, his interview with the personnel manager, the Bragby question, the visit to Nikolai's scriveners and the mystery concerning Juniper. He took pains to make reference to his role in relation to the wider activities of the conceptual initialisation department and, in turn, its dynamic purpose within the organisation as a whole. When Mr Johnson had finished, he sat back and smiled. He felt all talked out.

'That's all very interesting, Mr Johnson, but I'm still not sure that I understand exactly what it is you do. This concept engineer business – I don't want to sound rude, but it sounds a bit vague. Could you explain in more detail?'

Mr Johnson yawned. The candles were burning low; his head felt thick and soupy. 'I am sorry if I didn't make it clear,' he said. 'Let me put it this way. The overall strategic profile of the company is informed by the activities of a number of key functions.' He yawned more heavily than before. 'The synergy achieved by the interaction of these functions provides the motor, the organisational glue, if you will, for the company's core business.' The air was smoky and chemical-ridden. Only one candle still burned; slowly it guttered and expired. It was dark again. A silent blanket fell upon them. They sat in this way for some time. Mr Johnson's head nodded on his chest. He dropped off to sleep reluctantly. When he woke it was still quiet save for Bernard and Jackie's steady up-and-down breathing, which was arrhythmic.

Slowly he eased himself up from the seat and was about to turn round and go back to the main corridor when Bernard said sharply: 'Where are you going?'

Mr Johnson sat down again quickly. 'I was thinking about getting off. I must find Bragby before it's too late.'

'You won't find him that way,' said Bernard, and lapsed into silence. After some time, Mr Johnson felt thirsty again. 'I don't suppose you have any more tea?' he asked.

'You don't want much, do you?' retorted Bernard, but he rummaged again and handed Mr Johnson a glass jar. Mr Johnson helped himself. Very cautiously he turned his head round and saw that if anything the chink of light had grown even slighter and seemed further away. He handed the jar back to Bernard, who muttered as he accepted it.

'No lights down here,' he said, apparently unprompted. 'Nothing down here save what you can scavenge. No drinking water. No natural light. No visitors. Nothing.'

Mr Johnson didn't know what to say.

'Make the most of that drink,' said Bernard. 'There's none left after it's finished.' He laughed dryly. 'Just the two of us here with our cloths and bin bags.'

'While I'm here,' said Mr Johnson, keen to move conversation on, 'do you have any idea where I might find Leonard Bragby. I'm afraid that I keep drawing a blank everywhere I go.'

Bernard said nothing.

'Is he known to you?' asked Mr Johnson.

'You won't find him that way,' said Bernard after a moment or two.

'Which way?'

'Back that way.' Sitting forward in his chair, Mr Johnson became suddenly animated.

'Then I will find him the other way? Is that what you're saying?'

'Don't know.'

Mr Johnson sat back, deflated.

'You can try the other way, though.'

He sat up again. 'Where does it go to?'

'Nowhere much. But you can try it anyway.'

'When can I go there?'

'Soon.'

They both fell quiet again and Mr Johnson felt his eyes smart and his head swim. It had become oppressively hot in the cupboard. At length, Mr Johnson asked if it would possible to have some light. Bernard didn't answer at first but when pressed merely kept repeating 'no lights down here'. Then from out of the darkness Mr Johnson heard Jackie's voice once again. He had almost forgotten that she was there.

'For heaven's sake you old skinflint, light some more candles. I'm not having Mr Johnson sitting in the dark for a moment longer. I'm sorry, Mr Johnson. He'd sit in the dark at his own funeral, that one.'

Bernard, muttering, made a great deal of noise opening boxes and ransacking bags before another three candles were lit.

'Now that's much better,' said Jackie. 'All nice and snug. We can get a good fug up.'

She took a pouch of rolling tobacco and a packet of cigarette papers from a side pocket and expertly rolled a perilously thin cigarette which she offered first to Mr Johnson, who declined, and then to Bernard, who didn't. Then she rolled another for herself. In next to no time she had smoked it all; Bernard took longer with his.

'I don't want to press you, Mr Johnson,' she said, putting on a pair of glasses, 'but there are still a few things I need clarifying. This business about concept engineering, for one. You will have to explain it to me in more detail.'

Patiently, Mr Johnson went over the bare bones of his job, the department and its place within the organisation, his objectives and long-term ambitions, the central underpinning role of the Five Synergetic Elements, and the strategic importance of the Big Sell. He was pleased with the clarity he brought to bear on these difficult questions. Jackie had the look of someone for whom the pieces of a particularly fiendish jigsaw were finally falling into place and even Bernard had stopped muttering, though he was grinding his teeth furiously, and was at least looking in Mr Johnson's direction from time to time. But just as he completed his exposition, Jackie took her glasses off and scratched her head.

'As I said before, it all sounds very important. I am also beginning to see some of the connections between the different departments. But I am still a bit stuck on one point. Perhaps you could take the trouble to explain it to me again. What is it you actually do?'

Mr Johnson sighed. 'I'm sorry if I haven't been one hundred per cent clear,' he said. 'After all, I am still relatively new. I am very much in a learning curve at the moment.' An idea struck him. 'I tell you what. Rather than describing everything to you, why don't I draw it?'

He stood up. 'Do you have any paper? No? Not to worry. I'll open a cloth up. You don't mind? A pen.'

He felt in his pockets but he didn't have a pen about him. 'Do you have one? No? Not to worry. This cleaning fluid will do.'

Mr Johnson cleared a space on the floor and knelt down close to the light of one of the candles. With a smooth flow of fluid onto the cloth, he artfully contrived a schematic representation of the main activities of the conceptual initialisation department and the nature and extent of his own responsibilities, giving particular emphasis to the question of inputs, throughputs and outputs. He checked it against the impressionistic notes in his pocket. Compared to what he had produced on the cloth, they were perhaps as bad as Mark Mitchell had said. The diagram on the cloth, on the other hand, really did seem an accurate reflection of both the extent of his individual remit and the wider work and structure of the conceptual initialisation department. The presence of the Five Synergetic Elements was palpable. When he was finished he blew gently over the surface of the cloth, stood up slowly, and stepped back.

Jackie laughed. 'You'll not dry it that quickly,' she said. 'I would leave it there for a bit if I were you. Yes, that's very good,' she said, in response to Mr Johnson's raised eyebrows. 'Much clearer. Have you had a look at this?' she asked Bernard.

Bernard grunted and took a sip from his tin cup. 'I'll keep this when it has dried, if you don't mind,' Jackie said. 'It might come in useful when people ask me what's going on. You should pay more attention to things like this,' she shouted at Bernard, who turned away on his stool and pulled his cap over his eyes. 'He never listens to me, Mr Johnson. I can't tell you what a relief it is to have someone to talk to. I always take an interest in what's going on but he's not bothered. Sitting there with his cap over his eyes.' Bernard muttered again. 'You heard. Sitting there with your cap over your eyes. Wouldn't think we had a visitor to look at him, oh no.'

'I don't want to cause any trouble,' said Mr Johnson. 'In fact, I really should be getting off. Bernard said something about going the other way.'

'You stay where you are, Mr Johnson,' said Jackie quickly. 'We haven't had pudding yet. Bernard, give Mr Johnson a piece of that cake.'

Bernard sighed and felt around in the sportsbag, pulling out a hunk of brown sugar-crusted cake wrapped in clingfilm.

'Go on, Mr Meanbags, give it to Mr Johnson. No, it's not a problem, he's already had plenty. Filling his face like that, he ought to be ashamed.'

Mr Johnson was still hungry and he tore into the cake. It was delicious, but he ate too much and quickly became thirsty again. His mouth full of cakey mucus, he asked whether there was any more drink available. Jackie didn't say anything and Bernard looked away again. Mr Johnson regretted eating the cake and wished that he had been more sparing with the tea. It seemed impolite to ask again. Silence returned. In the light of the failing candles he saw that his lap was covered in crumbs. Instinctively he brushed them to the floor, at which Jackie, a horrified expression on her face, leapt up, grabbed a pan and brush, and swept them up.

'I'm terribly sorry. I wasn't thinking,' said Mr Johnson, reddening.

'It doesn't matter now,' said Jackie. Bernard glared at him. 'I expect you're the sort who scatters paper clips willy-nilly, aren't you?' said Jackie, though she didn't sound cross.

'I try not to,' answered Mr Johnson sheepishly.

'It's all right, I understand. They do get everywhere. I'm sure there are worse than you around.'

Jackie smiled maternally and sat back down. The candles expired in quick succession; the last to go sustained a brave red pinprick for a short while before the cupboard became utterly dark again. Jackie and Bernard breathed in soft counterpoint. Mr Johnson shifted his feet uneasily; his left shoe felt something irregular underfoot. He reached down and felt the cloth on which he had drawn the diagram. His fingers recoiled from the cleaning fluid, which was still wet. He didn't want to fall asleep again but under the circumstances it was hard not to. Once more his head lolled and his chin touched his chest. In many ways it was quite snug in there, even without any light. Sleep overtook him. Dreams rushed in quickly, odd, lumpy dreams of no discernible purpose, dreams fed on warm deep darkness and rich chemical smells.

When he woke, Jackie and Bernard's breathing had become more shallow and raspy. Mr Johnson was now extremely thirsty but felt much clearer in the head. There was only one thing he could do. He painstakingly eased himself out of his chair and inched forward. Although he couldn't see his hand in front of his face, he knew roughly where Bernard and Jackie were sitting and guessed that he would be able to steer a narrow but clear course between them. But just as he was about to pass what he imagined was Bernard's right foot, he tripped on something in front of him and fell awkwardly. Putting his hands out to steady himself, he succeeded only in leaning heavily on Bernard.

'I don't know what you're up to,' said Bernard, who didn't sound in the least surprised. 'You won't find anything that way.'

'I'm sorry,' said Mr Johnson firmly, 'but I am very thirsty and I must be on my way. You have both been very kind but it is time I said my goodbyes.'

Bernard said nothing, so Mr Johnson, beginning to feel a little foolish standing next to him, bent down to remove the obstacle. It was the vinyl sportsbag, which Bernard must have put there on purpose when Mr Johnson had fallen asleep. Before that it had been at his feet.

'You can put that down right away,' snapped Bernard, and Mr Johnson did, though not before he felt inside it and discovered another jar, full by the feel of it. Swiftly, he unscrewed the cap, sniffed it to be sure of its identity, and swigged down great grateful gulps. Sure enough, it was more iced tea. Bernard was out of his seat in an instant but by the time he wrested it from Mr Johnson's grasp, over half of the jar had been consumed. Curiously, Bernard didn't press the point but sat down quietly. When he next spoke, his voice sounded tired and defeated.

Mr Johnson tried to get some more information from him about where the other way led to but Bernard had merely taken up his litany of discontent once again.

'No lights down here. No windows neither. Nothing for the likes of us. Just the two of us down here with our cloths and bin liners. Spring, summer, autumn, winter. Cloths and bags, fluid and pads. Nothing. No vending machines. Acqua non potabile. No natural light,' and on and on, chuntering away to himself in the dark. The effect was quite hypnotic and soon Mr Johnson felt gritty eyed again. He fought sleep for a few moments but succumbed finally. When he woke up the cupboard was fiendishly hot. His forehead was slick and his shirt clung to his back.

'Good heavens, it's hot in here,' he said automatically. There was no answer, but a short while later he heard Jackie's voice once more.

'For the love of Adam, Bernard, light some more candles. Whatever will Mr Johnson think of us?'

Muttering, Bernard scrabbled about in his bag but before he managed to produce another set of candles, a new voice said: 'Here you are. What are you doing sitting in the dark like this?' and to Mr Johnson's astonishment the cupboard was suddenly flooded with electric light.

It turned out that there was a long fluorescent strip light behind him, although the switch was at the other end of the cupboard. At this end stood a young woman, in her early twenties by the look of it, also dressed in blue overalls and industrial footwear but wearing a red scarf on her head instead of a peaked cap. With her arrival and the sudden, unexpected illumination of the room, Jackie and Bernard seemed diminished and not a little shamefaced.

'I see you have a visitor. Aren't you going to introduce me?' said the young woman.

Jackie got up half-heartedly. 'Mr Johnson, this is our daughter Bernadette, Bernadette, this is Mr Johnson,' she said hurriedly, and sat down again.

'I don't know,' said Bernadette, 'I go away for a few hours and what happens? The house in darkness, cloths all over the floor, empty bottles everywhere. What on earth have you been doing?'

'Actually,' volunteered Mr Johnson, 'I should take some of the blame for the mess. I was trying to explain about my job.'

'You don't have to explain yourself, Mr Johnson. I know what these two are like,' Bernadette said, laughing. She whisked round quickly and in no time the cupboard was nice and tidy. 'Have they offered you anything to eat and drink?'

'We've given him some sandwiches and a piece of cake,' mumbled Jackie.

'Oh yes, they've been very generous, thank you,' confirmed Mr Johnson. 'I am rather thirsty, though. It does seem to be very hot in here.'

'Yes, the heating always comes on at this time. I'll turn the thermostat down. It's only on for the benefit of their old bones. I much prefer it cooler. What would you like to drink. Tea? Coffee? Something stronger?'

'Actually, a glass of water would be ideal but I don't want you to go to the trouble of boiling it up just for me.'

'Boiling it up? Why on earth should I have to do that?'

'I thought the water wasn't drinkable down here.'

'Who told you...? Oh, I see. Yes, very funny, Dad. Acqua non potabile, was it? Don't listen to him. The water down here is lovely.'

Removing a mop bucket from the sink, she poured Mr Johnson a tall glass of water which he drank in one go, then another and another.

'That's better,' he said, drying his mouth. 'Thank you.'

Bernadette had a frank and open face and Mr Johnson felt immediately that he could rely upon her to provide him with clear and unambiguous directions to continue his journey.

'I'm looking for Leonard Bragby but I haven't had much luck in tracking him down. Do you know anything about him?'

Bernadette scratched underneath her scarf. 'Bragby? Name's not familiar. I am afraid I see a lot of people come and go and in our job we don't always get introduced. Which department is he in?'

'That's the trouble. He used to be in straight sales and then conceptual initialisation but apparently he's moved around a lot since then. It is important that I find him, though, as I have some questions that only he can provide answers to.'

'Where have you looked so far?'

'Where haven't I looked, you mean,' laughed Mr Johnson. 'I've been up and down and side to side and even to Back Hawarden but there is neither sight nor scent of him. I was heading down the corridor when I saw the cupboard and stopped for a drink. But for all I know I might have been down that corridor already.'

'Yes, it's quite possible. A lot of these corridors look the same. You can try going up the back stairs,' offered Bernadette. 'It's unlikely that you will have been up there yet.'

'Bernard mentioned that way. Where does it lead to?'

'Plant stuff mainly but there are service doors to other levels. You'll need a guide, though.'

'Oh dear,' said Mr Johnson, his face dropping. 'Where will I find such a person?'

'Right here!' said Bernadette brightly. 'I'll be coming with you. I know these staircases intimately and I'll help prevent you from taking any wrong turnings.'

Mr Johnson was so grateful that he seized Bernadette's hand and pumped it vigorously.

'When can we start?' he said excitedly.

'Soon but not immediately. I have had a busy day and need a rest. I have also got some paperwork to do. In fact, you could help me with it, if you don't mind. I'd appreciate your input.'

She took off her scarf and shook down a curtain of dark black hair. Jackie came up with the cloth that Mr Johnson had marked and laid it on the draining board.

'Mr Johnson drew this for me,' she explained, and returned to her chair.

'I'll have a good look at that later,' Bernadette said to Mr Johnson. 'If you can bear with me while I get a bite to eat and don't mind giving me a hand with some work, we'll be off in no time. Will you join us for tea?'

'Thank you, but the sandwich and cake really filled me up. But you carry on.'

Mr Johnson sat back down on the chair while Bernadette opened and poured three tins of stew into a pan on a Primus stove. She stirred the contents of the pan slowly and when it had heated through decanted it into three white enamel bowls. She opened a camp stool up and sat down with

Jackie, Bernard and Mr Johnson. Jackie asked her how her day had been. Bernardette said that she had been extremely busy. Jackie said that she and Bernard had been rushed of their feet too. Mr Johnson thought about the time he had spent with them sitting in the dark but decided not to say anything. When they had all finished their stew, Bernadette cleared up and put the Primus stove away. She seemed to take on a lot of responsibility in the cupboard. Jackie rolled more cigarettes for her and Bernard and while they puffed away, Bernadette beckoned Mr Johnson to the end of the cupboard.

'I have a little cubby-hole through here,' she said quietly, removing a large cardboard box from one of the shelves. 'Mum and Dad don't know about it, so keep quiet.'

She climbed on to the shelf and through a small aperture that opened into a compact little room. Mr Johnson followed her and when they were both inside she turned round, leaned forward and lifted the box back onto the shelf.

'That's better – nice and private,' she said. 'It is important to have somewhere quiet to work.' The room was furnished with two office chairs and a desk on which sat a plastic stack tray and a desk tidy. There was no computer equipment as far as Mr Johnson could see. The room also had a low camp bed in it.

'When I'm working late, I like to sleep in here,' said Bernadette, seeing that Mr Johnson was looking at the bed. He felt suddenly embarrassed.

'You seem to have a very busy job.'

'I am busy. The cleaning is one thing but the paperwork is quite another. And then there is Mum and Dad to think of. They are both still of working age but they are not as young as they used to be. I find that I am doing more housework than I would like. I am afraid that it is getting to that stage where I am almost a parent to them, not the other way round. But I am not complaining – I don't have the time to.'

They sat down at the desk.

'I'd like you cast your expert eye over these, Mr Johnson,' said Bernadette, laying a large sheet of paper on the desk. 'I have been asked to audit the organisation's cleaning function and make some recommendations for efficiency savings and general improvements to working practices. I am happy on the whole with what I have come up with it but there is nothing like an objective view. It is the question of cost centres that I am finding particularly problematic.'

Bernadette highlighted a corner of the page with a fluorescent marker pen. 'Look at this, Mr Johnson. I've intimated that the cleaning function as a whole can be regarded as a cost centre in its own right but I am wondering whether I shouldn't break this down into a series of micro-cost centres consisting of myself, Mum and Dad. You see, the audit I undertook established that although our job descriptions are broadly the same, in practice our roles are rather different. None of us has formal responsibility for financial management yet responsibility seems to have defaulted to me. On the other hand, each of us makes demands upon the resource allocation for the cleaning function – I am thinking in terms of physical materials and time spent on jobs – and can properly be regarded as a buyer and a spender, each with our own self-regulated autonomy in terms of expenditure. Given that there are variances between the levels of resource diminishment within the cleaning function and that the day-to-day vagaries of the job tend to inhibit the capacity for accurate forecasting, I am increasingly inclined to devolve financial responsibility to individual members of staff rather than formalise it at a macro level. But I would be very interested to know what you think, Mr Johnson.'

Mr Johnson considered the diagrams and notes that Bernadette had produced.

'I should have brought my cloth with me. The Five Synergetic Elements are a very good model for this sort of work. Shall I go back and get it?'

'No, you might wake Mum and Dad up. They usually nod off after their tea. I'll look at it later. But really, what do you think?'

'I think that you are probably quite right to want to rationalise the processes down to the most basic level. My own experience in conceptual initialisation taught me that you cannot devolve autonomy enough, provided of course that there is a rational superstructure. On the other hand, my view is bound to be subjective – and I am not actually that experienced in such matters yet. Figure work isn't one of my strengths. Also, I have been identified as being an employee with an essentially individualistic approach to work, so perhaps I am bound to be in favour of a process that delegates responsibility to a micro-unit level. But the methodology looks good. I think that any process predicated on the principle of individual empowerment is axiomatically sound.'

'Thank you. I trust your judgement, Mr Johnson.'

A stray wisp of black hair brushed his face; they had moved quite near to each other over the paper.

'Needless to say, Mum and Dad can only go so far with this sort of thing. Mum is not too bad – she tries to keep abreast of what is going on. I think Dad has just given up. But I don't blame him.'

'You seem to have quite a developed managerial role,' said Mr Johnson. 'How did that come about?'

'It just happened, really. I was always conscious of looking for ways of improving the way we do things in the cleaning function. A couple of years ago I instituted a time and motion study and sent my findings upstairs. I think they were well received – suggestions for further audits came back and since then I have had to balance a hands-on cleaning role with an increasingly demanding managerial profile. To be honest with you, what I am trying to do now is delegate as much as I can. If I can empower Mum and Dad, maybe my own workload will ease a little – though experience would suggest otherwise. I suppose I have made a rod for my own back. But I am not complaining – I relish a challenge. Anyway, listen to me carrying on with myself – how are things in your line of work?'

Mr Johnson explained a little about his career and experiences to date and repeated what he had told Jackie about the role of the concept engineer. Unlike her mother, Bernadette seemed to grasp instantly what Mr Johnson was telling her.

'I am certainly seeing all aspects of the company's activities,' Mr Johnson said.

'And now you are looking for this Leonard Bragby. Is that part of your induction too?'

'Not formally, though I still haven't been given an induction programme as such so it might as well be. No, there a few things I need to clarify with him. Our career paths have some remarkable parallels, by all accounts. You said you haven't come across him.'

'No, but that doesn't mean a great deal. I hadn't heard of you, either, before you turned up.'

'Where are you going to take me?'

'On and on a bit further, into some areas that only the cleaners know of,' said Bernadette mysteriously. Then she laughed. 'You'll need a guide for some of the way, at least. Once you are though the plant stuff you should be back in more normal environments. But as for who works where and in what departments, I couldn't begin to help you. We are rather absorbed in our own sphere of work, I'm afraid.'

'Have you heard of Juniper and the Golden Clock?'

'Can't help you there, either. Is that another new department?'

'I don't think so. It's an information system of some sort.'

'Sounds interesting. It's probably a new sort of internet, or perhaps an intranet. I had a go on an internet once. I would be more sure if we had a connection down here. I have been on to the systems manager about it for ages. If you find out more about this Golden Clock, be sure to let me know.'

'I certainly will.'

Bernadette sat back in her chair.

'Well, one part of me is ready for bed. The other is keen to press on. Are you ready to go?'

Mr Johnson said he was. He felt quite tired again but wasn't sure how the sleeping arrangements would work out and thought it better to keep moving. They climbed out of the cubby hole and replaced the box. Sure enough, Bernard and Jackie were asleep again, although the overhead light was still on.

Bernadette whispered: 'We'll leave them be. No point in disturbing them.'

'Make sure you thank them for their hospitality on my behalf,' said Mr Johnson. 'The sandwiches and cake were delicious.'

'I will,' whispered Bernadette, and turned the light off.

She quietly opened the door at the back of the cupboard and they stepped into a narrow space at the foot of a long flight of stairs. Bernadette took a pad of yellow message notes from her pocket. 'The first part of the journey is quite straightforward but it gets complicated later on. After a certain point, we'll lay down these adhesive message pads at intervals in case you need to find your way back on your own later. Follow me now.'

They set off up the stairs. At first, as Bernadette had promised, the way was clear and memorable. But after ten minutes or so of gradual ascent, the stairs narrowed and finally gave out at a small chamber in which was fixed a metal ladder. This they climbed for about twenty feet and when they reached a narrow landing that they could only enter by lying on their sides, Bernadette placed down the first of her yellow markers.

'From this point on the going gets a little rough. You will need to keep your wits about you.'

They crawled along through a wide, low room that seemed like nothing more than a space between floors. Bernadette had taken a torch from her pocket and lit their way with it. There was no other illumination. Thick clusters of cable were fixed roughly to joists. The floor was thick with dust and wood shavings. Suddenly, Bernadette stopped and opened a panel in the floor.

'Careful here,' she said. 'We are going to clamber down onto the next floor.'

She swung agilely and dropped through the gloom to the floor below. Mr Johnson followed her gingerly; there was a drop of about two feet. When he was on the floor he dusted the shavings from his suit. Bernadette fixed another yellow note to the floor beneath the open trap. 'I will leave it open after I've come back,' she said.

She led him along a wide, dim corridor along which ran bulky metal ducts and old iron pipes. Bernadette set quite a pace and Mr Johnson marvelled at her energy. He wondered whether she ever slept.

'Where are we now, exactly?' he asked her.

'We are on one of the old cleaners' roads. It is deserted now but at one time, when there were more cleaners employed here, this road would be full of cleaners going to and from work at all hours of the day and night. At one time they even had their own bus service in here – look, there's one of the old stops.'

She gestured to the left and Mr Johnson saw that the wall at this point was recessed and contained a bench. Above the recess was fixed a faded sign reading 'Fare Stage'.

'No time to stand and stare, Mr Johnson. There is still some way to go.'

Placing yellow notes at regular intervals, Bernadette led Mr Johnson on deeper and deeper into a maze of tunnels and corridors, up and down ladders and narrow flights of stairs. He was glad that she had come with him. There was no way that he would have been able to navigate by himself. They passed through gloomy tunnels and beneath arches of crumbling brick and old ironwork. The further they went on the hotter it got. They paused more frequently and each time they went on again Mr Johnson found himself lagging further behind Bernadette. Finally, as they stepped through a low doorway into another dim chamber, he said: 'Bernadette, I really must sit down for a bit. I'm exhausted.'

She turned round and came back to him. 'I'm sorry,' she said. 'Once I get going, I simply don't stop. Mum and Dad are always trying to get me to slow down. Mum says that I will meet myself coming back if I'm not careful.'

They both sat down with their backs to the wall. Bernadette took a flask from her pocket and handed it to Mr Johnson; it was more iced tea in the American style. They passed each other the flask until the tea was finished.

'Where are we now?'

'We're still in the old cleaners' realm. No one comes down here anymore. Perhaps you can see why I have been laying a trail in case you have to find your way back. It's a real old maze. I don't come here much myself if I can help it.'

'I have never seen so much space given over to a cleaning function before,' said Mr Johnson. 'In most organisations there is little more than a couple of cupboards and a sink. How did the cleaning function here become so developed?'

Bernadette stretched her legs out in front of her. 'It just sort of grew over time. The cleaners used to be a much more powerful body than they are today. All these roads and tunnels and chambers, though they are now decrepit and abandoned, once contained houses, leisure centres, canteens and shops. There was practically a whole city down here at one time – at least, that's what Mum and Dad say. I've sometimes wondered whether they are just being nostalgic.'

'What happened to it all?'

'I am not really sure. People retired, died, moved on. The younger generation didn't want to carry on the trade of their parents – the usual reasons. I am quite unusual – I never had any doubt that I would follow Mum and Dad into the cleaning business. Another reason, of course, has been major structural changes to the organisation. Years ago, it seems, there was no question that the cleaning function should enjoy maximum resourcing and the cleaners benefit from the company's overall prosperity. That is why the cleaners had so many excellent facilities. Although I doubt whether it was really the golden age that Mum and Dad talk about, there is no denying that the cleaners down here had access to the best facilities available at the time – subsidised food and transport, new uniforms every month, coupon clubs, film shows, healthcare. There was even a little hospital round here somewhere. Then thinking changed. The cleaning function began to be pared down. New management and accounting techniques were brought to bear upon them. When the company entered a lean period, as all companies must, savings had to be made and axes were swung. In time, the very idea that the cleaners should inhabit their own city within the company and enjoy a social welfare system on the Scandinavian model began to seem, in certain quarters, preposterous. Now that whole world has vanished.'

She rose suddenly.

'Come and look at this, Mr Johnson,' she said, and went towards the middle of the chamber. She raised her torch and played its light upon the wall opposite them. 'Look – can you see the pictures?'

Mr Johnson strained his eyes. At first he could detect nothing but shaded depths of brick but gradually he could pick out faint images and shapes. Bernadette handed him the torch and he walked closer to the wall. Slowly moving the torch over the length of the wall, he saw that it bore a mural depicting cleaners in various heroic attitudes of work and leisure. Some carried mops and brooms over their shoulders, others were pushing vacuum cleaners, others babies in buggies. All were dressed in the same fashion as Bernard and Jackie, even the children. The artist had cleverly constructed the mural so that interior and exterior scenes blended seamlessly into one another. Where at one point a party of cleaners at rest lounged and smoked cigarettes in front of a row of tower blocks, in an adjacent scene a cleaner scrubbed intently away at a desk in an office, his colleague standing by with the cleaning materials. There were no awkward disjunctions; the whole series of scenes imparted a strong sense of cohesion and solidity.

Mr Johnson felt Bernadette at his shoulder. 'Remarkable, aren't they?' she said. 'I must admit that until I came across these paintings I had always taken Mum and Dad's stories with a pinch of salt.'

'It is such a shame that this whole world has disappeared,' said Mr Johnson. 'Don't you think so?'

'Yes and no,' Bernadette said. 'Subjectively speaking, of course – the cleaners enjoyed an almost enviable existence. But objectively and from a business point of view, I think that their way of life was unsustainable – though I would never say as much to Mum and Dad. Take this scene of the two cleaners in the office. That is overmanning pure and simple. You couldn't justify employing a cleaner to stand by holding the cleaning materials nowadays. And that wasn't the worst of it, by all accounts. Apparently there were at least three people employed at one time to count the number of bristles on all the brooms and sweeping brushes. Yes, I know, it sounds fantastic, doesn't it? The situation couldn't persist indefinitely. Efficiency savings had to be made. And do you know, Mr Johnson, although I shouldn't say so, I think that was right. The old way was very paternalistic and change resistant. Most of the cleaners didn't enjoy any variety in their work. If you were a sweeper, you swept; a mopper, you mopped; a bin emptier, you emptied bins. How things have changed. Although I sometimes think that there aren't enough hours in the day to do everything I need to do, I certainly can't complain about routine. Under the old system, there is no way that I would have been entrusted with the responsibility for working on the cost centre question, for example. And the more I look into these matters, the more convinced I am that the cleaning function has to keep pace with the macro rhythm of the organisation. If other functions must embrace organisational change, so must we. Does that sound clinical, Mr Johnson? I don't mean it to. I love Mum and Dad and will always do my best to ensure that they are fed and watered, have plenty of rolling tobacco, and don't have to work too hard. But I am conscious that one day I may have to take them to one side in the cupboard and tell them that there is no longer a role for them here. I hope that that day doesn't come but given the overall history of the cleaning function in relation to the broader developments that have taken place in the organisation, I wouldn't bet against it. Of course, I am telling you all this in confidence. Please don't ever repeat any of it to Mum and Dad. You can imagine how difficult it is combining the roles of daughter and manager. Well, I have carried on with myself, haven't I?'

She smiled at Mr Johnson and he smiled back at her. She lowered the torch and he felt out and touched her right hand. In the instant before she pulled it away her fingers closed round his.

'I think we had better move on now,' Bernadette said hoarsely. 'Are you fully rested?'

'Yes. I'm much better now.'

After the incident in the chamber, Mr Johnson kept his own counsel for the rest of their journey together. There was much less of a distance to cover after the break than before it. They went through more tunnels and corridors and finally descended a deep spiral staircase that ended at a small platform that looked down into a larger, lighter room.

'We are now at the border of the old cleaners' realm,' said Bernadette. 'This is where we must say goodbye.' She let out a low whistle and in a moment a small man appeared below them, crouching.

'This man will take you on the next stage of your journey. I don't think you can be too far now from where you want to be.'

'Do you really have to leave me?' asked Mr Johnson. He had become very comfortable in Bernadette's company and was sorry to have to say goodbye. 'Can I see you again?'

Bernadette took his hand and smiled. 'I am afraid we must part, though hopefully not forever. We both have important work to do and I don't think that we should blur any boundaries between the personal and the professional. But I have really enjoyed the time we have spent together.'

They shook hands warmly. Mr Johnson bent to kiss her cheek but she moved away and he banged his nose on her right ear. He coughed and looked away. Bernadette gave Mr Johnson the remainder of the yellow message pads and unfastened a rope ladder that was fixed at the edge of the shelf. Mr Johnson climbed down it and looked back up at her and waved.

'Take great care,' Bernadette cried from the shelf. 'Don't forget to mark your way.'

'Goodbye – and thank you once again,' shouted Mr Johnson.

'Goodbye,' Bernadette replied, and disappeared. For a moment, he was tempted to follow her. But he turned instead to face the crouching man who was poised on all fours at his feet, waiting, silent, staring. And looking back, he saw that Bernadette had drawn the rope ladder up.

CHAPTER SEVENTEEN
JUNIPER

Mr Johnson was in a wide and high brick chamber into which, from some unseen source, thin beams of dusty light penetrated at intervals. The floor was made from rough concrete and was strewn with rubble – old cardboard cable reels, dirty, warped plastic ice cream containers and collapsed box files.

'Hello, my name is Mr Johnson,' said Mr Johnson, extending his hand. His new companion didn't take it but only grunted and motioned across the chamber to a dim aperture on its far side. He sprang on to two legs and, still crouching, set off towards the aperture. Mr Johnson followed, picking his way carefully through the dusty rubbish.

After five minutes' careful progress, they reached the far side of the chamber and the aperture, which was now revealed to be a tall, narrow doorway surmounted by a pediment upon which could be faintly descried the words 'Come In' and 'Go Away' in red paint in a crude, unformed hand. Mr Johnson paused for breath but his companion, by a series of impassioned grunts and gestures, gave him to understand that time was running away from them and that they still had a considerable journey to make. They entered the doorway and with a last passing glance over his shoulder at the chamber, Mr Johnson mounted the first of a long flight of steps that wound mazily through crumbling brick walls, its progress interrupted periodically by narrow landings that showed yet more apertures and gullies.

Every so often, Mr Johnson stooped down to place a yellow note on the floor. He could get back to the point at which he had left Bernadette, at least. The ladder was another matter.

The travelling was hot work. After half an hour or so, Mr Johnson pulled on the other's elbow and motioned that he was thirsty. The guide pulled a plastic bottle from inside his anorak and passed it to Mr Johnson, who swigged greedily and steadily (it was American cream soda, a drink he hadn't had for years) before pulling the bottle back and setting off again.

They continued climbing until they reached an open landing from which they descended into another series of stairs to a narrow tunnel. Mr Johnson mopped his brow and paused for breath again. His new guide had not uttered a word throughout the journey. Mr Johnson was wondering when the trip would ever end when they emerged suddenly into a deep, warm red room in the middle of which sat a tall, floppy-haired, bespectacled young man at a desk.

Mr Johnson advanced to the desk and held his hand out once again. This man took it and shook firmly.

'You must be Mr Johnson. I am Juniper. Please have a seat.'

He made a dismissive motion with his hand to the guide, who scampered back into the tunnel and disappeared.

'Juniper. I have heard of you already. You are the man who keeps the Golden Clock, aren't you?'

At this Juniper laughed, and said: 'I wouldn't put it quite like that. Nobody keeps the Golden Clock, as such. But it is true that I am closely associated with its operation. How do you know about the Golden Clock?'

'Nikolai told me about it. He seems to hold it in great esteem.'

'Ah. Nikolai. Well, that explains things. We have been expecting you, Mr Johnson. You are still quite new, aren't you?'

'Yes. I am sort of in my induction period, although I have had at least two jobs since I started here. I am looking for Leonard Bragby. Do you know where I can find him?'

'I know all about Leonard Bragby. Why do you need to see him?'

'It was the personnel manager who put the idea into my head, although I have heard about him from a number of different people. It seems as though our respective careers have a number of curious parallels, although I of course haven't been here for as long as he has. I have the feeling that he might be able to provide a context for my experiences so far and perhaps offer some suggestions for the future course of my career.'

'Curious parallels, you say? That is interesting in itself.'

'How do you mean?'

'Nothing as such. What have you been up to since you joined?'

Mr Johnson outlined his experiences to date. Juniper seemed particularly interested in his rapid move into conceptual initialisation. He wrote something down on a piece of notepaper, which he put in his pocket.

'I thought that everything was going well for me but I appear to have done something to upset my manager and I am not sure how I will fare in the future.'

Juniper nodded slowly. 'I am afraid that you can never legislate against the whims and caprices of a line manager. You have made the right decision in putting some distance between you and the trouble you speak of. But what have you heard about Leonard Bragby?'

'Not a great deal. Actually, that's not true. Most of the people I have talked to knew or know of him. It sounds as though he has made quite an impression.'

'Yes, he has done one way or another.'

'Do you know him well?'

'You could say that.'

'Does he work round here?'

'In a manner of speaking. How much do you know about the Golden Clock?'

'Only the little that Nikolai told me. What is it, exactly?'

'That is not an easy question to answer. Suffice it to say, the Golden Clock is everywhere and it informs every aspect of our lives down here.'

'Down here? Nikolai referred to everywhere else as up there.'

'Yes, of course it is down here. You came from up there so this must be down here. But that is in relation to macro spatial considerations. As far as Nikolai is concerned we are up here and he is down there. It is possible to be simultaneously up here and down there, and, for that matter, down there and up here. It all depends upon where you are standing. In organisational terms we are down here in relation to certain functions and up there in relation to others.'

'Perhaps I went up there and down the other side. To be honest, I quite lost track after a while. It feels as though I have been up and down and from side to side.'

'I wouldn't worry too much about the geography if I were you,' said Juniper. 'There are more important things to think about.'

'What do you know of the rest of the organisation?' asked Mr Johnson. 'As far as I can see this section seems to exist on its own terms.'

'You mean that it appears to be cut off from the main currents? Yes, it is in many respects. Our existence down here is to all intents and purposes a quiet pool, maybe even no more than a droplet. They used to say that in a modern business organisation information perforce cascades from the senior managers to the lowliest member of staff, and yet I don't believe that here we are in fact even a droplet, come to think of it. More like a parched desert in many respects. Or at best an ox-bow lake. Which is why we have built the Golden Clock. Without it we really would die of thirst. We thrive on the connection it provides to the wider world.'

Juniper got up from his chair.

'Normally, strangers get no further than this desk but we have heard about you already and you have impressed me with your candour. Would you like to see it?'

'See what?'

'See the Golden Clock. Not all of it, of course – it's much too large and can't be traced all at once. But I can show you parts of it. Follow me.'

They stepped through a low doorway which led into another dusty tunnel, climbed a long flight of stairs and presently stepped out into a wide but low-ceilinged, gloomy chamber. Mr Johnson stooped low like a miner as he entered. In the middle of the room crouched numerous small forms bent intently over what seemed at first sight to be a random collection of disparate objects. Some of the workers were tapping, some fixing, some shaking and sifting, others polishing. Small well-tended fires burned in tiny braziers at the room's margins. The air smelt of metal and gum.

'I'm a tall fellow and all this stooping does me no good,' admitted Juniper as he led Mr Johnson towards the activity. 'But this part of the Golden Clock is certainly worth a look. You will see what I mean in a minute. I should say at the outset that nothing you have encountered here so far will have prepared you for the fact of the Golden Clock. There is nothing that I can do to help you comprehend it. You must suspend any preconceptions you have about the nature of phenomena and expel from your mind any business models or theories you have taken on board so far. Abandon yourself, Mr Johnson, and prepare to encounter the Golden Clock.'

Mr Johnson looked closely at a collection of objects near to where he and Juniper were standing. An operative stood back and bade him inspect them. Mr Johnson made a conscious effort to abandon his preconceptions and studied the scene as objectively as he could. He peered more closely and as he did he saw that far from being a disparate collection of objects, they were in fact linked together in innumerable subtle ways. There were many obvious physical connections – small boxes and cylinders attached to one another by string and masking tape or, in one striking instance, a long run of cardboard tubing looping up out of a hollowed-out old dictionary and passing three feet away into the back of a moulded plastic chair. But it was the suggestive affinities that most arrested Mr Johnson's attention. An empty water bottle with a nightlight strapped to its neck at first glance appeared to be an incongruous neighbour for an old transistor radio heavily bandaged with masking tape but when Mr Johnson bent his head to the radio and heard leaking from it faintly the immemorial hiss of the shipping forecast, he understood instantly that the bottle and nightlight could stand symbolically for a lighthouse and the empty soap dish glued to the side of a tomato box was in fact a little boat riding home to a safe harbour in the gloaming with a mighty storm on its heels; in short, that this entire sub-section of the Golden Clock was concerned with matters maritime. Looking more widely about him,

Mr Johnson thought that from the clutter he could detect configurations that referred inter alia to a Tribute to the Landscape of the Desert, Four Arguments for the Elimination of Television, A Quiet Day in the Tax Office, Rainforests, and Food. These, of course, were just initial impressions and he might have been mistaken. Doubtless there were other mood and theme areas; there was so much to take in and in any case workers were constantly hopping between the arrangements and making adjustments. Mr Johnson was overwhelmed.

'The assistants move and shift the objects according to the current exigencies. You have seen how the relations in the maritime section work. Shortly, the boat will be moored in a harbour. A new configuration of objects will represent its relationship to the price of fish and, for example, the domestic interests of the crew. A green leaf added to the scene is Ireland, a square of muslin, cheese-making. Are you with me? Imagine all the possible sets of relationships between matter and thoughts in every conceivable context. Every minute of every day and night we work to maintain the configurations. The work is endless because the permutations are endless.

'And this is but one small part of it. This is a good section to start off with since it is quite predictable and related. Later I will show you, as it were, one of the hearing parts of the site. It is not as obvious as this bit – fewer wires and boxes, more suggestions.'

Mr Johnson tried to organise his thoughts. The Golden Clock, even the small area he had seen, far outstripped his expectations. 'When I was with Nikolai, he suggested that the Golden Clock has an almost oracular function. It seemed to govern the working habits and practices of his department. How does that work?'

Juniper laughed and clapped his hands. 'Good old Nikolai. We let him see only a very small aspect of the Golden Clock. Come in here – I want to show you something.'

Juniper led Mr Johnson into a square room off the main chamber. Two men were crouched by a hole in the wall manipulating a system of levers and pulleys. On a table close by were piled bundles of paper and items of food and drink.

'If you were paying attention when you were with him, you would have seen Nikolai's staff producing reams of documentation. That is the core function of their work: the production of apparently endless reports and analyses on paper. We in turn take the documents and bring them down here for scrutiny.'

'What happens then?'

'We use them for fuel.'

'The food too?'

'Yes. Nikolai leaves out food and drink as offerings to the systems manager. They also are brought here. For how otherwise should we eat?'

'So the systems manager is based here? I have been hoping to meet him for some time. I have some questions to ask him. I haven't had access to the network since I started here.'

Juniper laughed again.

'There is no systems manager down here, not unless you think of Bragby as a sort of great, uber systems manager. Which he isn't, really. No, it is merely expedient for us to have Nikolai and his men believe in the existence of the systems manager. It provides a cohering and orienting focus for their work. And why shouldn't they believe in the systems manager? I know how hard they work up there. It is surely better for their endeavours to be put to a tangible end even if they don't know what that end is. And after all, a modest degree of fear is always a useful management tool.'

'The Big Committee?'

'Yes, and the Big Committee. I am the Big Committee, if you like. We use the Golden Clock to direct and rationalise their work processes. By implying a series of discrete relationships to it, we ensure that individuals retain a sense of empowerment and understand their own position in the greater scheme of things. We allow them their own meetings and sub-committees, so they do have a degree of latitude. From time to time I light a fire in Front Hawarden to keep Nikolai on his toes. He is a clever fellow but we can rely on his overall devotion to corporate imperatives. He knows when to stop asking questions.'

Mr Johnson was overwhelmed once more. 'I had thought about seeking a transfer to Nikolai's department once some pressing tasks had been accomplished but now I am not sure. I wouldn't like to think that all my hard work was merely going to end up in a brazier.'

'Of course you wouldn't. That's why you're here.'

'When can I see Bragby?'

'Soon. He is not ready for you yet.'

Juniper ushered Mr Johnson into a small side room off the main chamber furnished with two armchairs and a heavy desk. Illumination was provided by candles. Old cloth-bound books were packed into shelves at the back of the room. On the desk lay unfurled yellowing charts and plans.

'Sit down, please, Mr Johnson. I appreciate that there is an awful lot to take in, particularly given that you are still relatively new here. But I will be happy to provide you with any information you need. What have you made of the Golden Clock so far?'

'It is difficult to say since I have seen only a very small part of it.'

'You have, and that was one of the visual parts of the Golden Clock, which is, perforce, more obvious and explicable than some of the others. But don't worry if you haven't begun to grasp it yet. I am as intimately acquainted with the Golden Clock as anyone, yet I freely confess that I have much to learn about its workings. For example, I couldn't tell you what was happening right now in every one of its sections.'

'Nikolai said that the Golden Clock gave a different answer depending upon who posed the question.'

'Yes, within his limited conception of the Golden Clock, Nikolai is quite right. Although we firmly control the oracular function that Nikolai comes into contact with, it does nonetheless reflect in microcosm the larger shape and purpose of the Clock. Everybody has their own set of perceptions. The Golden Clock exists in many respects as a conceptual accretion of myriad subjective perceptions, if you follow me. As an overall conception, the best I can say is this: the Golden Clock is a system that facilitates the configuration of every conceivable phenomenological entity. That is probably how Nikolai would describe it, too. Just think for a moment of the implications of that statement. Imagine the billions of material and conceptual relationships being driven by human intention – humans seizing control of the reins of knowledge, of the philosophical underpinnings of knowledge, of the processes by which knowledge is created. A human-derived system that can replicate everything that has ever existed and everything that could possibly exist in every conceivable format. For Nikolai, the full splendour of the Clock remains unseen, unguessed, yet he divines something of its greater purpose. For those of us close to its working heart, the Golden Clock is nothing less than the total sum of all the world's possibilities – not just in terms of the world of work, either. I am sure that you grasped that much so far. Yet even we grasp it incompletely. Only Bragby fully understands the Golden Clock.'

'Did Bragby invent it?'

'Bragby first thought of it, certainly. The Golden Clock resonates with his spirit and purpose. Without Bragby, the Golden Clock wouldn't exist, though it has been built slowly over time through the endeavours of many. If it helps, you could say that the Golden Clock is the collective rendering of a deeply individualistic conception. It admits a multitude of paradoxes: the Golden Clock is at once a source of infinite wisdom and a stern instrument of control; it creates its own limitless configurations of phenomena, yet it wouldn't exist without incessant human intervention; it is at once greater and lesser than the sum of its parts. Are you with me?'

'Yes, I think so.'

'It resolutely insists upon its own identity. When I showed you the maritime aspect of the seeing section, did you think that you were looking at a randomly assemblage of found objects or an authentic seascape? I am not going to wait for an answer – I know what it will be. But the entire Golden Clock – at least its visible and tangible parts – is manufactured from just such materials. Everything the Golden Clock represents is achieved through substitution, yet substitution of such subtle and capable force that the perceiver is not conscious of witnessing an illusion but rather, like you, accepts the veracity and integrity of the situation thus presented. Yes, I know, it is hard to comprehend at first. I was in on the early development of the Golden Clock and know my way around it better than anyone except Bragby himself, yet it is only relatively recently that I have felt comfortable with my own conception of it. Now I feel that even if I do not fully understand it, I at least know it. I wouldn't expect you to reach this state of comprehension so soon. I would recommend prolonged exposure to the Golden Clock's seeing section before becoming acquainted with its more esoteric elements.'

'What other elements does the Golden Clock have?'

'It is difficult to say definitively. Put crudely, the Golden Clock can be divided into a number of sections that broadly correspond with the human senses. In addition to seeing, the Golden Clock has hearing, tasting, smelling and feeling sections, although these general definitions don't do justice to its complexity by any means. These five sections are more or less concrete as their essential imperatives determine. For ease of work, we use these definitions ourselves. There is also what can loosely be described as a thinking section. This is more of a meta-category, a means of identifying a conceptual thread that links all the other functions. The thinking section is the animating spirit that moves and guides the Golden Clock's disparate elements. It is the least tangible but the most important function. Only the most experienced operatives are allowed to work on the thinking section. Are you still following me?'

'Yes, I think so. Should I be making notes?'

'I shouldn't bother if I were you. It is next to impossible to accurately transcribe a verbal description of the workings of the Golden Clock. Goodness knows I have tried often enough. I even attempted to write a handbook concerning its proper usage once. But I found that when I came to read what I had written, all I could see on the page were meaningless swirls and scrawls. The Golden Clock isn't supposed to be written about. I am not a superstitious man but I sometimes wonder whether the Golden Clock itself intervenes whenever an attempt is made to write about it.'

'How many people work on the Golden Clock?'

'It is difficult to give an accurate figure. Staff come and go. As the Golden Clock has become larger and more sophisticated, so it has demanded ever more resources. At the same time, our working practices are constantly being refined and improved, so in some areas fewer people are required than before. But rest assured – the Golden Clock is attended to twenty-four hours a day. Some sections require more vigilance than others. There are seasonal factors to take into account, too. Christmas is always a very busy period, of course, what with the sheer proliferation of phenomena, Easter increasingly so. It is no mean task keeping on top of the Golden Clock.'

'How do you manage it? Does one person have overall responsibility for it?'

'Yes and no. Bragby, of course, sits at the centre of the Golden Clock, though his operational involvement is much reduced nowadays. On a day-to-day basis, you could say that I have a sort of executive responsibility for its smooth running. If, heaven forfend, anything were to go seriously wrong with it, responsibility for rectifying the problem would be mine. Believe you me, Mr Johnson, that is a responsibility I take very seriously indeed. The fortunes of all of us in here are closely tied to the fate of the Golden Clock. Even Nikolai and his department depend upon it, poor deluded fools. I am responsible for their welfare too. These are burdens not to be borne lightly. Of course, I cannot be everywhere at once. That's why I have a number of able deputies in key positions. I have learned to delegate as I've gone along. My deputies in turn have their own trusted subordinates. It is a fairly traditional management structure, I suppose, but one which admits a healthy degree of flexibility and latitude. Individuals become specialists in certain areas. They are able to make refinements and apply new thinking, provided they are in keeping with the spirit of the Clock. This is largely a self-regulating process since the Golden Clock knows when a modification is not appropriate and duly rejects it. Experienced operatives have learned over time what is and is not suitable. As I said before, I don't necessarily believe the Golden Clock has a mind of its own but it certainly possesses what you might call an independent operating principle. But I am talking at length and you look tired, Mr Johnson.'

'Yes, I am tired, although what you have been telling me has been fascinating. I have been exposed to a lot of new ideas since I started here but none of them has excited my interest as much as what I have seen and heard so far of the Golden Clock. I would like to find out more about it and perhaps see more of it in action. But I do need to speak to Bragby as soon as I can. How soon is soon?'

'Soon enough but not that soon. Bragby is an extremely busy man. I don't mean merely in terms of his workload, which would be reason enough to limit his available time, but because of his ceaseless thinking and wakefulness on our behalf. Bragby's conception and vision sustains us. It feeds the Golden Clock and it is responsible for every activity that takes place here. Without Bragby's perpetual mental effort on our behalf, we would lose the impetus to maintain the Golden Clock, which in turn would, piece by precious piece, cease to function properly, thus cutting us off from everything that gives us nourishment and purpose. Can you see how closely everything is linked, Mr Johnson? I think you can. Perhaps you can understand, then, why I can't just go up to Bragby and say, Bragby, here is Mr Johnson who wants to speak with you. For what if I were to disturb him in the midst of important brainwork? He might lose his concentration at a critical moment, and then where would we be? Believe you me, Mr Johnson, I know Bragby as well as anyone. I have worked closely with him, often under conditions of extreme pressure, especially in the early days, and know something of his thoughts. Yet there have been occasions when he has been unable to see me for days at a time. I don't worry about this. I accept that Bragby speaks to me when he is ready to speak to me. We all respect his sacred thinking time. We are in his thoughts all the time. He feels us through the Golden Clock, he senses the heat of our devotion and perceives our needs. Bragby is in all of us and we are in all of him. The Golden Clock tells him everything. But there I go again, and look at your tired eyes. Would you like to sleep now?'

'Yes, I do feel the need of sleep. Can I sleep in here?'

'Yes, for the moment. I have work to attend to but I will be back later. I will find somewhere more comfortable for you then. In the meantime, feel free to put your legs on the other armchair. Nobody will disturb you. My staff work quietly and efficiently. You will hear nothing more than a pleasant, low-level hum of productive activity. Look at your tired eyes.'

Mr Johnson must have dropped off to sleep before Juniper left the room. He woke with a start. The candles had expired. For a moment he didn't know where he was. He got out of the chair and groped his way to the door. Sure enough, Juniper's staff were, quietly and efficiently, hard at work. Mr Johnson couldn't tell at first exactly what configurations they were engendering. The light from the braziers threw the wide chamber into lurid orange relief and the workers cast grotesque shadows on the ceiling and walls. They crouched in clusters or alone, fixing, taping, screwing, attaching. But after watching them for a few moments, something of their movements and the way they were manipulating the objects suggested to Mr Johnson that they were busy configuring in the areas of Economics, Gardening and Ancestor Worship – although it was impossible to tell for sure. From time to time they would retreat to the periphery of the room and pull objects and materials from stout boxes and then return to their positions. Juniper was nowhere to be seen. He must have been attending to one of the more opaque sections, although from what Mr Johnson had gathered, the seeing section extended into other rooms. Juniper hadn't told him exactly how much space the Golden Clock took up. Mr Johnson imagined a network of objects and connecting materials wandering up staircases and across landings and extending through roof spaces and between walls. His imagination failed him when he tried to conceptualise the less tangible elements of the Golden Clock. Perhaps they only existed as purely subjective perceptual phenomena. Juniper had explained the workings of these elements reasonably clearly. Mr Johnson supposed that Bragby would be even more explicit. It hadn't come as a surprise to discover that Bragby lay behind the creation and development of the Golden Clock, given what Mr Johnson had already learned of him. In a way, it sounded as though Bragby really had made good in the end. It just went to show that it was always worth giving people a second or even a third chance, and Mr Johnson felt immediately reassured about his own prospects. There was nothing he had done that couldn't easily be explained away in terms of a misunderstanding, and if Bragby could accomplish so much in spite of all the opprobrium heaped upon him, there was no reason why Mr Johnson shouldn't also achieve great things. He felt terminally tired but his mind was racing. The Golden Clock, despite its apparent complexity and subtlety, offered a no less lucid explanation of the way in which the organisation worked than any of the other theories and models he had been exposed to so far. Mr Johnson shut the door of the office and found his way back to the chairs. His mind continued to race but his body must have gone back to sleep because he was conscious of waking with a start again. He felt that he had heard the door open and shut. This may have occurred in a dream. But awake again he had the strong sense of not being alone in the room. There was a warm presence near at hand, its shape and form undetectable in the darkness. Mr Johnson didn't feel afraid but he closed his eyes again, not that it made any difference given the darkness of the room. A hand passed over his face and the presence withdrew. Mr Johnson heard the door open and close again. Immediately he fell asleep. Later Juniper returned and bade Mr Johnson to follow him from the room. In the chamber outside work had reached a pitch of intensity. It was darker and noisier and the occupants appeared to be mostly involved in hammering activities. Juniper said nothing as he led Mr Johnson stooping across the room and through a door at the other side. Juniper's manner had changed since before Mr Johnson had gone to sleep. He looked troubled and Mr Johnson refrained from starting up a conversation. Juniper certainly didn't seem inclined to do so. They were walking down a narrow corridor lit by candles fixed into wall sconces. At the far end – they were about halfway down it – the corridor tapered to a fine point. The gloom and warmth pressed in from either side. Juniper stopped and gestured for Mr Johnson to overtake him. When he had done so, Juniper gave him a sharp shove in the back which sent him sprawling. 'Don't move until I say so,' snapped Juniper, breaking the silence, before running back up the corridor. Mr Johnson heard a door shutting to. The candles on the walls flickered in the draught but didn't expire. The sea change in Juniper's attitude was quite shocking. Mr Johnson wondered whether he had inadvertently said something to upset him or had slept for too long. Perhaps Juniper had been engaged in a particularly knotty question in relation to the Golden Clock. Whatever the cause, Mr Johnson felt no inclination to disobey Juniper's instruction to remain where he was, even if he could be sure that he could open the door at the top of the corridor, which he almost certainly couldn't. He lay where he fell and slept for a while. This time he dreamt strongly of oppressive, hot, confined spaces and when he woke he couldn't be sure that he had dreamed at all since the narrow corridor was, if anything, even more hot and oppressive. Juniper seemed in no hurry to get back. Perhaps he wasn't coming back and Mr Johnson had been set some sort of initiative test. He was very thirsty. The notion that he was playing a role in some sort of developmental game was quite amusing. One by one the candles began to expire. He really ought to decide what to do before the light went out altogether.

'What are you going to do?'

There was no doubt about it. Without light to see by there was no getting out of the corridor.

'What are you going to do?' repeated the voice, softly.

Mr Johnson looked up and around. The voice seemed to be coming from all directions. He was certain there was no-one else with him in the corridor.

'I don't know. Who are you?'

'Mr Johnson, Mr Johnson, Mr Johnson,' said the voice and tailed off. The quiet dark returned.

'Is it you, Bragby?' said Mr Johnson but there was no answer. The last candle went out. Soon after a rustling and shuffling commenced, followed by what sounded like very distant laughter, then nothing. Mr Johnson closed his eyes and curled against the wall. Clamorous dreams took him. The chatter of a thousand pub nights sat at the back of his consciousness, radio static dipped and played in waves across the foreground. A million insects swarmed. Goods trains clanked and shunted in distant sidings. From a deep source of memory, laughing children played by a brook in a summer field. Their happy laughter turned derisive before being drowned out by the sound of an old diesel engine and traffic hurtling past an open window. Church bells rang and helicopters swooped from the sky. In his mind a tiny voice said: 'Goodness me, it's noisy.' Then he fell in a swoon into a hammock strung between two trees in a courtyard filled with sunshine. The sounds diminished. The next thing he knew Juniper was standing over him shining a torch into his eyes.

'Get up,' he said. 'I've never known anyone sleep so much.' There was a kindly tone to his voice, however, and he gently took Mr Johnson's elbow and directed him out of the corridor and back into the main chamber. Mr Johnson blinked at the light, dim as it was. 'I've had odd dreams,' he said as they went back across to Juniper's office.

'Noisy dreams?'

'Yes. How did you know?'

'Because I left you in one of the listening sections of the Golden Clock. Word came down while you were asleep that you should go straight to the esoteric sections. It is quite unprecedented. I am sorry about the rough treatment. I wanted to see how you'd respond, test your durability, if you know what I mean.'

'Yes, I think so,' said Mr Johnson. 'I did wonder whether I was being set a test of some sort.'

They sat down in Juniper's office.

'Yes, it was something like that. You did well not to disobey my instructions, and neither did you get the screaming ab-dabs and clamour to be let out. Would I be right in thinking that you experienced a very personalised and particular sound environment?'

'Very much so. It's difficult to remember exactly what happened but I was conscious of being exposed to familiar noises that evoked very specific instances from my past. I wouldn't say that there was an objective shape to any of it but there was certainly a cohesive set of subjective impressions. They seemed to form a pattern. I can't be any more explicit than that.'

Juniper looked pleased. 'I must say, Mr Johnson, you are certainly getting to grips very quickly with the essential nature of the Golden Clock. You are demonstrating a very advanced level of explication.'

'It's strange, but I must say that of everything I have encountered here in terms of models and theories, the Golden Clock makes the most sense. I understand that it is deep and complex and that even experienced employees such as yourself have only a partial grasp of it, yet I feel comfortable in my relative lack of knowledge. I can see how, given time and patience, I will become more accustomed to its ways. I have had to take on board so many different ideas, theories and models that are transparently simple yet fundamentally complex that it is a blessed relief to encounter something that is transparently complex yet I suspect, and tell me if I'm wrong, is actually fundamentally simple.'

'No, you are not wrong,' said Juniper, who was rolling himself a cigarette. 'Smoke? No? No, it is quite true that the Golden Clock is actually very straightforward, as a conception, at least. The assembly and constant maintenance of it, of course, is quite another thing. But I think that is true of most phenomenological systems, don't you? The problem with the business models you alluded to a moment ago is that they are predicated on the assumption that people are too dim-witted to grapple with complex concepts and need to be spoon-fed childlike ideas in order to cope with the fact of being at work and coping with the demands it throws up. Hence the relentless use of acronyms, acrostics and mnemonics – you know the sort of things I mean. What Bragby's great genius taught us was that you should look at these questions from the other end of the telescope. Thus, what is apparently complex is actually straightforward. A neat inversion, but it is more profound than that. For we all know how dispiriting it is to learn basic business theories and models in a training context only to find that they provide as much illumination in a real life situation as a match does on a lonely moor at night in a howling gale. Yet people diligently plod on through this useless rubbish throughout their working lives. All that energy expended in the wrong direction. Do you follow me? But consider the unalloyed joy experienced by the humble operative who works on a middling section of the Golden Clock for whom the penny drops one day, the moment when they arrive at a developed conception of its function and purpose and surrender themselves to the notion that the Golden Clock is everything, nothing more and nothing less, and that they don't have to struggle to explain it or to divine its more occult purposes. It simply is, and so are they, and that is all. Perhaps I am not explaining this as well as I could. Bragby, of course would do a better job.'

'Where are we going to see Bragby? Is it very soon?'

'Sooner than before but not too soon. You must be patient in this matter.'

'Did Bragby himself suggest I go straight to the listening section of the Golden Clock?'

Juniper, who had got up from his chair and was rummaging around in a desk drawer, affected not to hear him. He sat down again and lit his cigarette with a match.

'Yes, you are very advanced, more so than I was at your stage. And the Golden Clock was nowhere near as well developed in those days. But to return to my earlier point, the woeful ways in which serious matters and concerns are dressed in petty banalities. The world of sales for example. Now, I think I am right in saying that you have some acquaintance with the sales function, Mr Johnson.'

'Yes, but not for very long. How did you know that?'

Juniper winked at him. 'We know all about you, Mr Johnson. We were expecting you, after all. But you'll be familiar with the terminology those fellows use, the aides memoire and cunning reworkings of popular psychology texts. So much theory with so little useful application to real life. I too have been employed in the sales industry, Mr Johnson. I too have taken on board motivational training strategies, learned how to be the best I could be, force-fed benefit burgers to unwilling customers. Yet none of this explains nor renders palatable the fearful process of laying oneself naked before a stranger and persuading them to part with their money for a product or service which you both know has no tangible benefit to them, to you or to the world at large. And the fear I have seen in the eyes of sales people. And the fear I too have felt.'

Juniper looked away sadly. 'It all seems so long ago now. But at the time I couldn't imagine how I would get away. You, Mr Johnson, have moved on sooner than most.'

'Well, it was more by accident than design. Even now I am a bit shaky about the exact circumstances but there was a resource allocation problem which never got addressed and one way or another I ended up in a different department. It was certainly more congenial. Most of the people I met in the sales office clearly wanted to be doing something else. As soon as I sat in the conceptual initialisation department I knew that I had to make the best possible impression in a short period of time.'

'That's a lucky escape, and not the usual route out, though there is a precedent.'

'You mean Bragby himself?'

Juniper said nothing but didn't contradict him.

'That is really the reason why I wanted to meet him. I think the personnel manager confirmed it for me. There do seem to be some parallels in our career paths, not that I am making any great claims for myself. And as I have said, for a while my career in conceptual initialisation seemed to be going extremely well but took a sudden nosedive for reasons apparently out of my control. I am still not sure when I can reasonably go back there, although I would like to make a success of the concept engineer role before I do anything else.'

Juniper looked hard at Mr Johnson and said, really to himself: 'And so clued up about the Golden Clock too. Yes,' he said, his voice rising, 'whatever the trajectory of your career here so far, it was on an upward trend the moment you sat down in the conceptual initialisation department. I suppose you are still a concept engineer, regardless of the problems you alluded to a moment ago?'

'Yes, I am. It says so on my business card.' Mr Johnson pulled the card from his breast pocket and showed it to Juniper, who looked impressed. Mr Johnson also pulled out the letter confirming his appointment. The circumstances that had led up to him receiving the letter and his arrival at the company seemed to belong to another time.

'Good,' said Juniper, 'because we always have the need of imaginative thinkers here. Not for the routine operative work, you understand, but for the strategic issues relating to the future development of the Golden Clock. I am not suggesting that you don't properly speaking still belong in conceptual initialisation but at least while you are with us we can find you some useful things to do – useful for us and for you, I hope. There is also the question of our relationship with other departments. There's Nikolai's crew, which you know all about, and the cleaners and certain other individuals who require very careful management. Such questions need to be addressed by people with high levels of tact and discretion.'

'I had almost forgotten about the cleaners,' said Mr Johnson. 'I spent quite a lot of time with them. They seemed to be very wrapped up in micro-management issues, Bernadette at least. They hadn't heard of you or the Golden Clock, however. What do you have to do with them?'

'Just as you have said. We set them vague management tasks to keep them focused on the issues at hand. Their cleaning remit stops short of this functional area which ensures we coexist peacefully. But actually setting their tasks is quite a job in itself. The daughter, certainly, can be a handful and won't be distracted by a threatening invocation of the systems manager. No, we don't reveal ourselves fully to them. They think they are reporting to a junior accounts executive. The man who led you here handles all the practical correspondence. He sits at the border just for the occasions on which she shows herself. But in fairness, Bernadette produces very high-level work. We'll be taking delivery of her latest report on the cleaning function cost-centre shortly. It will, of course, be used for fuel like Nikolai's work. But you, Mr

Johnson, with your broad set of experiences across the organisation, are perfectly situated to manage aspects of our external focus. If you continue to develop in the promising way you've begun, I may before long be able to offer you a position – if you want it. But perhaps I am being premature, and in any case, you already have a job title and a role you have said you would like to return to. I imagine you were very proud when they confirmed your appointment as a concept engineer.'

'Yes,' admitted Mr Johnson, 'I was. But as much as anything else I was pleased to be in an environment where I had a reasonable grasp on what was going on. But since spending time up or down here, I am still not sure geographically, I am less certain that I really did understand the underlying concepts that informed the structure and function of the conceptual initialisation department. For example, I learned about something called the Five Synergetic Elements quite early on which at the time made a great deal of sense and underpinned practically much of the work I undertook for the department. Yet since encountering the Golden Clock, even in modest way, I cannot see any virtue in the Five Synergetic Elements whatsoever. In fact, I am not sure I could even tell you what they mean exactly. It is difficult to tell now. There was also a project called the Big Sell, which was an effort to give strategic shape and direction to myriad disparate processes and activities. But again, it doesn't seem much of a strategy at all when set against the wonder of the Golden Clock.'

'I know what you mean,' said Juniper. 'I was familiar with the Elements you mentioned once, or at least I think so. There may have been six of them then. Or perhaps four. But it is the same with me – I couldn't for the life of me tell you what they were about. But I think that is a positive thing. It exemplifies one's capacity to quickly shed outmoded ways of thinking and absorb new, more progressive ideas. Quite simply, set against the Golden Clock, any idea or theory, however sophisticated, will inevitably be found wanting. They were always trying to introduce grand order-from-chaos schemes when I was up there. It is inevitable, I suppose, given the ever-proliferating number of departments, functions, teams and activities. At one time, everyone you met told you how they were engaged on this or that strategy which was nothing short of an attempt to calibrate the entire organisation according to this or that set of commercial imperatives, or that they were busy developing an information system that would provide an accurate snapshot of the organisation's activities at any given moment. The strange thing was, the grander the plans, the more parochial the arena of activity seemed to be. I'll bet my boots this Big Sell business you referred to is a known quantity only within the conceptual initialisation department, and perhaps with one or two people elsewhere. Beyond that, it will be of little interest or relevance. But to go back to your original point, yes, nothing touches the Golden Clock for sheer conceptual sense. It is simultaneously a practical set of processes and a tangible piece of machinery, and an eternally explicating business model. You really are learning quickly, and I must say you don't seem quite so tired now.'

'No, I feel I little better, although I think I've got what you might call structural tiredness. I feel weary to my bones, though my mind is switched on right now. What you said about the lack of relevance strategies such as the Big Sell have to the rest of the organisation was very true, although I didn't realise this when I was working on it. I can see know that it represented an attempt by the conceptual initialisation department to asserts its primacy in some way rather than being a strategy that grew from an organic need elsewhere in the company. I also suspect that it was an exercise in having an exercise. But I have only felt in this way since I have been exposed to the Golden Clock and seen what real work, with a purpose and a tangible outcome, and underpinned by sound theory, looks like. It has been quite an eye-opener. I would be interested in a position here at some point in the future. It certainly seems to be where the most stimulating work gets done. Again, I believed that the conceptual initialisation department was the very hub of the company but I can see that the eternal maintenance and development of the Golden Clock makes every other function and activity in the organisation seem small beer by comparison. I feel very strongly that I want to be part of it. But I wouldn't want to leave my current department under a cloud.'

'What you have said about the importance of the Golden Clock is very true, although of course everyone you meet will tell you that everyone you meet will tell you that they do the most important work in the organisation and then go on to say that in their case they really do do the most important work in the organisation. In our case, however, I can honestly say we don't do the most important work in the organisation, not, at least, for the organisation that lies outside the remit of this function and those immediately related to it. It is another case of looking down the telescope from the other end. When an individual tells you that their role or department is critical to the enduring life of the organisation, it almost always transpires that it is not. In our case, when we say that we are not the most important function in the organisation, it actually transpires that we are, though not for the same reasons that the people who say that they are and actually aren't imagine when they say that they are important. Do you see what I mean? But again, this is not a mere sophistical inversion. Imagine the disappointment for an individual engaged in work in a department which he or she believes to be central to the fortunes of the company when they unearth evidence that shows the situation to be quite the opposite. Or think about the relentless pursuit of pointless theories that I mentioned before. On the other hand, imagine how it must feel to toil away humbly for the greater good of the Golden Clock, secure in the knowledge that your efforts achieve only modest ends and that your activities are not subject to the glare of public scrutiny or the weight of corporate expectations, only to come to the wondrous, epiphanic realisation that the Golden Clock is by any objective and subjective reckoning the most significant accomplishment in the entire history of the organisation and by virtue of its existence, is axiomatically the most profound and meaningful enterprise the organisation undertakes, no matter that it is the concern of a relatively small group of people. When I said earlier that we are like an ox-bow lake separated from the main currents of activity, I might have been guilty of selling ourselves short. Imagine an ox-bow lake that has been drained and a mighty tower of ivory and gold erected on its bed and you will be nearer the mark. But I thought you said you were no longer tired.'

'I'm sorry, did I drop off again?'

'Yes, you did. Don't worry about it. I have some more work to attend to on the Golden Clock. You can nod off to your heart's content. I am going to be preoccupied for some time. But let me show you to your quarters first.'

Mr Johnson followed Juniper from the room and across the main chamber. They went into another corridor-style room similar to but not the same as the one that Mr Johnson had had noisy dreams in. This room also tapered at its end. Not far from that point cushions and a duvet were spread on the floor. It was simple but comfortable and Mr Johnson needed no second bidding to get under the covers. Juniper lit a tall candle and placed it in a holder on the floor. Then he tucked Mr Johnson in.

'I will be back later. You will have plenty of work to do before long, so enjoy the rest while you can. Are you hungry?'

'A little but I am tired more than anything.'

'Good. By the time you wake up, we will have taken delivery of another set of supplies from Nikolai's people. I will let you into a little secret: we so fixed the Golden Clock that when one of Nikolai's scriveners consulted it yesterday, it put into the poor fellow's head the notion that the only way the systems manager could be propitiated was by providing him with a particularly delicious brand of duck liver pate. We are expecting a regular shipping order of the stuff later on. You are not vegetarian, are you? I hadn't thought about your dietary requirements.'

'No, I'm omnivorous,' yawned Mr Johnson. 'But right now I could sleep for England.'

'Then I will leave you in peace,' said Juniper. 'Good night.'

'Goodnight,' said Mr Johnson, though before he dropped off it struck him that since it seemed to be dark in this department all the time, he might just as well have said 'good morning' or 'good afternoon'. No other thoughts struck him but when he woke up again he felt as though he'd been asleep for no more than five minutes. He was also extremely uncomfortable. The cushions had worked themselves away from underneath him and he was lying at an angle on the stone floor. This discomfort became the father to a set of other complaints. An itch got going behind his left knee. His toes felt awkward and chafed his socks. It occurred to him that he might well be in another section of the Golden Clock. He didn't want to be guilty of thinking too literally but perhaps this room was an element in the feeling section. But surely the feeling section would be more subtle than this. On the other hand, perhaps he was at a very low level of the feeling section. He thought back to what he had learned of the Golden Clock so far. Juniper had told him that the five sections of the Golden Clock corresponded broadly with the human senses, the visual section being the most comprehensible. He had also told Mr Johnson that the Golden Clock operated fundamentally on the principle of substitution. Mr Johnson could see how this thinking applied to the visual elements of the Clock and to an extent understood how it could explain the operation of the part of the hearing section that Mr Johnson had been exposed to since it was mediated through the agency of sleep. But he was at a loss to see how it could be applied to the operation of the feeling section, if this indeed were an aspect of the feeling section. Mr Johnson wondered whether, despite Juniper's advice, he should attempt to set down some of these thoughts on paper. But he had no pen and when he looked again at the notes that were in his pocket, they made less sense than ever. Perhaps the time for assiduous note-taking had passed.

The candle was still burning. Mr Johnson wondered whether he had been premature in telling Juniper how he felt he had apprehended the Golden Clock. Yet Juniper would surely have pulled him up if he thought he had been getting above himself. After all, Juniper had said that there was an opening there for Mr Johnson, if he wanted it; Bragby himself may even have heard about him by now. His body yearned for more sleep but his mind was hungry for thought. It oriented itself instinctively toward the Golden Clock. The Golden Clock was wonderfully comprehensible if only you approached it with the right frame of mind. It was all a question of balancing conceptual insightfulness with an understanding of its rudimentary mechanics. As he was trying to come to terms with what Juniper had intimated about a possible role in relation to the Golden Clock, Mr Johnson's body won and he fell to sleep. The next thing he knew, Juniper was leaning over him holding a candle.

'Tea is ready, if you are.'

Mr Johnson followed Juniper back to his office. On the desk a cold collation was spread – crackers, tomatoes, cheese and the deluxe pate that had been promised, courtesy of Nikolai. They tucked in together. Juniper didn't say anything while he ate. Mr Johnson was still tired and glad not to have to talk. When they had finished eating, Juniper asked Mr Johnson whether he needed more sleep. Mr Johnson did and pulled the armchairs together. Juniper lit more candles. He said that there was no rush and that everything would be revealed in good time.

'But tired as you are, you might be interested in this.'

Juniper opened a cupboard and brought out a large red ledger, which he gave to Mr Johnson.

'It's an account of the latest configurations. Just routine work but it is worth trying to get your head round it.'

Juniper opened the book towards its middle and paused on a page entitled 'Maritime and Related'.

'This is what you were looking at earlier. I would be interested to know how closely you think the entries correspond with the physical configurations you observed. It is the closest we get to book-keeping. No pressure – I expect you will be asleep in no time.'

Juniper left the office and shut the door. Tired as he was, Mr Johnson made an effort to study the entries. In a thick-edged box at the top of the page, a list of materials had been entered: 'Toilet-roll holders (12); comb (1); old torch (1); grass (dried) (3 small bags); vacuum cleaner bag (1)' etc. Beneath this a multiplicity of configurations had been entered in a tiny, tidy hand. Mr Johnson's eyes soon began to tire. A ship sat in port, took on its crew, left port. The galley was stocked with provisions from a supermarket (an asterisk next to this denoted a coded cross-reference to Retail and Multiples). A man stopped for petrol before driving past the ship and seeing it set sail, which reminded him of a holiday in Scotland three years ago. The boat disturbed a shoal of fish and a woman met another woman on the street and mentioned tinned mackerel and the fact that her husband was at sea. The captain thought about the lighthouse and the lighthouse keeper manipulated the controls, and so on and on in an apparently infinite sequence of loosely-related events and phenomenological entities, across dozens of pages, backwards and forwards through time until Mr Johnson's eyes snapped shut, but not before the book did. He slept, although running like a theme through his dreams was the notion that he was more tired than sleep would ever smooth out. He struggled instinctively against this thought but it took him high up and away from the deepest level of sleep and threw him upon a narrow ledge at the top of a tower, daylight filtering through the clouds. 'More sleep, more sleep,' a voice cried, deep down. 'More work, more work,' cried another near at hand.

He swam in and out of consciousness. At one point he sensed that someone was sitting on the edge of his bed trying to talk to him. He dreamt he was in his underpants and everybody was staring at him. Whoever was sitting at the edge of his bed moved away but the room was still full of commotion. There was much coming and going. Finally, Mr Johnson gave up on trying to sleep and raised himself up. He wasn't in his underpants after all. Neither was he in a bed. But a man was in Juniper's office going through the desk drawers and pulling maps and charts from tubes. He looked troubled.

CHAPTER EIGHTEEN
THE GOLDEN CLOCK

'What's the matter? Can I help you?' said Mr Johnson, straightening his tie and flattening his trousers.

'There's some sort of trouble with the Clock,' answered the man, who didn't seem in the least perturbed by Mr Johnson's presence. 'Reports came in saying that one of the configurations in a remote part of the seeing section made no sense whatsoever, in or out of its context. This has happened before and can usually be sorted out with some minor adjustments. But when we went down to look at it, the situation was more problematic than we thought. And Juniper is nowhere to be found. Who are you, anyway?'

'I'm Mr Johnson. I fell asleep in here, although I do have my own bedroom. I hope I haven't alarmed you.'

'Your own bedroom? You are honoured. We usually bunk up where we work.'

'I'm waiting to speak to Leonard Bragby,' said Mr Johnson, embarrassed by the exposure of his privileged sleeping arrangements. 'In the meantime, Juniper has been explaining the workings of the Golden Clock to me. I am slowly trying to get to grips with it. What exactly is wrong with the configuration?'

The man shut the desk drawers and replaced the maps and charts. Evidently he hadn't found what he was looking for. 'It is too complicated to go into here. One of the operatives on the section in question said that he felt a vague sense of unease that developed into full-blown uncertainty by four o'clock. It is hard to describe at a distance. If you are interested in how the Clock works, why don't you come down and see for yourself?'

'I'd like to. I am still new to its ways but I may be able to bring a fresh pair of eyes.'

He followed the man from Juniper's office and across the large chamber. They stooped lower than usual into a tunnel that led downwards away from the chamber. The journey lasted for over five minutes. At some points they had to crawl. They didn't speak to one another. The tunnel opened out into a round room that turned out to be the bottom of a deep shaft. Four sets of iron ladders ran up the shaft and they climbed one of these before stepping onto a ledge that opened into another large chamber where four men were engaged in work that looked similar to the work that went on in the seeing section that

Mr Johnson had become acquainted with upstairs. Another man stood away to one side next to a telephone on a desk. From the attitude of the men and the atmosphere in the chamber, it wasn't at all apparent that they had a problematic situation on their hands. They were calm, quiet and controlled, although this impression might have been engendered in part by the physical properties of the room. It was higher than the room upstairs and there was no need to stoop. The light was brighter, too. Large bicycle lamps were fixed around the wall at head height. There were no braziers. The chamber contained fewer objects than the one upstairs but there were more obvious links between the phenomenological entities arranged on the floor. A cursory glance suggested to Mr Johnson An Unexpected Holiday in the Autumn, The History of the Dutch, Paper, Urban Renewal and Cycling. Cycling had some obvious sub-connections with all the other elements except, as far as he could tell, Paper. What struck Mr Johnson was the discreteness of this particular room and any other connected rooms that lay through the doors that led off it. He had suspected that there must be more to the seeing section than had met his eyes but he hadn't been prepared for the distance between its constituent parts. As far as he understood it, the seeing aspect of the Golden Clock presented a unified visual rendering of all possible phenomenological configurations. To his mind this implied an actual physical connection between the chambers where the material configurations were laid out. Yet they were some distance from the main chamber upstairs and there were no obvious physical connections. Everything was contained within the room.

'It's a long way from the other part of the seeing section,' Mr Johnson said to the man who had spoken to him in Juniper's office, but he didn't get an answer because this man was busy talking to the man by the telephone, who had the receiver in his hand. This was the first telephone that Mr Johnson had seen in this section. It looked similar to the telephones in Nikolai's area and also lacked an obvious connection. But Mr Johnson decided against saying anything about it.

'Any luck with Juniper?'

'No, still nothing,' said the man by the telephone.

'I don't like this at all. We can't just make changes to the configurations without permission from a higher authority.'

'No, I agree. But equally, we cannot let the misconfiguration go unattended without jeopardising the functional effectiveness of its cognate neighbours. We are not talking about a slight adjustment to shape or spatial situation here.'

'I know. Are you quite sure there hasn't been an error in the interpretation?'

'Horrobin is looking at it again. We have been over everything repeatedly and keep drawing the same conclusions.'

'Who picked it up originally?'

'Wormald. He's writing his report up now.'

'Good. That will be the first thing Juniper will want to see. I wish we could track him down. I feel uneasy without him here to see for himself what's wrong.'

'I'll try again but I don't hold out much luck. The telephone system has been erratic all week anyway. Most of the time there's not even a signal.'

'Have you spoken to the systems manager about it?'

'I've tried but frankly it's like calling out into the wind on a stormy night. The words just fall back on themselves. I know that there is a lot of work going through at the moment but when you are stuck in an outpost like this, you need to have speedy, connective technologies immediately to hand. I'm worried that we have lost valuable time on this one already.'

'Don't worry too much. You have done everything you can with the resources available. Juniper will understand. The main thing is to try and resolve this situation as quickly as possible to everybody's satisfaction and to at all costs avoid a knock-on effect on the Clock at large.'

All through this exchange Mr Johnson said nothing but listened and observed. He was impressed with the dedication of the operatives and the ways in which they thought through the possible courses of action they could take. It was clear from what they said that they had only a moderate degree of autonomy. The extent to which they invoked Juniper's name proved that much. They were also apparently in the dark about the true nature of the systems manager. It hadn't occurred to Mr Johnson that some of the employees on the Golden Clock might also be in his thrall, although when he thought about it he could see that it made sense from a management control perspective. He reckoned these men were somewhere in the middle of the hierarchy. But at the same time they were obviously articulate, conscientious and diligent, had a strong grasp of the technical issues and knew enough about the Golden Clock's workings to identify a failure in its smooth operating and to assess the possible consequences of this failure on the rest of the system.

'It's not just the seeing section I am worried about,' said the man who had led Mr Johnson to the chamber. 'It's what might happen if the fault spreads into one of the less tangible sections. Imagine a disruption to the contextual configurations in the feeling section.'

'It doesn't bear thinking about,' said the man with telephone, who had replaced the receiver on the cradle. He looked troubled. 'Do you remember that time when the hearing elements were being constructed and I opened a channel of political and leisure aural suggestions without attaching them to the appropriate nuances and echoes in at least sixteen other cognate contexts?'

'Good lord, yes. If I remember rightly, we had to rebuild it from scratch.'

'Exactly. I was new then, of course, but I learned my lesson soon enough. If you don't pay attention to detail, you might as well give up the job. When you are working on something as complex and inter-related as the Golden Clock, you can't afford to stop thinking about permutations, implications and ramifications. This is a case in point.'

'Yes,' said the other man, 'it's the attention to detail that's the key. That and knowing when it is appropriate to take remedial action. I have had my own salutary lessons on the Clock recently. Only last week ago I overstated an allusive aspect of the thinking strand in terms of its symbolic, suggestive relationship with a fairly straightforward piece of plain hearing. Basic schoolboy error – I was busy and probably a little tired, and I simply neglected to do the mathematics. Again, an apparently minor oversight quickly became a full-blown crisis. The thinking strand was temporarily suspended and they had to get Bragby himself to conceptualise a solution out of nothing.'

The other man whistled. 'Straight to the top, was it? I don't envy you. The worst I have ever had is a stern word or two from Juniper. Were you in big trouble?'

'Not as such but it was a bit embarrassing. I didn't see Bragby directly, of course, but Juniper made it clear that his mind was somewhat exercised by what I had done. Apparently they had to put extra people on keeping-him-awake duty and the hard thinking took over two days. Thankfully everything is back to normal now. But you can see why I'm so keen to get this situation sorted out properly. I can't imagine that they would be as tolerant again so soon.'

'Yes, I can see that a lot of responsibility rests on your shoulders. But I don't wish to pass on responsibility. I am over this immediate section and should carry the can when things go wrong. Neither of us wants to be hauled up before the authorities. But I am afraid that they are as likely to say, "why didn't you do something when you had the chance" as "why did you do that?". It's a very difficult one to call.'

'Yes it is, particularly given the unforgiving time parameters we are working within. With every second that passes, the likelihood of a major disruption to the seeing section of the Golden Clock grows. We must act, and soon.'

'Of course we must. But we keep returning to the same question: how do we proceed without Juniper? Quite simply, we may not be mandated to perform the sort of remedial work required to restore sense to the configurations. I don't suppose you had any luck upstairs with the plans?'

'No, nothing specific enough, I'm afraid. A lot of the charts and plans haven't been updated for a long time, anyway. The Golden Clock changes so much that I suppose they have difficulty keeping on top of the admin side of things. But it's a nuisance when you need accurate and relevant information quickly.'

'I know, I've had the same experiences. I sometimes think that it is ironic that we are engaged on the relentless configuring of all possible relationships between all conceivable phenomena and yet we have no accurate and up-to-date documentation that refers to the explicit condition of the system in the here and now – the irony being that the process of rendering such phenomenological relationships appears to militate against our capacity to produce such an administrative infrastructure, which is nonetheless a phenomenological fact in its own right. Do you follow me?'

'Yes, I do. I suppose it's the same everywhere – everyone is just too busy to provide an objective concordance that explains and codifies the subjective daily experiences and practices of work. Or is it a subjective concordance that explains and codifies objective experiences? I must be losing my sharpness.'

'You probably need sleep. I know I do. We do seem to be working harder than ever.'

'Yes, I do feel the need for sleep. But while Bragby stays awake, we also must do our best to stay awake.'

'You're right. Going to sleep isn't going to get this problem sorted out. What are we going to do?'

'I'm really not sure. We do keep coming back to the same question. If only Juniper were here.'

Another man joined them by the desk. From their conversation, Mr Johnson assumed that this was Wormald with his report. The man by the telephone looked it up and down and handed it to his colleague, who nodded at key points and handed it back to Wormald. Apparently it had covered all the main points and gave a clear and unambiguous explanation of what had gone wrong and when. Wormald disappeared from the chamber. The two men resumed their deliberations. They seemed unaware of Mr Johnson's presence, as did the other two men in the room busy with their careful manipulations. He didn't want to intrude but he felt that the longer the men discussed the problem, the less likely they were to devise an appropriate solution. He stepped towards them and introduced himself to the man with the telephone, whose name was Bramley. It turned out that the man who had brought Mr

Johnson to the chamber was called Holhouse.

'I've listened to what you have been saying and it strikes me that you are in a difficult spot in terms of decision making.'

The two men nodded.

'I don't know a great deal about the Golden Clock but I would be very happy to help you in whatever way I can. What exactly is the problem with the configuration?'

'It's difficult to say exactly,' said Bramley. 'Wormald felt uneasy this morning and said that the more he looked at the configuration in question, the less sense it seemed to make. From there it is a short step to conceptual dissonance and downright incongruity.'

'Is the configuration in question in this room?'

'Yes and no. It's a very small sub-element of the urban renewal and regeneration area.' (Mr Johnson was pleased that he had identified just such an element.) 'Basically, it concerns the suggestion of a horse at rest on a piece of wasteground adjacent to a block of condemned flats and a mill that has been converted into apartments for young professionals. Six small children are crossing the wasteground on their way to the shops. It is summer and a fair has recently been held at a park nearby. So far so good. The presence of a horse can be explained by the fact of the fair or with reference to the organic rural culture that exists in certain housing estates in Ireland. But look now. The horse is up and about and appears to be wearing a saddle. He begins to manifest the qualities of a racehorse rather than a tired beast of burden. Whilst at rest he was explicable. Active, he is less persuasive. Do the children come over and attend to the horse? No, they appear to have no interest in him. Their clothes, their demeanour, the purpose of their journey all militate against the likelihood of their being organic ruralists keeping alive country culture in the harsh environment of the inner city. A closer scrutiny of the fair that was held recently in a park close by reveals that it was prevented by a local by-law from exploiting live animals. No licence that permitted the use of horses or any other creatures had been issued. As time passes he is more and more a horse out of context. He emanates incongruity; he is increasingly a distinctive seeing element at sea in an alien context. Before long, any attempts to establish a set of contexts around him seem futile, half-hearted essays in inconsistency and irrelevance and merely serve to sharpen the horse's distinctiveness, which is, of course, anathema to the innate conception of the Clock, unless it were to be presented in the overall horse category. Which it isn't. Of course, you could argue that in a system that seeks to provide a visual representation of every conceivable phenomenological configuration, the aspect I have just described surely has its place; and you would be right, save for one thing: the thinking strand of the Golden Clock, that part of the system that most closely corresponds to the organisational glue model, is not sufficiently developed in this instance to persuade the perceiver of the veracity of the situation. Does this make sense? I know that you are new to the ways of the Golden Clock. What I mean is, the perceiver brings to the Golden Clock a set of hierarchical perceptions, ranked according to commonly accepted notions of rightness. Yes, of course a racehorse may be resting on a patch of wasteground adjacent to a condemned block of facts and a converted mill. But to admit the possibility of such a configuration most certainly does not imply that it will work as a credible element in the seeing section; not, as I say, without a strong intervention from the thinking strand which perforce provides a subtle and insinuating argument in favour of the veracity of a configuration that teeters on the edge of incongruity – at least, most of the time. Do you follow me? But the dangers we have outlined are very real. If we were simply to remove the horse aspect from the configuration, we might unwittingly be throwing into doubt a whole set of minor but related suggestive configurations that had sprung up in the meantime. On the other hand, if we were to allow the distinctive horse to prevail, he might overrun the rest of the section and wreak goodness knows what havoc on other parts of the Clock. Before we knew it, there would be horses everywhere, and what sort of a unified representation of all the possible configurations of every conceivable phenomenological entity in all the senses known to humankind would that be? It's not all about horses, for heaven's sake. Can you see how important this is?'

'Yes, I think I can. It seems to make sense even given the limited understanding I have of the operating mechanisms of the Golden Clock. What I think you are essentially concerned about is maintaining the conceptual consistency and overall integrity of the Golden Clock in theory and in practice.'

'Yes, yes,' said Holhouse. 'I don't know you, Mr Johnson, but you do demonstrate a sophisticated understanding of the underlying principles. You have said that Juniper has already shown you parts of the Golden Clock. What would you recommend we do?'

'I am not sure but perhaps I can make a couple of observations which may or may not be germane to the issues at hand. First, as I mentioned earlier, this part of the seeing section of the Golden Clock does strike me as existing somewhat independently of the rest of the section. For example, the material representations of the phenomenological configurations in this room have no obvious relationship with configurations in other rooms. I don't mean only in terms of its relationship with the main chamber upstairs but with any other configurations in the rooms which lead off from here.'

Holhouse and Bramley nodded.

'Now, as far as I understand it, the seeing section of the Golden Clock — and, for all I know, which admittedly isn't very much at this moment, the other sensory sections — acquires conceptual integrity through the suggestive and allusive relationship between its constituent parts.'

Holhouse and Bramley nodded again.

'But with the best will in the world and with any number of invocations of the thinking strand, if the actual physical connections haven't been established, then surely the dynamic relationship this particular area has with the rest of the section is axiomatically flawed? Am I on the right track? I am? Good. As I say, I'm still new to all this but I do like to think that in the short time I've been with the organisation I have been able to divine something of the intentions behind the more significant processes and theoretical models that carry weight here. In fact, I did say to Juniper that more than any other, the Golden Clock was the process — I don't mean to devalue it by using such a workaday term — that seemed the most clear and unambiguous. I am not sure whether I have covered two points here. Perhaps I should add that although I understand your concerns about the primacy of the horse, perhaps you are overstating the extent to which it might be interpreted as an incongruous racehorse rather than a beast of burden with an explicable provenance in terms of its positioning in an aspect of the urban renewal and regeneration depiction. Perhaps I'm being naïve, and correct me if I'm wrong, but didn't you begin to feel uneasy about the horse when you saw that it had a saddle? You did? Good. In that case, might it not be the case that you were projecting your own notions of what the possession of a saddle constitutes rather than making an objective judgement of the visual representation that confronted you? In other words, you immediately assumed that because the horse wore a saddle, it was a racehorse. Yet horses of all kinds wear saddles, even horses at rest on an urban wasteground. I might also say that the horse at rest aspect of the impression threw you off the scent somewhat. You took it for granted that the horse was an inert element in the scene and when it evinced signs of life by getting to its feet, you jumped to the conclusion that it was a creature accustomed to intense activity, that is to say, a racehorse. But what if it was clear from the first configuration that the horse was a racing animal? You probably would have accepted its presence and oriented your thinking about the scene as a whole accordingly. I'm not sure if I am making sense but it seems to me that a combination of inadequate mechanical structuring and conceptual misinterpretation has led you to this crisis point. I wouldn't go as far to suggest that there isn't a problem but I would hazard a guess that the situation isn't as insoluble as you suspect. It's not my place to say as much but I think a little low level tinkering with the configuration and an adjustment of your own attitude to the scene presented should resolve the situation to everyone's satisfaction. But what do you think?'

Bramley and Holhouse looked at each other.

'God, he's good,' said Bramley.

Then he addressed Mr Johnson.

'Everything you have said makes perfect sense. You told me that you might be able to bring a fresh pair of eyes. What you've actually done is bring a fresh sense of sight. And how apposite given that we are engaged in the seeing section. Could you specify exactly how we should progress from here?'

'I'd be happy to try but I would like to look closely at the configuration first. Would that be possible?'

It would be. Bramley and Holhouse led him over to the northern corner of the room and squatted down next to a combination of found objects. Mr Johnson scrutinised the arrangement and shortly divined the pattern that had been described to him. The horse was a fine animal, wrought from an empty toilet roll holder and a tangle of cotton. Evidently the saddle had been suggested by a dark mottling on the middle of the empty toilet roll which had become visible when the cardboard cylinder had been turned over when the horse got to its feet. The other elements in the scene were clear enough. The children were represented by rubber thimbles, the gentrified mill by a brown chocolate bar wrapper with gilt trimming. A dirty soap dish stood for the condemned flats. Bramley and Holhouse were right — in many respect, the scene was incongruous. The horse was magnificently out of place. But with a little judicious tinkering, order could be restored with no consequences for the stability of the rest of the system.

'May I?' said Mr Johnson.

Holhouse and Bramley assented. Mr Johnson lifted the horse from its setting, which caused both men to raise their eyebrows and look at each other in astonishment, and set it down two feet away in the middle of An Unexpected Holiday in Autumn.

'You see?' he said. 'Is that still incongruous? Imagine that you have gone on an unexpected holiday in autumn. The day is wet, moisty, as the visual configuration suggests.' (A small plastic cup half filled with water sat next to a piece of brown masking tape, which was a country road. Two matchboxes were cars; three inches away and partly obscured by a plastic bag was a desk tidy filled with pens, or, as Mr Johnson took it to be, a cathedral poking its towers above the surrounding hills.) 'What could be more characteristic of an unexpected holiday in autumn during wet weather than to see from the passing car, the windscreen wipers beating back and forth, a racehorse at rest in a field? At the moment the car passes, the horse gets up. But you are not surprised by the presence of a saddle because you have no reason not to think that the horse may be a racehorse. This is the countryside, after all. Can you see how your expectations have informed your perceptions? Later, perhaps, the car drives through the city. The horse, or perhaps a different horse, is observed in a new setting. But the occupants of the car are already attuned to horse-perception. It might strike them as curious that a horse is in the city but I would warrant that they have the conceptual wherewithal to accommodate the fact of it, and in any case, the question of the saddle ought to preclude any deeper crisis of incongruity developing.'

He paused for a moment.

'Perhaps I am teaching you to suck eggs here' – Bramley and Holhouse dissented vigorously – 'but it does strike me that perhaps you have strayed a little from conceptual first principles. Again, I know only a little of the intimate workings of the system but I like to think that I have a grasp of the overarching design.'

Mr Johnson began to feel returning to him the self-confidence that had inspired him in the presentation suite. He felt that he was getting back on top of the issues and turning theory turn into practice with his very words. The instinctive grasp of the underlying conceptual principles of the Golden Clock was fast becoming a strong practical application. In this one small corner of the system he could see how his micro actions connected to the macro elements as well as to all the inter-linking bits and even some of the spaces between. He explained this to Bramley and Holhouse. They were all ears.

'By maintaining awareness of the importance of the relationship between small scale actions and larger conceptual principles, the physical configuration resolutely insists upon its own theoretical solidity, which is, as far as I understand it, and correct me if you think I am heading in the wrong direction with this, the very principle that informs the functional imperative of the thinking strand in terms of its dynamic relationship with the more tangible, sensory-derived elements of the Golden Clock. The thinking strand weaves a web of coherent interpretation from a tangled mass of often disparate phenomenological data. But it does not exist *a priori*. It is given conceptual substance from the available evidence and the shifting perceptual intentions of the viewer. Which is a key issue in this context – I might be being a little bold in saying this but perhaps the pair of you are too close to the issues.'

Bramley and Holhouse looked at each other with rueful expressions. They didn't demur.

'But now that the horse has touched tangibly its cognate neighbours and insisted upon its own congruity within its original context, I don't think you should worry about a knock-on effect anymore. Sometimes there is no substitute for a little distance and a fresh pair of eyes – though I would hesitate to say a fresh sense of sight. Does that make sense?'

'Yes, Mr Johnson, it all makes perfect sense,' said a voice at the door. It was Juniper. He was smiling. Juniper walked over to join them by the desk.

'I didn't know you were here,' said Mr Johnson, feeling suddenly abashed. 'How long were you listening?'

'Long enough to help make my mind up finally about you, Mr Johnson. We knew that you possessed an unusually sophisticated grasp of the underlying principles of the Golden Clock but we could never have dreamt that you would be able to demonstrate this in practical terms so soon – and so effectively.'

'I don't know what we would have done without Mr Johnson, Juniper,' said Bramley. 'He made an adjustment to the configuration that we hadn't considered and showed us how it affected all the cognate configurations. Then he explained his actions in lucid, theoretical terms.'

'I know, I heard him.'

Mr Johnson was keen to play down his role in the affair although he was feeling extremely proud.

'It was nothing really. I simply placed the horse in a different context and explored some of the interpretative implications.'

'Don't be modest, Mr Johnson,' said Juniper. 'As these gentlemen could tell you, there is much more to adjusting a misconfiguration than merely placing an object in another context. The success or failure of a reconfiguration depends to a great extent upon the attitude and depth of understanding of the reconfigurer. You of all people must understand this – your first exposure to the Golden Clock, after all, was mediated through a filter of subjective impressionism. Do you remember what you asked me about the oracular function?'

Mr Johnson nodded.

'So it is with the operational side of things. Every operative brings their own set of skills, experiences, assumptions and prejudices to their work. Not all of them are allowed to configure, let alone reconfigure. I'm sure I don't need to explain to you the difference between routine configuring and schematic extension and the sort of work you have just undertaken. No, I thought not. You are very advanced, Mr Johnson. And I think that these fellows owe you a debt of gratitude.'

Bramley and Holhouse looked away embarrassed. But Juniper smiled at them.

'Don't worry. There won't be any comeback. I of all people understand how easily problems arise in this line of work. Just go easy on the horses next time.'

Bramley and Holhouse thanked Juniper and Mr Johnson and left the room, presumably to compose themselves. The other operatives were attending to their tasks, apparently oblivious to the drama that had unfolded before them.

'I think your work here is done for the moment, Mr Johnson.'

When they had stepped out of the chamber, Juniper said: 'I didn't want to overstate things in there but that was a real let off. The Golden Clock was in grave danger for a while. I wasn't going to say as much in front of Bramley and Holhouse but I think, Mr Johnson, that you have saved the Golden Clock from a wholesale malfunctioning. Yes, really. Bramley and Holhouse understood the perils that could ensue from a mishandling of the reconfiguration but their conception, of course, only extends so far. If the horse incongruity had spread through the seeing section, there would almost certainly have been a catastrophic roll out of intense ambiguity into the other broad elements. Precariousness and instability would have infected every operative, however senior, and the thinking strand would have disintegrated. The whole system would have been cast in darkness – and so, therefore, would we. Quite apart from the devastating cultural impact on all who work here, we would have been without food or fuel since our connection with Nikolai's department would have been severed. They in turn would be thrown into confusion and chaos. And what would the cleaners do then? No, Mr Johnson, it is clear that you have come to us at the right time. There is work for you here, let no one say otherwise.'

They descended the iron ladder and crawled back up the tunnel.

'How do you feel?' asked Juniper when they reached the top and stood stooping once more in the main chamber.

'Exhilarated. And tired. In fact, I don't think I've ever felt as tired in my life. Although I wasn't at work in the chamber for long, I expended more energy on that one task than on all the other work I've done while I've been here.'

'Of course you did. The Golden Clock demands just such an expenditure of effort. For people at your level, it is brainwork of the highest order. The physical placement of material phenomena is the least of it. After what you did, you will need rest and plenty of it. But not yet.'

'No?'

'No. I think you still have something to do.'

'Do you mean Bragby?'

'I don't need to answer that, do I?'

'When can I see him?'

'Very soon now. Are you still clear about what you want to see him about?'

'I think so. It feels appropriate. Perhaps more than ever now.'

'Why do you say that?'

'I'm not sure. Perhaps because of the work I've just undertaken on the Golden Clock. I do feel more closely involved with the life of this section.'

'Come into the office with me. There's something I want to talk to you about.'

They went inside and Juniper shut the door. Juniper sat behind his desk and Mr Johnson in front of it. Mr Johnson could hear outside the eternal activity of the Golden Clock. Even the air in the office smelt of metal and gum. Juniper was talking to him about higher level operations. After the intense mental activity in the chamber, Mr Johnson's senses were dulled. His thoughts wandered like stray sheep.

'But in essence, you thought about the situation differently,' said Juniper. Mr Johnson opened his eyes wide.

'Yes, I think I did. That makes sense.'

With every minute that passed, Mr Johnson was less sure about what exactly he had done. But it had felt significant. He had saved the Golden Clock, apparently. He had put theory into practice. He had felt a cream ribbon of understanding extending from his mind into the field of operation. The theories were unifying, the models shining in crystalline relief. He heard Juniper ask him what he had made of the ledger and Mr Johnson said that the finely detailed entries were to his way of thinking as close an approximation of the actual condition of the Golden Clock as it were possible to render, though he wondered how such a rendition of the less tangible elements of the system would appear. Mr Johnson asked whether the red ledger would have helped Bramley and Holhouse. It seemed to fulfil the admin requirements they had spoken off. But Juniper said that the ledger wasn't for everybody's eyes. Operatives could know too much, and in any case, it was essentially a retrospective record and in no way provided an accurate snapshot of the condition of the Golden Clock at the present moment. Juniper also referred to something called 'deep conceptual auditing' and said there would be time enough for Mr Johnson to become acquainted with it. Juniper wasn't surprised that Mr Johnson had instantly grasped the essence of the information in the ledger, even in his tired state. Mr Johnson heard himself begin to summarise the relationship between the theoretical and material components of the Golden Clock as it was revealed in the red ledger, when quite suddenly Juniper said: 'It's yours if you want it.'

'I'm sorry?'

'The Golden Clock.'

'But the Golden Clock belongs to Bragby.'

'No, Bragby's relentless thinking feeds the Golden Clock. Bragby developed the Golden Clock from nothing. But Bragby doesn't own it.'

'Then neither can I.'

'But you can think it. Maybe not immediately. I don't know. But nobody has demonstrated such a conceptual grasp as you. I certainly didn't. Only Bragby has thought on that level.'

'But I'm not qualified to think about the Golden Clock at that level. I am still relatively new here.'

'You are already thinking about the Golden Clock, Mr Johnson. And the Golden Clock is thinking about you. I am not suggesting that you assume control over it today, or next week, or even next year – although I would wager that if you were to, it would be sooner rather than later. But you are young, you have ideas, you know how to effect change. The men respect you already – yes, news will already have spread. It is yours if you want it.'

'What does Bragby think about this?'

'Bragby doesn't think about anything in such specific terms. If you asked what Bragby felt about it, I might say that he feels a great sense of imminent resolution. He feels appropriate and at peace. I might also say that he feels as though he is being gently absorbed at last into the thinking strand. I am guessing, of course. Does this make sense to you?'

'Yes, I think so. But I am so very tired. I can't go on snatching scraps of sleep.'

Juniper looked away sadly. 'We are all tired, Mr Johnson. I can't promise that that will ever change. Bragby, of course, is more tired than anyone.'

'Does Bragby ever sleep?'

'No. Bragby cannot sleep. No, that's not true. Bragby could sleep, and therein lies the danger. Bragby mustn't sleep. If Bragby sleeps, he may sleep for ever. As much as our work has been focused on the Golden Clock, it has been devoted to keeping Bragby awake. Sometimes this has seemed like a cruelty. But Bragby himself understands why he must stay awake. If he stops thinking, then what you saw today will be common practice throughout the Golden Clock.'

'Then if I were to assume such a position in relation to the Golden Clock, I too would be unable to sleep.'

'I am not going to make any rash promises to you, Mr Johnson. But I should say that when that day comes, your own position in relation to the Golden Clock would be less individuated than Bragby's. For one thing, we would work more closely together. You would feel comfortable about delegating certain responsibilities to me and other senior members of staff. For another, everybody's skill levels will be higher. Yes, there will be more work to do and complicated new processes will have to be learned. But the organic life of the section would have reached a sufficiently evolved stage to be able to cope with whatever demands are thrown at it. We anticipate being able to sit comfortably on speedily emerging new technologies and managing changes to the work culture. Things do change in here, despite what you might think.'

Juniper paused to roll a cigarette and light another candle.

'To your mind, the Golden Clock might seem something of a fixed entity in terms of its structure and shape but I can assure you that it is subject to any number of refinements, modifications and improvements over time. I don't mean modifications of the type you just made – you performed a conceptual intervention to an active process strand – but changes to the overarching mechanisms and the means by which raw materials are procured and fitted. As time passes and our technological proficiency improves – and, of course, the possibilities offered by available technology increase – we see that the Golden Clock of today is an infinitely more sophisticated creature than, say, the Golden Clock of a week ago or when it was first conceived. This is quite right, of course – our own working culture here is very different, the relationships between teams and individuals more developed. And it will change again. It could be that we are drawing to the close of one period in the history of the Golden Clock and are about to enter another. I think you know what I mean by that. I'm sorry, Mr Johnson, did you drop off?'

'I don't know. Perhaps. I know that you were explaining more about the Golden Clock. Perhaps I was comprehending it in my sleep.'

Juniper smiled. 'Quite possibly. It wouldn't surprise me given all that has passed today. I was talking particularly about how your closer involvement in the workings of the Golden Clock would affect you and about the mutability of the Golden Clock in spite of its apparently fixed and solid state. Would you like me to recap?'

''No, I think I have a grasp of both of those areas,' said Mr Johnson, stifling a yawn.

'Would you like some proper sleep?'

'Yes, I would, although I don't want to miss anything.'

'Don't worry about that. If I were you, I would have a good sleep while you can. Goodness knows it looks like you'll be busy enough later on.'

'That sounds ominous.'

'It wasn't meant to. But you will have plenty on your plate and if things work out as I hope and expect they will, you won't have much time for sleep, not formal sleep, anyway. I ought to be honest with you at the outset. But don't dwell too much on the detail. You are probably used to working flat out by now. At least you will have the satisfaction of knowing that the prodigious mental and physical efforts you will expend on behalf of the Golden Clock will be towards a productive end, in professional and personal terms. I bet you haven't been able to say that about any of the projects you've worked on here hitherto.'

'No, I couldn't. But I am a little worried about assuming overall control of the Golden Clock, if indeed it comes to that. I haven't had any formal management experience so far. I am still relatively new, after all.'

'I don't think that's a problem in the least. Bragby himself wasn't greatly experienced in such matters when he first turned his great brain towards building and developing the Golden Clock. He acquired authority and respect through practical demonstration. Talent will always out. The men know that there is no aspect of the Golden Clock, however arcane or hidden away, that Bragby hasn't comprehended. There is nothing that anyone call tell him about the Golden Clock that he doesn't already know. And how many managers could you say that of?'

'Not many,' admitted Mr Johnson. 'In fact, I can't think of any.'

'Exactly. Now you may well say to me, how can I, Mr Johnson, be expected to acquire such knowledge of the Golden Clock when my formal acquaintance with it has been so cursory? What level of authority and respect could I expect to command from the men? And you wouldn't be wrong to ask those questions. All I would say to you is this: if Bragby wishes it, it shall be so. All manner of things will follow from that. And I should add: the Golden Clock would wish it too. That would be enough. In any case, I suspect that you were familiar with the conception of the Golden Clock long before you ever encountered it or had even heard of it, if that makes sense. Our innate confidence in your instinctive ability married to the practical evidence you have already provided more than adequately qualifies you for such a role. We don't stand on ceremony in here. There are no interminable induction programmes or training courses to complete first. If you are capable, you will be rewarded. If you are eminently capable, you will be rewarded at the highest possible level. But look, your eyes have closed again and I'm going on with myself. Have that sleep we talked about.'

Mr Johnson opened his eyes. Juniper was smiling at him again.

'Yes,' Mr Johnson said, 'I think I did drop off that time. But I still heard everything you said. You have reassured me somewhat. Perhaps if I take things one step at a time I will be all right. But there does seem to be an awful lot to learn.'

'Of course there is a lot to learn. That will never change. And it is worse for fast learners like ourselves.'

Juniper winked at Mr Johnson.

'We will never stop learning. The Golden Clock will never stop growing. And you must think that I'll never stop talking. Have a good sleep.'

'I'll try. One more thing – what do I need to do next? Will I be able to see Bragby soon?'

'Yes, very, very soon now. Sleep first, questions later. I will wake you in time for the meeting.'

'What meeting?'

'The Golden Clock reiteration meeting. It is a regular fixture in the working week. We review developments, plan for the future, restate our objectives, that sort of thing. It has a motivational value, too. I know, it sounds like any other meeting. In many ways it is, save for it being concerned entirely with our individual and collective relationships with the Golden Clock. It is important that you attend – it will soon become central to your working life. And there are other reasons, too. But I won't say it again – sleep first.'

Juniper blew the candle out and Mr Johnson fell to sleep straight away in the chair. It seemed that Juniper had been gone for only a minute when he woke Mr Johnson and told him that the meeting was about to start.

'Do you feel better for your sleep?'

'I don't know. It is hard to tell anymore.' In truth, he didn't know whether he was asleep or awake. 'Was I asleep long?'

'Long enough. I felt bad waking you up but it's time for the meeting. It is almost time for many new and wonderful things. Follow me.'

CHAPTER NINETEEN
THE LOOM

They went out of Juniper's office and crossed the main chamber to a smaller room. Save for a couple of operatives, the men stopped what they were doing and followed Juniper and Mr Johnson. Others were appearing through the arches that surrounded the main chamber. The small room quickly filled up. Candles were lit and Juniper squatted down at the end of the room opposite the door, the men, with Mr Johnson in the middle, squatting before him. Mr Johnson wondered why there were no chairs in the room, or indeed in any of the working areas of the Golden Clock that he had encountered so far, and assumed that it was to encourage efficient use of time. He certainly wasn't going to get too comfortable on his haunches, although the men seemed used to it. The room was packed and hot. When the last of the men had entered and the door closed, Juniper commenced the meeting. He talked about work that had recently been undertaken and projects that were coming up. It was hard to take in the details. Much of what Juniper said dealt with the specifics of configurations that Mr Johnson could barely conceive of. He supposed that this ought to concern him but because of the heat of the room or the confidence Juniper, and presumably Bragby, felt in him, he decided not to worry. There would be adequate time to get to grips with the finer points, after all. Juniper touched on questions relating to the supply of paper for the braziers and cleaner liaison. Mr Johnson thought it unlikely that he would have to devote too much attention to such questions. On the other hand, if Bragby was intimately acquainted with every aspect of the functioning and structure of the Golden Clock, then Mr Johnson could be reasonably expected to familiarise himself with the processes by which materials were requisitioned from Nikolai's department and the cleaning interface, even if only to a modest extent. The men were all ears, although no-one was taking any notes. There was no mention of an agenda either. Mr Johnson's eyes closed in spite of himself. When he opened them, the mood in the room had changed. The men were on their knees and the candles had been put out. Mr Johnson also dropped to his knees. Juniper's voice rang clear in the darkness. He had moved on to the essence of the Golden Clock itself.

'What has the Golden Clock brought us? You don't need me to tell you, I know, but there is no harm in revisiting first principles. For what principles they are. Oh, my good friends and esteemed colleagues, what is the Golden

Clock if not the whole sum of everything, the organic embodiment of light, knowledge and truth?'

The men rocked gently in approbation.

'Its gleaming, radiant sharp face and then the deep bass and thrum of its brass internals. I am speaking actually and symbolically. You know all of this, the sense of the surface of things and then the untouchable interiors. How our knowledge has been gathered and all the approximations and permutations ordered so that a mighty enduring tower may be built even here. Yes, especially here. Something that explains everything. Who gave us this? Bragby gave us this. Why must he not sleep? Because his will and thought sustains the Golden Clock and so sustains each one of us, even Bragby himself. Yes, for we are all part of its eternal organic life. But I don't need to tell you all of this. You know and feel it instinctively.'

'Yes,' the men said, 'yes, we know it and we feel it.'

'For if we didn't know it and feel it, where should we be? Without the eternal mental vigilance of Bragby and our own unceasing activity, the Golden Clock would fail. For even the Golden Clock is vulnerable and no more than the sum total of the accumulated interventions of purposed human agency. Yes, even the Golden Clock. It is at once greater and smaller than ourselves and so are we in relation to it. Just think about it for a moment quietly.'

Silence fell upon the chamber. Some of the men shook gently with silent sobs.

'Danger,' whispered one man at length, 'there was great danger, I hear.'

'Yes,' said Juniper, rising on his haunches so that he was above the men and Mr Johnson, 'news certainly travels quickly round here. What you have heard as rumour may now be confirmed as fact. The Golden Clock was in danger. Yes, my friends and colleagues, in great danger. We all know only too well the hazards we face on a daily basis, the perils entailed in the relentless configuring and adapting. Yes, yes, perils and hazards. And who among us is qualified to even contemplate a misconfiguration, let alone modify it? There is no answer to that, I know, save for Bragby himself. No, Wormald, not even I, not so swiftly, at least. But there is one among us now who looked at a gross misconfiguration on the Golden Clock and without hesitation moved to correct it and not only that but ensured that the tandemic implications in the cognate areas were wholly congruous. Yes, I know, it is remarkable. But Mr Johnson here, he did this.'

The men around Mr Johnson looked at him as if for the first time.

'Just picked up the horse and re-set him, as cool as you like,' they said. 'Didn't even need to consult with Juniper first.'

'Without delay or demur,' Juniper went on, 'he adjusted the configuration and brought clarity to a question of great murk and ambiguity. And who, my dearest people, who among us could do that save one, save Bragby himself? Who save Bragby has ever demonstrated such an instinctive grasp of the nuances and subtleties of the Golden Clock, that great entity without which we should surely die of thirst? Not even I, who has been intimately present at all the stages of its development. I say this entirely without rancour. It fills my soul with gladness to welcome to the Golden Clock a new and talented operative. No, not merely an operative, and no disrespect to you my friends, and I'm sure none has been taken – not an operative, I say, but a comprehender, a great changer, an initiator, an imaginer. I don't know. Words fail me – for once. I know, I never thought that I would say that. But think, all of you, of what he has done. And now, good, good operatives and friends, he has one more appointment to keep, and who knows what changes shall be wrought as a consequence? But we must greet change without fear for all change is good change when governed by the conceptual constancy of the Golden Clock. For that is what has happened in the case of Mr Johnson. The Clock knows and it responded to his gentle touch and nimble mind. He knew how to touch it in the right way – softly, though not like a lady.'

Juniper made a signal and the men rose to stooping height. Some of the men next to Mr Johnson drew closer to him. Suddenly Juniper cried, 'Hold him down,' and Mr Johnson was pinned to the floor. The crowd parted and Juniper stooped towards him swinging a lantern. The men who were holding Mr Johnson down stroked his face tenderly.

'It is soon now. Are you ready?'

'Yes, I think so.'

'It is yours if you want it. Do you understand what that means?' said Juniper, holding the lantern so close to Mr Johnson's face that he squinted and turned away blindly.

'I think so, yes.'

'Then it is time.'

The men lifted their hands from him. Mr Johnson got up from the floor and dusted himself down. They took him through a side door and down a tunnel before leading him into a square canvas construction in the middle of another chamber lit at the periphery by braziers, and sat him on an armchair. To his left was a wall made out of old box files. The men removed themselves from the canvas construction.

Mr Johnson could hear someone on the other side of the boxes breathing quietly. Dimly in the background he heard music made from flutes and guitars strike up.

'Bragby?' whispered Mr Johnson in the gloom. 'Is that you?'

The breathing continued, low and metronomic. Mr Johnson sat still and quiet for some time. Then a voice muttered: 'Shadowment, shadowment.'

'Bragby?' repeated Mr Johnson.

'My shadowment. You, Mr Johnson, in the heart of The Loom, swathed in my shadowment. I was wondering when you'd turn up.'

'Is this The Loom? What is it?'

'The Loom is all and all is in The Loom. You, in the heart of The Loom, are warm, have seen things. This tiredness, I feel it in you.'

'Yes I am tired. I need rest. I have been working very hard down here and elsewhere.'

'Plenty of rest. You need to speak to me. I know all about it.'

'Yes, I need to speak to you. Our respective paths, some similarities. My induction programme.' His eyes smarted even in the heavy dark. His head felt full of metal and wood. 'I am tired. I need to speak to you. There are matters which concern us both.'

But when he tried to put his mind to it, Mr Johnson wasn't sure anymore what it was exactly he wanted to ask Bragby about. He couldn't very well ask for the Golden Clock just like that. Everything else was vague and out of reach. Even the Golden Clock seemed far away. The warm and dark ate up his thoughts. He needed rest and plenty of it. He sat still. Bragby was murmuring softly to himself. The effect was reassuring, lulling. At all costs, he must keep Bragby awake. At all costs he must stay awake. But Bragby's lulling voice lulled him deeper and deeper and it was difficult to tell anymore whether he was listening to Bragby in his sleep or awake himself and listening to Bragby in his sleep or whether he was asleep and he was listening to Bragby listening in his sleep to him while he thought he was awake. But Bragby never slept.

'Warm, dark Loom, resolutions, decay. My people, feel the heat of their devotion. My hands working the grid and the lights pimple pricking. From department to department, deeper and dark, fuggy Loom. Bring them out, bring away, downhere, upperthere, come in, come in. Good people, keep from going to the bad. Keep them safe. These and others.'

Fighting against the weight in his head and on his eyes, Mr Johnson strove to resolve his thoughts. 'There are five synergetic functional elements,' he began. 'Feel – Felt – Found. All the Ds.' But if Bragby heard him at all, he gave no sign of it. He had probably heard it all before.

'The braziers working and the feeding, relentless, the permutations and configurations. The Golden Clock tells us everything.'

'The Golden Clock? I have seen and worked on the Golden Clock. I know that you built it. I think we need to talk about it.'

'Always this way, the fug and the murk. Good people driven bad. Resolution and decay. They know not of what is this and others. All is in this and this is in all there is. Like dark doom and murk. Bring away, away. Always this way. Bring to the light-in-dark.'

'Yes, the light in the dark.'

'I had a conception of The Loom and was aware of its interconnectedness, of the organic relationship between all its elements and points. I felt all The Loom and The Loom felt me moving within it.'

His murmurings resolved themselves into clearer statements and Mr Johnson pricked up his ears in the dark.

'I brought them rich achievements and they called me greedy for challenging their shifting. The thousand small ways by which a man may meet his death. A loose stair carpet. A forgotten nut in a jet engine worked loose. The impermanence and the decay. Do you see? Always the shifting and sorting and change. I wonder. Did you ever miss a sales target, Mr Johnson? I never missed one. I was the best performer they ever had. They told me this. I needed no approbation. Do you know how they rewarded me? For every target I exceeded, they would increase the next one by the same percentage.'

'I also started in the sales office, I think. Our respective paths have much in common, show many parallels. I was told this. I think. I need to speak with you about my induction. I was told that talent would always be rewarded and the organisation welcomed enthusiasm. For me, communication, commercial and growth. I have learned about the Five Synergetic Elements but they are less and less clear with every passing day. The Golden Clock is clearer but fading. I need you to explain something to me but I cannot remember what it is now. It is a case of knowing where to go next or not. They told me about you in the buds.'

'The things they tell you. A chain of broken promises shattering infinity. Remove at the source, nip in the bud. They told me many things. Bring away, away. Better here. Everything we need here.

'This dark place, tunnels and walls. In this 1972 dark. I think... sound aesthetics, the summoning up of rooms of old. Mr Johnson, somewhere I possess every studio recording made by Jethro Tull. That folk prog thrub. I am not proud. What has this got to do with work? What has work got to do with this? But here. Yes, here is old thrub and warm. Warm Jethro Tull lulling warm room.

'I cannot perceive you yet you seem surprised. A film of gloom, doubt, cast across your visage like clouds eating up the sunshine. The clouds played hide and seek with each other over the wolds.'

'How did you know about the sunshine and the clouds?'

On the other side of the table a hand removed two boxes at head height.

'Sit nearer to me. That doom. The tiredness in you, I sense that. The lie about logical ordered thought. In The Loom, for example. All the up and down and round and round work. More like spirals of being. I feel that you understand this too. Come closer to me. Many of them up there now imagining that they are proceeding sequentially on a rational escalator, accumulating experiences and knowledge, the slow amassing numbers and data fields. Information and chaos. Then for what?'

'The Loom. Yes, that makes sense.'

'Warm dark fuggy mug. Better here. Quiet here. Hear think better. Muggy fug. Yes, I know all about the meetings. As plate blue sky in metal the green afternoon. You are warm.'

'Yes, I am warm.'

'This dark obscuring cloud. Play Jethro Tull softly, calming. Still warm 1972 evening, quiet red wine night, guitars and woollen drums and thin carpet. Static vinyl warmth, the gasses fizzing and spitting, the rain. The goods trains roll back along the viaduct past the upper-floor windows, the dirty lace curtains flapping, the sill crumbling. We wore heavy overcoats, torn badges, sent west, east, north and south. We rolled our own. The shadows and the gloom played shrouds and gauntlets with the sun. The rain swept over the town like a glove. These thoughts are unendurable. Time before all this. Time before all. Goodness yet. Not even sure if wanted back. Everything here. Safe and warm here. The Golden Clock tells us everything.'

'Jethro Tull?'

'I feel you drawing warm to something. You developed early an understanding of the Golden Clock. This thing identified in you. My time, diminished, the networks rusting. From upthere, come in, come in. My commitment undimmed, they call me greedy. I bring great riches and they know not it or that, laboured here, come gather, my networks upperhere bring great richness, but you have seen all this. Wore many hats, but at senior level they look away and despatch, north, south, east, west, they change to newness and we must go, dive down away, bring whom we may. But you, on to something, have seen things, you are warm, come near. You have listened and smelt and tasted and touched and heard and thought and all the great workings have been unified by your own conception. Come closer. Tired and warm. Tired and worn. I feel this in you, passing my hands.

'There is money here, let them not otherwise. I bring them great riches but how do they reward me? For every increment, a percentage, the slow shifting and shuffling, like hide and seek, bring away, away. They said to bring them out and away. The things they say. Sun and clouds. Fug and mug. Better here, dark here. You are warm. Sit nearer to me.'

One by one all the boxes were removed and Mr Johnson felt the canvas structure being lifted away. He saw at last Bragby dark and hunched on a low stool at his side. On the periphery his men crouched waiting, their eyes yellow in the light of the braziers.

'Money for all. I touched its surface and felt its pimpled walls, gave way. What brings you here? I know what brings you here. Our paths are remarkable, the curiousness. My time diminishing. My belly soft. They draw away. The pimpling and then this, unharnessed and far away. All the quarters. All yours. You understand the Golden Clock. North, east, west and south. My time rusting, year on year. In all this time, old Loom!'

Mr Johnson felt Bragby's warm and searching breath on his face. 'My induction – how?' he began, but the words died on his lips. Bragby sighed and his head hung heavy on his chest. His breathing was slow and rhythmic. 'Don't go to sleep,' said Mr Johnson. 'Please don't go to sleep.' Bragby's people looked away. Moths span madly in the stagnation. The braziers flamed and went out. The music slurred to a halt. The dark chewed the air. Bragby was asleep. The moment had passed. Mr Johnson bore no malice. He was lifted or shuffled rather back and away from Bragby, whose diminishment was indicated by the detectable decline of a star of darker massy black to a pin prick spot and then pop, though Mr Johnson could hear him snoring gently as if he were close at hand. The moment had passed and there seemed to be no reason to be sorry for that. Mr Johnson was actually laughing as Bragby's men hoisted him up in the soft old armchair. The light was better now; illumination was provided by yellow bicycle lamps strung from a joist above them. Juniper's face swam into view. 'It's The Loom, you see,' he cried, and disappeared. The chair was leaking its filling. Mr Johnson laughed and laughed. The men seemed to dance around him. 'Don't tickle me, please don't tickle me,' he said, as one enormous fellow with a sly face and a lazy eye paddled his hands back and forth from Mr Johnson's tummy. 'Stop it, stop it,' he cried in delirious agitation. It was all he could do to stay in the chair until it appeared that the dancing men were actually tickling the chair itself, which was even more ticklish than Mr Johnson, so over and over he went in giddy wonder until he landed upright, still in the chair, and saw the men now many feet above his head pointing down and smirking, their sharp white teeth flashing. Mr

Johnson pointed back. 'I told you not to tickle me,' he shouted. 'Don't go!' The faces were disappearing one by one from the ceiling. 'Don't tickle me!'

'I won't tickle you,' said a voice, but it wasn't Bragby's or Juniper's. 'It's Mr Johnson, isn't it? I wondered when you'd show up.'

Mr Johnson yawned and looked about him. He was in a large but sparsely-furnished office. Bright sunshine poured through broad windows. A chunky, bespectacled man resembling a well-fed, hyper-active child stuffed into the suit of a senior executive stood before him. The man beamed at Mr Johnson from one side of his mild floury face to the other and extended a pudgy paw.

'I'm Sir Colin,' he said, pumping Mr Johnson's hand firmly. 'Excuse me one moment.' He stood on the arm of the chair and reached up to the ceiling where he moved a large, square polystyrene tile back into position. 'That's better. We shouldn't have any more trouble from that quarter.' He climbed down. 'Now then. You are late for your induction with me. Don't worry – I'm not offended. How's it all gone so far?'

Mr Johnson looked up at Sir Colin and tried as best he could to gather his thoughts.

'I can't say, really. It has been difficult keeping track of everything. I have met so many different people and they have all had very different things to say. Everybody seems to think that what they do is more important than what everybody else does. The personnel manager told me that in some ways my induction would never end, and I'm beginning to think she was right.'

'Well, Mr Johnson, formally speaking, your induction ends here. According to the checklist, I'm your last port of call. So you can tick me off and be done with it.'

'But I have never been given a checklist, Sir Colin.'

'What? Never given a checklist? That's no good. All inductees get a checklist. Inductors certainly have one.'

Sir Colin went to his desk and returned with a piece of paper.

'Look – here's my name. Last on the list – induction period over. You really should have been given a copy, it's most irregular.'

'Everything seemed a little chaotic when I started. I wasn't even connected properly to the computer network.'

At this Sir Colin raised his eyes to the ceiling.

'Mr Johnson, I can only apologise for our dilatoriness. It sounds as though you have been shunted from pillar to post. I hardly dare ask whether you have been able to form a clear idea about the way we work.'

'Not a very clear one, but I've certainly been granted a lot of fascinating insights into the organisational culture. I don't know whether this was the right approach to take but after a while I concentrated on getting to grips with the work of the conceptual initialisation department. There was a resource allocation problem in sales, you see, and I never did any work as such in that department. During my short time here so far, I have seen a lot of people from many different departments and functions but I'm still not one hundred per cent sure how everything fits together. I had hoped that Bragby would clarify things for me. Our careers apparently have a number of curious parallels. He did clarify things eventually, but not in a way that will be useful to my career in the long term. He made sense at the time but it's dissolving even as I speak. Even the Golden Clock seems less real somehow now, and I became very involved with it during my time down there. Or was it up there?'

At the mention of Bragby, or the Golden Clock, or possibly both, Sir Colin raised his eyes to the ceiling again and Mr Johnson decided not to pursue the point.

'Perhaps you could put me in the picture a bit more. I think that I could see everybody in the organisation every day of the week and still not emerge with a clear overview.'

'You are right,' said Sir Colin. 'It is quite a task getting to know your way round when you are also learning on the job, as it were. And we've got some people here who can talk for England but don't always explain things properly. But when it comes down to the nub, it's actually very simple and all the inductions in the world are so much flying chaff by comparison. Allow me to explain.'

Mr Johnson felt fixed into the old chair and didn't demur but just returned Sir Colin's kindly smile. He was all ears.

'What you must remember at all times, Mr Johnson, is that everything in life depends upon how you look at it. It's really that simple. Take this place, for example. Never forget, Mr Johnson, that we are a flat organisation, yet an organisation that possesses many ridges and declivities. Does this sound like a paradox? Perhaps it is. Let me explain in the best way that I can.'

Sir Colin picked up a square, smooth plane of wood.

'Look at this board. Appears to be perfectly flat. And so it may seem. But wait a minute. Let's put it under the microscope and see what happens.'

Mr Johnson got up stiffly and Sir Colin led him over to a workbench at the back of office where, sure enough, a large microscope sat. Following Sir Colin's lead, he peered closely through the lens.

'You see,' Sir Colin cried triumphantly, 'it's not really flat at all, is it? It's pitted and potted. If you were tiny enough to live in one of those holes, you could be forgiven for thinking that you lived in one of the deepest valleys in the Himalayas. Similarly, if you lived on one of those ridges, you would regard the world below you with the benign superiority the Man in the Moon surveys the earth.'

He stepped back from the microscope and tapped the wood for emphasis.

'And so it is with us. From a macro point of view, we are a flat organisation. From a micro point of view, we are structured according to a multitude of strata and an infinite subtlety of gradations. Man exists at once in a micro and macro condition. It's the principle of simultaneousness,' Sir Colin added, clutching the wood to his chest.

'Simultaneousness,' repeated Mr Johnson slowly. 'Yes, that makes a lot of sense.'

'Think of it like being in two places at the same time or two very different trains hurtling down parallel tracks. The trains might not even be aware of each other but sure enough they are both rattling along at the same pace. The two trains might be going to different stations, one might be a passenger train, the other a freight train – it doesn't matter. What counts is the mutuality of the phenomena. Do I make myself clear? Do you know, Mr Johnson, I get so impatient with corporate jargon and management speak. I firmly believe that the essence of modern business practice can be reduced to a few short parabolic statements. That's how I see my role in the company – a storyteller pulling together the frayed threads of an old tapestry in order to weave a new narrative.'

Mr Johnson didn't feel the need to say anything else. He smiled at Sir Colin, who was hopping excitedly from foot to foot.

'Golden yarn trailing from the sky... yes, it takes an artist's eye and hand to weave a story all can understand. Let them spout their management speak! They call me a figurehead, but Mr Johnson, which part of a ship is the first to reach the land? Quite.'

He remembered himself and stopped hopping. 'But I go on, and you look tired.'

'Yes, I've been meaning to have a proper lie down for some time. I've been very busy recently and snatching sleep when I can.'

'Go and get some proper rest. What day is it today? Wednesday? Right, off you go. Get off home and don't come back until Monday. Is there a Mrs Johnson?'

'No, there isn't.'

'Never mind. A serious partner?'

'No, not at the moment.'

'Not to worry. Here's a tenner – no, it's on me. Go and treat yourself. Buy a couple of nice chops, bottle of wine, rent a film, indulge yourself. What am I thinking of? Ten pounds won't cover that little lot, will it? Here's another ten. No, I absolutely insist. We expect our employees to work hard, Mr Johnson, but we are not inhumane. I know when a man's body is crying out for recuperation. Now, off you go. I don't want to see you again until next Monday.'

'It's very kind of you, Sir Colin. But there's one thing I need to mention before I go.'

Mr Johnson reached into his trouser pocket, pulled out the offending notes that the personnel manager had given him and handed them to Sir Colin.

'I think I might still be in trouble about these. I can't in all conscience go home with a potential disciplinary case hanging over me.'

'Ah, the famous notes,' said Sir Colin. He went over to his desk and picked up the vinyl presentation case. Mr Johnson started.

'Where did that appear from? I thought I had lost it.'

'Looks like someone's taking care of you. It was sent up to me a short while ago.'

Sir Colin gave the offending notes a cursory glance.

'Now then. We could put these notes back in this case, or…' He gestured over to the wastepaper basket. Mr Johnson smiled and nodded and Sir Colin screwed up the notes and threw them away. Then he took all the other notes out of the presentation case and threw them away as well before handing the empty case to Mr Johnson.

'Nothing like a turning over a new leaf,' he said with a wink. 'But ten-out-of-ten for your candour. Come on – home.'

'But what about The Loom? Perhaps I should find out more about it before I go home.'

'Enough! You'll have plenty of time to find out everything you need to know. Try not to get too bogged down in minor details. In any case, I'm sure I'm not wrong in thinking that you have had to take more than enough on board already. I won't say it again, Mr Johnson – home.'

He couldn't argue. The afternoon sunshine streamed gloriously through Sir Colin's windows and Mr Johnson squinted as they shook hands on the threshold of the landing.

'Until next Monday, then.'

'Yes, you'll come back raring to go. Take care, now. Don't forget: simultaneousness.'

'I won't – How do I get to the main reception area from here?'

Sir Colin smiled. 'I'm not going to give directions to an experienced and valued employee like you. You'll find it easily enough.'

He was right. Mr Johnson tucked the presentation case under his arm, and went through a door on the landing and down two short flights of broad stairs, which opened into a small, tidy reception area furnished with low vinyl-seating for guests and embellished by two large, shiny plants. He nodded and smiled at the two women behind the desk, waved at the security guard who emerged from an anteroom, straightened his tie, pushed open the front door and found himself once again outside The Loom.